DAWSON'S WAR

A NOVEL OF FRIENDSHIP
UNDER FIRE

B. K. MARSHALL

This Book is a work of Fiction. Names, characters, places and incidents are a product of the author's imagination or are used fictitiously. Any resemblance to actual events, locals, or persons, living or dead, is coincidental.

Copyright © 2020 B. K. Marshall
All rights reserved.

ISBN: 9798636654513

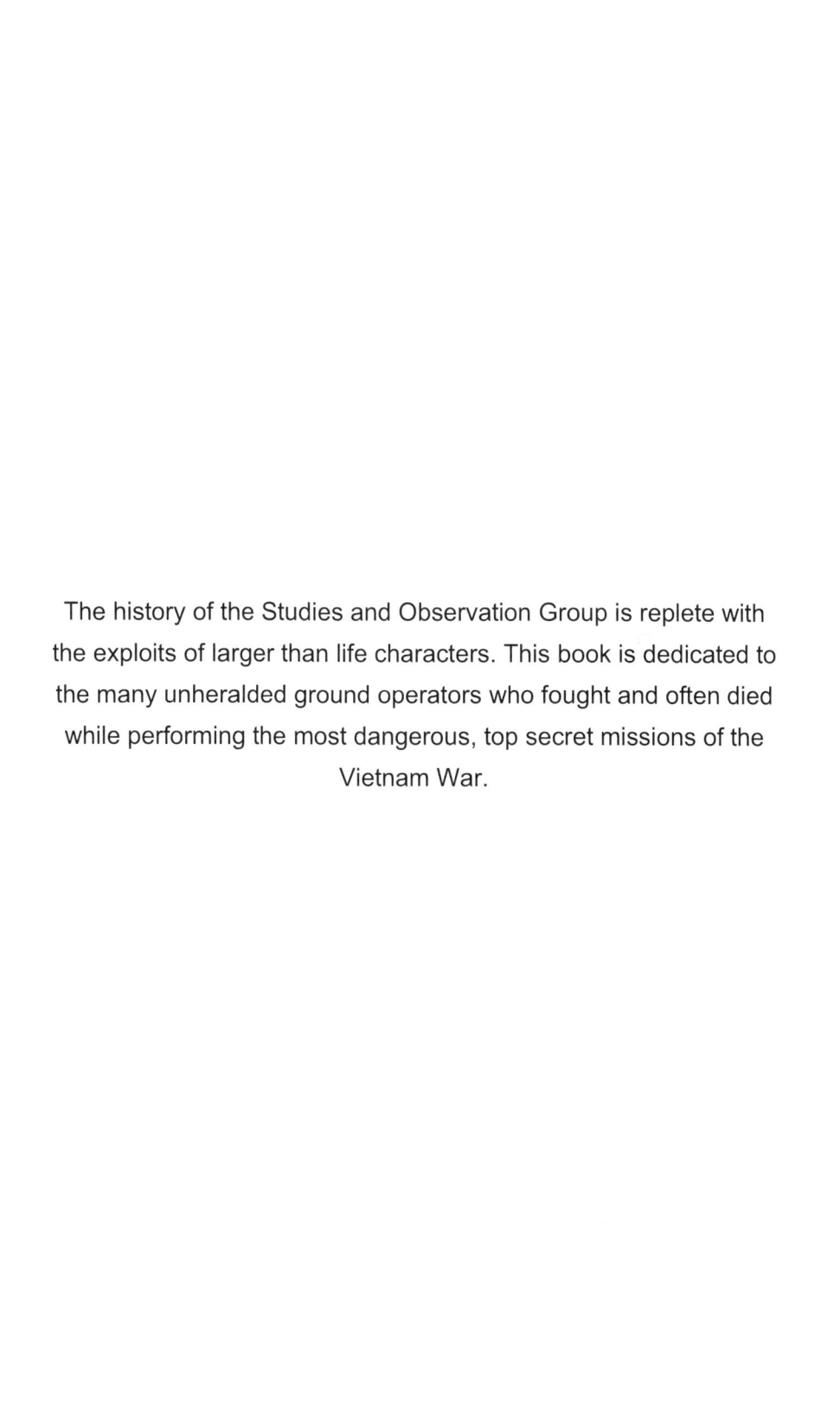

The history of the Studies and Observation Group is replete with the exploits of larger than life characters. This book is dedicated to the many unheralded ground operators who fought and often died while performing the most dangerous, top secret missions of the Vietnam War.

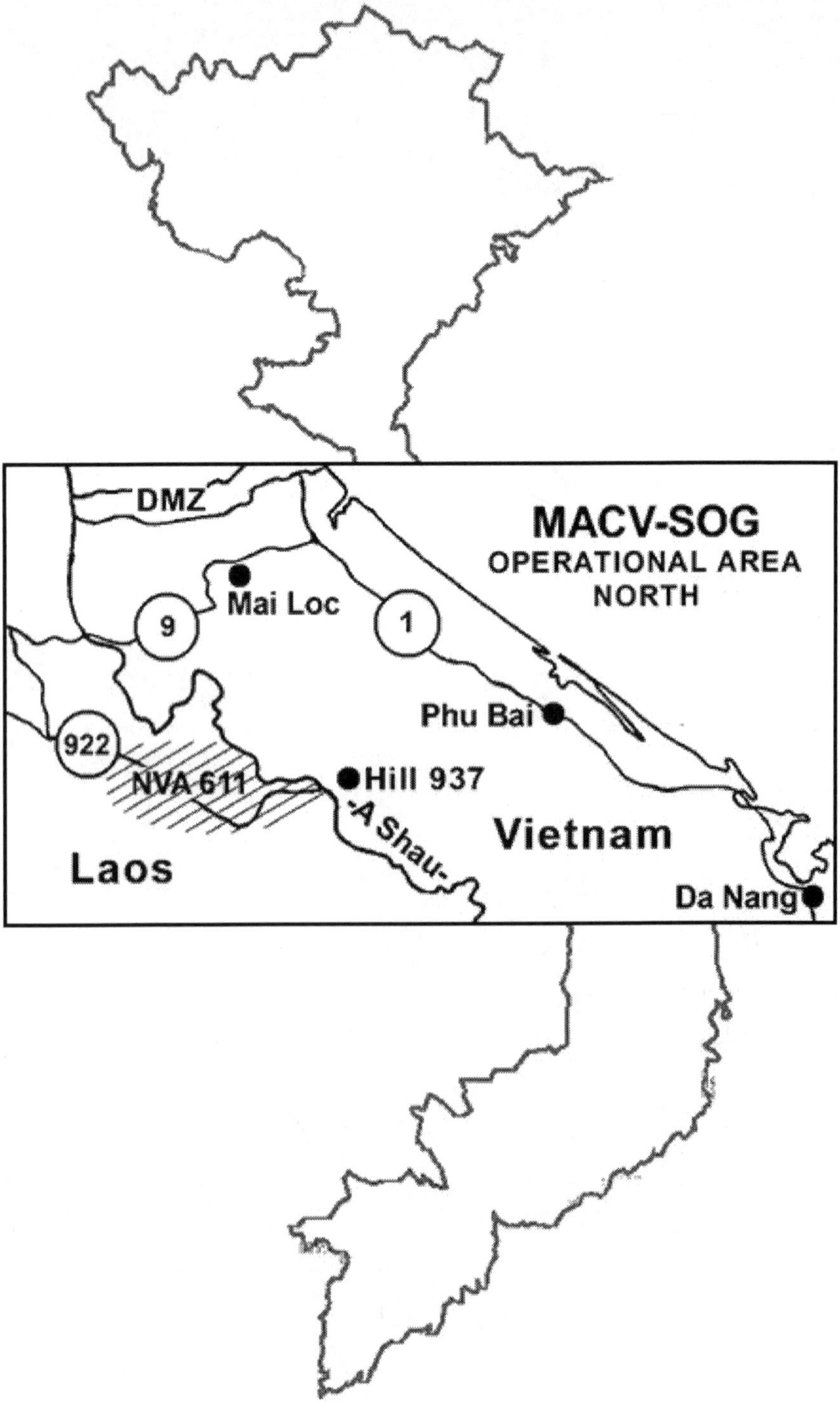

DMZ
MACV-SOG
OPERATIONAL AREA
NORTH
Mai Loc
9
1
Phu Bai
922
NVA 611
Hill 937
-A Shau-
Vietnam
Laos
Da Nang

Prologue

TWO HELICOPTER GUNSHIPS were attempting to suppress the enemy's fire as the team fired bursts from their CAR-15s to slow their advance.

"You gotta bring it in tighter. It's not doing any good." The American radioed the air controller as a burst of AK rounds hit the tree he was using for cover.

"Roger that. Get your heads down." The men on the ground continued to fire as four of their team were hoisted up through the sparse jungle on ropes hanging from a helicopter. Moments later ammo cans filled with sand attached to ropes dropped from the second helicopter and crashed through the canopy thudding to the ground. The three men abandoned their fighting positions and ran to the ropes. One went down hard. The others instantly moved toward him, but he was back up and running a second later. They unhooked the ammo cans and secured themselves to the ropes. Sporadic rounds were hitting the trees above their heads as the NVA troops continued to advance. Finally, the gunships brought their fire closer. The enemy abandoned the assault and found safety from the hail of bullets at the base of large trees. The chopper pulled the last team members up and out of the jungle. As the sound of the helicopters receded, the North

Vietnamese assembled and counted heads. With their mission complete they began the walk back to their base camp.

Dangling three thousand feet above the mountain jungle the team could see the pockmarked earth surrounding the abandoned Khe Sanh combat base off to the North. They had crossed the Laotian border into South Vietnam. Continuing east the chopper eventually hovered over the Marine Base at LZ Stud. As it lowered, the men, oscillating below, were dumped on the PSP runway. The team leader unhooked himself, grabbed the rope and ran to the chopper. He tossed the rope to the crew chief and clapped him on the shoulder. Then he moved to the cockpit, pounded on the door and gave the pilots a thumbs up. The chopper that had extracted the first four members of the team was idling a ways down the runway. Feeling exhausted for the first time he walked the distance.

"Everybody all right?" he called above the noise of the rotors.

By the spring of 1968 enemy countermeasures along the Ho Chi Minh Trail in Laos had become so effective that survival defined success for the recon teams of MACV-SOG.

CHAPTER ONE

ALAN DAWSON'S FIRST attempt to acquire a college education was unsuccessful. Enrolled in a small liberal arts school in central Pennsylvania, aided by an athletic scholarship, he attended classes and went to fraternity rush parties. His enthusiastic participation in the latter brought him to the attention of the administration and he was asked to leave after six weeks.

Returning to his modest home just outside Philadelphia, Dawson's strict Protestant parents offered constant reminders of the embarrassment his failure had caused them. He had been raised to be the first in the family to graduate from college. A new plan was devised. Obviously too immature to be on his own, he would live at home and commute to a large university in the city. He filed the application and was accepted to begin the next semester. Life at home was not going well. So, in early December, after the latest family episode of 'As long as you stay in my house you live by my rules,' Dawson parked his mother's car by the curb in a neighboring town and stared through the windows of the Army recruiting station. He entered and was immediately surrounded by posters and pamphlets featuring stern-looking men wearing green berets. A competent sergeant explained that with a two year enlistment he would be assigned where the army needed him. If he enlisted for three years he would be guaranteed the school of his choice. Dawson interpreted that to mean a two year enlistment would send him to Vietnam with the infantry. So, he chose three years. He took a battery of tests, carefully marking "Strongly Disagree" on any questions about enjoying camping or hiking. The scores qualified him to choose from a huge list of schools. With the sergeant's help he choose the Intelligence Analyst School at Ft. Holabird, MD. After a trip downtown for a physical, he signed the enlistment agreement.

A couple of days before Christmas his father said he was writing the check for the college tuition. The announcement that Alan had joined the army was as welcomed as the news of the Kennedy assassination. He worked as a shipping clerk in a local factory while he waited for his enlistment date. On March 6, 1966 Alan Dawson was sworn in as a $78 a month Private E-1 in the United States Army. He boarded a troop train bound for Ft. Jackson, South Carolina. The train had a three hour layover in Washington, DC. The new recruits headed to local bars and got drunk. The first day of army life was just like college.

The train arrived at the Ft. Jackson reception station. There the new recruits were given a partial pay and had their hair cut off. As uniforms were issued the troops walked under a sign stating "You are Now the Best Equipped Fighting Man in the World." After hanging around for a couple of days they loaded on to a bus for a trip to Ft. Gordon, GA.

Basic training was a lot of running and a lot of hollering. Pvt. Dawson made his first and only trip to the orderly room on the second day. He had not elected to have a saving's bond automatically deducted from his pay. A sergeant explained that with 100% participation in the program the commanding officer got to fly a small minuteman flag below the American flag in front of the building. This was apparently very important to the captain. He corrected his error and returned to running and hollering. The most anticipated event of basic training occurred in the beginning of week seven. The infiltration course. Trainees got to crawl under barbed wire while machine guns fired real bullets over their heads and pyrotechnics blew dirt in their faces. The troops were very excited. Unfortunately, Dawson was on light duty with an upper respiratory infection and was unable to attend. Two days before they graduated from basic the trainees cleaned and turned in their weapons. He believed he had carried a rifle for the last time.

The Army Intelligence School at Ft. Holabird was located between a yeast factory and a General Motors B body plant in southeast Baltimore. In the summer of 1966 the soldiers endured sweltering nights on sweat soaked sheets and the stench of yeast. During the day they attended Intelligence Analyst classes in air conditioned buildings. The students favorite classes, the DAME course, Defense Against Methods of Entry, and the DASE course, Defense Against Sound Equipment actually taught them how to break into buildings and how to bug rooms. The aerial photography classes consisted of looking at photos through a device called a stereoscope. It was supposed to add depth to the photos. Dawson could never make it work because he wore glasses. After class students would go have a drink at the local bar on Dundalk Avenue or on special occasions they would take a bus to East Baltimore Street and visit the strip clubs. On $78 a month Dawson was always broke so he spent most of his off time playing softball or working out at the post gym.

Midway through the course, there was a serious traffic accident and a call went out for blood donors. Dawson was a match so he volunteered. While he was recovering in the dispensary, he saw a notice on the bulletin board. It detailed how the requirements for Officer's Candidate School had been changed. Enlisted personnel could now attend OCS without two years of college if they met certain other requirements. He pulled the paper down and stuck it in his pocket. The next day, after reading the notice several times, he left class early and went to the orderly room.

"First sergeant, I'd like to apply for OCS."

"You're going to have to see the CO about that," the first sergeant replied.

"When can I see him?"

"Maybe right now. Let me check." Returning in a few seconds, he said,"Go ahead in." Dawson entered and saluted the captain.

"So, why do you want to go to OCS?"

"Because I can't live on eighty bucks a month, sir," he replied.

"That's probably the least bullshit answer I've ever heard," the captain belly laughed. "I'll have the first sergeant give you the paper work and you can use one of the typewriters in the office to complete them when you're off duty." Dawson was amazed with how easy that was. Over the next 3 days he hunted and pecked his way through the application. One section raised his concern. List three branches of the Army you are applying for. You must include one combat arm. After some thought he entered Intelligence, Signal and Armor as the combat arm. He figured Armor would have the least possibility of ending up in the jungles of Vietnam. He turned in the paperwork and returned to classes, softball and the gym.

A week later, the first sergeant called him to the orderly room. He was directed to be interviewed by an OCS review board. He entered the room and stood at attention before a four officer panel. A lieutenant colonel, a major and two captains. They were very intimidating. He was questioned about his background, patriotism and how as a military officer he would motivate his subordinates. To the latter he found himself repeating words his high school football coach had used in pre-game pep talks. Abruptly, he was dismissed. As he left the room, he lingered to listen through the door.
"That kid's not officer material."
"That's not our job. Our job is only to determine if they're qualified. It's the school's job to wash them out," an older voice replied.

Ten days before completing the Intelligence Analyst course Dawson was back in the captain's office.
"Congratulations private. You have been accepted to Officer's Candidate School," the captain said handing him a small stack of papers. The sense of accomplishment he felt was quickly extinguished as he read the words: Infantry Officer Candidate School, Ft, Benning, Georgia.
"Sir, I think there is a mistake," Dawson said, extending the papers back to the captain. "This says Infantry OCS." The captain

took a look at the papers, thought for a few seconds and replied.

"Intelligence branch is too small to have it's own OCS. Our officers go through Infantry OCS and then on to Intelligence Officers Basic. Don't worry. The Army is not hard up enough to need infantry officers who wear glasses." The captain answered with authority. The answer made sense. And since Dawson wanted to believe it, he did.

In a few weeks he was settled into the Infantry OCS barracks at Ft, Benning, Ga. In a repeat of basic training he was once again called to the company commander's office. This time he had failed to volunteer for the Airborne, Rangers, and Special Forces. And this time it was about some little green flag for 100% participation. The captain's fatigues displayed the Combat Infantryman's Badge, jump wings and a 173rd Airborne combat patch. He wasn't fooling around, and made it clear that Dawson would either volunteer right now or he would be sent to the first infantry unit leaving for Vietnam. He also pointed out that no one who wore glasses was qualified to serve in these elite fighting forces. Pvt. Dawson, now Officer's Candidate E-5 Dawson signed the paper.

If there was such a thing as a well-oiled machine in the U. S. Army, Infantry OCS was it. Watching the organized formations of double timing candidates each carrying an infantry blue clipboard with a Win in Vietnam sticker on the back, converge on Infantry Hall each morning was quite impressive. The constant harassment by TAC officers, offset by highly professional classroom and field training, created an atmosphere of organized chaos. Each day candidates were given more tasks than they could possibly accomplish. They had to prioritize them and the TAC officers always made sure that their decisions were wrong. As they got deeper into the training, they were becoming more efficient. Midway through the twenty-four week course most of the candidates who weren't going to make it were gone. For those that remained, spit shining floors, always running when outdoors, bellowing TAC officers and punishment pushups for the most minor infraction had become an easily endured norm.

Surprising himself, Dawson was fitting in quite well. His high school athleticism allowed him to easily overcome the grinding physical requirements that hampered many of his peers and he found the classes both interesting and informing. Keeping a low profile he had managed to evade the wrath of most of the TAC officers. Most, but not all. There was one, a short, round face TAC officer who seemed to take a particular pleasure harassing Dawson. His name tag read OBERLONG. 2nd Lt. Oberlong. Dawson was careful to avoid him. Returning from class one evening, Dawson found his shined floor scrapped up, the mattress overturned and his perfectly folded socks and underwear dumped out of the chest onto the floor. This had happened to other candidates. So, it wasn't unheard of. But it wasn't the norm either. Dawson spent a couple of hours after lights out with a flashlight putting his room back in order. Returning from PT the next morning, Dawson heard a voice behind him.

"Tired this morning, candidate." It was Oberlong. Dawson turned and came to attention.

"No Sir."

"I heard you were up after curfew last night," Oberlong questioned. Dawson did not reply.

"Were you up after curfew last night?" Oberlong demanded.

"Yes Sir."

"Get down to my level." Dawson bent his knees till his face was directly in front of the TAC officer's. "Do you think you're better than me candidate?"

"No, Sir," Dawson lied. Oberlong was screaming now. His face was red. As he yelled, his spit was hitting Dawson in the face. Two TAC officers stood a dozen feet away.

"Frank's getting carried away," said the first.

"If he's not careful that kid's going to kill him," replied the other.

"I'd pay to see that," they laughed. Together they approached the still raging Lt. Oberlong. "We gotta go Frank," one said placing his hand on Oberlong's shoulder. Dawson was angry. A quiet, seething anger.

Things quickly got back to normal. Dawson avoided Lt. Oberlong and it seemed like Oberlong was avoiding him. Weeks passed. The company was out on a range for a day long class titled "The Infantry Platoon in the Assault." The instructor was explaining that in Vietnam, when you are ambushed, you are in the kill zone and you must immediately assault into the ambush. This had been a common teaching point in many of the tactics courses. During a break Dawson asked the instructor why it was always assumed that you would walk into an ambush? Why didn't they have courses on how not to walk into an ambush?

"That's a good question," the instructor replied. "Maybe after you get back from Vietnam you can teach that course." Dawson wondered why he bothered to ask. What did he care about infantry tactics since he would be returning to the Intelligence Branch?

On the day before graduation, the candidates gathered around the steps to the mess hall in civilian clothes. Technically, they had been discharged the day before from their enlisted service and tomorrow they would reenter the army as commissioned officers. It was an excited group. Within the hour they would receive orders for their first duty assignment. Dawson was thinking about returning to Ft. Holabird. Not on sweaty sheets and $78 a month. This time he would be living in the air-conditioned bachelor officer's quarters, simply called the BOQ, with $300 a month to spend. It had been worth the hard six months. Many of his classmates, some of them good friends now, were hoping to be sent on a bus ride across Ft. Benning to the high towers for paratrooper training or the demanding ranger school. Others with higher ambitions wanted the ultimate prize. Special Forces, the Green Berets.

The company commander appeared on the steps. He congratulated the troops on their successful completion of OCS and urged them to "Give 'em hell in Vietnam." Then he proudly announced that he had received orders to the 101st Airborne Division, the famed Screaming Eagles, and was returning to the fight in Vietnam. The troops cheered. He turned it over to the first sergeant, who jokingly reminded the men that tomorrow was his pay day. It is a tradition that each newly commissioned officer rewards the first sergeant with a silver dollar as he gives them their first salute. Then the company clerk began to read the orders and pass out the paperwork. Most of the orders were to basic training posts. Ft. Dix, Fort Polk, Ft. Gordon. Many of the gung-ho soon to be 2nd lieutenants were openly disappointed. It was going very slowly and got to be boring. Dawson was annoyed that the orders weren't coming in alphabetical order and almost missed his.

"Dawson, Alan. Airborne School, Ft, Benning, GA en route to the Special Forces Officer Course, Ft. Bragg, North Carolina." Finally, some one had gotten decent orders. His classmates applauded and patted him on the back. Dawson removed his glasses. Looking at them, he remembered the captain's words,

"No one who wears glasses is qualified to serve in these elite fighting units." He shook his head.

CHAPTER TWO

HAVING A WEEK of casual company before jump school began, Dawson ventured down to the sparkling lights and plastic flags of the used car lots that dotted Victory Drive in Columbus. He bought a four year old Chevrolet Corvair. The car Ralph Nader had labeled "Unsafe at Any Speed." He didn't care. It had decent tires, ran OK, only cost a few hundred dollars and besides he figured he wouldn't need it very long. Being able to just get in the car and go where he wanted created a great sense of freedom after a year of training.

The first thing 2Lt. Dawson learned in parachute school was that the training instructors, called black hats, logically, because they wore black baseball caps, took great joy in dropping the brand new 2nd lieutenants for push ups. At the end of the first week Dawson was standing around during a break.
"Hey, lieutenant." Dawson looked up to see a black hat, who had dropped him more than a few times. "You from Philly?" the staff sergeant asked.
"Yes, sergeant. How'd you know?"
"You say wader instead of water," Sergeant Williams laughed.

"I'm from Germantown."

"I used to play pickup basketball at the Sedgwick courts."

"Surprised the brothers didn't mess you up."

"Oh, they did," Dawson smiled. "Too much talent for me."

During the middle of tower week Dawson and Williams were having a couple of beers after training at an off post bar. Williams was wearing a tee shirt with the 1st Air Cavalry insignia on it.

"Why were you with a leg unit in Vietnam?" Dawson asked referring to the fact that the 1st Air Cav was not a parachute division.

"I was in the 82nd at Fort Bragg. My unit didn't go to the Dominican Republic so they sent me here, to Benning, when they were putting units together to make up the 1st Air Cav. I deployed with the unit by boat to Vietnam and a month later I was in the Ia Drang Valley," Sergeant Williams explained.

"Jesus! You were in that mess?"

"Went in to reinforce on day two. The first day they spent about five hours shuttling the battalion in and by the time the last slicks. . ."

"What are slicks?" Dawson interrupted.

"In Vietnam troop carrying helicopters are called slicks. The gunships, that provide cover are simply called guns. Anyway, by the time the last slicks were landing, they were dropping off troops and picking up casualties. When I got there it was pretty much under control. In Vietnam most people get killed when the shooting first starts, then everybody eats dirt until you get airpower. We got airlifted out to the fire support base the next day. The battalion north of us nearly got wiped out. I knew it was bad, but I didn't know how bad until I started getting letters from my mother. When you're in country you don't know shit about what's happening."

"So, they got ambushed on the LZ?" Dawson asked, thinking about his training.

"Yeah. They prepped it with air and artillery, but it didn't make no difference. They got pinned down as they were landing."

"Did they assault into the ambush?" Dawson had to ask even though he knew the answer.

"Fuck no. You can't assault an ambush. Well, you can. But only once. When you get ambushed they can see you. You can't see them. There're shooting at you. You're shooting at trees. Besides, Charlie's got AKs with 30 round magazines. You got a Matty Mattel M-16. If you stick more than 18 rounds in the magazine it jams up." Sergeant Williams was getting pissed just thinking about it.

"That's what they taught us in OCS. When you get into an ambush you're in the kill zone and must immediately assault the enemy," Dawson said.

"Ain't none of them ever been in a firefight," Williams asserted.

"You should be teaching tactics not parachute jumping. We only had a couple of instructors who had actually been in Vietnam."

"I'm happy here." Williams didn't sound happy. "They'll probably send me back there in September. "Where're you going after jump school?"

"Ft. Bragg."

"82nd?" Williams asked.

"No, Special Forces," Dawson replied.

"That's crazy. You volunteer for that shit?"

"Not exactly." Dawson grinned.

The next week was jump week. The soldiers were staged in the ready room at Lawson Field. They put on their parachute harnesses, received safety checks and were loaded into a World War II vintage C-119. Dawson realized, for the first time, that he had never been in an airplane before. As the plane flew the short distance to Fryar Drop Zone he was surprised how low they were. He could clearly see cars on the road below and thought that if he put on his glasses, which he had carefully wrapped in a wash rag and secured in his breast pocket, he could probably make out the car models. The jump master was shouting commands. The troops stood up and hooked their static lines to the wires above their heads. Equipment checks made, the command came to "Stand in the Door." Moments later shouts of "Go, Go, Go" were heard above the noise of the plane. The troopers exited the plane from the rear doors on both sites. As Dawson stepped from the plane he felt an instant of panic as it appeared that he was going to slam right into the tail fin of the split boomed plane. He didn't. He felt his harness tighten as he swung down under its opening canopy. A bull horn on the ground was imploring the jumper with a malfunction to activate his reserve. About a half dozen reserve chutes appeared in the sky. Dawson hoped one was the soldier that actually had the malfunction. Then he hit the ground. It wasn't much of a parachute landing fall that he had just spent two weeks practicing hundreds of times. More of a crumple. But he was on the ground safe and uninjured. He gathered up his parachute, piled it into the kit bag and lugged it to the rally point where busses were waiting to return them to Lawson Airfield.

The weather wasn't cooperating. Windy and rainy. Jump schedules were set, broken and set again. It got pretty hectic in the ready room but they finally completed the required five jumps. A scratchy recording of "Blood on the Risers" was playing as the students assembled for graduation on Friday morning. They were awarded their parachute badges with special recognition being given to second generation paratroopers.

With his jump wings and an extra $110 a month parachutist pay Dawson drove his Corvair to Philadelphia for a two week leave. Arriving home, it didn't take long for his father to confront him.
"So, I guess you think you're a big deal now?"
"Not really."
"When I was in World War Two, paratrooper officers had a life expectancy of about two minutes. Where're you going next?"
"Fort Bragg. It's in North Carolina."
"What are you going to do there?
"Special Forces school."
"What's that?"
"The Green Berets."
"What are you nuts?"
"That's where they're sending me."
"That's bullsiht! You think I'm stupid. Nobody gets into the paratroopers or rangers or, what'd you call it? special forces, without volunteering." Dawson knew it was useless to explain. "You know you're going to end up in Vietnam?"
"Yeah, probably."
"Let me tell you something. World War Two was clear cut good vs. evil. The people who died, died for something. This Vietnam thing is just like Korea. A lot of people's children are going to get killed for nothing and their parents are going to be heart-broken. How could you do this to your mother? If you have a brain in your head you'll flunk out of that school."

Of course, relationships between fathers and sons being what they are, that was all the motivation Dawson needed. A few days early, he backed the Corvair out of the driveway and headed to Ft. Bragg. For the first time, he was looking forward to the challenge.

The students, primarily 2nd lieutenants, a few captains and one major, entered a darkened auditorium in the John F. Kennedy Center for Special Warfare. High in the left corner of the stage was an illuminated skull wearing a green beret and the words Think Dirty. "The Ballad of the Green Berets" was playing in the background. Suddenly the room went black and immediately a spotlight shown on a single speaker. When he was finished the room went black again and a second speaker was spotlighted at the other end of the stage. It went back and forth like this until the orientation was over. It was a dynamic presentation and the students were impressed as they would be for most of the next twelve weeks.

The goal of the course was to teach the officers how to command a Special Forces A Team. The backbone of the A Team are pairs of highly trained non-commissioned officers. A large portion of the course was dedicated to familiarizing the officers with the capabilities of these sergeants. The Special Forces employed the T-10 steerable parachute. A more maneuverable version of the army's standard chute. The students made numerous jumps to get familiar with it. Most of the rest centered around equipping, training and leading indigenous people recruited to form light infantry units. The students were broken down into small groups each with its own advisor.

The first field training exercise was a long difficult compass course with each student performing on his own. The next day the class size was visibly smaller. The course went on like this with students disappearing. There were no grades. No stated expectations. No one ever said so and so washed out because he failed this or that. Students just disappeared without a word. The advisor was a ghost. No matter where you were or what you were doing the advisor would show up out of nowhere. One morning, Dawson's group was on a simulated patrol behind enemy lines. Suddenly one member of the group ran out of formation and started yelling and screaming. The advisor appeared.

"Dawson. You're in charge," he commanded. Dawson put the men in a defensive perimeter and sent two of them out to recover the screaming soldier, bring him back and calm him down. That done, Dawson looked up. The advisor had vanished. Dawson wondered if he had handled the situation correctly. His advisor never offered critiques. He also wondered if the course was set up this way or if it was just how his advisor did things. The only thing he was sure of was that the advisor was the one who made the students disappear. It was very disconcerting. But, at the end of the course, Dawson was still there. He was a Special Forces qualified officer.

CHAPTER THREE

"GOING FISHING THIS afternoon, Brownie?" Lt. Colonel Forbes asked the sergeant major.

"Yes, sir," he replied.

"Another one?" the colonel said, nodding at Dawson.

"School's out, sir." The sergeant major laughed. The commander looked at Dawson, shook his head and walked into his office. "The colonel's not real fond of 2nd lieutenants," he said handing Dawson a slip of paper. Compared to the stern colonel, the sergeant major was almost jovial with a round face that smiled easily. "You're being assigned to A-Team 504 as the XO. That's the executive officer. In case they didn't teach you that."

"Oh really," Dawson mocked back, smiling.

"Here's the building number. Outside, Dawson looked around at the maze of tan wooden buildings. He checked the building numbers until he figured out how they were organized and soon enough found the building. He entered and was directed to a small office. Dawson was expecting to meet the captain who commanded the team. Instead another 2nd lieutenant was sitting behind a desk smoking. He put out his cigarette and stood to shake hands.

"I'm Bob Hudson."

"Alan Dawson. I've been assigned as the XO," he said, not sure who this guy was.

"I'm the team commander. Not enough captains to go around. Here's how this works. For three months you'll be the executive officer just like I've been for the last three. Three months from now another class will finish. I'll be sent to Vietnam and you'll become the team leader. Three months after that you'll go to Vietnam," Hudson explained. They talked for a while about how to get equipment, other logistics and schedules. Then Hudson said, "Let's go meet the men that are here."

They moved to the team room and everybody casually took seats around a large table. "This is Lt. Dawson," Hudson announced. They acknowledged Dawson with hays and nods. "This is Master Sergeant Bradford. He's opps and intel. He was with the Marines in the Pacific during World War Two. Then he joined the Army and was with the 18th Airborne in Korea where he got the silver star and he has a tour in Vietnam. Sergeant Kramer is weapons. He has two tours in Vietnam. Sergeant White is demo and was in Operation White Star, our secret little war in Laos that nobody is allowed to know about. They named it after him. Just kidding," Hudson laughed. "Then he had a tour in Vietnam. Sergeant Allison just finished a year of training at Fort Sam. He's our medic and Sergeant Connelly just finished communications school. He's our commo man."

"Well, I mopped tar for a roofing company while I was in high school." Dawson laughed thinking Holy Shit! The team members laughed with him.

The next day the team was scheduled for a daylight equipment jump. Dawson was amazed as they loaded their rucksacks and M-16s into their private vehicles and drove to Green Ramp at the adjacent Pope Air Force Base. No standing around in lines. No practicing parachute landing falls. No piling onto busses. Just get in your car and go with an automatic weapon in the trunk. At Green Ramp Sgt. Kramer taught Dawson how to attach his rucksack below his reserve chute with quick releases and fasten the drop line. They had their briefing, rigger check and climbed aboard the plane. The team flew to Saint Mere Eglise and jumped into the sparse scrub of the drop zone. They carried their gear to a spot where Lt. Hudson was with his car and a deuce-and-a-half. As they rode in the back of the truck to get their cars Dawson asked Sgt. White if they made all their jumps like this.

"Mostly. But if Col. Forbes shit cans you to the 82nd Airborne you'll be up at 5 in the morning standing around with your thumb up your ass waiting to jump at noon. Sir," White said with grin.

"Sergeant Major Brown told me he has a real thing for 2nd lieutenants," Dawson stated.

"Yeah. Wait'll you see. When we have a formation he makes the 2nd lieutenants stand in the back. If you have to report to him he won't let you in his office. You have to stand outside and report through the window." Dawson thought White was exaggerating, but a couple of days later there he was standing in the back of a command reveille formation.

The team maintained a rigorous training schedule combining parachute drops, field training exercises and cross training. Toward the end of the year they had to get ready for their I. G. inspection. Hudson put Dawson in charge. The I. G. is the most important inspection the Army has. Doing poorly can cost an NCO a promotion and ruin an officer's career. Dawson set about learning the requirements. The team equipment had to be laid out in a specific order on shelter halves. He inventoried the team's equipment and found a lot of it missing. He asked Bradford about it and was told that they had probably lent it to other teams and never gotten it back.

"What are we going to do?" Dawson asked.

"Borrow it from some other team," Bradford replied.

"Who?"

"Don't worry about it, lieutenant. We got this." But he did worry about it. More than a little bit. When he approached Kramer and White they were equally unconcerned. The day before the inspection Dawson was in with Hudson telling him about the missing equipment when they heard a lot of activity in the team room. Entering the room, he saw Kramer and White unloading not only the missing equipment, but most of the equipment they needed from White's pickup. It all looked brand new.

"Where did you get this stuff? Dawson asked.

"From the team that had the last inspection," White laughed. "And they got it from the team that had the inspection before them."

"You mean."

"Yep. The inspectors keep looking at the same shit in different buildings." Everyone laughed.

"Well, we should just change the numbers on the building that way we wouldn't even have to set it up," Dawson said relieved.

"Now, you're learning, lieutenant," Kramer said as he carefully put a Nikon camera down on the table. "We're going to make a Special Forces soldier out of you yet." Of course, they passed the inspection.

As a Christmas present from the United States Army, Lt. Hudson received his orders to Vietnam. Dawson became the team leader. Between passes and leaves the team was inactive until the beginning of January. A couple of days later, Dawson was summonsed to the orderly room. He had been very, very careful to avoid Ltc. Forbes and his mind was spinning trying to figure out which of the things he had done wrong had come to the colonel's attention. With trepidation, he approached Sergeant Major Brown.

"A little cold for fishing," he said. Trying to keep things casual.

"Lieutenant, haven't seen you in ages. Guess you've been smart enough to stay under the radar. You've got a briefing in the XO's office." He motioned to a door to his left. Dawson joined a small group of soldiers sitting around the room and noticed a map taped to the wall with a magic marker line drawn from Ft. Bragg to someplace in Virginia. A major entered. Dawson flinched to jump to attention but no one else moved so he remained seated.

"We are going to run a field training exercise for some National Guard Special Forces units at Camp A. P. Hill, Virginia," the major announced. The gist of the briefing was that Camp A. P. Hill was basically a hunting lodge for Pentagon generals and that it had come under the scrutiny of congress. E Company had been tasked to hold an FTX there to show that the camp had military value. A-504's job was to take a convoy of supplies and equipment some 300 miles to the camp then oversee the airborne insertion of the National Guard troops. Dawson got the team together and told them about the exercise.

"So, you're telling us we're a bunch of truck drivers?" Msg. Bradford complained.

"Yeah. That's about it."

"Can't you get us out of this?" asked White.

"Sure. I'll just go tell the major we've got better things to do. Who is he? Anybody know him?" Dawson inquired.

"Major Hanson," Kramer replied. "Arrogant S.O.B. He was a captain S-2, S-4 or some shit for the 1 Corps Mike Force when I was there in early '65. A real hard ass that's never set foot in the woods. Spent most of the time shacked up with a Vietnamese girl in Da Nang. Is he going?"

"To use his own words he's the Ground Commander," answered Dawson.

"Be his first time," Kramer said.

A few days later, everything was set to go. Surprising no one, Bradford, Kramer and White weren't going with the convoy. They were driving up in Bradford's station wagon. The motor pool had supplied the team with a couple of drivers. With no communication between the vehicles and a straight shot up Route 401, Dawson decided to take the rear truck just in case there were stragglers. He climbed into the passenger side.

"I'm Dawson," he said assuming the driver could see his rank on his field jacket.

"Specialist 4 Jennings, sir."

"I haven't seen many Spec. 4s in E company."

"Oh, there are plenty of us, sir. We've graduated from the Special Forces Qualification Course and are waiting for a slot in one of the specialty courses to open up."

"How long will you have to wait?"

"That's the thing. We're in a race against time to see which comes first our orders to school or our orders to Vietnam."

"What happens if you get orders to Vietnam?"

"Then we'll probably get assigned to one of the airborne units."

The four deuce-and-a-half trucks pulled out of Ft. Bragg at 8 AM. By the time they reached the North Carolina, Virginia boarder the temperature had dropped and a combination of rain, sleet and snow was falling. The canvas top vehicles had no heaters or defrosters and they were placing the palms of their hands on the windshield to clear a spot for the driver to peer through. On a long down hill slope a car skidded into the rear driver's side of one of the trucks. The right side of the car's roof was peeled away as if opened with a can opener. The truck had a small scratch. No one was hurt. Luckily, the motor pool drivers had the necessary paperwork and they were back on their way in less than an hour. As conditions worsened the convoy moved forward at a crawl. It was well after dark when they entered the steep hills of the city of Richmond. In a crowded residential neighborhood one of the trucks hit a parked car. They finally found the owner, filled out the paperwork, and were prepared to leave after almost two hours.

"Where's Jennings?" Dawson asked anyone within earshot.

"He's in with the hookers," came a reply.

"Hookers?"

"There's hookers in that house," said one of the motor pool guys pointing.

"Go get him." A few minutes later, Jennings appeared.

"Lieutenant I . . ." Dawson cut him off.

"Don't say anything. Can't wait to tell the major I'm sorry we're late, but we stopped off at a whore house in Richmond." By 9 PM, after driving around Camp A. P. Hill for a while, Dawson spotted

Bradford's station wagon parked in front of what look like a large house. Instructing the drivers to secure the trucks, he climbed the steps to the porch and entered. It was warm inside. Soldiers from his and couple other teams who had different roles in the exercise were scattered about on chairs and at tables. Beer cans everywhere.

"Get lost lieutenant?"

"Fuck you, White."

"There's food in the kitchen." White gestured to the back. Dawson got some food and a beer and found a seat. Three or four or five beers later he climbed the stairs to the second floor and found a bunk. Exhausted, he fell asleep immediately.

The next day he met with the major who ordered him to go reconnoiter the drop zone.

"Hey, Sgt. Bradford, lets go check out the drop zone. You can drive."

"They have a couple of jeeps from the camp. I'm almost out of gas."

"Let's go. Your car's got a heater," Dawson said flashing an Army credit card. " Sgt Connelly. Care to join us?"

"No."

"Sure you do. You're going to have to run the commo for the drops," Dawson said, wincing through his hangover. They drove off base and got gas.

"Is it OK to use a government card to put gas in your car?" Connelly asked.

"Nobody used it to put gas in their car," Bradford admonished. Connelly was a quiet guy. The kind of guy you didn't know whether you liked or not. But he was decent at his job.

"Where's the drop zone? Sir," Bradford asked.

"Three-four klicks north on the same road where we're staying." The drop zone was tight. A little more than 200 x 300 meters. Surrounded by trees. Tight but doable. Flight track due south to due north because of a clump of trees in the southeast corner. No power lines. They returned to the house and hung out with not much to do. More drinking that night. The next day was more hanging around. Just before sundown, they set up the drop zone. At 9PM Dawson made contact with the aircraft. They lit the pots to mark the drop zone. It was windy. The pilot made a pass to see the lights and circled around to make the drop run. Dawson checked the wind meter. The little plastic ball was blown to the top of the tube.

"Pretty windy," Dawson said to Kramer.

"The major won't be happy if you scrub the jump," Kramer replied.

"13 knots max. I'd push it to 15 maybe 16. It's over 20. These guy can get hurt if they blow into the trees. I gotta cancel this thing."

"It's your ass, sir," Kramer shrugged. Dawson told the pilot. They gathered up their equipment and returned to the house.

The major was livid. Who the hell was some 2nd lieutenant to cancel his drop. The team could hear him ripping Dawson a new one as if they were in the room. Eventually he returned. The team just looked at him. Not even a wise crack.

"Get a couple of deuce-an-a-halfs and drivers. I gotta go to Richmond Airport to pick up the National Guard team," Dawson told Kramer. Returning from the airport he dropped the team off at the drop zone around 4AM.

The major hadn't calmed down much by the next day. He kept telling Dawson that the team scheduled to jump tonight was coming all the way from Alaska. As if where they came from had something to do with wind speed. They set up the drop zone exactly the same as the night before. Dawson made contact with the pilot and the team lit the pots. The plane flew over the drop and circled for the drop run. Dawson checked the wind speed. It was the same as the night before. As the plane approached the pilot spoke over the radio.

"Pretty windy up here. Are you sure you don't want to call this thing off?" Dawson hesitated. Looked at Sgt. Kramer.

"Drop them," he said into the handset. The night sky was bright and they could clearly see the plane and the jumpers as they were blown to the west past the drop zone into the forest beyond. Oh, Jesus Dawson thought. "Did all jumpers exit?" Dawson asked the pilot making sure everyone was accounted for. The reply was affirmative.

The major was happy. None of the Alaskan Special Forces members were injured. They spent all of the next day cutting parachutes out of trees. That night Dawson and Kramer were in the corner of the room drinking beer.

"That was a real bullshit move. Jumping that team," Kramer said. "You let that major scare you. You're lucky nobody got hurt. If anybody did, you can be sure that the major would have been the first to put all the blame on you. Pull a stunt like that in Vietnam you'll be putting bodies in plastic bags," Kramer finished.

"I know," Dawson said quietly.

CHAPTER FOUR

AS DAWSON WAS helping pack up the trucks for the return to Fort Bragg, a voice behind him asked,

"Are you the asshole that dropped those guys in a hurricane?" He turned to see another lieutenant, built like a linebacker. He could have been on a poster in the recruiter's office.

"Yeah, so what," Dawson replied.

"We were stuck for a whole day cutting parachutes out of the trees."

"If you have a complaint, go tell the major." Dawson had heard enough about it.

"Word is he's the one who caused the screw up."

"Yeah, well I was the Drop Zone Safety Officer. That makes it my fault. I recognize you from the officer's course," Dawson said checking the lieutenant's name tag.

"I didn't see you there," the lieutenant said.

"That was the idea."

"I'm Walt Zobel," he said extending his hand.

"Alan Dawson." They shook.

The weather cooperated on the trip back to Fort Bragg. No

traffic accidents, no visits to a whore house. Amazingly, that stop in Richmond seemed to have been kept quiet. In just under 7 hours they unloaded the trucks on Smoke Bomb Hill. The team resumed their normal training schedule. A week later a rumor emerged. A team was going to be selected to hike the Appalachian Trail. With the National Guard being called up to confront race riots and the Vietnam war getting less and less popular, the Appalachian Trail seemed like a safe place to take publicity photos of rugged Green Berets being welcomed by patriotic citizens. Even if they did live in poverty. Early Monday morning Sgt. Bradford approached.

"Lieutenant. They want you in the orderly room."

"Were not going on any Appalachian Trail exercise," White said.

"You better get us out of this, Sir," Kramer chimed in. As he walked to the orderly room, Dawson was thinking of reasons why A-504 was the wrong team for this job. They had just got back from A. P. Hill. Bradford was too old, although, he probably could still out hike the rest of them. His Vietnam orders couldn't be far off. Same was true for most of the team.

"The old man wants to see you," said Sergeant Major Brown. No smile today. Dawson turned toward the colonel's office. "Outside through the window." Brown pointed.

"Sir. Lieutenant Dawson," he said saluting outside the window. No answer. He held the salute and stood there at attention. Finally he heard a voice from inside.

"Why did you stop my convoy at a house of prostitution, lieutenant?"

By the time Dawson got back to the team house the details of his encounter preceded him. The team was relieved that they weren't going to the Appalachian Trail.

"Hey, lieutenant. We heard Forbes just wanted you to drop by so he could tell you what a great job you're doing," White said. Everyone laughed.

"Don't worry, Sir. The colonel's not going to do anything to you because anything he would do could slow down your orders to Vietnam and he wants all of you 2nd lieutenants out of here as fast as possible," Bradford explained. More laughter.

"Oh, that's a relief," Dawson said sarcastically.

"Don't worry, sir. What you did is no big deal," Kramer said laughing. "A while back two crazy lieutenants took live ammo on a survival exercise. They shot a deer and got caught by the game warden. So they turned their weapons on him, tied him to a tree and stole his truck. Compared to them you're an amateur."

Dawson was picking up a few things at the PX when he ran into Zobel, the lieutenant who had complained about the A. P. Hill parachute drop. The two started talking. During the conversation Dawson mentioned that he was looking for a place to live. Quarters at Ft. Bragg had been a constant problem. First he had stayed in the BOQ. It's painted cinderblock walls and stark furniture made him feel like he was in the army twenty four hours a day. Then he shared a house with a couple of other officers but between people washing out of the officer's course and getting overseas orders he had been bouncing around from place to place. For the last two weeks he was back in the BOQ. Zobel was in the same situation. He had just lost a roommate and could use someone to share the rent. Dawson agreed to move in.

A couple of days later he drove the Corvair, loaded with his meager belongings out the main gate, turned east on Honeycutt Road and drove to Woodburn Drive, the first road off the base. The house, a small one-story ranch with a garage, backed up to a wooded area of the fort. He climbed the brick steps up to the front door and knocked. The door opened.

Hey, Alan," Zobel said as if they were old friends.

"Walt."

"I'll give you a hand with your stuff." When they were done Zobel handed Dawson a beer.

By the time there was a pile of empty beer cans in the kitchen, Dawson learned that Zobel had worked his way through two years of college as a ski instructor in Vermont in order to qualify for the army's OCS program. His goal was to wear the green beret and serve his country. His father was an Air Force master sergeant stationed at McGuire Air Force Base in New Jersey. Zobel learned that Dawson shouldn't be here because he wore glasses.

Daily training and work with the A-Team kept up at the same pace but with most of them now anticipating Vietnam orders the intensity dropped. Dawson and Zobel became pretty good friends. They met a couple of nurses who lived down the street. Over beers they discussed small unit tactics they use could in Vietnam and since neither really knew what they were talking about it all made perfectly good sense. They took to running with back packs containing sand bags to build up stamina for their deployment. While running, Dawson kept remembering Sergeant Kramer telling him,

"The only way to get in shape to hump the mountains in

Vietnam is to hump the mountains in Vietnam." Dawson wasn't sure if that was true or if Kramer just wanted to avoid exercise.

"We have to go the Pentagon," Zobel exclaimed. Dawson had just walked through the front door.
"Why?"
"They are cutting Vietnam orders for us as general replacements not to the 5th Special Forces Group."
"So what?"
"So what? They can just assign you to any unit that needs people."
"Good. Maybe they'll make me the savings bond officer."
"More likely they'll make you a rifle platoon leader of some leg unit made up of dope smoking draftees."
"Couldn't be any worse than Forbes." Dawson tried a joke. "How do you know this?
"Brownie told me."
"Sergeant Major Brown?
"Yeah. This is really serious. We can drive up Sunday. Go to the Pentagon Monday and get someone to make sure our orders are for the 5th Special Forces Group and drive back Monday night. We have to get there before they issue our orders. Just get a pass for Monday."
"How do you know they will change our orders?"
"I asked my dad and he made a few calls. He has pretty good connections. He told me this is what we should do."
"Thought we were going to see the nurses this weekend?"
"Fuck the nurses."
"That was the plan."

When they got to the Pentagon they found out that they had to go across the Potomac to Infantry Branch at Ft. McNair. Luckily, there was a shuttle. At Ft. McNair they entered a huge room filled with desks. A large picture of troops marching in the World War Two victory parade looked down over the room. They filled out forms detailing who they were and why they were there. After a wait of more than an hour they were escorted to see an adjutant captain. Zobel explained why they were there.

"So, you two want to stay together?" the captain questioned.

"No. We want to be assigned to the 5th Special Forces Group." Zobel was explaining that they wanted to do what they had been trained to do. Dawson was thinking the captain probably thought they were a couple of queers. When Zobel finished talking, the captain started shuffling papers and making notes. After about five minutes he looked up and said,

"All right gentlemen. I'll see what I can do." And that was that. They caught the shuttle back to the Pentagon and wasted half an hour looking for the Corvair in the parking lot.

A few days later Dawson told Kramer about his trip.

"You didn't have to do any of that. You hand carry your records. When you get to Cam Ranh Bay don't report. Just get a hop to Nha Trang and show up at 5th Group headquarters. They'll take care of your assignment."

"Oh, so when I get to Vietnam, I just go AWOL. And how to I get a hop to Nha Trang?"

"Just like you do everything here, lieutenant. Look for a Special Forces sergeant and ask him what to do." They laughed.

Zobel got his orders and Dawson's followed ten days later. In the top paragraph both read:

Asg to USAR Trans Det APO San Francisco 96375 for further asg to 5th SF Gp (Abn) APO San Francisco 96240.

The trip to Ft. McNair had not been a waste of time.

Zobel was ordered to Vietnam three weeks before Dawson. As always, he had a plan. They both had a 30 day leave coming. Zobel's father could get them a free ride on a military plane from Maguire Air Force Base to Homestead Air Force Base near Miami. From Miami they would fly to Nassau in the Bahamas for a couple weeks of diving and drinking. Dawson would return to Ft. Bragg for his remaining time and go home for a visit before he left for Vietnam. They set it up.

Before going overseas soldiers had to re-qualify with their weapon. Dawson and Zobel were given qualification cards and loaded on a bus. They filled out their scorecards on the way to the range, before firing a shot. Of course, they scored Expert. Once there, they joined another unit and used their ammunition helping them out.

On the day their leave began, they turned in the house keys at the real estate office. Dawson had packed up the Corvair with his stuff and dropped it off at the trailer where Sergeant Kramer was living. Kramer drove them to the airport. In Philadelphia they were picked up by Zobel's father and younger brother and driven to his home in Tom's River, New Jersey. His father, Walter Sr., was a nice guy. Dawson liked him. He and his son showed a lot of affection for each other. It was different than the relationship Dawson had with his father. Not better. Just different. Dawson told himself. Anyone could see that Walter Sr. was extremely proud of his son. They hung around for a couple of days

There's a small rocky beach just north of the airport and west of the town of Nassau on New Providence Island. Looking north, at low tide, you can see white ripples in the ocean as portions of the reef are exposed a thousand yards offshore. Swimming from the beach the rocky bottom turns to white sand with occasional clumps of sea grass. As the floor drops away to forty, fifty, sixty feet the water is so clear that it fools the brain into thinking you are suspended in air and could plunge to the bottom. Approaching the reef the depth recedes to thirty feet and the mountain of coral extends to the surface. Drawing closer, you can identify staghorn, elkhorn, the occasional boulder of brain coral, along with sea fans of fire coral waving in the current. Everywhere tiny damsel fish are darting through the branches. Blue tangs and butterfly fish pick at the polyps while sharp billed parrot fish scrape algae from the limestone leaving barren white streaks. Bigger fish, lightning fast jacks make strikes at the reef feeding on the small inhabitants. Barracuda hang motionless in the water then in a blur move and reappear yards away motionless again. If you look away form the reef you may see a large shark moving by. Snorkelers, unencumbered by breathing apparatus, can spend hours lying on the surface watching the world below. The weather was perfect. Dawson and Zobel swam out to the reef each morning towing a small yellow one man air force survival raft with a couple of canteens of fresh water. They would use it for rest breaks and return to shore in the afternoon.

It was the beginning of spring break and college students were flocking to Nassau and Paradise Island. Mostly daughters of parents who paid for airfare and hotel rooms. Their sons were left to carpool to the drunken ruckus of Ft. Lauderdale. They sat on the beach of Paradise Island sipping pina coladas and rum runners in front of the Resorts International and Britannia Beach hotels which were joined together by a shared casino. Security was tight. It was rumored that the mysterious billionaire Howard Hughes was occupying the entire top floor of the Britannia Beach. Guests had to show their room key for access to the hotel and beach. Dawson and Zobel quickly learned to swim around the jetty at the eastern end of the island and walk the half mile up the beach to join the students. They bragged to the girls about being green berets and more often than not often managed to spend the night in the hotel.

The two weeks came to an end. Dawson and Zobel shook hands goodbye at Miami International Airport. Zobel flew home to Tom's River and Dawson flew back to Bragg.

"What the hell's going on?"
"I have no idea sir," Kramer replied. "They just told us to load up our equipment, rifles and ammo, and assemble on the parade ground." Field caps only. No green berets. Within the hour they joined a couple of hundred other soldiers near the flag pole. They sat around in little clusters. No one seemed to be in charge and they were told nothing. The Reverend Martin Luther King had been assassinated three days before and there was rioting in Washington, D. C. The rumor mill was in full operation. They were going to Washington. They were going to protect the White House. They were

going to protect the Pentagon. After sitting on the field for a day and a half, whatever was planned was cancelled. They heard someone had decided Green Berets shooting rioters would be a publicity nightmare.

Dawson stayed with Sergeant Kramer for his last couple of weeks at Fort Bragg. The only activity of any importance was Sergeant Major Brown's retirement party. Of course, 2nd lieutenants weren't invited.

"Have you ever heard of SOG," Kramer asked. They had had a few beers.
"Just that it's some super secret thing."
"When you get to Nha Trang they will probably try to get you to volunteer for SOG."
"I didn't even volunteer for this."
"Yeah, well if you want to stay alive stay out of SOG."
"What do they do?"
"They get people killed. Take my word on this one."

When his time was up, he offered his Corvair to Kramer. He didn't want it so he gave it to Sergeant White and flew home to Philadelphia. When his father learned that he had spent most of his leave time in the Bahamas he complained that he wasn't spending more time at home. After a week Dawson flew to Seattle and spent a day visiting the Space Needle and the aquarium, finishing up with dinner at the marina restaurant nearby. The next day he went to McCord Air Force Base and flew to Vietnam via Alaska on a Northwest Airlines troop charter.

CHAPTER FIVE

DAWSON WAS SITTING on the beach at the sprawling Cam Ranh Bay base. Over the last two years he had heard hundreds of sentences that started with the words, When you get to Vietnam . . . The war that didn't seem like much when he had joined the army still didn't seem like much now that he was in it. The South China Sea rolled ashore with small one foot breakers. Not yet used to the heat, he was forced into the water every few minutes. The swimming area was protected by a shark net. Someone blew a whistle, a white banner was lowered from the flag staff and replaced by a large red ball. Swimmers exited the ocean. A strange looking helicopter with a square cabin and no tail rotor appeared from behind the dune. It flew out over the sea and hovered just beyond the shark net. A shooter leaned out of the cabin and fired two rifle rounds into the ocean, presumably at a shark. Then departed. The red ball was lowered, replaced by the white banner. People re-entered the sea. They were the first shots Dawson heard fired in Vietnam.

Entering the officer's mess hall and club, dressed in jeans and a tee shirt, he was asked for his military ID. The building was so long that the far end disappeared in cigarette smoke. He noticed that most of the officers wore stateside military fatigues. Going through the cafeteria line, he emerged with two cheeseburgers and two cans of beer, and found a seat at a rare empty table. By the time he had finished the first beer and half of a cheeseburger two young officers asked to sit at his table. He nodded. They were very excited to have been assigned to the 1st Infantry Division which they kept referring to as the Big Red One. Finally, realizing they were ignoring him, one asked Dawson where he was going,

"5th Special Forces Group," Dawson said, without looking up. The rest of the meal was spent in silence. Dawson got another beer, left the building and drank it sitting on a pile of sandbags.

The next morning he stood in line D-F to get his orders. A civilian clerk returned his file with his assignment packet clipped on the front. He exited the building and sat at a picnic table. Reading the paperwork, he was surprised and irritated to see he had been assigned to the 4th Infantry Division. Included in the paperwork were instructions to locate the escort officer for transport to Pleiku. His first instinct was to rush back inside and get it straightened out. But after two years of intense training he knew better than to rush into anything. He tried to convince himself that it was an easily corrected mistake, but all he had to do was look around at the huge size of the replacement operation to realize he was caught in an impersonal machine. Eventually, he went back inside anyway and stood in line at the information desk.

"Can I help you, sir?" a spec 5 asked.

"Yes, I had orders to the 5th Special Forces Group and now I have been assigned to the 4th..."

"The line down there at the end," the specialist interrupted pointing. They have lines for everything, Dawson thought. He walked down and joined the long line of unhappy junior officers. As he stood there he listened to conversations between men who until moments ago were complete strangers. Some were explaining their case for assignment change. Others confidently assuring them that their case was just. Focusing on the front of the line, he could see two clerks at the counter constantly shaking their heads. Most in the line were turned away in less than a minute. If the conversation became heated a major would appear and put an end to it. Every once in a while someone from the line would be directed to one of the desks behind the counter. In his mind, Dawson called it the ray of hope desk. After a half hour, not totally convinced that his undertaking was useless, but sure that he was tired of standing in line, Dawson left. He walked to his quarters, placed his folder and orders in the top of his duffle bag, put on a wet pair of cut off jeans and went to the beach.

The next morning, he sat outside reading his orders. When he finished he threw them in a nearby trash can. He opened his file and for the first time noticed a letter of reprimand for stopping at the whore house in Richmond signed by Colonel Forbes. He ripped it out, threw it in the trash, went to the mess hall and ate a fried egg sandwich, then spent some time on the beach. Later that afternoon he packed his half-full duffle bag, put on his stateside fatigues and taking Sergeant Kramer's advice set off to find a Special Forces sergeant. He walked along the sandy road next to the ocean toward the enlisted billets. When he got to a busy area he sat down on a pile of sandbags and waited and watched. Soon enough two soldiers appeared wearing green berets. One carried a kit bag the other a duffle bag. They both had Third Group flashes on their berets. One was in jungle fatigues. Dawson assumed it was his second tour.

"Excuse me gentlemen," he said standing.

"Lieutenant."

"You going to Nha Trang?"

"Thirty klicks. Straight up Highway One. You can walk it, lieutenant." Highway one. "The Street Without Joy." Dawson had read Bernard Fall's book about the French debacle in Indo-China.

"I'll wait with you for the limo, sergeant." They laughed and walked a hundred meters to a small square of PSP. A helicopter landed. The sergeant yelled,

"Nha Trang?" The pilot nodded. After a short flight the pilot set down. They piled into a jeep and drove under an arched sign that read "5th Special Forces Group (Airborne)" onto a wide dusty street and came to a stop.

"You know where the orderly room is, sir?"

"I figure it's in that building that says HEADQUARTERS in two foot high letters," Dawson replied, nodding over his shoulder. "Thanks for the ride."

Entering the building, Dawson approached a spec 4 sitting behind the closest desk to the door.

"How ya doing?" not giving the specialist time to reply. He continued, "I just arrived from the 7th Group with orders to join the 5th," sounding a lot more sure of himself than he felt. A lieutenant a couple of desks away interrupted,

I'll take care of you." Dawson walked over and handed him his file. "Where's your replacement packet."

"My orders are to the 5th so I just came here."

"Guess you didn't like your replacement orders," the lieutenant replied. Realizing he wasn't fooling anybody, Dawson said,

"No. Not particularly."

"Don't worry. We got you now." Very relieved, he stood watching as the officer efficiently rifled through his file and stacked other papers from his desk. "Your pay may get a little screwed up because the army won't know where you are for a few days." He kept moving papers around. "Congratulations."

"For what?"

"You can get rid of that brown bar," referring to Dawson's 2nd lieutenant's bar. "You're in a combat zone so I can wave 50% of your time in grade. You're promoted to 1st lieutenant as of right now. I'll take care of the orders." He reached in a drawer and handed Dawson a silver bar. "We don't want any 2nd lieutenants around here." Dawson pinned it to the red flash on his beret. Noticing, the lieutenant said, "When you draw your jungle fatigues you'll have to leave them for a while to get the name tag and patches sewn on but they'll change the flash on your beret while you wait."

"Thanks." He had a dozen how do I, what do I, where do I questions but he had learned that in the army, with patience, the answers would come to him. The lieutenant handed him a folder.

"You can get checked into the BOQ out the front to the right." They shook hands as he left.

"Better put your beret on, sir," a passing sergeant said. "This may be a combat zone but it's not an asshole free zone."

"Hey, thanks for the warning." He complied, then turned right. After a few steps a bright area across the wide street caught his attention. People were standing around eating ice cream. Who would have thought there would be an ice cream parlor in the middle of

Special Forces headquarters? He almost laughed out loud. Pausing to take in the view, he began to notice a difference in the green uniforms moving about the area. Some wore carefully pressed jungle fatigues with shined boots and berets. Others, wrinkled fatigues with dirty boots and floppy jungle hats. He figured that the former worked at the headquarters and the latter were in from the field. Two striking captains stood together. They had to be 6 foot 3 inches tall. Blonde hair and blue eyes. Their immaculate uniforms were adorned with pistol belts holstering 45s. Dawson immediately dubbed them the palace guard. Much too pretty to get dirty he thought. As he turned to resume his walk to the BOQ he noticed two other men. Jungle fatigues with no insignia whatsoever, bare-headed. One carried a thick grip pistol in a shoulder holster. A Browning nine millimeter. He stopped and watched as they walked down the street. It might have been his imagination but he thought others took quick looks trying to act casual. They walked directly in front of the palace guard without incident. Maybe they weren't noticed. Or, more likely, the rules did not apply to them.

He entered the BOQ. Two lieutenants were seated at opposite ends of a couch. An E-5 was helping a third at a small counter. Dropping his duffle bag, he sat in a matching chair. The sergeant came around from behind the counter limping on a stiff leg.

"Got stitched by an AK," the sergeant said tapping his bad leg to no one in particular. The lieutenants ignored him. Dawson saw the combat infantry badge on his fatigue shirt.

"They gave you this shit job while you rehab?"

"That's about it, sir,"

"Where were you when you got hit?"

"A-245, Dak Seang. Just north of Dak To. Routine patrol. Just got unlucky, sir."

"Well, none of us here have ever been in combat," he gestured pointedly around the room. "Hopefully we'll be luckier than you were." The other three lieutenants disregarded Dawson's comment and carried their bags up the stairs to the second floor.

"Need a room sir?

"Yeah, I just got here an hour ago."

"Oh, you'll be here for a while. You have to go through orientation training."

"What's that?"

"Didn't you read the papers they gave you?"

"No, not yet."

"They want you to get used to the climate and take your malaria pill. Monday is pill day. Tuesday is shit day. You'll get some classes on how to treat the locals and go on a couple of one day field exercises. Wanna a beer, sir?"

"Sure." The sergeant went through a door behind the counter and returned with two beers. Handing one to Dawson, hiding the other behind the counter, he said,

"You know you pissed off those other lieutenants?"

"I didn't like the way they treated you like some bellhop."

⌒The next morning Dawson lay in bed reading the paperwork. After a while he got up and got dressed. Down the stairs he was disappointed that the stiff-legged sergeant had been replaced by a PFC. He checked the camp map and walked to the quartermaster where he drew two sets of jungle fatigues, jungle boots, green tee shirts and shorts. From there he went to the tailor shop just down from the ice cream parlor run by Vietnamese. They knew what to do and as promised, removed the red flash on his beret and replaced it with the 5th group flash in just a few minutes. Hungry, he pulled the folded map out of his pocket and located the officer's club just past the headquarters building. He entered and walked up a long dark stairway to the second floor. It was early in the day and there were only a few other people seated in the large room. He went to the counter, ate a couple of fried egg sandwiches and left.

Returning to the BOQ he saw the sergeant from the night before outside with another man both dressed in civilian clothes.

"Hey lieutenant."

"Johnson," Dawson replied, remembering his name from his fatigue shirt.

"This is Sergeant Cooke." They shook hands and talked.

"Want to go see Nha Trang?" Johnson asked.

"Sure. I don't have anything else to do."

"Do you have civilian clothes."

"Yeah. When are you leaving?"

"Right now."

CHAPTER SIX

FIVE MINUTES LATER, he returned in jeans and a collared polo shirt. They walked to the main gate. Johnson's limp was less noticeable now. Cooke signaled a Lambretta taxi and they climbed onto the benches in the rear. In a few minutes they were in the city streets clamoring with pedestrians, bicycles and scooters. Just like all the Asian cities you could watch back home on TV. Dawson was uneasy. He had been in Vietnam for six days and other than the sounds of aircraft he hadn't seen any evidence of a war, but he had heard two years of stories about Viet Cong tossing hand grenades at American soldiers in civilian areas. Cooke and Johnson certainly weren't worried about it. The Lambretta labored up a steep, winding, crowded street and stopped. They got out and looked down the steep street. As he turned, Dawson was confronted by a huge white statue.

"Jesus!" he said.

"No, Buddha," Johnson laughed. Rising above them the statue of Buddha seated in the lotus position had to be more than forty feet high looking down over the city. It was breathtaking. They climbed the steps to the base of the statue and wandered around just like tourists on vacation.

"Let's go to the blow bath," Cooke said, starting down the wide stone stairway.

"What's a blow bath?"

"You're gonna love it, sir." Johnson and Cooke were laughing. They got in another Lambretta. Cooke gave instructions and they were off, down the hill to a less crowded part of town to a massage parlor. They each paid and were given towels and a plastic bag. In a small curtained changing booth Dawson stripped, hung his clothes on hooks, wrapped one towel around his waste and put his wallet in the plastic bag. Stepping out, hanging the other towel around his neck, an older Vietnamese woman led him to a steam room. It was way too hot inside. The thick steam blinded him. Johnson entered and disappeared into the steam. Dawson drew a quick breath of fresh air through the open door. He stood there trying to breath the bleach tainted air until the woman finally returned and led him to the relief of a shower. From there he was taken to a massage table surrounded by bedspreads hanging over ropes for privacy. He lay down on his stomach and put a towel over his butt. A young Vietnamese woman entered wearing pajamas and began to massage him. She was probing deep into his muscles. He was surprised how strong she was. He was also surprised how pretty she was. She put her hands together, like praying, and pounded up and down his back, her hands making a clacking sound. Occasionally, she would call out saying something to another girl on the other side of the bedspreads. After quite a while she leaned close to him and said,

"You pay me?" Dawson did and she was naked. As she climbed up on top of him she called out to the other girl and they giggled.

"How'd you like that, lieutenant?" Johnson asked.

"Most fun I've had since I joined the army."

"You probably got special treatment since you were paying in green backs. You need to change them into piasters."

"What's that?"

"Vietnamese currency."

Three artillery rounds could be heard as they passed over and slammed into the side of a hill a hundred meters from where they were standing. Dawson heard a whizzing sound that ended with a thud as it hit a tree and fell to the ground. It was thick piece of brown metal a few inches long. Part of the shell casing. He walked down the hill and carefully touched it to make sure it wasn't hot. He went to pick it up. The razor sharp serrations on the sides cut the hell out of his fingers. He wiped the blood on his pant leg and picked it up avoiding the edges. It was heavy. Looking off into the hills he realized somewhere out there, people, outside of the safety of the base camps, were getting slaughtered by chunks of metal like this. It made his blood run cold. He walked back up the hill and rejoined the class.

Orientation was over and it was time to get his orders. He went back to headquarters. The same spec 4 was still sitting at the desk closest to the door. Dawson told him why he was there. This time he had to wait almost a half hour before he was shown to a captain's small office. He entered and came to attention.

"No need to report. Have a seat," he said. "I've got your paperwork. You the one who came here from Cam Ranh replacement without orders?"

"Yes, sir."

"Guess you'd like to pick your assignment again," the captain said.

"If you need an assistant, I'd be happy to stay right here," Dawson said picking up on the joke.

"Unfortunately, I don't. But I've got an unconventional assignment for an unconventional lieutenant. Your are being assigned to the Studies and Observation Group, FOB 1, at Phu Bai," he announced.

"What's the Studies and Observation Group?"

"It's better known as SOG." Dawson felt just like he did when he picked up the piece of shrapnel.

"I thought you had to volunteer for SOG, sir."

"You just did, lieutenant."

Dawson walked out of the headquarters building and turned right toward the BOQ. Johnson was there and he told him about his orders.

"Oh, you're fucked," he said adding "Sir."

"What does SOG do?"

"They get peopled killed." Dawson remembered that he had had this conversation before with Kramer at Ft. Bragg. "There's a lieutenant staying here tonight from SOG. If you're around here when he shows up I'll point him out."

"Can't wait."

John Miller was dressed in unmarked fatigues, wearing a green beret with a first lieutenant's bar when he and Dawson met. Now, they were drinking at the officer's club.

"What does SOG do?"

"If I told you. I would have to kill you," Miller said using the annoying cliché. I'm the only lieutenant one-zero at FOB 1," he boasted.

"What's a one-zero?"

"A recon team commander. The team leader is the one-zero. The assistant team leader is the one-one and the radio operator is the one-two. The indig are numbered zero-one, zero-two, zero-three to however many there are."

"Who runs most of the recon teams?"

"Sergeants. Mostly E-7s."

"What do the lieutenants do?"

"They're either staff or hatchet force platoon leaders. You'll get a full briefing at Phu Bai." Miller was tired of the questions.

The next morning Dawson made a quick stop at headquarters.

"Can you tell me where someone is assigned?" He asked the Spec 4.

"What's his name?"

"Walter Zobel." The spec 4 walked over to a row of file cabinets and bent to opened the lowest drawer on the right. Z for Zobel. Dawson thought.

"He's at FOB 2, Kontum, with SOG."

"Thanks for your help."

Later that day he met up with Miller, now armed with an M-16 and wearing bulky web gear. They found a jeep to drive them the short distance to the air base and spent two hours doing nothing, waiting for a flight to DaNang. Finally, they were directed to a C-130 sitting on the runway. The plane was loaded with cargo. They climbed up the tail ramp, threw their bags into the back of a jeep lashed to the floor of the plane and sat in the front seats.

"Why's this plane painted black and green instead of brown and green?" Dawson asked Miller.

"It's an air commando blackbird. They fly classified missions."

"So, they paint it a different color so nobody knows what it is?"

"Exactly."

"Where we going? China?" The flight was taking longer than Dawson expected.

"It's about three hundred miles to Da Nang," Miller replied. Finally, the plane landed, taxied and as the tail gate lowered a military three-quarter ton truck painted black pulled up behind the plane. A staff sergeant wearing a bush hat got out and waited for the ramp to hit the tarmac. The plane's engines shut down.

"Hey, lieutenant. Welcome back," he called to Miller. "Give me a hand with this stuff." They loaded a few boxes into the bed of the truck that already contained a dozen cases of beer. At the last minute Dawson ran back to the plane and retrieved his duffle bag from the back of the jeep. A couple of minutes later they were out of the airbase and after another couple of minutes they were in the crowded city streets of Da Nang. Sitting alone in the open back of the truck, Dawson felt like a target. Realizing he was probably being overly cautious, he still took off his beret and shoved it in the side pocket of his fatigue pants. As they drove down a main city street he was surprised to see a Chevrolet agency and the Bank of America. Further along he saw a dark masonry building with white globe lamps flanking its large wooden doors. It looked like a police precinct station house right out of the TV show "Dragnet." They turned onto a side street and after a couple more turns were in a area of larger two story houses crowded together, surrounded with palm trees. By the look of them, upkeep wasn't a priority. They stopped in front of a house surrounded by what could generously be called a ramshackle wall consisting of a white four rail fence backed by sheets of plywood. On top of that was a two-by-four frame covered with cyclone wire fence extending its height to eight feet. In front, extending into the street, was a small security hut surrounded by sandbags topped with a piece of corrugated aluminum and pieces of canvas to protect the carbine armed Vietnamese guard from the weather.

"What is this place?" Dawson asked as they walked through the gate.

"House 22. SOG's safe house," Miller answered.

"Doesn't look very safe. What's it for?"

"You come here to get transportation to the forward operating bases. It was getting dark as they entered the house. It wasn't much brighter inside. There were maybe a dozen other soldiers inside. None of them paid them any attention. Dawson followed Miller past a couple of tables where people were eating. Back towards the kitchen they climbed the rear stairs to a large room with a line of metal bunks strewn with personal items and a variety of weapons. Stowing their gear, they went back down the stairs to eat. Later, someone set up a movie projector and was showing stag films. Dawson drank a couple of beers while he watched then went upstairs and turned in. The next afternoon they took a jeep back to the airbase and made a quick fifty mile helicopter flight to Phu Bai.

CHAPTER SEVEN

TWO AMERICANS STOOD outside the aid station of FOB 1. Blood was still oozing through multiple holes in their green tee shirts. They were surrounded by a half dozen slightly wounded Cambodian soldiers. Those more serious had already been transported to the medevac hospital. Earlier that morning, while moving up a hillside in an area southwest of the Ashau Valley, the SOG hatchet force had made contact with the enemy. They tried to rally the mercenaries into an organized defense. The task, difficult to accomplish on the practice field, proved impossible under enemy fire. The Cambodes, as they called them, retreated down the hill leaving the Americans exposed. The NVA detonated a Chinese claymore, a trash can lid sized explosive device which spew hundreds of nails, screws, nuts, bolts and other assorted pieces of metal toward the Americans. Beyond the lethal range of the weapon, each received multiple superficial wounds. What followed was the suppression of emery fire by aircraft and the extraction of the troops by helicopter.

"Hey, Leon," Miller called to one of the wounded soldiers. Preoccupied with poking at one of the wounds in his chest, he didn't reply. "Don, are they Americans?" he asked the other, a shorter, muscular man with a closely shaved head, gesturing toward two body bags laying by the side of the aid station.

"No," the man replied shaking his head. Miller continued walking. Dawson followed silently behind.

Compared to Cam Ranh Bay and Na Trang, FOB 1 at Phu Bai was more of a hole in the wall than a military base. Located less than ten miles south of the imperial capitol of Hue, it consisted of a couple of dozen wood buildings with corrugated metal roofs crowded together. To the rear of the compound stood a sixty foot rappelling tower. They entered Miller's sleeping quarters.

"You can take that bunk. It's empty." Dawson dropped his duffle bag on the metal springs of a gray air force cot. The mattress was rolled at the top.

"No air conditioner?"

"We got electricity. A little refrigerator. A hot plate," Miller said pointing. "This is pure luxury."

"And enough weapons and ammo to start a war." Everywhere Dawson looked there were ammo cans and loaded magazines. An M-16 and a carbine were propped up against the wall. A military 45 on a table. Hand grenades some sitting in opened round black cardboard containers, some just loose, were scattered around the room. "Guess I won't be getting a weapons card." Referring to how weapons were controlled in the states.

"Nope. Not here. You should probably go to the TOC. That's the tactical operations center."

"I know that."

"And tell them you're here."

"Where is it?"

"Across from the dispensary." Dawson left.

"The next time your people run on us I'm gonna call an air strike right down on their ass. Do you understand?" That got Dawson's attention. An American was yelling at a Vietnamese man dressed in a green beret, black shirt, tan vest with some kind of medals pinned to it and mirror sunglasses. He looked more like a pimp than a soldier. Trying not to stare, he continued to the TOC. Inside a lieutenant logged him in, had him fill out a couple of pieces of paperwork and told him he would receive an operational briefing the next day. Back in his quarters, he told Miller what he had just witnessed.

"That wasn't a Vietnamese. He's a Cambodian. Terrible soldiers. No discipline at all. Six Nungs from my recon team could take a company of Cambodes."

"What are Nungs?"

"Ethnic Chinese who live in Vietnam. Good aggressive fighters. They'll probably give you a whole platoon of Cambodes," Miller said, thinking it was very amusing.

The next morning, Dawson was waiting to be briefed in a small room in the tactical operations center. After a while an officer entered.

"Stay seated. I'm Captain Stevens, the S-2, intelligence officer. You're Lieutenant Alan Dawson?" he asked, looking at a sheet of paper.

"Yes, sir."

"Ok, I'm going to explain your responsibilities for operational security. I see you have your final Top Secret security clearance." Sill standing, he started reading from a card. "This entire operation is classified Top Secret. You may not discuss this unit, its operations or your duties with any unauthorized individual. Furthermore, this operation is designated limited access on a need to know basis, which means you cannot discuss it with any person who is not assigned to this unit even if that person has a top secret security clearance. Violations are punishable under the Espionage Act." Looking up he asked, "Do you have any questions?"

"No, sir," Dawson answered. The captain placed the paper on the table, handed Dawson a pen and had him sign the form.

"That's it," he said and left the room. Dawson sat there wondering if the briefing was over. He was about to leave when a major entered and slid into a chair across the table.

"Dawson?"

"Yes, sir."

"I'm Major Capra, the S-3 operations officer. Thank you for volunteering for SOG," he said with a wry smile. Obviously knowing that officers were being assigned to the so called all volunteer unit. "Do you know what SOG stands for?' he asked.

"Special Operations Group?"

"That was our original name but it was changed. Now it officially stands for the Studies and Observation Group. That makes it sound like we are a bunch of bird watchers. Not that it fools anyone except maybe the congress and the press. Since we got into this war the use of ground combat forces inside North Vietnam, Laos, and Cambodia has been strictly forbidden. The President of the United States, by top secret executive order, has lifted that restriction for SOG. You've heard of the Ho Chi Minh Trail?"

"Yes, Sir." Major Capra got up and got a map from a cabinet. He spread it out on the table.

"The North gets all of its supplies from China and the Soviets. There's a railroad that runs out of China to north of Hanoi. The

Russian equipment comes in by boat to the port at Haiphong," he said, pointing out areas on the map. "Instead of bringing their supplies straight down across the DMZ into South Vietnam, they truck it west into northern Laos and then bring it south. Sort of like they are allowed to go out of bounds, but we aren't. Make sense?"

"Yes, sir. I thought we were bombing the infiltration routes?"

"We are. But those routes are almost as long as the state of California, most of it is dense mountain jungle. So without ground spotters the bombing just kills a lot of trees. That's where SOG comes in. We insert recon teams to find the supply routes and mobile strike platoons and companies, called Hatchet Forces, to attack those supply lines. Capra looked up from the map to get a reaction.

"I guess the North Vietnamese aren't real thrilled with that," Dawson offered. Not knowing what else to say.

"This is dangerous work. Without a doubt the most dangerous in this war. To support our ground teams we have a complete package of communications and air support dedicated to providing them whatever they need on short notice. From FOB 1 you are going to be working targets in Laos. The code name for Laos is Prairie Fire. When you are the commander on the ground and you believe your unit is in grave danger, you can, at your sole discretion, declare a 'Prairie Fire Emergency.' Those words will immediately trigger the scrambling of all assets to extract your unit. No other ground commanders in this war have that authority. No one up the chain of command can challenge your decision. I'll never do that and I don't care if there is a general officer sitting in my chair, you are in command and we're getting you out. You'll have a lot to learn but I want to assure you that you're not going to be alone out there. Oh, and one more thing. Our operations are conducted with plausible deniability. That means no uniform insignia, no dog tags, no identifying personal items such as wallets or ID cards when you are in Laos. Or as we say, across the fence."

Major Capra got up and got a stack of business cards out of a drawer. He fanned them out like a deck of cards and held them out to Dawson.

"Pick one," he said. Dawson did. The major took it back, turned it over and placed it on the table. It contained one word, Shadow. "That's your operational code name. Congratulations Shadow. Welcome to SOG." They stood up from the table and shook hands. The briefing over, Dawson started to leave.

"Lieutenant."

"Sir?"

"Just because you have a silver bar on your collar doesn't mean you know what you're doing. Because, right now, you definitely do not. Pay attention to your sergeants. If you don't, you'll not only get yourself killed, but you could get them killed too. And, believe me, we need them more than we need you."

CHAPTER EIGHT

"GET YOUR ASSIGNMENT?"

"Yeah. 2nd Platoon, Company A," Dawson replied.

"I figured that," Miller said. "Did you hear me ask that guy about the KIA yesterday?"

"The one with the shaved head?"

"Yeah. Well, it turns out that he was hurt worse than they thought. He's in the hospital."

"So, I got his platoon? The one that ran on him?"

"Yep," Miller laughed.

"That's just great! Where do I find A Company?"

"The Cambodes live in two barracks on hammocks for racks. There isn't an orderly room or anything."

"Who's the company commander?"

"They don't have one. They've just been using whoever is available. Most operations are single platoons anyway, so they really don't need one."

"What are the chances I have a platoon sergeant?"

"That's Rogers. Staff sergeant. Square built guy with a crew cut."

"I think I know who that is," Dawson said remembering the American and the pimp. "Where can I find him?"

"Wherever you find a rum and coke," Miller chuckled.

Dawson walked to the rear of the camp toward the Cambode barracks. Two men were standing next to a conex container.

"Sergeant Rogers?" The men looked up. "I'm Dawson. I became your platoon leader about a half hour ago."

"The lieutenant's not coming back?" Rogers asked.

"He's in the hospital. That's all I know."

'This is Specialist Sacco," gesturing to the other man. He's your radio operator. It's just the three of us and the Cambodes." The men shook hands.

"What are they doing now?" Dawson asked.

"The Cambodes?"

"Yeah."

"They're cleaning their equipment from the operation. We'll inspect them later on. Anything you want us to do, Sir?"

"I've been here less than twenty-four hours. I don't even know what I want to do."

"Do you have your equipment?"

"No."

"Let's take care of that right now."

After a half hour of digging through conex containers and a trip to supply they were done.

"Think you have enough stuff LT?" as Rogers had decided to call Dawson.

"How about a helmet and flack jacket?"

"We don't use them."

"What? Do you think bullets bounce off you?" Dawson joked.

"No," Rogers replied. "We definitely don't think that." There was an ominous tone in his voice. Dawson knew he hit a nerve, but he didn't know which one.

"Have you got a kit bag?" directing his question to the supply clerk.

"No, Sir." He walked away and returned in a few seconds and produced a beat up old duffle bag. "You can take this."

"Thanks."

They carried it all back to Dawson's billet and set the ammo, grenades and weapons on the floor. Then dumped the contents of the duffle bag on his rack.

"Know how to set this stuff up LT?"

"I don't even know what some of it is."

"Got a beer?"

"Check Miller's fridge," Dawson said pointing. Sacco checked and shook his head. Rogers pulled a floppy brimmed bush hat out of the pile and handed it to Sacco.

"Take this over to Mamason and have it cut down. A little bigger than normal because the lieutenant wears glasses," Rogers instructed Sacco. "Get some beer on your way back."

"Sure thing, Sarge."

"Ok LT, here's the deal. You dress in three layers. Your fatigues, your web gear and your back pack. Suppose you're on the run and you have to get lighter. The first thing you do is lose the back pack. Next off is the web gear. That leaves your fatigues. So the most important stuff goes in your fatigue pockets. Map, compass, signal mirror, strobe light, pen flare gun, the essential things you need to signal an aircraft to get extracted. Are you going to wear jungle fatigues or tiger fatigues?"

"I have a choice?"

"Yeah. Whichever you want."

"Tiger fatigues look cool, but I'll go with the pockets."

"Put 'em on and I'll show you where everything goes." An hour and a half later they were done. Sacco had returned with beer and his cut down bush hat and left to inspect the Cambodes. Dawson's fatigue pockets were full of survival equipment tied down so it couldn't be dropped. His web gear was set up. They fastened black electric tape tabs to the bottom of his magazines for easy access. He attached a sling to his M-16 and hooked it through a snap link that was in turn fastened to a loop on his web gear. "That about does it LT. You're good to go."

"Christ, I feel like a bride getting fitted for her wedding dress," Dawson joked. "How many rounds do you load in your magazines?"

"Twenty. Why?"

"A sergeant in jump school, who was in the Ia Drang Valley shootout, told me if you loaded more than eighteen it would jam up."

"He had one of the old M-16s." Rogers picked up the rifle. "They added this plunger to the receiver. After you insert the magazine and load the first round you use this to make sure it's seated," he demonstrated.

"That's kinda Mickey Mouse. Speaking of Mickey Mouse, why do we carry these cheap canvas back packs instead of jungle rucksacks?"

"Jungle rucks are too big for the Cambodes. If you carried something different the bad guys would know exactly who to shoot."

"Now, that makes more sense than just about anything I've ever heard since I joined the army. Of course, they could just shoot the tall guys."

"You'd be surprised how difficult it is to gauge height in the uneven mountain terrain."

"There's some things you should know about the Cambodes, LT." Rogers and Dawson were walking through the camp to check on Sacco's inspection. "They're Buddhists. You can't touch their head. They don't sleep in bunk beds because they can't put one spirit above another. You can't take their picture without asking. Some of them think the camera captures their spirit. Others don't care. Oh, and they wear Buddha bags around their neck. That's a rolled up cloth necklace that has a bunch of religious charms in it. When they are in danger they put it in their mouth for protection."

"You forgot the part about they don't fight."

"The big excuse for that is that they were expecting to fight on the border of Cambodia. Some genius decided to send them to I Corps. Now they are far away from their families and they aren't happy.

"Who's the guy with the sunglasses you were jacking up yesterday?"

"Oh, you saw that. That asshole is their company commander. We pay him more than they pay me. He never goes in the field and he comes up and starts blaming me that two of his people got killed. I'm just starting my second tour. My first was with a hatchet force out of FOB 2. We had Nungs down there. This was my first Cambode operation. Compared to the Nungs, they stink. The Nungs were loyal, They had your back."

"So, if they're not loyal and not going to fight why hire them?"

"Because they couldn't find anybody else to do the job. They don't have a problem with fighting. They can be vicious so long as they're winning."

"How do you make sure they're winning?"

"That's your job, lieutenant." Dawson let that sink in.

The Cambodian barracks was a maze of hammocks strung between roof posts dimly lit with assorted light bulbs hanging from lamp wire strung along the rafters. Some of the men had tapped into the wire with safety pins to get light nearer their hammock. It was miraculous it didn't short out or burn down the building. Their weapons, equipment and personal items were piled under and around the hammocks. Dawson focused on the weapons. It looked like the squad leaders had green folding wire stock Swedish K nine millimeter submachine guns. There were a couple of Browning automatic rifles. The prize weapon was a single M-60 machine gun. Most of the others had 30 caliber carbines. Stopping in front of one of the soldiers, Dawson took his carbine. He ejected the magazine and pulled back the operating slide. It slid out in his hand. Checking to make sure there wasn't a round in the chamber, he replaced the slide and wiggled it.

"No good," the Cambodian soldier said with a wide grin.

"No good," Dawson agreed.

"What do you think, LT?" They were back outside the barracks.

"I think those carbines went up San Juan Hill with Teddy Roosevelt."

"Sir, they weren't made until."

"I know, until World War Two," Dawson said cutting Sacco off. Then he paused and asked, "If we go out on operation will they give us a couple more Americans?"

"At least one," Rogers said.

"Good. You know, if I had to go up against an AK-47 with one of those carbines, I'd probably run too. We have to increase the fire power."

"We can't get M-16s for the Cambodes. They still want deniability. They just started letting us carry them."

"Yeah. I know. Can you get us a couple of M-60s?"

"Sure, LT. I'll just go over to supply and ask for two machine guns."

"That would be a start. Are there pre-placed M-60s and ammo in the defensive bunkers?"

"We can't just steal them."

"There's weapons and ammo laying around all over this place like it's fucking Christmas. Must be a way."

The next day Sergeant Rogers had scheduled a training march. Dawson picked up his web gear and put it on. Rogers had him set it up with ten magazines in two M-14 ammo pouches, seven magazines in a canteen cover, three grenades fastened to the sides of the ammo pouches and another five grenades in an ammo pouch. Add two plastic quart canteens and it was very heavy. Dawson thought about getting rid of some of the stuff for training, then decided he better get used to the weight. Putting on his newly-cropped bush hat he walked to the Cambode barracks. Rogers and Sacco had the troops milling around outside. They had their web gear paired down to one ammo pouch and a couple of canteens.

"Going to war, LT?" Rogers and Sacco laughed.

"Just thought I'd try it out. If it gets too heavy I'll give some of it to you." They walked through the camp with the Cambodes trailing behind. Then across Route 1 and the parallel railroad tracks. On the other side Rogers and Sacco organized the Cambodes.

"What's that?" Dawson asked, pointing back to a compound next of the FOB.

"That's an ARVN basic training camp," Sacco replied. Their objective was about three kilometers away. A hill that rose out of the flat plain about two hundred meters high. It was hard to tell if it was natural or man made. In the center a road about ten meters wide had been bulldozed up the steep slope from bottom to top. The sides and back dropped off abruptly. It was hot. Over one hundred degrees hot. Rogers and Sacco had green triangular bandages rolled up and tied around their foreheads to stop the sweat, and another tied as a bandanna to wipe their faces. Dawson had neither. When his bush hat became saturated, the sweat poured down his face clouding his glasses. His web gear hung heavily on his shoulders.

"The lieutenant's not doing too well. Wanna call a break?" Sacco said to Rogers.

"No, let's see what he's made of." A half hour later Dawson was still plodding along half-blind from his sweat-soaked glasses.

"Hey LT. How about a break?" As Dawson drank half the water out of a canteen, Rogers produced a triangle bandage.

"Here you go LT." Dawson used it to clean his glasses. He shoved his bush hat in his side pocket, grabbed the bandage by the ends, spun it around and knotted it around his forehead.

"If you tighten your web belt you can transfer some of the weight off your shoulders to your hips," Rogers advised. Dawson made the adjustment. Put his web gear back on and felt an immediate improvement.

"Thanks Mom."

"Baby sitting lieutenants. That's what I do."

They proceeded to the base of the hill and climbed the steep slope. About half way up Dawson stopped, mostly to give his screaming thigh muscles a break, and asked Rogers,

"ARVN rifle range?" Looking off to his right at the base of the hill.

"Yeah, they're useless," Rogers replied. Almost immediately they heard the zing of a couple of rounds go by. The ARVN on the range were firing pot shots at then. They moved the Cambodes to safety on the opposite side of the road. Out of the line of sight.

"Think I'll see if this thing works," Dawson said shouldering his M-16.

"That's not a great idea, LT." Dawson ignored him, moved to the edge of the road and blew off a magazine in three short bursts toward the rifle range. Unimpressed, the firing from the ARVN increased.

"Get me the sixty," it was the closest thing to a command Dawson had issued since he was commissioned. Sacco grabbed the Cambode gunner and pulled him up the hill to the lieutenant. Taking the gun Dawson lay on the ground, opened the bi-pod and seated a hundred round belt of ammo. He then proceeded to fire bursts at the rife range working them closer and closer to the firing positions until some of the ARVN got up and ran.

"Holly shit, sir. That's gonna cause a big problem," Sacco said. The Cambodes chattered and grinned from ear to ear. Dawson handed the gun back to the Cambodian.

"Trung uy number one."

"What'd he say?"

"He loves you, LT," Rogers laughed.

That night, after a couple of beers, Dawson turned in. He had trouble getting to sleep thinking about what Rogers had said about the Cambodes. "They can be vicious so long as they're winning." The next morning he walked down to the Cambode barracks. Rogers, Sacco and another man were there.

"Hey, LT. This is Specialist 4 Healey from third platoon. He's coming with us on our mission."

"What mission?"

"I heard they're sending your platoon out for an in country operation, lieutenant," Healey said.

"That's news to me." He shook hands with Healey. "When is this supposed to happen?"

"You'll probably get the op order later today."

"What do you want us to do. sir?" Sacco asked. It was a pain in the ass question.

"I don't know. Go make sure the Cambodes have bullets in their magazines," Dawson said to blow him off. A few seconds later he asked, "Hey, Healey how many M-60s have you got in the third platoon?"

"I think we have two, sir."

"Can we borrow one?"

"They aren't going anywhere. I don't see why not."

"Why don't you go get it?"

"Now?"

"Yeah, now would be good." Healey just looked at him. "I'd appreciated it if you'd go get it," Dawson said.

"The platoons are both in this barracks," Healey said. It's probably right inside."

"So just go get it," Dawson said. Then to Sacco who hadn't moved either, "Go get our M-60, please." Turning to Rogers he said, "These guys have problems with English?."

"Move!" Rogers said forcefully. Healey and Sacco disappeared into the barracks.

"Nothing like a little command presence. Thanks."

"What are you up to, LT?" Rogers asked.

"I was thinking about what you said about the Cambodes only being effective if they're winning. In our walk up the hill yesterday, I saw that the machine gunner and assistant carried the ammo belts slung across their chests like in a movie. Let's have them carry the ammo in the cloth pouches slung over their shoulders but not around their neck. Oh, and also, get rid of the slings on the guns."

"It's a lot harder to carry the gun that way," Rogers said. "What are you trying to do?"

"I'm thinking our time may be better spent winning than trying to round up a bunch of reluctant fighters. If they run on us they'll probably drop the guns and ammo instead of taking it with them. You any good with an M-60?"

"Oh, I see where you're going with this. Why not just go all the way and turn them into arms bearers? After that act you pulled yesterday on the ARVN rifle range I think you should definitely take one of the guns." In spite of himself, Rogers grinned.

"I'll be too busy being in charge," Dawson laughed. "Let's form up the kids, take them across the tracks and see if we can turn this into an immediate action drill."

CHAPTER NINE

AS HEALEY HAD predicted, late that afternoon Dawson and Rogers were in the TOC getting briefed. The mission they were assigned was defined as both training and operational. Because of the platoon's poor performance on the last operation, the first part of the mission was to increase the platoon's combat effectiveness. They were going to be inserted into a small peninsula on the coast southeast of Phu Bai less than half way to Danang. There had been reports of local Viet Cong units bringing supplies ashore by boat and it was the sight of a suspected arms cache. The second part of the mission was to find and destroy the cache.

Early the next morning Dawson, Rogers, Sacco and Healey were busy distributing rations, ammo and inspecting the troops. They decided Rogers would take the radio, Sacco and Healey each running squads. When finished they walked to the helipad and the four Americans and twenty-four Cambodes loaded into three Korean war era H-34 Kingbee helicopters, flown by Vietnamese pilots, and made the short trip to the landing zone. They approached from the land side to the rear of a high rocky hilltop and disembarked, shielded from view of the peninsula. After performing commo checks they got organized and picked their way around boulders to the other side of the hilltop. Going was slow and difficult. Some of the boulders were as much as twenty feet high and they often had to detour around sheer drop offs of about the same size. It took them two hours. Before them stretched the peninsula running due north. The rocky field extended for another five hundred meters, then descended to a lush green jungle. The jungle, three kilometers long and barely a kilometer wide, was surrounded by bright blue ocean water. It was quite a beautiful spot. Looking down they could see a small fishing village on the western shore.

"Lieutenant." It was Sacco calling down from a huge flat top boulder behind them. "You should see this." Dropping their gear and slinging their M-16s, Dawson and Rogers worked their way around the boulder and climbed to the top with difficulty.

"How, the fuck did you get up here?" Dawson asked.

"Look," Sacco said. Pointing to an extinguished campfire. "It might be a signal fire for the boats."

"Maybe people were roasting marshmallows. Did you find any condoms?" Rogers said dismissing the idea of a signal fire.

"Charlie's not going to climb all the way up here when he can just stand on the beach and turn on a flashlight. Only Americans are that dumb," Dawson added.

"Well, somebody built the fire."

"Probably Marines." They laughed.

By the time they got back down off the boulder the shadows were growing long.

"You wanna RON here, LT?" Rogers asked.

"What's RON?"

"Rest Over Night. Didn't they teach you anything?"

"I don't like it here. If we get in a firefight the bullets will ricochet all over the goddamn place."

"No sign of enemy activity."

"That's what Custer said."

"Probably a better chance one of the little guys will fall off a cliff taking a piss in the middle of the night."

"Alright, you win. Let's set up here."

The next morning they were sore from sleeping on the rocks. There was a tree line less than a hundred meters to their east and fifty meters down the hill. They worked their way through the rocks and entered the trees. Glad for the shade, they took a break. Dawson and Rogers took a look around. The wooded area was only flat for a few meters then dropped off sharply down to the water. There was no sign of a trail. Back on their feet they moved along the edge of the rocks staying concealed by the trees. There was little ground cover so movement was easy. Before long they came to the end of the rocks, moved into the jungle, up the slight hill to the crest of the peninsula and set up a perimeter.

"I wouldn't get too close to the fishing village, LT."

"Why not?"

"I don't think we can trust the Cambodes. They might start shooting the place up."

"That's all we'd need. If they were really serious about finding a weapons cache they'd drive a platoon of Marines down here and kick it over. We don't have much room to operate."

"That's so you can't get lost."

"Funny. We're going to need water by tomorrow. The map says

there's a stream between us and the road to the village. Why don't we move west a hundred meters at a time and have Socco and Healey run clover leaf patrols. That should satisfy the training requirement. If they run into a trail tell them not to cross it. Just come back and report it."

The platoon moved west with two squads making circular patrols. After a couple of hours, both Sacco and Healey returned reporting they had found a high speed trail. They formed up as a single unit and moved forward cautiously. The trail was wide enough to move carts but it didn't show any signs of recent use. Small vegetation grew in the depressions. They moved forward crossing the trail and soon found a small fast flowing creek that was marked on the map. Setting security, they watched the creek for a while. When they were sure there were no signs of activity each squad in turn filled their canteens. When done the unit moved east back into the jungle a few hundred meters and selected a small rise to RON. They set out two listening posts and placed claymore mines. The night was uneventful.

The next day, they proceeded north staying well inland of the village. The jungle became denser. They moved with Dawson, Rogers and two squads in column. Sacco and Healey's squads moved on the flanks, the thick jungle forcing them to stay within ten meters of the column in order not to get separated. A single point man walked slightly ahead keeping in sight. The air was still. It was hot, buggy and boring work. Dawson was feeling the weight of his equipment. He stopped to apply insect repellent to his face and ears and turned to offer it to Rogers.

A short burst of fire. Some single rounds and another longer burst. They hit the ground as the point man ran back past Dawson.

"Rock and roll," Dawson yelled dropping the repellent. Sacco and Healey immediately grabbed the machine guns from the Cambodes and laid down fire. Dawson and Rogers blindly fired their M-16s into the thick jungle. After a few seconds the Cambodes decide to join in, adding the firepower of two dozen carbines. Dawson called Cease Fire. The Cambodes kept shooting. Rogers, Dawson and Healey kept calling Cease Fire and gesturing stop with their hands. Eventually, the Cambodes stopped firing. "These guys don't know the meaning of cease fire?" Dawson asked Rogers.

"How the fuck would I know? The only other time I was out with them they wouldn't shoot at all." Setting a quick perimeter they moved forward cautiously. After twenty meters they came upon a trail. Two VC, black pajamas, light equipment, no rice bags, were down. Both carried Chinese SKS carbines.

"Locals. Didn't know we were here," Rogers said. They policed up the weapons and searched the bodies. One had an NVA belt with a red star buckle. Sacco took it for a souvenir. Dawson looked at the trees across the trail. He could see bullet scars high up on the trunks from the platoon's fire. He pointed it out to Rogers. "Well, at least they were firing."

"Let's get out of here. That trail probably goes around to the fishing village and I'm sure they heard us. Let's head back up hill. But first we have find my insect repellent," he joked. Rogers shook his head.

"That's probably a good idea." They moved about three hundred meters and set up on what they agreed was a defensible knoll.

You should probably call in a situation report," Rogers advised. Dawson pulled the map and code matrix out of his side pocket to encode the coordinates. "Don't tell them about the SKSs. Maybe we can trade them for another M-60."

"Can we make radio contact?"

"I think we're high enough. Just use the long whip," Rogers said, handing Dawson his backpack. Dawson unfolded the antenna and screwed it into the radio.

"What's our call sign?"

"You don't know the call sign?" Sacco said overhearing and trying to look appalled.

"What is it?"

"Coast Walk."

"Honeycutt, Honeycutt this is Coast Walk. Over," pause. "Honeycutt, Honeycutt this is Coast Walk. Over."

"This is Honeycutt. Go ahead Coast Walk."

"Sitrep, over."

"Wait one. Go ahead Coast Walk." Dawson gave his report. "Copy that. Wait one." Another voice spoke.

"Coast Walk. This is Comanche. Over."

"Roger, Comanche. Go."

"Move to the village on the coast and search it for enemy and supplies." Dawson hesitated. The voice came back on the radio. "I say again, Move to the coastal village and search it for enemy and supplies, this is Comanche. over."

"You're breaking up. Say again." As Comanche started to talk Dawson turned off the radio. He leaned over and tapped Rogers. "Let's take a walk." They got up and after a few steps, Dawson asked, "Who's code name Comanche?"

"That's the commander, Major Barton."

The commander of what?"

The commander of the FOB."

"I was afraid you were going to say that."

"Why?"

"He just ordered us to search the fishing village."

"You can't do that. The Cambodes might start shooting civilians."

"I know. You already told me."

"What did you tell him?"

"I told him he was breaking up."

"He's not going to believe you."

"I know. Listen, whatever you do, don't say anything to Sacco. I don't trust that little weasel."

"Good instincts, LT. What are you going to do?"

"I don't know."

"Maybe you could just tell him the truth."

"Think he would believe it?"

"No, he'd probably think you're chicken shit."

Dawson put down the hand set. Rogers walked over and sat down.

"What'd they say?"

"We're being extracted in the morning."

"That's it? What did you tell him?"

"I just told him I didn't think mixing up the Cambodes and civilians would have a good outcome."

"Who did you talk to?

"I don't know. As soon as I told him he said he was pulling us in the morning."

"Just like that?"

"Yep."

"Had to be the operations officer. Major Capra. He was my hatchet force commander at FOB 2. He knows what he's doing."

"That's everybody," Dawson yelled over the noise as he climbed aboard and sat in the door. The H-34 lifted off. At a couple of hundred feet the pilot rolled it abruptly to the right. In a second Dawson was looking straight down at the ground. He felt his body go weightless and his ass started to lift. At the exact instant his mind told him he was about to fall right the hell out of the helicopter he felt a hand grab his web gear pulling him back. He turned to see Rogers grinning and shaking his head.

CHAPTER TEN

"SO A LOT of good people got killed and we accomplished nothing. That's exactly what happens on high priority targets." Rogers was finishing the story. "As soon as you get a general involved everybody's too busy covering their ass and nobody is taking care of the poor bastards on the ground." Dawson couldn't help staring at the panther tattoo on Rogers' forearm as he practically strangled his rum and coke. They each had another drink in silence. Dawson returned to his quarters.

"Where've you been?" Miller asked while rearranging his web gear for about the twentieth time since Dawson had arrived, "I'm taking the team across the fence tomorrow."

"I just had a couple of drinks with Sergeant Rogers."

"You know he was on SOG's first Bright Light. Bright Light is a rescue mission."

"Yeah, I know. He just told me about it."

"Really. I heard it was a fiasco. What did he say?"

"They had a high priority mission to rescue a POW. It was the midway through Rogers' first tour out of FOB 2. Major Capra, I guess he was a captain then, was the company commander. There was supposed to be a captured American pilot held in a little village by about a dozen guards Instead they landed in the middle of an NVA battalion and got into a huge firefight almost immediately. One of the helicopters got shot down. They called in airpower and instead of gunships they got a couple of jets. One dropped two bombs right on the company and blew up another chopper that was on the ground and killed a bunch of our own people. Of course, they didn't rescue the pilot."

"That's why I stick with recon," Miller said, fooling with his web gear some more. "You have a lot more control if you know what you're doing. You have to be really careful when you select your landing zone. Choose high, rough terrain away from any water source. Then work your way down toward their base camps. That way if you make contact it will only be with small security patrols," he explained confidently.

"Are you Lieutenant Dawson?" He turned to see a major.
"Yes, Sir."
"I ordered you to search the fishing village." Oh shit. Dawson thought. This must be Major Barton. The FOB commander. "You seem to have had a radio problem."
"Sir?" he replied, deciding to play out the lie.
"I think you could use some RTO training. Let's see if you're capable of carrying Captain Coulter's radio. You leave tomorrow," he said. It could have been worse, Dawson thought. On his way out, Major Capra, the operations officer who had briefed him on SOG stopped him. "I served with Sergeant Rogers at Kontum. He's a good man. He told me it was the right call not to get the Cambodes mixed up with civilians. The commander will get over it. Just stay away from

him," he said quietly.

The next day, about the same time, Miller's recon team was inserted in Laos about 15 kilometers southwest of the A Shau Valley, Dawson was looking past his jungle boots. He watched as the rice paddy filled terrain turned to sloping hills and then steep mountain jungle. Sitting in the door of the Huey, this time holding on carefully, he looked back and saw a line of helicopters swinging like toys on a pendulum. As the mountains rose so did the helicopters. He felt a chill. The chopper rolled to the left and the ground disappeared from view for a few moments. It steadied and then they were flying between two mountain ridges. Dawson thought they were very exposed, but before he could figure out the logic they slowed and dropped into a large light green field. The long blades of grass were blown down by the wind from the rotors. Hovering a few feet above the ground, careful not to turn an ankle, he climbed out holding the strut and began to follow the captain around.

The mountain jungle was a steep shaded place. High above, the vegetation thrived in the sunlight. It was there that the birds and the animals lived. At ground level tree trunks were swarmed by thick vines. They walked among ferns growing from the rotting detritus of the forest canopy. The jungle floor was reserved for scavengers, large predators and the dying. As they climbed the steep hills they wore away the ground cover, exposing the slippery red clay, forcing them to hang on to vines to avoid falling. Every so often the tree canopy would disappear and they would enter a flatter area of thick elephant grass. The blades extended well over head, but offered no relief from the sun's heat and limited visibility to a couple of meters.

Twelve days later, Dawson was still following the captain around. At first he had been intensely alert, expecting gunfire to erupt at any second. Now, trudging the jungle floor his mind wandered. After two years of training and watching hundreds of World War Two movies he had expected nothing less than to be constantly repelling attacks, valiantly over-running enemy positions and rushing out under a hail of fire to rescue fallen comrades. But now, in actual combat, they were just walking up and down hills at a pace far less demanding than most of the training exercises at Fort Bragg. Although he didn't realize it at the time, he was, in fact, learning about the life of an infantryman, a grunt. He didn't know where they were. He didn't know where they were going. He was just one of a long line of soldiers carrying a heavy load of killing equipment waiting to unleash it on the so far unseen enemy.

Each morning their encampment became a little more relaxed. For the first couple of days the Cambodes strung their hammocks close to the ground, talked in whispers, alert for any foreign sound. Now on the thirteenth day they set up their hammocks high enough to hang clothing that needed to be aired out, openly cooked and chatted. Suddenly, there was a commotion. Cambodes were calling out loudly. Some had their Buddha bags in their mouths. The first sergeant had been killed on patrol. The captain, visibly upset and angry, instructed a platoon leader to assemble his men. Within minutes they were hurrying down a well-worn trail. Dawson, steps behind the captain, worried about being ambushed. After traveling a couple of hundred meters they came to a halt. The trail sloped gently down to a saddle between two small hills sharply rising up on the far side. At the bottom, next to the trail, lay the first sergeant. A bullet had entered the top of his head. Small slivers of white bone fragment could be seen where it exited in the back. The captain knelt beside the body. Tears ran down his face. This wasn't the movies where scores of anonymous people died. This was a war of personal anguish. The platoon leader put his unit on line, swept up the far slope and returned, finding nothing. Separating his equipment, they placed the sergeant's body on a poncho and carried him back to the camp. Later that day a chopper came in to retrieve the body and they returned to walking up and down hills. Everyone was a little more on alert. Two days later, the mission over, they found a field of elephant grass. The helicopters came in and returned them to the FOB.

The mattress on Miller's rack was rolled up. His personal property had been removed. Dawson got a sick feeling in the pit of his stomach. Offloading his pack and web gear, he went to look for a beer but the refrigerator was gone too. He took that as a sign that Miller had moved to new quarters. Relieved, he pulled a canteen from his web gear and took a drink of what remained of the mountain water. He sat on his rack for a few minutes then pulled the PRC-25 radio out of his back pack and set off to return it.

Captain Coulter was talking to Major Barton in front of the TOC. They saw him and looked up. Shit, Dawson thought.

"Sir," he said acknowledging the commander. Then, "Captain Coulter, where do you want me to put this?" holding up the radio.

"Just give it to anybody in the company." As he walked away he heard Major Barton ask Coulter,

"How'd he do?"

"Fine," was the reply.

Later, showered, shaved and dressed in clean everything he set out to find a beer and something to eat. Entering the club, there was Rogers and a rum and coke.

"I was startin' to miss you, LT. How you doing?"

"Good. A little sore from humping those mountains."

"Find anything?"

"Not much. On the third or fourth day we came down a steep hill to a little flat rise and stumbled into a pretty good size bunker complex. All the foxholes were dug almost exactly the same size. Like they were dug by a machine. Square corners. They had cut branches to camouflage the piles of dirt around the bunkers, but they were dead so it looked like they hadn't been used for a while. No trash laying around so it wasn't Americans."

"Heard you lost the first sergeant."

"Yeah. That was weird. Nothing happening on the whole operation and then he gets killed."

"He fought in Korea. Special Forces since the beginning. His tour was up next month."

"You knew him?"

"Had a few drinks with him."

"That's no surprise." Dawson got a beer. "I only knew him to see. Never talked to him."

"You know Lieutenant Miller's gone."

"Yeah. Where'd he go?"

"MIA. His whole team."

"Oh, shit. You know when I saw his stuff was moved, I was worried at first, but then I convinced myself that he just found new quarters. What happened?"

"His team had a clean insert and radioed a 'Team OK.' That was their last radio contact. After a couple of days they put in a bright light team and found some expended cartridge shells and blood trails just west of the landing zone but nothing more. The Americans were listed MIA."

"I'm really sorry to hear that. Miller thought he was pretty good at this stuff."

"We have to or we couldn't do it," Rogers said shaking his head. They sat drinking in silence. Dawson's food came. He could only eat half of it. His stomach had shrunk while he was out in the field. So he made up for it by drinking a couple of beers too many.

The next few days were boring. Some of the Cambodes had been sent home on leave. The weather was so hot that they spent an hour around noon lying on their racks sweating. No operations had been scheduled and they were running out of make-work jobs.

"Good morning, Sergeant Rogers."

"Nothing good about it. It's hot as hell already. I can tell by that shit-eating grin you're up to no good, LT."

"Can you get a jeep?"

"Yeah. Why?"

"Let's go see Hue."

"You wanna go sightseeing?"

"I'd call it a recon. But, Yeah. Have you been there?"

"No. It got blown to shit during Tet."

"I know. I watched it on TV at Fort Bragg. Don't you want to see it? The Imperial City. The Perfume River."

"Not especially."

"Go get a jeep. It's only a twenty minute ride. Better than hanging around here trying to look like we have something to do.

Tell Sacco some bullshit about why he's in charge."

After a brief disagreement about who would drive, with Rogers prevailing, they were heading Northwest on Highway One beside the railroad tracks with Dawson in the shotgun seat. The two lane street wasn't crowded, mostly Vietnamese civilians walking, some bicycles and Vespas, and the occasional military vehicle. They passed a large Army base west of the road. It contained hundreds of tents and some hardback buildings set on rolling hills.

"They built this for the 1st Air Cav when they went in to relieve the Marines at Khe Sanh. Now it has units from the 82nd and 101st," Rogers said.

"What's it called?"

"I don't know."

"You're not much of a tour guide," Dawson laughed. Continuing on, they came to a large Buddhist temple with a pagoda like steeple. Dawson got out and took pictures. As the ever-present railroad tracks split off to the west, the city of Hue came into view. They moved forward to a spot were they could view the narrow Perfume River flowing beside the walls of the citadel and a bridge over the water at the southeast corner of the fortress leading to a large gate. As they started to cross the bridge the were immediately stopped by a group of military looking guards wearing helmet liners with the big letters "QC" painted on them.

"Who are these guys?" Dawson asked.

"QC, Vietnamese National Police. They're not known for their sense of humor," Rogers replied.

"I.D., I.D." The QC demanded their identification. They were sitting there in a black jeep with no military markings and fatigues with no insignia trying to enter a city that had been the scene of a slaughter just a few months before.

"This is a great idea you had, LT." Dawson took off his bush hat and reached into the side pocket of his jungle fatigues and put on his green beret with the single silver bar.

" Trung uy. OK. OK," the QC waived them through.

"Why did you bring your beret?" Rogers asked.

"So you could take my picture."

CHAPTER ELEVEN

"SIR, EVERYBODY HAS been looking for you!" Sacco exclaimed as the jeep pulled into the FOB.

"Who's everybody?" Dawson replied, instantly annoyed.

"Major Capra and Sergeant Peterson from recon."

"Alright, I'll take care of it." They drove on to the motor pool. "Where did you tell him we were going?" Dawson asked Rogers.

"I told him we were going to check out a training site."

"Good. I'll stick to that story." After stowing his M-16 in his quarters he walked to the TOC and entered operations.

"Hey, Dawson," Major Capra called almost pleasantly.

"Sir."

"Sergeant Peterson's recon team is down a man. How about you straphang with him on his next operation. It'll give you a good chance to get your feet wet in recon."

"Sure, Sir. Anything else?" he replied, thinking about Miller's team.

"No, that'll do it. You'll find him somewhere around the recon barracks." Dawson left relieved he wasn't asked where he was for the past couple of hours. He was thinking no one had said anything about him shooting up the ARVN rifle range and it didn't seem like anybody knew or cared what he was doing with the Cambode platoon. So far, SOG was a bullshit-free version of the army. All you had to do was stay alive.

It took him a while, but he finally found the sergeant in his quarters. He was a staff sergeant, slim build, three or four inches shorter and about five years older than Dawson. Unsurprisingly, he was repacking his web gear.

"Sergeant Peterson. I'm Lieutenant Dawson. Major Capra told me you could use an extra man for an operation," Dawson called through the screen.

"Come on in. I didn't know they would assign me a lieutenant." Dawson entered and shook his hand. "I hope you know how recon works," he continued as if giving a rehearsed speech. I'm the team's One-Zero, the team leader. In recon rank doesn't matter. We go by experience. Spec. 4 Morrissey is the One-One, assistant team leader. You will be the One-Two. The radio operator. There is no second guessing the One-Zero on a recon team. Is that clear?" Peterson finished. It was pretty obvious to Dawson that this guy knew he was getting a lieutenant and was none too happy to have someone who out ranked him on the team.

"Well, I just spent two weeks following Captain Coulter around with a radio. I can be a good PFC so long as they don't cut my pay," Dawson smiled, trying to reassure the sergeant. It didn't work.

"Hatchet force isn't recon. Go get your web gear and backpack. Let's see what we have to do to straighten it out." Dawson left and returned in a couple of minutes. Peterson was opening pouches, pulling stuff out and putting it back. "This isn't too bad." He sounded disappointed. "Where's your medical equipment?"

"All I have is a couple of field dressings, an ace bandage, a rubber tourniquet and some band aids."

"You're missing some stuff. I'll be back.," Peterson said, leaving abruptly. Dawson looked around for a place to sit but the only chair was piled with junk. After a few minutes he sat on the concrete floor.

"You the lieutenant?" A big guy, young, probably Dawson's age barged into the room.

"Yeah," Dawson replied getting up. Confirming his earlier suspicion that Peterson knew his new radio operator was an officer.

"I'm Morrissey, the One-One, Sir."

"Hey, how are you doing?"

"Just fine, sir," he said with a smile.

"Probably a good idea to drop the lieutenants and sirs while we're working together. Just call me Dawson."

"Yes, Sir. Sorry, Dawson." They laughed.

"How long have you been running recon?"

"Couple of months. I've been on three missions. One in country. Two across the fence."

"I've been on none. I'm here to learn."

"I see you've met the . . ." Peterson returned.

"Dawson." Dawson interrupted knowing Peterson didn't want to call him by his rank.

"Dawson," Peterson repeated. "Here's your medical equipment," he said. Pushing some M-16 magazines across the table to make room, he began a show and tell. An olive drab can a little longer and narrower than a beer can contained and I. V. bottle of serum albumin blood expander. He got a sheet of paper and dumped a bunch of pills on it. Compazine to control severe nausea and vomiting. Lomotil to treat diarrhea by slowing down the movements of the intestines.

Dextroamphetamine sulfate to keep you awake in an escape and evasion situation. Codeine to stop a cough. Darvon for pain relief. And finally, four syrettes of morphine to control pain from serious wounds. "A narcotic collection like this would probably get you a few years in prison in the states," Peterson finished up. He grabbed a roll of black electrical tape and the can of blood expander and wrapped it around a rear canvas strap on Dawson's web gear so that it would ride behind his neck. Then he carefully slid the pills off the paper into a Tupperware container. Holding it up he said, "You can put your ace bandage and maybe a dressing in here to keep the pills from rattling around. It fits in a canteen cover and will keep everything dry."

"Thanks."

"Be here at 0900 tomorrow and we'll take the Nungs out and teach you the immediate action drills. Web gear, rifle. No back packs," Peterson said dismissing Dawson.

"Got it. Thanks again."

"I'm gonna take the radio for a walk again. This time with a recon team. The One-Zero is an E-6 named Peterson. Doesn't think much of lieutenants or at least not of me. Short guy. Probably only an inch taller than you." Dawson winced as Rogers, without turning to look, punched him in the arm spilling some of his beer. "He gave me a bunch of drugs to fill out my med kit."

"Darvon, compazine and speed. That's the cocktail for hung-over chopper pilots. Don't take any of the speed," Rogers advised. "Some guys have gotten hooked on it. They get out in the mountains and wonder if they're about to climb a one pill hill or a two pill hill. Makes them jumpy and they start hearing things."

"What kind of things?"

"Oh, you know, like they hear the wind blow bamboo trees together and they imagine it's the wood stock of an AK-47. Then they shoot at nothing and give away their position.

"What's this guy Peterson like?"

"I don't recognize the name. Maybe I'd know him to see."

The next morning Dawson, Peterson, Morrissey and five Nungs crossed the highway and the railroad tracks. The Nungs were taller than the Cambodes and didn't smile as much. They were stronger, with stern jaws and long hair, obviously imitating the Beatles. They gave off the impression that they took their job seriously. Peterson showed Dawson the line of march. A Nung with an M-16 was the point man, followed by another Nung with an M-79 grenade launcher. Then came Peterson, the One-Zero. Dawson would follow him with the radio. Behind Dawson were two more Nung riflemen. Then came Morrissey and another rifleman. The last Nung was designated the tail gunner. It was his job to walk backwards obscuring their tracks while covering the rear. Their separation was three to five meters except for Dawson with the radio who would stay within two meters of the One-Zero, Peterson explained.

They practiced Immediate action drills. Pre-planned maneuvers a recon team would perform when they had a surprise encounter with an enemy force. The purpose was to break contact and create separation between the team and the enemy. If the point man made contact he would fire his complete magazine at the enemy, then turn and run to the rear, reloading on the way, setting up just behind the tail gunner. Then the grenadier would fire his M-79 and run to the rear. The rest of the team would follow, leapfrogging to the rear. If the team was still in contact they would repeat the maneuver. They practiced differed variations of the drill in case the team made contact with the enemy from the flanks or from the rear. It was approaching noon and getting very hot. Peterson pressed on. They practiced the drills with a designated casualty. The man or either side would grab the wounded team member under the arms and drag him to the rear while the rest of the team performed the drill. By the time Peterson was satisfied, everyone was soaked with sweat and guzzling from their canteens.

"What do you think Dawson?" Peterson asked. Dawson's first thought was to offer a positive evaluation. He hesitated, realizing evaluation wasn't the job of a radio operator. So, he simply replied,

"I understand what I have to do." Peterson seemed satisfied with the answer.

"Immediate action drills don't solve the team's problem. They just keep the enemy's head down giving the team a little time and distance to regroup and decide what to do next," Rogers explained. "Problem is in most cases the One-Zero doesn't have enough information to know what to do next."

"Why not?" Dawson asked.

"Look at it form the point man's position. He's moving along and he sees the enemy and they see him at the same time. They all go to fire their weapons but the point man always fires first because all he has to do is flick his thumb to take the M-16 off safe. With an AK-47 you have to let go of the pistol grip, snap down the safety on the right side of the receiver, re-grip and fire. Bang. He loses. So you run the drill and regroup. The One-Zero asks the point man what he saw. He's probably going to say, 'Beaucoup VC.' Which can be anywhere from one to ten thousand." Dawson laughed at that. "Yeah. That's true," Rogers continued. "But even if he tells you he just saw two you still don't really know what you are up against because there could five hundred more right behind them."

"So what do you do?"

"When I was here in 1966 the NVA supply lines were guarded by local rear echelon security troops. They didn't have any real experience and they were scared to death of SOG teams. They'd shoot and run away. Or just run away. You could make contact, stay in the area, set ambushes, call in air strikes, and make bomb damage assessments. Back then we didn't even call them recon teams. They were spike teams. Twelve men including a machine gun. We were hunting them. Now it's totally different. When you hit the ground, you aren't hunting them. They're hunting you. Look at all the equipment the NVA had to bring in for the siege of Khe Sanh. The Air Force was running a half dozen Arc Lights every day to try to stop them."

"What's an Arc Light? Dawson interrupted.

"A B-52 strike. Didn't they teach you anything at Fort Bragg?" Dawson shook his head. "They bombed the hell out of the place and the NVA still kept moving all the weapons and ammo they needed down the trail. This isn't some peasant walking from Hanoi to South Vietnam with a basket on his back like they teach you. Today they're running truck convoys and the trail is guarded by anti-aircraft, hardcore infantry and sapper units. They're well-equipped and organized.

"This is real encouraging. What do you do?"

"You make contact and run your immediate action drill. But when you break contact you don't sit around and decide what to do next. Because you made that decision before the mission began."

"What's that?"

"They used to tell you to break contact and continue with the mission. Now you break contact, declare an emergency, request air support, get to an LZ and get the fuck out."

"But if you end a mission because of two enemy aren't you going to get in trouble?" Dawson asked. " Seems like you should, at least, stick around a little longer and see if there's more."

"Thinking like that will get you killed. If there's two there's more. A recon team is carrying sixty pounds of equipment, staying off trails, moving slowly through rough terrain. The NVA aren't carrying much more than an AK-47 and a couple of magazines. They're running down high speed trails trying to locate you. And when they find you, and they will find you, they aren't afraid to fight. You make contact. You get out."

CHAPTER TWELVE

THE NEXT MORNING Peterson, Morrissey and Dawson went to the TOC to receive an intelligence briefing on their upcoming mission. Targets were defined as a six square kilometer area where B-52 strikes would be suspended while his team was on the ground. Captain Stevens showed them on the map. Just north of the A Shau Valley the Vietnam, Laos border turned due west. Their target was in Laos, bound on the north by the southeastern corner of NVA Base Area 611 and on the east by a mountain ridge that formed the western side of the A Shau Valley. After describing the target Captain Stevens turned him over to a staff sergeant, with his arm in a sling, for a detailed briefing.

"My name is Fallon. I got dinged up on a hatchet force operation out of Kontum last month," he said motioning to his arm. "So, I haven't been here long. But, I've been here long enough to know that you're probably not going to get into this target," Fallon stated bluntly. "There's too much anti-aircraft in base area 611 and the A Shau. They found this spot right in between where they hope they can insert you. We had a team in there a year ago. They wandered around for six days and didn't find anything. I doubt that's the case now." Fallon continued with the usual, ambiguous information about squad size enemy units moving on trails that could apply to anywhere in Eastern Laos. "Oh, this is important, about six months ago a recon team mined the area. They posted the location as here," he said pointing to the map. "They reported planting three toe poppers on a high speed trail. You never know how good their location is, so be sure to give it a wide berth."

"Glad you remembered to tell me," Peterson said. "What do they want us to do?"

"See this road running just south of the border? It's Route 922. Except for the occasional bomb crater, which they repair in about twenty minutes, it can take truck traffic. So I'm guessing a road watch. But, there's probably a lot of commo wire running all over the place so they may want you to set up a wire tap. That's up to Major Capra."

"When's the last time we had a team to this area?"

"That's what I was just about to get to. I marked the map, about six klicks west and ten klicks north of your target is where one of your recon teams got shot up last month. If you look at the contour lines you can see that they inserted the team in a low flat area. Now look at your target area. In the center you've got an east, west line of thousand meter high hill tops with steep finger ridges running north down to the road. You want to pick a landing zone as close to the hill tops as possible and work your way down."

"But we will still have to fly over 611 or the A Shau so they'll know we're coming."

"I think they know you're coming before we do."

"What!" Peterson exclaimed startled.

"I probably shouldn't have said that. But we can bomb the hell out of the Ho Chi Minh Trail and we never seem to hit anything. But put in a recon team and suddenly there's enemy all over they place. After a while it doesn't look like a coincidence."

After Fallon's briefing, Peterson said he had a bad feeling about this mission. Dawson followed Morrissey's lead and kept his mouth shut. Then they moved to the operations office where a lieutenant instructed them to gather information on the NVA traffic on Route 922.

"Do you have any questions?" the lieutenant asked, finishing up his briefing.

"No, sir," Peterson lied, wondering why they needed to put a team into such a high risk area. He got up to leave.

"Sergeant Peterson." It was Major Capra. He motioned them into his office and closed the door. "Do you have your target maps?"

"Yes, Sir."

"Give me one of them." Peterson separated the team's maps and placed one on the desk. "You see this line of hilltops?"

"Yes, Sir. Sergeant Fallon in intel pointed them out to us. We're supposed to infiltrate somewhere near hill 1263," he said pointing to a spot on the map. "And move north and find a spot to observe Route 922."

"Well, if you do that you're only going to find out one of two things."

"Sir?"

"One. They are running a shit load of trucks through the area. Which we already know. Or two. They have the capability of hunting down and killing a recon team. Which we also already know." Peterson turned his head and stared intently at the major. "I want you to go in just like the plan. But, instead of heading north to the road, I want you to move to the south. We are bombing the shit out of 922. The NVA need an alternative route. They can't go north because then they would be in Vietnam and we could hit them with a division of Marines. So it only makes sense that they try to build a road in this low ground in the southern area of your target," he said sweeping his finger across the map. "For now, this is just between us. Do you understand?" the major asked, looking at each of them.

Yes, sir. But what if they ask me the target objective during the pilot's briefing?"

"You are to perform a road watch on Route 922."

"What about the forward air controller? If I run into trouble they'll be looking for us in the wrong place?"

"Don't worry about that. I'll make sure the Covey rider knows where you are. As soon as they see the helicopters the NVA are going to assume that you are heading north and they will activate their security teams. But, don't assume for a minute that they don't have the area to the south protected. If you start seeing a lot of activity don't be afraid to declare an emergency. Are we straight?" They all nodded.

"That ever happen before?" Dawson asked, on the way out, breaking his silence. Peterson just shook his head.

That afternoon while Peterson was making an aerial reconnaissance of the target, Dawson went to supply to get new batteries for the radio and returned to his quarters. He checked and rechecked his equipment. It didn't dawn on him that it was what he had made fun of Miller for doing. Morrissey was issuing rations and checking the Nung's equipment. After a couple of hours Peterson returned. They gathered in his quarters. Dawson started folding his map so the target area could be seen through the clear plastic case.

"We're not going to RON in this target," Peterson stated. That got Dawson's attention. The sergeant showed them the primary and secondary LZs he had selected. Both were near the crest of the hill tops. One a small elephant grass field. The other an old slash and burn farming area. He ended by stating again, "We're not going to RON in this target."

At 0800 hours the next morning, they had their pilot's briefing. Then they loaded into two helicopters. Peterson, Dawson and three Nungs in the first, Morrissey and three Nungs in the second. As they got airborne they were joined by two gun ships. Seated in the door, Dawson took out his compass. They were flying a little south of west. When they flew over a mountain top fire support base the choppers turned due west and began to gain altitude. As they continued to climb, it became more difficult to see the steep sides of the mountains and the scene below appeared to flatten out. By the time they leveled out they were very high. Dawson knew some of the hill tops were over a thousand meters. He had made a few parachute jumps from three thousand feet. He thought they were a least that high over the mountains. He put the two together and concluded that they were at six or seven thousand feet.

"That's the A Shau Valley." Peterson pointed south, hitting him on the shoulder, yelling above the noise. Dawson turned his head and nodded. He could see a long narrow depression. Lighter green at the bottom. Looking back as the valley started to disappear he thought he saw a puff of black smoke in the air. It was about the same altitude as the helicopter, not that far behind them and maybe fifty meters away. He wondered what it was. Soon enough there were more black puffs and he realized it was anti-aircraft fire. The black smoke was flack, explosions of shrapnel. There weren't a lot of them. Certainly nothing like he had seen in the movies of air raids during World War Two, but there were enough to move him a few inches back from the open door. Being new, he didn't know if this was a cause for concern or something that was normal on missions into Laos. He quickly got his answer as the helicopter pulled right and began to gain altitude once again. They continued to pull right and finally leveled out. Dawson pulled out his compass. He guessed right, they were heading east. A half hour later they were on the ground at Phu Bai.

"Were the LZs hot?" Dawson asked Peterson.

"They didn't even get that far. The pilots scrubbed the mission. Told you we weren't going to RON," he laughed. "Let's get a beer!"

The Nungs went back to their barracks and immediately started to cook the rations they had been given for the mission. The Americans went to Sergeant Peterson's quarters. He got three bottles of Vietnamese Ba Muoi Ba beer out of his refrigerator, opened them and passed them around.

"We were lucky today guys. I had a really bad feeling about that target. That S-2, Fallon wouldn't even look me in the eyes during the briefing. Then with Major Capra sending us south, it all just seemed wrong. Hopefully the next mission we get is a long way from the A Shau."

"I'll drink to that," Morrissey said. Dawson drank, then leaned down and opened his back pack, pulled out the radio and put it on the table.

"I guess I won't be needing this anymore," he said.

"Hey, lieutenant, sir," Peterson said. Finally finding something to call him. "Your were a trooper. I was afraid you'd try to pull rank. But you fit right in. You can carry my radio anytime."

"I'll take that as a compliment, sergeant, as long as you have another beer," he laughed. They drank and talked the nervous chatter of infantrymen just spared from battle.

"Sergeant Peterson. Major Capra wants to see you," a Spec 4 said, poking his head through the door.

"Ah, what the hell, he doesn't need a sit rep from me." Peterson put down his beer and followed the specialist. He wasn't gone long.

"They are going to try to put us back in again."

"That's bullshit," Morrissey said. Dawson was stunned. Ironically, his first thought was that he shouldn't have opened the third beer.

"They are going to fly us south. Straight across the A Shau, then turn north once we cross the border." Dawson took the radio off the table and put it back in his back pack.

"What time are we leaving?" he asked.

"1400 hours," Peterson replied..

CHAPTER THIRTEEN

BY THE TIME they assembled on the runway it was after 1400 hours, but it didn't make any difference because the choppers didn't show up for another hour. Back in the air, they flew west directly over the A Shau Valley, then turned to the north as they entered Laotian air space. Over the target, the helicopters flew in a wide circle as the gunships skimmed over a large green area near the edge of the mountain jungle. There was no anti-aircraft fire. Their chopper went into a swerving dive. After several maneuvers it rapidly slowed and then hovered a few feet above the ground. The team jumped into the elephant grass and quickly took up defensive positions. The second chopper came in with Morrissey and his Nungs, offloading them about thirty meters away. After two or three minutes they linked up. Dawson radioed a Team OK and asked Covey for their location. He quickly decoded the letters into numbers, plotted their position on the map and moved to show Peterson.

"Fuck, we're no where near the LZ I requested. Let's get into the tree line." They moved quickly through the elephant grass, foregoing stealth for the cover of the jungle. Then continued straight up the hill through thick vegetation for a couple of hundred meters and set up a perimeter. It was 1630 hours. Dawson checked in with Covey again.

"What'd he say?" Peterson asked.

"He said that there was no fire on the insert and that he was going to RTB for happy hour."

"Return to base," Peterson interpreted. "So much for the idea that we aren't going to RON." He pulled out his map. "You figure we're about here?"

"Yeah, if Covey gave us the right coordinates, there should be a trail a couple of hundred meters west of here."

"Let's move east, away from the trail, and find a place to set up." He signaled Morrissey and the team formed up and moved out slowly and silently, weapons at the ready. The vegetation was thick. At times visibility extended as far as ten meters. Most of the time less than half of that. Thirty minutes later, the team had only moved about a hundred and fifty meters. They found a small knoll consisting of dense vegetation and trees with thick trunks. Although surrounded on three sides by higher ground the immediate area slopped down in all directions. Peterson designated it their RON. They made a circular patrol about fifty meters around to insure that there weren't any trails in the area. Finding nothing, they returned to the knoll. Morrissey immediately placed the Nungs into a perimeter and set up the claymores. The Americans each spread out a thin piece of green nylon groundcover, removed their back packs, opened their web gear and laid on their stomachs. Dawson put his backpack with the radio just in front of his head, more for protection than quick access.

"Did you turn off the radio?" Peterson whispered.

"Yeah, right after Covey pulled out."

"Make sure you turn it on at first light so we can make contact and have our location ready to send."

"Got it." Dawson looked around trying to memorize the Nungs' positions, imagining how he would react if they were attacked from different positions. At this latitude it got dark fast. He remembered Captain Coulter telling him it doesn't get dark in the jungle mountains. They just turn off the lights. Adjusting his rifle so it was between his head and the radio, he placed his right hand on the receiver.

He opened his eyes, turned his head, shifting his weight, and looked up through the trees. The sky was a couple of shades lighter than the black jungle. False dawn. That time just before the sun announced its appearance. He didn't even realize he had fallen asleep. He started to hear the Nungs move. In a few minutes, with more light, he could see them with weapons at the ready. He undid one of the straps of his back pack and turned on the radio, then turned the volume all the way down then back up two clicks. Remaining vigilant, the Nungs started eating. He pulled out his map and note pad, wrote down the numbered coordinates of their position and coded it into letters. Morrissey signaled the Nungs and they retrieved the claymores and repacked them. Peterson pushed up on all fours, looked at Dawson and nodded at the radio. Dawson shook his head, Yes.

"We're ready to roll," Morrissey said quietly, joining them with the Nung team leader.

"We'll head east and let the terrain dictate when we turn south," Peterson directed. The Nung left to inform the point man. As they were assembling two low blasts of static sounded from the radio. He pulled out the handset and offered it to Peterson who shook his head. Dawson keyed the handset and whispered,

"Covey, Covey this is Hard Case. Over."

"Good morning Hard Case. How are things going with you this morning?" Glad he had made sure the volume was set to low, Dawson replied,

"Quiet so far. Ready to copy location? Over."

"Roger that. Go ahead Hard Case." Dawson read off a string of letters using the phonetic alphabet.

"Copy that. Anything else for me?"

"That's a negative. Over."

"Well, then, stay safe. I'll check back with you around mid-day." Dawson turned off the radio to save battery life and fell in behind Peterson.

They walked in a semi-crouch, careful not be make a sound or leave any tracks. Pausing now and again to listen intently for any foreign sound. Their weapons swept the area as if attached to the movement of their eyes. Traveling at a rate of only twenty steps per minute, up and down steep hills and the sides of ridgelines was grueling work. In order to move a hundred meters on the flat map they were forced to walk two or three times that distance because of the unevenness of the terrain. Just after noon, they approached a deep draw. Peterson gave a circular signal with his hand and Morrissey moved the Nungs into defensive positions. They sat silently for a while. When Peterson was sure they were secure he tapped his lip a couple of times and the Nungs began to eat. He and Dawson sat at the base of a large tree.

"You better turn the radio on. Covey will be up soon," he whispered. "This draw doesn't look this steep on the map. If we try to cross here it will take the rest of the day to get to the other side."

"It's not a draw. It's a canyon. Maybe it's time to head south,"

Dawson offered. He turned on the radio, then poured water from his canteen into a dehydrated ration. He taped it back up and put it in the side pocket of his pants.

"No, see," Peterson said pointing to the map. "If we head south here the west side drops off and that will leave us stuck on this thin ridgeline. We'd be sitting ducks with no way to get to an LZ."

"That leaves us with going over the top."

"Yeah. If there's a trail that's not on the map that's exactly where it will be." He signaled Morrissey to join them. "Let's back up thirty, forty meters then loop around the top of the draw. Tell the guys to be careful there may be a trail."

"There may be a lot more than a trail," Morrissey predicted.

CHAPTER FOURTEEN

THE POINT MAN crouched, lowered his arm and gave the stop signal with the palm of his hand. Peterson moved forward and returned almost immediately. Walking past Dawson, he conferred with Morrissey. A Nung moved out to each flank. Returning, he motioned for the point man to cross. The trail was wide and well-worn. It took two steps to cross it. The rest of the team followed. The tail gunner did his best to obscure their tracks. They climbed up and turned east. As they were moving above the top of the draw, Covey came up on the radio. Dawson moved up and put his hand on Peterson's shoulder. As Peterson turned, he pointed to the radio and mouthed the word Covey.

"Let them wait. It will keep them in the area until we're done with this." They moved east then made their way back down the hill and spread out just above the trail. As they rose to cross, the left flank guard signaled with a hand to his throat. The point man moved back. The team lay prone aiming their weapons down at the trail. Dawson pushed himself flatter into the ground wishing himself part of the jungle. He opened his ammo pouch, put a second magazine on the ground and thumbed his safety to auto. Seconds went by. Very slow seconds. He pulled his eyes off the trail and located the point man to his left. To his right, he couldn't make out Peterson without raising his head. Nothing was happening on the trail. He was starting to think it was time to call a false alarm and get moving when he realized they were there. Through the vegetation he saw an arm, part of an AK-47, then a helmet liner woven with leaves for camouflage. Then another and another. They were moving cautiously and slowly. Then maybe a fourth. He wondered if they were going to shoot them. He focused on the second man placing him in his sights. A single shot, definitely an M-16 got it started. Then a roar of automatic weapons fire. Dawson dropped his target with a short burst as a B-40 rocket slammed into a tree sending splinters flying. No other discernable targets, only flashes of movement, he emptied his magazine at the trail and reloaded. Firing died down to the occasional shot. No fire was returned. Peterson called out and the team moved to the trail. Three bodies, three AKs and a rocket launcher were scattered over ten meters. To the east, a blood trail indicated at least one had gotten away.

"This guy's got a pistol," Morrissey said.

"Tokarav?" Peterson questioned as he moved to the body.

"No US 45."

"Damn you can get a month's pay for a Tokarav. He's probably an officer," Peterson said, as he knelt down by the body. He removed an official looking piece of paper, written in Vietnamese, from his map case and carefully put it in the dead mans shirt pocket.

"What's that?" Dawson asked.

"It's a Project Eldest Son notice. We've been putting exploding AK rounds and 82 millimeter mortar rounds in NVA ammo cashes. When they use it, it blows up and kills them. That was a forged NVA command notice that says some of the Chinese ammo is faulty."

"Who says we don't play dirty."

"Let's get out of here," Peterson motioned south. No stealth now, the team moved as quickly as they could down the hill. After a couple of hundred meters he signaled a halt.

"Give me the radio. I'm going to declare an emergency."

"I've got it," Dawson said not giving Peterson a chance to respond. "Covey this is Hard Case. Over." Nothing. "Covey this is Hard Case. Over."

"Hey there Hard Case. This is Covey. Where you fellows been?"

"We are in contact. I repeat. We are in contact. We are declaring a Prairie Fire Emergency. I repeat. We are declaring a Prairie Fire Emergency. Over." Dawson said in a slow purposeful monotone as if instructing a child.

"Roger that. Do you have casualties?"

"Unknown at this time. We are on the move."

"What's your location?"

"About a klick west of our last reported position. Heading to an LZ. Over."

"Roger that. I'm scrambling assets. Stay safe. I'm here if you need me."

"Yeah, roger that."

"Next time I tell you to give me the radio. Do it." Peterson was pissed. "Where did you learn how to do that?"

"All I've been doing since I got here is talk on the radio. Sergeant Rogers told me to always exaggerate when you need an extraction."

"Well, let's hope you did. Exaggerate, that is." Peterson pulled out his map. "We've got this marked trail to the east. The fucking canyon to the west and contact on the trail behind us. So they know we are heading south."

"They may think we're heading for the high ground. We hit them from the north side of the road," Dawson speculated.

"Yeah, and maybe the guy who left the blood trail crawled up in the bushes and died. The only option we have is to head south and get to this flat open area. Unless we run into something in between it's just a question of who gets their shit together first. Covey or the North Vietnamese."

The moved quickly. More ready to fight than hide. In a half hour, they had covered a klick and were approaching the end of the forest. The ground cover thinned out and visibility increased. Peterson asked for the radio and this time Dawson gave it to him. After a brief conversation he returned the handset.

"The choppers are forty minutes out. Let's keep going." As soon as they started a shot was fired from directly in front of them. How far was anybody's guess. "Make sure the magazines are full and let's move five and four abreast," he said to Morrissey. They moved out in the new formation that focused their firepower forward. The immediate action drills they practiced weren't an option now. Any resistance would be met with force. Another shot was fired.

"What are they doing?" Dawson asked Peterson who was now on his right in the rear line.

"They're trying to turn us. They must not have enough troops for an ambush." They kept moving. Morrissey signaled a halt. Fifteen meters away, in a clearing, they could clearly see two NVA soldiers. They were just standing there. Each armed with an SKS carbine. The Nungs shot them. They moved on policing up the rifles and in seconds reached the end of the forest. Crossing a worn down area they entered dense eight to ten feet high scrub mixed with elephant grass.

"There's the major's road," Peterson said pulling Dawson back onto the worn area.

"Where?"

"You're standing on it." Dawson still didn't see it. He thought the over hanging trees had starved the plants of sunlight. But as he looked closer he saw it winding along the edge of the forest. In the distance he could see a low area where logs had been placed to keep vehicles from getting bogged down. Peterson took a few pictures. From beyond the logs someone fired a few ineffective shots at them. They hurried into the brush and caught up with the team.

Back in their normal column formation, they pushed through the thick undergrowth leaving a trail a blind man could follow, until they came to a flat area consisting mostly of elephant grass.

"This will do," Peterson informed them. He switched back packs with Dawson and contacted Covey. Morrissey and one of the Nungs guarded the trail they had left. The rest of the Nungs stomped down the tall grass so they could be seen from the sky. Dawson, having nothing to do, joined them.

"Hey. That's enough. I can't hear a goddamn thing with you guys making that racket." They took up defensive positions uselessly staring into a solid wall of elephant grass. "Covey's going to make a pass. Lay out a panel and see if you can get a mirror on him." Dawson had his signal mirror wrapped in the orange panel for protection. He pulled it out of his breast pocket and spread it on the ground in the center of the cleared area. He listened to the plane coming closer, finally saw it and put the mirror to his eye, walked the dot up the elephant grass and put it on the O-2's windshield.

"OK, he's got us," Peterson called. They heard some automatic weapons fire from their northwest. "Covey says he's taking fire."

"Tell him there's a war going on down here," Morrissey responded. The sound of the engine receded as Covey pulled away.

"Probably coming from where the canyon runs down to the road." Dawson checked his map. "Yeah, there's water there. Good spot for a base camp. All small arms fire. Nothing heavy. If they had anti-aircraft they would have had enough troops to ambush us." With Covey gone the enemy directed their fire at the team. They could hear the fast bursts of AK-47s and the slightly slower pounding of an RPD machine gun. A few rounds zipped over their heads, but shooting into elephant grass was like shooting into water. The rounds enter at full force but are quickly slowed until they fall harmlessly to the ground.

"He's bringing in the gunships. Give me a location."

"Tell him 315 degrees. 200 meters." Peterson radioed the instructions and Covey fired a marker rocket.

"How's that look?"

"I can't see shit. Sounded OK." Two gunships attacked the area. It was impossible to hear if the ground fire had stopped over the sounds of the attacking helicopters.

"Slick coming in." The chopper hovered over them, the skid about five feet off the ground. When motioning the crew chief to bring it lower failed, they threw the Nungs' backpacks into the ship and boosted them up. Morrissey stepped into Dawson's hands. They all scrambled inside. Immediately, the helicopter took off. It grew quiet on the landing zone. A minute passed. Then another.

"Think they forgot us?" Dawson asked, not totally in jest. Just as he moved to guard the path they had created, the gunships went back to work on the target. The other slick swooped in, hovered lower than the first, and they easily climbed aboard. Well aware that being shot down during extraction was one of the greatest dangers recon teams face, they still felt an immediate sense of relief and elation to be off the ground. Even the Nungs smiled.

CHAPTER FIFTEEN

"WHAT THE HELL'S going on?" Peterson asked as they entered the FOB. The Cambodes were in formation in the center of the camp, dressed in a mix of civilian clothes and fatigues. Most held small cloth bags. They were angry, yelling, some shaking their fists.

"They're celebrating our return," Morrissey joked. Armed Americans were scattered around the area. Dawson saw Major Capra and approached.

"Hey, sir. What's up?"

"Barton is firing the Cambodes."

"All of them?"

"All of them."

"Where are they going to go?"

"Probably to the nearest Viet Cong recruiting station. How'd it go out there?"

"We found your road."

"You did? Are you sure?"

"Well, actually Peterson did. I stood on it and didn't realize it was a road."

"That's the difference between sergeants and lieutenants. Can it support truck traffic?"

"Yeah, absolutely. They even had logs in a low part to keep trucks from getting stuck in the mud."

"As soon as this shit's over make sure you get together with Captain Stevens for your debriefing. Major Barton will be glad to hear this. Finding that road is a big deal. We needed a success."

"I doubt if the major will be glad to hear anything from me. He's still pissed that I didn't go into the fishing village. Where is he?"

"He's in the TOC protecting his girlfriend."

"The woman in the áo dài? I've seen her around. What's up with that?"

"He's the commander. It's none of my business," Major Capra said, sounding like there was a lot more to this story. Dawson looked over and saw that a recon team was guarding the entrance. The Cambodes were herded to the main gate, searched for weapons and released. In an hour, the FOB was quiet and definitely undermanned. Peterson, Morrissey and Dawson went to the TOC and took seats around a table for their mission debriefing.

It's difficult to overstate how incredibly boring a recon mission debriefing is. There are a dozen questions about every trail and stream the team encountered. What are the location coordinates? How wide? Direction? Type of soil? Vegetation? Overhead cover? On and on. It often sounds like a report from a National Geographic field trip. Enemy contacts are devoid of tactics, focusing on the numbers and equipment. Teams are asked if the enemy looked well fed and if they had haircuts. After two hours of this, Peterson's recon team was more than ready to get out of there and go have a beer. As they were wrapping, up Major Barton and Major Capra appeared.

"Good job men," Major Barton said. "The road you found may

be very important. Peterson, Dawson we're sending you to SOG Headquarters tomorrow for further debriefing."

"Guess they don't want any input from spec 4s," Morrissey said.

"Guess not," Dawson jokingly replied,. "Where's SOG Headquarters?"

"Saigon," Peterson said. "We'll get a night on the town."

"And maybe another one in Nha Trang. I've got something I have to check up on. I'll catch up with you guys later." He ducked into the S-3.

"Where's the major?"

"I'm right here, Dawson. What do you need." Crossing the room Dawson spoke quietly.

"I haven't been paid since I got here, sir. I don't have enough money to go to Saigon."

"Follow me." They walked down the hall to the S-1 office. "Wait here," Major Capra said as he entered, leaving the door open. He walked over to a desk and spoke to someone who quickly got up and opened a combination lock on a foot locker in the corner of the room. Seconds later, Major Capra returned and handed Dawson a stack of five hundred piaster notes.

"Thanks. Do I have to sign for this or anything?"

"Don't ask stupid questions, lieutenant. Try not to spend it all on Saigon tea."

"Well, ok, thanks."

"Guess you're out of a job, sergeant."

"That makes two of us, LT." Dawson sat down next to Rogers at the bar and asked,

"Why did they fire the Cambodes?"

"That's above my pay grade. Coulter took his temporary duty team back to Okinawa. So they're short of cadre. The Cambodes were lousy soldiers. Probably a bunch of reasons."

"So, they just up and marched them out the gate?"

"No. It had to be planned. They held it pretty close. I think they were afraid we'd get into a gun battle with them if it got out. The QC rounded them up and put them on a train south. It had to come from higher up. Can you imagine Barton trying to explain to Chief SOG that he can't run operations because he fired the mercenaries?"

"Have any idea what you are going to do now?" Dawson asked.

"No. How about you?"

"So far I'm just the designated RTO. While you've been hanging out drinking, I've spent twenty of the last thirty days in the woods."

"That's good. You need the experience," Rogers laughed.

"Yeah. Well I'm off to Saigon tomorrow."

"What for?"

"Peterson and I are going to SOG headquarters to brief them on something very important we found on the mission."

"What did you find?"

"Sorry, can't tell you it's top secret," Dawson teased.

"Fuck you, LT."

"Just a road."

"A new road?"

"Yes."

"That'll get you a trip to Saigon every time. Try not to do that again."

"What's wrong with a trip to Saigon?"

"A couple of trips and you'll become a go-to guy."

"So?"

"They always get the go-to guys killed."

"Sergeant Peterson's the one-zero. I'm just the lowly radio operator."

"Yeah, but you're a lieutenant. Officers always get more credit than they deserve."

Their food came and they ate in silence. Dawson was weak from hunger. He realized he had to discipline himself to eat more in the field. When they finished, the pretty Vietnamese bartender brought them another beer and a rum and coke.

"You ever eat anything other than fried egg sandwiches, LT?"

"Yeah. LRP rations," Dawson laughed. Halfway through his beer he pulled out the wad of cash Major Capra had given him. Separating a bill he asked Rogers, "What are these things worth?"

"Three dollars and eighty cents. Where'd you get all that?"

"My pay's screwed up. Capra gave it to me to go to Saigon."

"That's out of the foot locker," Rogers exclaimed.

"Yeah. How'd you know?"

"Every Special Forces team in Vietnam has a ton of cash."

"Where do they get it?"

"When a mercenary gets killed or just doesn't show up they leave him on the roster and keep collecting his pay."

"Sounds like a good idea to me. Guess they'll make a fortune by firing the Cambodes." They laughed and ordered another round of drinks.

"You guys were supposed to be here yesterday." Peterson and Dawson exchanged glances. They were in a non-descript five story apartment building on Pasteur Street in Saigon that served as the headquarters for MACV-SOG.

"We had to scrounge rides from Phu Bai. It took all day yesterday. If you needed us sooner you could have sent a private jet," Dawson pushed back, pissing off the captain.

"Well, we're here. We got here as fast as we could," Peterson said, to calm things down.

"You can't take your weapons upstairs." They placed their pistols on the desk. "Are they loaded?"

"Of course," Dawson was antagonizing again. "What about these?" he said raising a gym bag that contained civilian clothes.

"Tell you what. Put your guns in the bags and leave them here. You can pick them up on your way out. They're waiting for you on the fourth floor."

"Why try to start a fight with the captain?" They were walking up the stairs.

"I don't know. How did he think we'd get here yesterday?"

"You're just jealous he has a desk job."

"You're probably right," Dawson laughed.

The welcome on the fourth floor was a lot warmer. They had been told to wear jungle fatigues with insignia so everyone assumed the lieutenant was in charge. Dawson was very careful to make sure they understood that the sergeant one-zeroed the operation. They met Colonel Singlaub. He was referred to as Chief SOG. He congratulated them and hung around while Peterson pointed out the route the team had taken on a big map. They were asked a lot of questions about the enemy soldiers' uniforms and the condition of the road. After about an hour, they took a break for coffee. When they resumed, a civilian in a suit and tie stood in front of the map and formally addressed the group.

"All right gentlemen. Let's evaluate what we have heard here. This new section of road is nineteen kilometers due west of the Northern extreme of the A Shau Valley and the Special Forces camp at A Luoi, that was abandoned in 1966 as a result of enemy pressure. The airfield was briefly reopened this year to support an operation of the 1st Air Cavalry Division. If the road the recon team found was extended to A Luoi it would be of tremendous value to the enemy because it would add over ten kilometers of road that would not be subject to ground attack. Fortunately, this solution is not available to the enemy because of this terrain feature." He continued. Pointing at the map. "Dong Ap Bia or hilltop 937 greatly restricts the enemy's ability to construct a road in this area making it next to impossible to move supplies into the floor of the A Shau Valley. According to the reporting by the recon team, this road is very low-maintenance and not heavily traveled, if traveled at all. The North Vietnamese constructed this road as a diversion hoping we would find it, spend assets destroying it and thereby take pressure off Route 922."

"So we only found the road because they wanted us to find it." Peterson said. They were re-armed and back out on the street.

"That condescending, little prick. Who, the fuck, was he? The CIA terrain specialist? Hill 937 greatly restricts the enemy's ability to construct a road," He mimicked. "Who talks like that? He's one of those people you'd like to punch right in the mouth just because he's breathing."

"Guess you feel strongly about this," Peterson laughed. "At least we got a trip to Saigon. Let's find a hotel. I'll let you pay for it with Capra's money." Dawson fished in his side pocket and came up with a scrap of paper.

"The Eden Roc on TU Do Street. Sergeant Rogers says it's got a great bar full of hookers."

"Where is it?"

"Rogers said it's between SOG HQ and the river."

"Where's the river?"

They walked down the street in the opposite direction from the air base. There were a good number of people around, but not what you would call a crowd.

"Is it my imagination or are there a lot of eyes on us?" Dawson asked.

"I was thinking the same thing. Probably the berets."

"Or maybe the guns. I don't see anybody else carrying." They ducked into an alley, put their weapons and headgear in their bags and returned to the street wearing bush hats.

"That did it. We disappeared," Peterson observed. They continued and in less than a mile they came to the corner entrance of the Rex Hotel. It looked pretty fancy, with a couple of QC milling around outside. A sign advertised a roof top bar.

"Think they'll let us in?"

"Let's find out," Dawson said. They walked between the QC and into the hotel lobby. Nobody bothered them. Following a sign, they took an elevator.

If you had to be in a war zone, this was the place to be. The roof top bar of the Rex Hotel, although only six stories high, completely removed you from the dirt and bustle of the streets below. Looking past the twisting Saigon River, a thousand different shades of vivid green were reflected in the rubber tree plantation. Dawson and Peterson sat at a table, taking in the view, eating shrimp and drinking Heineken. It wasn't busy, just a few people scattered around. They were the only ones in uniform. As the afternoon wore on, and the shadows on the plantation began to lengthen, the tables began to fill up. They moved to the bar.

"You guys special forces?" a man in his forties wearing a maroon polo shirt and khakis pulled up a stool beside them.

"Tourists," Dawson said, knowing his shoulder patch gave them away.

"This place will be mobbed in a half hour when the five o'clock follies end."

"What's the five o'clock follies?"

"The military press briefing. It's held everyday downstairs. Most of the war correspondents are staying here. At least the ones that aren't shacking up with Vietnamese girls in villas."

"Why do they call it the follies?"

"Because the press doesn't believe a word the military tells them. Unless you want to get bombarded with questions you better get out of here before they arrive. Most of those guys have never seen a real green beret."

"You with the press?" Peterson asked.

"No. Construction. RMK. We built the embassy and most of the bases here."

"Thanks for the warning," Dawson said, and asked for the check.

"I've got your check. You guys work too hard for your money."

"Thanks. We appreciate it." After a pause, "Hey, do you know where the Eden Roc Hotel is on Tu Do Street?"

"Right around the corner. Down one block and one block east."

"Thanks again."

"Hey, fellows. Just remember you're still in a war zone. It's a different kind of war than you're used to, but it's still a war."

CHAPTER SIXTEEN

DRESSED IN JEANS and a black tee shirt, Dawson strapped on his shoulder holster. He checked the magazine of his Browning 9mm, slid it into the holster and fastened the snap. Retrieving a crumpled bush jacket out of his bag, he shook it, put it on and checked himself out in the mirror.

"All you need is a pair of Ray-Bans and the CIA would hire you in a minute," Peterson joked.

They had checked into the hotel a little after 1800 and grabbed a couple of hours of sleep. By 2200 they were ready to check out the night life. During the day, the Eden Roc looked more than a little worn, but it came to life at night. Five foot neon letters projected its name. The entrance's wide open doors bathed in red light attracted lonely GIs and women hungry for the cash they had in their pockets.

Dawson and Peterson sat at the packed bar drinking beer, rejecting the young girls, dressed in mini skirts and boots, who descended on them the moment they sat down. A five man band pounded out American pop songs making it hard to talk. Finally, they took a break.

"You ever been in one of these places?" Peterson asked once the noise subsided.

"Never."

"There's a couple of bars like this in Da Nang. See those little green shots the girls are hustling. That's Saigon tea. They have a quota they have to sell before they can leave with a customer. Then you make a separate deal with them. The drinks can cost you a lot more than the girls. Trick is to pick up a girl who's already sold a lot of drinks."

"Well, you finally taught me something useful." They clicked glasses and laughed.

During the next set, a girl with a pretty face and a lot of cleavage approached Peterson. Dawson watched as he bought her a Saigon tea. After a while he handed her some money. She took it to the end of the bar and gave it to a tough-looking guy with slicked back hair. He looked at a strip of paper and started yelling at her. She handed him more money. Dawson figured she tried to hold out. When she returned Peterson tapped him on the shoulder.

"This is Linh. I'm going to take her to the room. You gonna be OK on your own?"

"I'm not alone," Dawson replied tapping his side feeling the pistol underneath.

"Let's hope you don't need that. I'll see you later."

"Have fun."

He ordered another beer and looked around. The crowed had thinned out and the band was taking apart their equipment. He wondered how long the girl would stay in the room, not wanting to go barging in. He thought maybe he should get another room. He still had plenty of money left.

"You buy me Saigon tea?" He started to shake his head, no, but as he turned to look he saw a very pretty girl. Tall for a Vietnamese. Short dress, nice legs, white go-go boots.

"Sure, sit down," he said pulling back a stool. She got her drink and he paid.

"What's your name?"

"Linh." Guess they're all Linh he thought.

"You name."

"Alan."

"You GI?"

"No," he lied. Not really knowing why. Of course, she didn't believe him. Changing the subject he said, "What's in that?" pointing to her drink.

"Tea." She took a sip. Dawson tried a little more small talk.

"No hieu biet," she said. Dawson realized she didn't speak much English. He tried again and they both laughed , neither understanding what the other had said. Her eyes shinned and she smiled. After a while, she put her hand on his arm. "Alan, you have room?" He was surprised she remembered his name.

"Yes, but my friend has a girl there." Seeing a questioning look he said, "No room." Trying to make it simple.

"You want go Linh room?"

"Absolutely." Then "Yes." Making sure she understood.

"You pay bar five hundred." He gave her the money and watched as she gave it to the slick hair guy and returned.

"We go now." He followed her out of the bar, down a hall and out the rear entrance. Stepping into a brightly lit area with a bunch of motor scooters he saw a QC and stopped.

"No sweat. No sweat," she said pulling his arm. She started a Vespa and kicked it off the stand. He hesitated thinking she had meant a room in the hotel. Ah, what the hell, he thought and climbed on behind her, putting his hand around her waist, touching her for the first time. She was driving fast down side streets. He tried to keep track, but after a few turns he was lost. It was probably less than five minutes when she pulled into an alley beside a long one story concrete building with a half dozen louvered metal double doors. She chained the Vespa to a pole and opened one of the sets of doors with a big key. It was a surprisingly large room with a high ceiling, no windows, sparsely furnished, with a bed, a cabinet, a couple of chairs and a small table.

They had an awkward moment. Dawson wasn't sure what to do, he gently put is arm around her. For hanging out in a smoke-filled bar, she smelled fresh, a slight whiff of perfume. He leaned over and ran his nose up the smooth skin of her neck. She pushed her body into him then moved away and Dawson realized business was business. He took care of her and she moved across the room, pulled papers and money out of her boot, added it to Dawson's and locked it in the cabinet. Returning, she led him to the bed. He sat at the bottom. Slowly, she pulled the little dress over her head and stood there in pretty matching pink underwear. Next went the bra revealing her breasts with perky brown nipples. A few seconds later he saw her long narrow strip of straight, black hair. Dressed only in go-go boots she did a little pirouette then came to him and pushed his jackct off his shoulders.

"No good. No good." She recoiled, seeing his pistol.

"It's Ok. Ok," he said wrapping it in his jacket and placing it beside the bed. She calmed down in a few seconds. Dawson undressed, laid with her on the bed, took off her boots and kissed her everywhere. She responded in kind. When they were finished she wrapped herself in a towel and gave one to Dawson. He wrapped it around his waist. Taking his hand she let him outside to a small concrete enclosure, with a hole in the ground. They relieved themselves and moved to a large urn containing water. She washed herself and then cleaned Dawson arousing him again. She laughed, grabbed it, and pulled him back inside. Laying on the bed he ran his fingers over her body being sure to touch any spot he might have missed the first time. He heard a vehicle pull up outside and stopped to listen. She pulled his hand back. That made him smile. There was a soft knock on the metal doors.

"Tien, Tien." It was an American voice. Then the sound of a key in the lock. Panicked, she jumped up pointing wildly at his clothes and ran to grab her dress. Dawson chose safety over modesty and grabbed the Browning. A man entered, wearing fatigues, an Air Force major.

"Who are you? What are you doing here?" he demanded using the authority of a field grade officer, but still sounding stupid. Of course, he knew exactly what was going on.

"Right now, I'm just the guy with the gun," Dawson answered, trying to act casual. Like he pulled guns on people everyday.

"Go! You go!" Linh was yelling and crying. The major moved to the other end of the room and sat in a chair.

"No, problem," Dawson said, laying the pistol on the bed and getting dressed. Not being one to do anything the easy way he added, "As soon as I get my money back. I paid for the night." She understood that and vigorously shook her head. The major got out some money and started to get up.

"Stay there. Give it to her." He was dressed now, holding the pistol at his side. Motioning her over, he took the money and put it in his pocket without counting. He had pushed things far enough. "Good bye Linh, Tien. or whatever." he walked out the door and closed it.

Outside he breathed deeply. His first thoughts were about the girl, but his training kicked that out of his mind as he tried to figure out the way back to the hotel. The air force jeep was sitting there and he thought about borrowing it, then rejected the idea. Stealing a major's jeep was probably a lot more serious than screwing his girlfriend. Walking to the end of the alley, he turned right. It was the only turn he was sure of. He listened for traffic, but the only sounds were the occasional dog barking. There were no street lights. Saigon was designed on a grid so he decided to walk in a constant direction hoping to find something familiar. As he walked, staying in the shadows, wary of the QC, he thought about the rules from orientation. Being alone, out after curfew, in an off-limits area. It reminded him of his college advisor asking him if there were any rules he didn't break just before he got tossed. You could probably add carrying a concealed weapon to the list. He wondered if the Get Out of Jail Free cards the sergeants talked about at Bragg actually worked. Eventually, he crossed Pasteur Street. He almost missed the sign buried behind a tree. He followed it and was surprised to pass SOG headquarters. They had traveled farther on the Vespa than he realized. He thought about going in and asking for a ride, but decided that, with his luck, he would run into the captain he had had words with that morning - actually yesterday morning. Passing the Rex

Hotel, he remembered the guy who paid their bill saying, down one block. east one block. The welcoming red lights to the entrance had been turned off, but the neon letters spelling Eden Roc still lit up the area. The lobby was empty except for a sleeping clerk. Upstairs, he quietly entered the room. Peterson and the girl were sleeping. He undressed and slid into the other bed falling asleep in seconds.

When he awoke, the girl was standing there looking at him curiously. Totally unconcerned with her nakedness. He recognized her by the big boobs. Peterson came out of the bathroom in a pair of jeans. Dawson pretended to sleep as she got dressed. Peterson gave her a hug and some money and she left. he turned and asked,
"So, how'd it go last night?"

An hour later they were in the coffee shop eating French bread and trying to drink what may have been the world's worst-tasting coffee.
"We probably should have gone to the Rex. I don't think food is high on this place's agenda," Peterson said. Dawson was too tired to care. They walked the mile to SOG headquarters and got a jeep and a Vietnamese driver to take them to Tan Son Nhut.

On the flight back to Phu Bai he though about Linh , imagining what it might have been like to spend the whole night with her. It made going back to the world of steep mountain jungles and dangerous missions a little more difficult.

"Didn't they feed you in Saigon?" Rogers joined Dawson at the bar.

"Nope. They had me too busy taking care of the ladies."

"That's a whole different world down there. LT."

"Yeah. It's brutal. Imagine that after shuffling papers in an air conditioned office all day you still have to go out and find a Vietnamese girl at night?"

"It's not as great as it sounds." Rogers cautioned.

"You don't think so?"

"No. You're forgetting they still have to make time to write letters home to their wives about the horrors of war."

"That's hilarious. What have they got you doing?"

"Nothing."

"Nothing?"

"Well, we cleaned out all the crap the Cambodes left behind in the barracks and today we tried to get rid of their jerry-rigged lighting without getting electrocuted."

"Sounds like a good job for Sacco."

"You're tough, LT. After I got shocked a couple of times we cut the power and just tore the wires out. Now the lights won't go on at all."

"Why am I not surprised?"

"Oh, by the way, we found a PRC-25 radio they had hidden away."

"In the barracks?"

"Yeah."

"Battery work?"

"Good as new."

"Set to Honeycutt frequency?"

"I didn't look."

"What'd you do with it?"

"Kept it. We can use a spare."

"I should probably give it to S-2."

"Why, you think the Cambodes were spies?" Rogers said sarcastically. "S-2's not going to do anything with it."

"Either are we. They fired the hatchet force. Remember?"

The next morning, Dawson took the radio to S-2 and gave it to Sergeant Fallon.

"The Cambodes were probably trying to figure out how to get it out the gate. You can get a lot of money for one of these on the black market," he said.

"Who'd buy it?" Dawson asked, quickly realizing he had asked a stupid question.

"The VC. Who else? The ARVN sell half the shit we give them."

"Half!"

"No not half. That's an exaggeration. They probably only sell forty eight percent."

"The frequency on the radio isn't set to Honeycutt. Any way to find out who's on the other end?"

"No. If we asked ASA they'd just use it as an excuse to run a big security investigation on the camp and try to hang somebody for letting a radio get loose. And god only knows what else they'd find."

"Great way to run a top secret operation."

"Hey, Sir, everything in Vietnam leaks like a sieve. I always try to tell you guys that in the briefings. The only safe thing you can assume is that if you know it, the North Vietnamese know it too."

"OK. Well thanks for that. Can I take the radio?"

"Sure. What do you need it for?"

"Hey, I can get it out the gate," he laughed and left.

He didn't get far.

"Dawson."

"Sir," he replied and followed Major Capra to his office.

"Have a seat." Dawson put the radio on the floor and sat. "How'd the briefing go in Saigon?"

"Sergeant Peterson was in charge. He gave the briefing. He's probably more qualified to tell you how it went than I am."

"I already talked to him. Now I'm asking you. How'd it go?"

"I think they were happy with how we performed the operation. Chief SOG sat in on the first half of the briefing. After he left, some civilian in a suit got up and said we didn't find shit."

"Why?"

"He said there was some hill, Hill 937 I think. It also had a Vietnamese name, fifteen klicks east that made it impossible for the NVA to complete the road to the A Shau Valley. He said the road we found was just a diversion to suck assets away from Route 922."

"Anything else?"

"No, that's about it, sir."

"OK. You can go." Dawson picked up the radio and started to leave. "Hey, did you have a good time in Saigon?"

"Yes, sir."

"Good. Because, where we're sending you, you won't get an opportunity like that again for a while."

"Oh, Great. Where am I going?"

"The commander's at a big meeting in Da Nang. I'll let you know when everything is finalized."

"Hey, LT, heard you robbed an Air Force major at gun point!"

"Fuck you, Rogers. Who told you that shit?"

"Sacco knows someone on Peterson's team."

"Somebody should send Sacco on a one-way recon mission to Hanoi."

"So what happened?"

"I'm sure whatever you heard is a lot more interesting than what really happened."

"You're not going to tell me?" Of course, Dawson told him every word.

After food and a few drinks, Dawson told Rogers,

"Capra says I'm being reassigned."

"Yeah, I heard."

"What do you mean, you heard?"

"They're sending some hatchet force people to Mai Loc."

"Where's Mai Loc?"

"Just below the DMZ in the middle of the country. Our FOB 3 was at Khe Sanh. When they closed down the Marine base, after the siege, they moved what was left of the FOB to Mai Loc and told them to build a launch site."

"You going?"

"Not me LT. I'm smart enough to stay away from places where they don't have running water and toilets."

CHAPTER SEVENTEEN

TO THE MEN OF SOG their target areas were defined as six square kilometer areas often consisting of steep mountains and dense jungle, exaggerating their size. But, to the pilots who provided support, they were mere moments of air travel. Even though their maps were divided by kilometers, Americans still thought of distance in terms of miles. At the DMZ that separated North and South Vietnam the country was only forty miles wide. It was only thirty miles from Phu Bai to the A Shau Valley. In fact, the entire deadly area of northern I Corp could be stuck in a sixty mile box. To put this into perspective, the allies traveled one hundred miles to cross the English Channel on D Day, then marched six hundred miles east to Berlin.

MACV-SOG's FOB 3 was located on the southern perimeter of the Marine combat base at Khe Sanh. A formidable structure consisting of deep bunkers with overhead cover, connected by trenches, it withstood the seventy-seven day artillery bombardment launched by the North Vietnamese. When the siege was lifted in early April, the high command decided to abandon the base. In May, the Americans and their Bru montagnard fighting force loaded onto trucks and traveled east on Route 9 sixteen miles to the Cua Valley near the village of Mai Loc. Here they were dropped off next to a small Naval construction unit of Seabees that had arrived just days before. It was an interesting choice of location for a top secret unit tasked with running the most classified missions of the war in that it offered no area security and zero infrastructure. The fact that the port of Dong Ha, a few minutes of flight time further east, offered roads, airfields, electricity and security made the decision even stranger. But in true military fashion, no one over the rank of sergeant seemed to think it was a stupid idea. So there they stood, in the middle of nowhere, with their equipment piled around them, watching the trucks pull away.

A helicopter landed on a partially completed runway. Dirt, stirred by the whirling blades, blew through the cabin as the chopper shut down. After two weeks of work, the Mai Loc launch site was nothing more than a few tents, not even protected by sandbags, surrounded by a couple of strands of concertina wire. Dawson stepped out, carrying a duffle bag. Looking around, he saw hills to the south and mountains to the west. The rest was a flat plain. He followed the helicopter crew though a rudimentary gate, guarded by a grinning, dark-skinned, Asian.

Another camp. Another major. This one less full of himself than most, comfortable in command. Probably had been a sergeant before getting commissioned. He put Dawson in charge of a hatchet force platoon. There weren't many officers above the rank of first lieutenant assigned to the camp and those that were had ways of finding very good reasons to visit Phu Bai, DaNang or Saigon on a regular basis.

Dawson pulled the poncho liner up over the pillow. The gray metal cot sat on the dirt floor of a twelve man tent. His shaving kit and personal items were in a wooden mortar shell box kept off the ground by four C-ration cans placed under the corners. His web gear, weapons and the duffle bag he lived out of were next to it on a small wood pallet. He stepped out of the tent squinting in the bright sunlight.

"Whatcha doin' dummy?" the strong, densely built Bru montagnard laughed. It was Thoung, his Bru platoon leader and interpreter. Dawson had taught him to say dummy. He had no idea if he knew what it meant.

"Digging ditches. Filling sand bags. Same thing you're going to do," he replied.

"No good, No good."

"Gotta get you something to hide behind if the VC show up." They walked over to a large pile of dirt the Seabees had bulldozed for them. The other Bru from the platoon were filling sandbags and carrying them over to reinforce the trenches. At Khe Sanh most of the Americans who worked with the Bru had been on temporary duty from the 1st Special Forces Group on Okinawa. Their six month tour ended with the move to Mai Loc. The Bru and the new Americans were getting used to each other. The Bru were native mountain tribesmen the Americans had hired as mercenary soldiers who were extremely loyal, would stand and fight, but they were not known to be aggressive fighters. So far they seemed to be very friendly, constantly smiling and laughing, almost childish.

"Hey, Thoung. Why does it take six tahan to fill a sand bag?" Dawson asked, holding up his fingers, letting him know that he knew that tahan was the Bru word for soldier.

"No six."

"Yeah. One to shovel, one to hold the bag, one to tie the bag, one to carry it and two to watch," he said acting out the actions, pointing to his eyes for the last.

"No two to watch. Two to rest," Thoung laughed.

The days at Mai Loc were full of building fortifications by day and drinking at night. After a couple of weeks, Dawson approached the major.

"Excuse me, sir. Do you have a minute?" The major looked up, obviously having no idea who he was. "Lieutenant Dawson, sir. Do you know Major Capra down at Phu Bai?" They talked for a minute or two and Dawson returned to working in the dirt.

The helicopters were landing on the runway. Dawson walked to the gate. He looked past the pilots and saw a couple of Americans carrying duffle bags.

"Sergeant Rogers. Stopping by for a visit?" he called out.

"Fuck you, LT. I should have known you had something to do with this."

"I have no idea what you're talking about."

"That's bullshit."

"You're gonna love it here," he laughed. Rogers wasn't amused.

"You better have some rum in this dump."

"Oh, I bet I could find more than a couple of bottles in your duffle bag." Dawson led him to his tent. Pointing to an empty bunk he said, "Here you go. Home sweet home."

"You're a fucking riot, LT."

After a day of working on the fortifications, Rogers was still in a foul mood. They sat in the front seats of one of the only two jeeps at the launch site drinking beer and warm rum and coke watching the North Vietnamese shell the Marine base at Camp Carroll a few klicks to their north just below the DMZ.

"Probably 122 millimeter rockets," Dawson offered as an ice breaker.

"Who ordered you to work on the camp bunkers?" Rogers asked, changing the subject.

"Nobody. This place is really weird. You get up in the morning and just see what needs to be done and do it. I've met two other platoon leaders. One's a rodeo rider from Montana. If we have a company commander he's not here. I sure haven't gone to the major to ask about it."

"You think maybe you ought to find out if these Bru can fight?" Rogers said gesturing at the black columns of smoke rising on the horizon. "You know, just in case they have to shoot somebody," he paused for a while then said, "You know sooner or later they're going to have to do what they're getting paid for."

"Ok. I got your point the first time. You know, you've really got this wise old sergeant act down. You're only a few years older than I am, for Christ sake."

"Do you want to take the Bru out for some live fire training tomorrow?" Dawson asked Rogers trying to get back in his good graces. They were placing sandbags around a machine gun bunker.

"Beats the hell out of doing this."

"What do you think we can use for targets?"

"Sandbags," Rogers laughed. I'll go see if I can get the Seabees to cut some plywood into strips. You better check to see if they have enough replacement ammo."

"How much do you think we'll need?"

"If we let them fire ten magazines, two hundred rounds each. You do the math."

Late the next morning, they moved across the runway, into a field and set up a row of targets. Dawson let the Bru fire on full automatic from a standing position without instruction on the first targets. Not surprisingly, they fired from the hip expending the whole magazine with a single pull of the trigger not doing much damage to the plywood.

"I thought these guys were trained," Rogers complained.

"Looks like that's our job. At least they have M-16s." They taught the Bru to shoulder their weapons and fire short two or three round bursts. Their improvement was obvious by the increase of the number of holes as they moved from one target to the next.

"They're quick learners," Dawson said, on the way back to the compound.

"Somebody probably worked with them before. They've been sitting in bunkers at Khe Sanh for three or four months. Probably not a lot of training going on there. They just need some practice, LT."

"Probably a good idea to do it again tomorrow."

"And the next day. And the next day."

After the third day, Dawson and Rogers were eating dinner in the mess tent. The food was pretty decent considering the conditions.

"Lieutenant." It was the major. "I hear your people shot up twenty-five thousand rounds of ammunition in the last couple of days."

"Yes, sir. That's probably about right."

"Can they hit anything?"

"Yes, sir. They're getting pretty good."

"Pretty good will have to be good enough until we get a resupply."

"Yes, sir."

"Are you ready to take your platoon across the fence?"

"No, sir. Not till we do some patrolling."

"Ok. Do what you can locally. There's a valley with a steep ridgeline southeast of here that the marines just cleared. Terrain is like you'll find in a Prairie Fire target. They didn't get much resistance. I'll set up a mission for your platoon there next week. You can use it to train knowing there's a chance you'll make contact," the major said.

"There for a minute, I was a little worried that 'Yes sir,' was the only thing you knew how to say, LT," Rogers joked quietly so the major didn't hear.

The Vietnamese cook stopped serving dinner. The mess tent had emptied out and now was refilling with drinkers. They took a couple of drinks, walked to the mortar pit and sat on the newly-stacked sandbags.

"So, how do you want to handle this patrol training?"

"I don't know," Dawson replied.

"That's what you should have said when the major asked you if the Bru could shoot," Rogers said, only half kidding.

"We could teach them squad rushes, leapfrogging, that kind of stuff."

"That shit doesn't work in the mountains. Why don't we just bring the Bru out with their gear tomorrow, make them jump up and down to be sure nothing makes a racket. We can run a short patrol teaching them to be quiet and maybe figure out a point squad. If that's ok with you, LT."

"Fine with me."

The next morning, the Bru were assembled on the air strip in full battle gear. Actually, assembled is too strong a word. They were clustered in little groups. Dawson told Thoung he wanted to make sure the soldiers' equipment was quiet.

"OK. OK. Quiet," he replied, and started calling out to the troops. They started shaking and bouncing up and down. When a soldier's gear made noise, others near him would laugh and point then strip off his gear and fix the problem. In a few minutes they were done.

"Tahan quiet now, trung uy," Thoung told Dawson using the Vietnamese word for lieutenant.

"That was good."

"Tahan know quiet. Go find VC, tahan quiet," he said putting his hand across his mouth. "Tahan fight VC long time. Trung uy come Vietnam. Go home. Bru stay Vietnam."

"What's he saying, LT?"

"He says Americans come and go, but they're here to stay."

"Yeah. He probably figures that by the time we know what we're doing we'll pack up and leave."

"He may be right. Let's set up the point squad."

"Maybe you could just ask him?'

"Hey Thoung."

"Trung uy?"

"Have point man?"

"RaLang. RaLang pa pan ai," he called out. A slim muscular Bru carrying a CAR-15 quickly walked over. "RaLang be point man," Thoung stated firmly.

They broke the platoon down into two large squads and a point element and moved east away from the camp and the Seabees. The open field soon turned into farm land and rice paddies divided by thick hedgerows which offered ample concealment for any enemy threat. Forced to walk in the open, they were exposed. The Bru's normal chatter subsided. Quiet and vigilant, moving cautiously, weapons at the ready, having the appearance of a formidable fighting force was their only means of deterrence. Dawson gave directions to Thoung who relayed them to the men with hand signals which the men passed on. After a while, Dawson and Rogers caught on to the signals and started using them. Two hedgerows converged forming the sides of a wide cart path. The platoon split into parallel columns on either side ready to disappear into the thick vegetation at a moment's notice. Dawson had them do just that. Then he, Rogers and Thoung walked along the path inspecting their positions. They were silent, difficult to see, weapons pointed at the path. He nodded his approval and had them return to their columns. They continued on. The hedgerow on the north side of the road ended revealing a large expanse of rice paddies. As they moved into the open area two men, a few hundred meters away, fled across the dikes. Weapons came up, waiting on the order to fire.

"VC?" Dawson asked.

"Tahan don't know. Maybe just Vietnam," Thoung patted his chest above his heart.

"Scared?"

"Scared," Thoung repeated.

"Let'em go."

They worked their way through some thick scrub traveling south, circled back to the familiar field being careful not to duplicate their route and returned to the camp in about an hour.

"I was pretty impressed with the Bru today." They were sitting in the jeep. Nobody was shelling Camp Carroll this evening. "Did you notice they brought their M-16s up to their shoulder, like we taught them, when those two Vietnamese took off?"

"What surprised me was that you didn't grab a machine gun and shoot them yourself. Remember the ARVN training range." They laughed.

"You know, they were good and quiet. Alert. Even though there hasn't been any signs of enemy activity in the area they still took it seriously. What did you think?"

"They were fine. Especially when you compare them to the Cambodes. Speaking of taking it seriously, you got a little far from camp today without a radio, LT."

"Yeah, I know. That was a stupid mistake. I realized it as soon as we saw the Vietnamese."

"It could have been a major mistake. What if someone got hurt and we needed a medevac? If we're going to get out of sight of camp we should have a radio. It might help if you tell me what you plan on doing before you just go and do it." Dawson knew he was right, but Rogers wasn't done. "Another thing. There's no way just the two of us can run this platoon on a real operation. We need at least one more American."

"I know that but, I don't know who to ask other than the major and I don't want to do that because if he says no, that's the end of discussion. I'm starting to miss that weasel Sacco. Why don't you see if one of your NCO buddies wants to straphang?"

"No problem. They're all at Phu Bai. I'll leave tomorrow." That lifted the tension.

"That's not going to happen. It's time you make some new friends. Besides, tomorrow we're going to check out our machine gunners and M-79 grenadiers to find out if they're any good."

"Oh. Somehow I didn't get the training schedule."

"Ok, I got it. Most of the time I just do what I think is right at the time."

"That's pretty obvious, LT."

CHAPTER EIGHTEEN

THE MACHINE GUNNERS were accurate, so long as they used the bipod and kept the legs collapsed to keep them from shooting high. They were able to lay down a solid base of fire without a lot of instruction. The tracers started a little brush fire, but luckily they were able to stomp it out. The grenadiers were a whole different story. They wanted to fire the grenade launchers like they were shotguns, aiming straight, and blast away with 40mm high explosive rounds. The concept of lobbing rounds over a hill or into a bunker was totally foreign to them. Problem was, neither Dawson or Rogers had enough practice to be good at it either. So they finished up and went back to camp.

"What do you want to do now, LT?"

"Let's call it a day. If it's ok with you, we're going to go check out Bang Son village tomorrow."

"What sightseeing again. Like Hue?"

"No. This is a patrol. It's about two, two and a half klicks just west of north. There's a lot of forest between here and there. Supposed to be a sketchy area."

"Whatever you say, LT."

"Take the rest of the afternoon to go make friends. Try to find one that's a medic and knows how to fire an M-79."

The next morning they were busy, getting a day's rations for the troops, claymore mines and, of course, a radio. Dawson stopped by the mess tent. He generally avoided breakfast. A few men were sitting around talking and drinking coffee. He got a cup and approached four men at a table.

"I'm taking a platoon out locally for a day long training patrol. I could use some help. Anybody want to come along?"

"I wouldn't mind coming along," a voice behind him said.

I'm Lt. Dawson. Who are you?"

"Specialist Jennings, sir." Dawson thought he looked familiar. "I drove you to Camp A. P. Hill, sir."

"The hookers in Richmond!"

"Yes, sir."

"Special Forces is a small world. What are you doing here?"

"I just got in country. Went through the 5th Group Orientation. They sent me to FOB 1 and they sent me here. Got here yesterday."

"You volunteered for SOG?"

"I got orders to Vietnam before a slot for a specialty school opened up. When I got to Cahm Ran they told me if I volunteered for SOG I could stay in Special Forces. So, that's what I did."

"Have you got an assignment?"

"No, sir."

"How about field gear?"

"Got that at Phu Bai."

"Get your stuff."

"Where will you be, sir?"

"Just look around. The place isn't that big." Dawson turned to leave then turned back again. "By any chance, are you any good with an M-79?"

"Yes, sir."

"Good. See you in a few minutes."

"Where you been, LT? We're ready to go."

"Been busy. Where's the radio?"

"Tahan have radio," Thoung replied.

"I'll carry it." The soldier unpacked the radio and gave it to Dawson who put it in his back pack carefully fitting the whip antenna through the slits he had cut in the flap to hide it from the enemy.

"Ready now, LT?" Rogers faked exasperation.

"In a minute. Here he comes now."

"Who's that?"

"Just some guy I picked up this morning. At least one of us knows how to make friends. Sergeant Rogers. Specialist Jennings. Jennings, Rogers is the platoon sergeant you do what he says no matter what I say." Rogers laughed at that. The two started talking. "Hey, we gonna stand around all day?"

The platoon spent two and a half hours in the forest. The ground cover was sparse, the terrain fairly flat, so they moved two squads in parallel columns. Each had a machine gun forward with a sergeant nearby. The point squad formed a loose triangle. RaLang came to a halt and signaled Thoung to come forward. Dawson joined them. They could barely see the village hidden in a clump of trees surrounded by a wide expanse of rice paddies. Right down the center of the paddy ran a wide raised road about three hundred meters long leading to the village.

"You could drive an eighteen wheeler across that thing, LT."

"We could set up M-60s on either side of it for cover," Jennings suggested.

"Put your squad in a defensive perimeter to watch our backs," Dawson told him. After he left, Rogers asked,

"You're not thinking about crossing that, are you, LT?"

"Absolutely not."

"Well, that's a relief."

"Not unless I've been on the other side first."

"Here we go. What are you thinking?"

"See how the rice paddies look like they go on forever to the west, but to the east they get narrower as the ground rises. I think they end by the side of the village. We can circle around to the back door."

"You wouldn't take the Cambodes into the fishing village. Now you want to take these guys in here. What's the difference?"

"The fishing village wasn't within striking distance of where I sleep."

"That's a point."

"VC stay here?" Dawson asked Thoung. They had a short conversation using English, French and Vietnamese words in the same sentences.

"What did he say?"

"He says the VC come here to eat and get food."

"Pretty far west for VC."

"He means NVA. To them the VC and the NVA are the same thing. They aren't real fond of the South Vietnamese either. Let's work our way east and see if it looks like we can enter the village without getting exposed."

"Maybe you should call it in?"

"That's a good idea." Dawson flipped up the whip antenna and pulled out the handset. After a little back and forth he told Rogers, "They're trying to find somebody in charge." Then he was back talking.

"What did they say?"

"Find out if there are NVA in the village. Count how many there are. Take an inventory of their weapons, but don't get into a fight."

"That's brilliant."

They moved slowly, trying to see behind every tree and bush that might conceal an enemy. The Americans in a crouch trying to make themselves less noticeable. It was almost 1400 hrs. In the middle of the tense march Dawson realized he hadn't stopped to let the Bru eat. Too late now. They came to a well-worn trail. It seemed to enter the village without any break in the cover of the forest. Truth be told, he would have much rather encountered an obstacle, returned to camp and had a beer. Beer trumped danger any day. He signaled the platoon to stay put and moved down the trail with part of the point squad. Within ten meters they were in back of the first hooch. Leaving the others in place, he returned to the platoon and put his hand on Thoung's shoulder.

"You tell tahan no shoot mama-san. No shoot baby-san. Man with gun OK." Thoung moved off and whispered to the Bru. As he told them they looked up at Dawson and shook their heads yes.

"OK , trung uy. Tahan understand."

"Ready?" he said to Rogers and Jennings. They nodded. "Be careful of booby traps. Don't pick up anything."

The village was immaculate. Like something out of a travelogue. Perfect little thatched huts. Some with decorative trinkets hung by the doors and drop down shutters over the windows. The pathways were edged by thin logs and covered with a dark brown mulch. Where the trees parted and sunlight hit the ground they had planted small gardens. A strand of gray commo wire crossed one of the openings. The was no trash anywhere. Or people or animals for that matter. No dogs barking. The place was as silent as the soldiers who were now moving down the paths. It was as if the place was built for display and abandoned.

"Where are the people?" Dawson quietly asked Thoung.

"Bunkers," he whispered back, pointing to the ground.

They were almost to the wide road that crossed the rice paddies when they saw the first person. A very old lady stood in a doorway defiantly glaring at them. The look on her face was unmistakable. Hatred. There was a small covered water buffalo pen by the road. Dawson imagined the animals were glaring at them too.

"Jennings. Now you can set up your two guns on either side of the road. Spread your men on the bank. Aim back at the village and cover us while we cross the road. Don't shoot anything by accident and don't yell at anyone. Do it in silence. When we get across we'll cover you." They crossed and assembled on the other side where the road narrowed without any problem.

"What now, LT? Back into the forest."

"No, let's just keep walking slowly down the road."

"You kidding? That's asking to get ambushed."

"Just until we're out of sight of the village. Then we can move into the forest and set up our own ambush. See if we can catch them running parallel to the road to ambush us." It was a great idea, but the enemy didn't play along. So after a while they got up off the ground, gave the Bru time to eat and made their way back to camp.

"I wonder how many people were hiding in the village?" Dawson asked as he opened a beer.

"Who knows. Say four per hooch. So maybe a hundred.

"That old mama-son didn't like us much."

"What did you expect them to do, come out waving American flags, LT?"

"That would have been nice."

"I was surprised you didn't kick over a couple of hooches to see what was inside."

"That's a job for the Marines. I'm sure it's what they expected. Hopefully, appearing out of nowhere and sweeping through silently had a bigger effect than a bunch of yelling soldiers messing up their shit."

"Passing through like the angel of death."

"That's beautiful. No, more like giving them the impression we have better things to do."

"You do, LT."

"What's that?"

"Get me a couple of bottles of rum. I'm running out."

The next day, they went back to filling sand bags. Late in the afternoon Dawson appeared with his web gear and CAR-15.

Going back to visit mama-san?" Rogers joked.

"No Phu Bai."

"Not without me!"

"Sorry, they only gave me one ticket."

"What for?"

"You told me you needed rum."

"Bullshit. Why are you really going?"

"They want to debrief me on the village."

"What did you do? Tell them Ho Chi Minh was hiding in the basement."

"Something like that. Did you see the commo wire in the village?"

"Yeah, I saw it."

"You did? Why didn't you say something?"

"I figured some lieutenant might want to start yanking on it without knowing what was at the other end."

"Thanks for the vote of confidence. Be back tomorrow," he said, as he turned to walk to the helicopters on the runway.

"Hey, LT," Rogers called after him. "Don't forget the rum."

Dawson sat shivering in the air conditioned S-2 office at Phu Bai. He had just finished describing the village to Fallon.

"The commo wire really doesn't mean much unless you find a phone. They use it for a million different things. Every village like that grows rice for the North Vietnamese Army."

"We know that?"

"Sure. If it's more than they can possibly eat what else are they going to do with it?"

"Sell it?"

"Besides the fact that the NVA would kill them if they tried, farmers can't sell rice in Vietnam."

"I thought rice and rubber were their major products."

"Rubber still is. But, we give them so much rice it killed the market."

"Why would we give the Vietnamese rice?"

"It's the USAID Food for Peace program. Haven't you ever been to the market in Hue or even right here in Phu Bai?"

"No."

"There's pallets of bags of rice all over the place on the black market. Everything we give these people from Food for Peace ends up on the black market. The rice comes from Texas. Vietnamese farmers can't compete with free rice."

"Why would we send rice from Texas to Vietnam? It doesn't make any sense."

"Sure it does. The president is from Texas, so he keeps his farmers happy by having the government buy their rice. That keeps the price up of for them. Now the only thing the Vietnamese farmers can do is give or sell their rice to the North Vietnamese Army so they don't starve and can keep fighting. And that keeps the defense contractors happy."

"That's pretty cynical."

"Well I doubt anybody sat down and figured it out like that. Our government thought it would be good to feed people around the world. Probably with a little push from the agriculture industry. But no matter what the intentions may have been, the end result is that it feeds the enemy and the war goes on."

"Who knows about this?"

"Everybody but the people who are getting shot."

Dawson got up to leave. He stepped out the door and immediately returned.

"Forget something?" Fallon asked.

"No. Major Barton is in the hall. We don't get along and I want to avoid him. He's with that woman."

"Oh, his little Vietnamese honey. He's going to stay in Vietnam forever. No way he's going to give that up to go home to his wife and kids."

"He's married?"

"I don't know. I just made that up."

"What's she doing in the TOC? Isn't that a pretty big security breach?"

"Sure is. Why don't you go ask him about it?"

"Yeah. That's what I'll do. Hey, while I'm stuck here did anybody take action on that road we found south of Base Area 611?"

"What road?"

"You know, the one with Peterson's recon team that we went to Saigon about."

"Oh that one. It's in the area intelligence summary that's available to all military branches and intelligence services. You're listed as an indigenous paramilitary unit with impeccable reliability. Information not confirmed by other sources."

"So what does that do?"

"Not much."

"Great. At least you're honest.' Dawson peeked into the hall. The major and his girlfriend were gone. "Ok, thanks. By the way I need to take a few bottles of rum back to Mai Loc. Where can I get some?"

"The black market," Fallon laughed. "Go to the club and just ask until you find somebody who says yes. Then just take some."

"Ok. I'm going to get out of here." He didn't get far. Six steps down the hall to be exact.

"Lieutenant Dawson. I thought you were at Mai Loc?" It was Major Capra.

"Yes sir. I am. They just sent me down here for a debriefing."

"Why?"

"I don't know. I guess they don't think anybody at Mai Loc can read or write." They talked for a while and Dawson told him that he needed to get some rum for the mess tent at Mai Loc. The major sent a spec. 4 to get it. After a while he returned with a liquor box with four two liter bottles of rum.

"That enough?" Capra asked.

"That's great, sir. Thanks."

"Tell Sergeant Rogers not to drink it all at one time." The major grinned.

CHAPTER NINETEEN

"TRUNG UY WALK same, same elephant," Thoung said.

"Maybe if you let one of the little guys carry the radio you'd be quieter, LT," Rogers said quietly, trying not to grin.

"I'll pay more attention to it from now on," Dawson replied, not responding well to the criticism.

True to his word, the major had set them up with a mountainous, in country operation to check out the Bru's patrolling skills. They had been inserted by helicopter three days before. So far, the results were excellent. The Bru moved easily up and down the steep ridges carrying their heavy load of weapons and equipment. They were quiet, alert and blended in well with the surrounding jungle. At night they worked efficiently with the Americans to set up their defensive perimeter and in the morning they left the position undisturbed.

For the first three days, they practiced moving over different types of terrain, identifying potential enemy points of attack and moving their weapons to counter those threats. On day four, that changed. They needed a re-supply of water. On Prairie Fire missions it was well known that the enemy often waited for a hatchet force to move to a stream and often used that for the site of a deadly ambush. There had been no signs of the NVA in the area. The only thing the platoon had found were discarded C-rations and other litter left behind by the Marines' recent sweep of the area. With the threat of enemy contact diminished, the Bru had started to relax. Before they moved out of their overnight position Dawson explained to Thoung that they were going to head downhill to a stream between two ridge lines and cautioned him that the Bru had to be alert.

The movement down the steep grade made it difficult to maintain any semblance of a fighting formation. They halted often to reorganize and reposition the machine guns. After descending almost five hundred, meters RaLang came to a halt at a high speed trail. Dawson conferred with Rogers and Jennings and decided to use it to teach the Bru how to set up an immediate ambush. They moved the squads up quickly and had the Bru lay prone in camouflaged positions. Establishing security to the flanks and rear their firepower was focused on the trail. Dawson moved along the line with Thoung. He was being very careful not to move like an elephant. The Bru had, once again, performed well. The ammo bearers were beside the machine gunners. It was one of those things that sounded simple, but often got screwed up. Satisfied, they returned to RaLang who was positioned in the center and Thoung told him to cross the trail. As he started to move forward he suddenly stopped, turned and put his hand to his throat. Enemy! The right flank had flashed the signal. RaLang, Thoung and Dawson quickly dropped to the ground. Focusing their weapons on the trail. They thumbed the safeties to full automatic. And waited, hearts pounding, adrenalin beginning to flow. Seconds later, the enemy began to come into view. They were moving carefully, camouflaged fatigues, M-16's at the ready, web gear, flack jackets and steel helmets. United States Marines! Dawson's mind reeled. In a split-second he thought to yell out a warning. What would he say? Don't shoot, Americans. If they saw the Bru they would surely think they were the enemy. Then he decided to let them walk by and hope or pray that the marines didn't see them. Ready to yell for a cease fire if the first shot was fired. He started breathing again and watched them. An M-79, a radio, riflemen. He didn't keep count. No machine gun. Then they were out of his sight. The platoon remained frozen. Two minutes, five minutes, ten minutes passed. Dawson flipped the antenna up out of his back pack and tried to make radio contact with somebody, anybody, but they were too far down between the ridge lines. Rogers moved up.

"What the fuck," he whispered.

"No good. No Good," Thoung shook his head. "Tahan no can do shoot marine."

"What are you going to do, LT?"

"We still have to get water."

"You gotta let somebody know what happened."

""If we climb back up the hill to make radio contact we'll just have to come back down for water. It's probably only another hundred meters to the stream. Let's get that over with and then I'll call it in."

The banks of the stream were steep on both sides so they set up a semi-circular security perimeter. The Bru gathered up their canteens, hung them off of sticks and passed them down to three men who filled them. As they moved by, Dawson could see questioning looks in their faces, and he knew they were wondering how the Americans had screwed up so badly by putting Bru and Marines in the same place. When the canteens were full they returned them to the troops and collected more. It wasn't long until they were almost finished. Two M-60s opened fire almost simultaneously, followed by the crackle of M-16s. In seconds it grew to a thunderous roar. Dawson jumped up and started to move forward fearing they were engaging the Marines. A B-40 rocket exploded in the tree above his head knocking him to the ground. It wasn't the Marines. He heard an NVA RPD machine gun begin to fire, but it was silenced before it got off a dozen rounds. The firing died out after just a few seconds. Over the next minute there were single shots and short bursts. All from the Bru's M16s. Then it was over. Dawson moved to find Rogers.

"What the fuck happened?"

"We caught a bunch of NVA creeping down the hill. They must have seen our tracks on the trail and thought we were the Marine squad. They had no idea what they were up against," Rogers explained.

"Did you get them all?"

"Jennings is checking that out now."

"Anybody hurt?"

"Not that I know of. You got a pretty good gash behind your ear, LT." Dawson felt the back of his head and was surprised when his fingers ran up under a flap of skin. While Rogers was patching him up, Jennings showed up with a couple of Bru carrying several AKs, an RPD and a B-40 rocket launcher.

"Did you get all of them?" Dawson asked for the second time.

"I don't know for sure, sir."

"Prisoners?"

"No, sir. The Bru took care of that."

"Where's Thoung?" Jennings went and got him. "Everybody OK?"

"One man, tahan die," Thoung said.

They passed out the last of the canteens, crossed the stream and began the arduous task of climbing the ridge. The Bru distributed their fallen comrade's equipment and wrapped him in a poncho. Then they cut a strong pole from the jungle and used it to carry the body. It was obvious they had done this before. No one had to caution them to be alert now. If there were enemy in the area they gave them a wide berth, respecting the fire power of the hatchet force. Finally, able to make radio contact, Dawson relayed a sitrep. Then they moved to a small hilltop and set up for the night. The next morning they moved to an LZ and were extracted to FOB 1 at Phu Bai.

CHAPTER TWENTY

"WELL, I SEE you brought the boss with you this time, sir," Fallon said, referring to Rogers.

"Yeah, it seems I still need a babysitter," Dawson replied pulling at the bandage behind his ear. It came loose and he pulled it all the way off. "This is nasty. Where's your trash can?"

"You should keep it covered, LT."

"If you put it on right, it wouldn't have fallen off. It's starting to get more than a little bit painful."

"It's supposed to hurt. You should probably get it checked out."

"Yes, mother."

"Are you guys always like this or is this just for my benefit?" Fallon asked.

"Let's just get this debriefing over with so I can get some real medical attention."

When they finished, they headed over to the club for a drink.

"I don't miss this place," Dawson said.

"Yeah, well, I wouldn't miss it either if you didn't get me sent to that shit hole, LT."

"Does that guy Fallon strike you as a little weird?" Dawson

asked.

"Everybody in Special Forces is a little weird. Especially you, LT."

"No there's something about him that's different."

"I heard he has a masters degree from some expensive school. Did you see the picture of his wife on his desk?"

"That girl in the blue bathing suit is his wife?"

"That's what he says."

"She's a knock out. If it's really his wife. He said he was wounded in Kontum. Do you know he was at FOB 2?"

"No."

"I thought you knew everything. Let's eat something."

"I hope you brought your own rum, Sergeant Rogers." Major Capra said from behind them. "What happened to your head, lieutenant?"

"He got up when he should have got down, sir," Rogers replied before Dawson had a chance to speak.

"I thought we were in a firefight with the Marines," Dawson explained.

"We're not going to say anything about the Marines," the major warned.

"Sir?"

"Shit rolls down hill in the military. You should know that by now. Having you and the Marines in the same AO could have been a disaster. No Marine colonel is going to take the blame if he can blame a Special Forces major. You did a good job out there. Both of you."

"I didn't do anything, sir, except let them walk by," Dawson said.

"In that case, doing nothing was exactly what you should have done. There's no reason to think that they know you were there."

"They probably heard the gun fire from the firefight, sir."

"That could have been anybody. There is to be no more talk about any Marines. Do you understand?"

"Yes, sir."

You better get over to the dispensary and get your head sewn up. You'll get a Purple Heart for that."

"I'd rather get my pay straightened out. sir."

"That's still screwed up? Do you need any money?"

"No, sir. Nothing to spend it on at Mai Loc."

"Go get it fixed up and come back and eat. I'll make sure they don't charge either of you." After the major left Rogers said,

"What are you crazy, LT? You just turned down money."

"I'm going to the dispensary. I guess you'll be here when I'm done."

Dawson returned less than an hour later.

"How'd it go, LT?"

"They stitched it up and gave me some darvon. Son of a bitch started out by swabbing it with alcohol instead of water. Lit me right up." They ate, had a couple of more drinks, and turned in. The Bru slept in the empty Cambode barracks. The lights still didn't work.

When Dawson awoke, his head was throbbing. At first he thought it is was a hangover, but as he got up he saw the pillow was full of blood and lymph. He went to supply and got a new set of jungle fatigues, underwear and socks. Showered and in clean clothes he threw out the dirty, blood soaked-clothes he had worn on the operation and went to the dispensary to get his wound treated again. That done, he went to the mess hall.

"You look like shit, LT."

"Yeah, the back of my head swelled up and one of the sutures ripped out. They cleaned it up again and gave me these," he said, producing a bottle of yellow tetracycline tablets.

"Thought those were for the clap."

"Apparently they're for everything. They want me to hang around here to make sure it doesn't get infected."

"How long."

"Probably just a month or two."

"Keep wishing, LT. The Bru are set to go back to Mai Loc this morning, but they don't have enough helicopters to move all of them at one time. I'll send Jennings back with the first group and hang around for the choppers to return and go back on the second lift. I'll take your back pack with the radio. You won't be needing it."

"If I knew how long they were going to keep me here I'd fly back with Jennings, get my ID and some clothes and fly back."

"Why?"

"I'd go to Nha Trang to hang out and recuperate."

"That's the problem with you lieutenants. You think this war is your own personal party."

"No. You have to be a field grade officer or above for that. Just look at the major parading his girlfriend around."

"You better keep quiet about that, LT, or you'll be the one on a one way mission to Hanoi."

After Rogers left, Dawson had nothing better to do than lie around and think about how bad his head hurt. He had taken a couple of darvon, but they upset his stomach. That evening, he drank a half dozen beers, but that didn't help either. When he awoke the next morning, he was surprised to see that he had slept almost twelve hours. The slight hangover between his eyebrows distracted him from the pain in the back of his head. He got up, got dressed and headed to the S-2 office.

"Got a minute sergeant?" Fallon was sitting at his desk.

"Sure. What do you need, sir?"

"How's your arm?"

"Oh, it's, actually, the shoulder. It's getting better. I can go without the sling a few hours a day."

"You said you were wounded at Kontum?"

"I was stationed at FOB 2, Kontum, out on a hatchet force mission in Laos. Why?"

"By any chance did you know a lieutenant named Zobel? He would have gotten there around the middle of April."

"Yes, sir. He was my platoon leader."

"Really. We rented a house at Bragg and went diving in the Bahamas on leave together. How's he doing?"

"He's back in the States."

"Why?"

"He stepped on a toe popper."

"How the hell did he do that?"

"We had been in contact and the yards didn't want to move, so he grabbed a couple of them and was pushing them forward when he stepped on a mine we had planted."

"He's pretty gung-ho."

"He was very gung-ho."

"Did he get hurt bad?

"He's had a couple of surgeries."

"Where is he?"

"Valley Forge Army Hospital in Pennsylvania."

"Phoenixville. I grew up near there. Any idea how I can get his address?" Fallon routed through his desk.

"Here's a letter he wrote me. It's got a return address."

"Can I read it?"

"Sure. Go ahead." As Dawson was reading he saw Fallon open a letter. Start reading, crumpled it up and throw it away.

"Are you just throwing that letter away?" he asked realizing it wasn't any of his business.

"It's from my wife. I read it till I got to the word irresponsible."

"Is that her?" Pointing to the bathing suit picture on his desk.

"Yeah."

"If I were you, I'd try to stay on her good side.

"We're probably past that."

"Sorry. Let me have a pen and paper I want to copy Zobel's address."

Zobel's letter sounded pretty upbeat. He wrote about how the thin rows of metal plates in the sole of his jungle boot, designed to protect from punji steaks, had saved his foot. He was confident he would have a near complete recovery and return to Special Forces. Dawson opened a canteen cover on his web gear and put the slip of paper with Zobel's address in the tupperware container that contained his narcotic collection. Then he sat around doing nothing until he couldn't stand it anymore. Finally, he walked to the TOC to check on his pay. To his surprise, he left with a pocket full of money and headed to the dispensary.

"This is looking better, sir," the medic informed him. "How's the pain?"

"A lot better today than it was yesterday. I'm going to head back to Mai Loc tomorrow."

"You should hang around here until the weekend and I'll take the stitches out."

"I'm sure somebody at Mai Loc can do that."

"It's up to you, sir. Keep it clean and take the tetracycline. If it swells up again you're only going to have to come back here. Doesn't make much sense to go back tomorrow."

"Doesn't make much sense walking around the woods shooting at each other either. But we do it." Dawson smiled. "Thanks for your help. I appreciate it."

"What are you doing here, LT?"

"Nice to see you too, sergeant."

"I thought you had to stay in Phu Bai for a few more days. How's the head?"

"It's better."

"Well, it's probably good that you're back. I'm going to the FOB at DaNang tomorrow."

"What for?"

"Promotion board."

"When?"

"Thursday."

"What day's today?"

"Monday. I'm leaving with the helicopters late tomorrow afternoon."

The sun was setting. Dawson and Rogers were sitting in the jeep drinking.

"Do you think you'll get promoted?"

"At the rate E-7s are dying on recon teams I should have a good chance."

"I guess that's one sick way to look at it. Just think, then, pretty soon, you can get promoted to master sergeant and sit around drinking coffee, telling us what it was like to be in the real Special Forces."

"Most of those guys fought in Korea."

"Yesterday's hero."

"You're tough, LT," Rogers said, shoving his arm. Dawson's head jerked and he winced.

"You OK?"

"Yeah. So long as I didn't just pop a stitch."

"Maybe you're not so tough. I'll make sure Jennings baby sits you while I'm gone."

Saturday afternoon Dawson went to the aid tent to get his stitches removed.

"Have a seat. I'll be with you in a minute," a sergeant said without looking up. Obeying, Dawson sat on a folding metal chair. The dirt floor tent was well-lit. The sergeant was writing at a desk. Beyond him were six cots. Two were occupied with bandaged patients. One had an IV stand.

"I'm Sergeant Nolan, the camp medic. What happened to you?"

"B-40 hit a tree. I got hit with shrapnel or a chunk of the tree."

"Whoever stitched this up did a shitty job. Soon as it swelled, this stitch was bound to rip out."

"They did it at FOB 1."

"Those guys are busy down there. They usually do a good job," Nolan said, backing off of his criticism.

"Those Bru look like they belong in a hospital," Dawson said referring to his patients.

"Yeah, they do. Problem is, if they get sent to a Vietnamese hospital they just stick them in the hall and let them die."

"They do?"

"Yeah, the Vietnamese hate the Montagnards."

"The Bru aren't real fond of the Vietnamese either."

"I've got tags that say 'Keep in US Channels' that you can use for medevacs, but nobody bothers to carry them." Sergeant Nolan got a pair of scissors to remove the stitches, explaining he was going to pull the knots back through the holes so they would bleed and clog up to prevent infection. Dawson wasn't sure if this was how it was done or if the medic was a sadist. As he was finishing up one of the camp's radio operators came into the tent.

"Sir, is your code name Shadow?"

"Yeah. Why?"

"You have a FLASH message, sir."

CHAPTER TWENTY-ONE

DAWSON FOLLOWED THE radio operator to the TOC tent and read the message.

"What's this about?"

"You haven't heard, sir? FOB 4 was attacked yesterday." Dawson's first thought was of Rogers.

"Where's the major?"

"He was at the commander's conference in DaNang but he left before the attack. He's at Phu Bai. They're sending two Marine CH-46 helicopters to transport your platoon to Da Nang for security in the morning.

"What do you know about the attack?"

"Just that a lot of Americans were killed, sir"

Dawson went to round up Jennings and Thoung.

"Hey, We have to take the platoon to DaNang."

"When?" Jennings asked.

"Tomorrow morning. FOB 4 got hit."

"Bad?"

"Supposed to be. They told me there are Americans KIA, but I don't have any details."

"Rogers is there."

"I know."

"Da Nang beaucoup Vietnam," Thoung said.

"Yeah. Beaucoup," Dawson affirmed.

"No Good."

"What's he saying, sir?"

"He's not happy that there are a lot of Vietnamese in DaNang. Give these guys three days of rations in case they can't feed us. The ammo they have should be enough. Oh, and be sure to bring Rogers' web gear and weapon."

The next morning they loaded the platoon into the two big tandem rotor Marine helicopters. The crew chief made them unhook their weapons and hold them pointing down with the tip of the barrel resting on the floor. The CH-46s were extremely noisy inside. Besides the roar of the twin engines they emitted a piercing, screeching sound. Dawson tried to talk to Thoung but soon gave up. Even the Bru's constant chatter was impossible and many sat with their fingers in their ears. Not only loud, but fast, the helicopters landed on the FOB chopper pad in less than an hour. The troops scrambled out. The helicopters took off. While his ears cleared, he looked around. The camp was big. Much bigger than Phu Bai. It was located on a rectangular piece of ground that ran from Highway 1 to the ocean on the east. A high rocky hill looked down over the southern perimeter. A military base of some sort bordered it on the north. Clusters of orderly hard back buildings with corrugated tin roofs were visible from the high point of the chopper pad. He had half expected to see the bodies of enemy soldiers hanging in the wire surrounding smoldering ruins. If anything it looked peaceful rather than the scene of a vicious attack.

"Sir," Jennings called. "Do you want me to put the Bru in a perimeter?"

"No, just move them off to the side in case any other choppers come in. I'm going to wander around and see if I can find somebody in charge." He started walking east on a crushed limestone road toward a large U-shaped building. In front the American Flag and Vietnamese flags flew on separate poles identifying it as the camp's headquarters. He turned left and saw a low building surrounded by a barbed wire fence that he assumed was the TOC. A solitary figure approached wearing a bush hat and web gear with a side arm.

"Major Capra."

"Dawson. That your platoon?" He asked nodding toward the chopper pad.

"Yes, sir."

"Have them take up positions along the POW camp."

"Where's the POW camp, sir?"

"Haven't you been here before?"

"No, sir."

"Those trenches and bunkers along the north wall," He said pointing.

"The Bru would love to shoot up a camp full of enemy POWs."

"See that they don't."

"Doesn't look like much happened here, sir."

"Follow me. Sappers infiltrated the camp and hit it with satchel charges, grenades and small arms." Past the TOC they turned toward the ocean. "This used to be the supply area and ammo dump." It was totally destroyed. "You can see they pried the air conditioners out of the TOC and threw explosives in through the holes." As they passed the TOC there were three heavily damaged buildings. Two had their side walls blown out and the roofs had collapsed. "These were the senior NCO barracks and the transient barracks. Most of the losses happened here."

"How many people got killed, sir?"

"At least a dozen maybe as many as twenty. They don't have all of the reports from the hospitals yet. There is a marine medevac unit a mile down the road. Some went there. Some went all the way to the China Beach hospital. They're still trying to figure out who's where."

"Were you here during the attack?"

"No. I was here Thursday for the commander's conference. We went back to Phu Bai around 1700 then I came back with a reaction force early the next morning. It was pretty much over. A few enemy that didn't escape were still hiding in the camp and had to be eliminated, but that was about it."

"Sir, Rogers was here for the promotion board. Have you seen him?"

"No, but I know his name isn't on the casualty list. You better go back and get your troops deployed."

"Yes, sir. Kind of like closing the barn door."

"What?"

"You know. Closing the barn door after the horses already got out." Maybe the major had never heard that expression. "Are you staying here, sir?"

"No. This place has become one big blame game. I'm leaving later today."

"Who will I report to?"

"I don't think that's been determined. The new Chief SOG was here yesterday and he tasked FOB 1 to supply additional security. You're it for now."

"All right, sir. But I don't want to get stuck here doing nothing. It's not like we can just bum a ride back to Mai Loc. I've got forty guys over there. We're going to need an air lift."

"Give it a couple of days, lieutenant. If you're not needed contact me."

"Oh. One more thing, sir," Dawson said knowing he was pushing the major's patience. "Where is their club?"

"Toward the beach. Just before you get to the recon barracks. Why?"

"It's probably a good place to start looking for Sergeant Rogers, sir."

Dawson walked back to the helipad, moved the platoon to the north boarder of the camp and had them take positions in the trench and bunkers facing the POW camp. They were done in a few minutes.

"Hey Thoung, Jennings," Dawson called out. They joined him. "I don't know if there are any mines in the ground between the trench and the wire so have everybody stay on this side." As soon as he spoke two Bru moved out of the trench to retrieve a small parachute that was stuck in the wire. It had been used to suspend a flare that was dropped to provide illumination during the attack. Thoung quickly called them back.

"Well, that may answer the mine question, but keep them back anyway. Just in case."

"What want Tahan do now?"

"Watch for VC."

"No have VC. VC go."

"Yeah. I know," Dawson agreed.

"Sir, did you hear anything about Rogers?"

"No. Major Capra is here. I asked him if he knew anything. He said he's not on the casualty list. I'm going over to the headquarters building to find out who's running security and see if there's a commo net we should join. Then I'll go look for him."

As he entered the headquarters building, Dawson left the quiet outdoors and came upon a near frenzy of activity. Ignored, he stood just inside the entry observing. Voices were raised. Normal requests were being stated as demands. Many began with the words "Who was responsible for . . .?" It was almost as if hyper-vigilance would make up for the lack of vigilance that had resulted in the attack. Officers and senior NCOs were trying to retrieve their shattered image of competence.

"Who are you?" some captain demanded.

"Dawson, sir. I brought a security platoon down from Mai Loc."

"Do you have a rank, Dawson?"

"Lieutenant," he replied purposefully avoiding calling him sir again.

"Where'd you say you were from?"

"Mai Loc. It's the launch side for FOB 1."

"What do you need, lieutenant?"

"I need to get linked up with whoever is in charge of camp security."

"That's Captain Sanders. He's in the TOC, but it's been put off limits to non-assigned personnel."

"Ok, sir," Dawson said, abruptly turning away and walking back outside, cutting off the conversation. Everyone inside had much better things to do than assist his security platoon - like saving their careers. He also thought today was a good day not to be Captain Sanders.

Taking the route Major Capra had led him on earlier, he walked past the destruction and continued toward the ocean. Earlier, from the helipad he had thought the camp was big, walking it proved him right. It was the length of a couple of football fields from headquarters to the Recon team and hatchet force billets. To his right, there was a lot of activity around the mercenary mess hall. He turned left and wandered around the recon team huts. Groups of Americans were recounting their experiences during the attack. His inquiries about Rogers were met with shrugs. Same thing in the mess hall. The club was locked. Walking back on the long road along the north side of the camp his platoon came into view. Some of the Bru had spread out ponchos on top of the bunkers and were playing cards. Others were heating water in canteen cups by burning little chunks of C-4 explosive. Their equipment and weapons were scattered all over the place.

"Any word on Sergeant Rogers?" Jennings asked.

"No. What the fuck are you doing?"

"Sir?"

"This looks like a fucking refugee camp. All we need is for one of these assholes from headquarters to show up and see this. "Thoung papa nai."

"Trung uy," Thoung answered as he walked over to Dawson.

"Tahan play cards, cook?"

"Yes, tahan play cards, cook. OK?"

"No. Not OK."

"No have VC, trung uy."

"Maybe no have VC. Have dai uy. Have tieu ta," Dawson replied, using the Vietnamese words for captain and major.

"Oh. Trung uy beaucoup sweat tieu ta," the lieutenant is afraid of the major, he said with a big grin. "Thoung fix." He started calling out to the Bru. Dawson heard the words trung uy and tieu ta. He shook his head and laughed, knowing Thoung had told the tahan they were doing this for show. He watched RaLang cover a piece of burning C-4 with sand and pour the water out of his canteen cup over it and wondered if it actually went out or would just keep burning until consumed. Along with the chatter and laughter he heard ammo belts being loaded into machine guns. In a couple of minutes the Bru looked like they were ready to repel a communist onslaught. Dawson wondered how to explain to Thoung that something between playing cards and fingers on the trigger would be fine.

"Hey, I'm sorry, sir. I didn't want to get you in trouble," Jennings said sounding sincere.

"Yeah, I don't need any help from you to do that. This is ridiculous. These guys have a field of fire of about ten feet between the bunkers and the POW camp," he exaggerated. "I don't care how good the NVA sappers are, they aren't coming through that maze of concertina. How about moving some sand bags around and put two machine guns near the end where they can at least sweep from the main gate across to the helipad."

"Where tahan go glom?" Thoung asked Jennings.

"What did he say, lieutenant?"

"He wants to know where the tahan can take a shit." There was a latrine farther down the road near the recon barracks. Afraid to let the Bru walk around what may be a trigger happy camp, they took turns escorting small groups back and forth. The idea of making Rogers take the Bru to the bathroom struck Dawson funny. He was worried about him.

A jeep pulled up and Captain Sanders, the security officer, got out and introduced himself. He was in pretty good spirits for someone who was about to get blamed for the attack on the camp. Dawson actually told him that.

Oh, no," Sanders replied. "I've only been here a couple of weeks. It's the secret to success in the army. Keep changing assignments. That way anything that goes wrong is always the last guy's fault. We just got a new Chief SOG. He was here yesterday. The first thing he said was "I just took command.' So nobody can blame him. Of course, nothing ever gets fixed that way. But, I didn't invent the system. I just live with it."

"What, the hell, happened? It looks like they just walked in and blew the place up."

"This was an inside job. Thursday we had a commander's conference and the NCO promotion board. There were a lot more people in camp than usual and, of course, they were all drinking. The enemy knew exactly when to attack. Just after I got here, they replaced the Nung security guards with Vietnamese QC. They all disappeared. Most of the local workers live in the villages south of here. For months, maybe years, they have been taking a shortcut through the wire in the southeast corner of the camp rather than walking all the way up to the main gate. We found explosives they smuggled in before the attack in the indig mess hall. Once the sappers snuck past the hatchet force barracks the rest of the camp was pretty much undefended. So, like you said, they just walked in and blew the place up."

"Hard to believe," Dawson said.

"Not really. Look at the layout of the camp. You come in off the road and you have the helipad, then headquarters, the TOC, supply, the motor pool, billets, mess halls and clubs, all the pretty stuff in the front. Then in the very back, you have the guys with the guns all crammed together like they want to keep anybody that gets dirty out of sight. It's as if it was designed to be put on display in New Jersey. Not in the middle of a war zone."

"Then why do they have us here guarding fifty million rolls of concertina wire, where nothing is going to happen, instead of the line of bunkers in front of headquarters and the TOC?"

"That's what I came here to tell you. The Nungs who were replaced by the QC are coming back to work in the morning. So, we don't need your platoon. You're being flown back tomorrow, lieutenant."

The screech of the helicopter was still in his ears as Dawson entered Mai Loc's mess tent, got a beer and sat down at a table.

"What are you doing here? he asked.

"They closed the club at Da Nang, LT," Rogers replied.

CHAPTER TWENTY-TWO

LONG BEFORE THERE were Roman legions, there were three essential elements to a battle plan. Enemy, weather and terrain.

It started to rain. At first, none of the soldiers at Mai Loc thought much about it. But it didn't stop. It rained right through the tents. They put engineer stakes at the four corners of their cots and hung ponchos above them to stay dry. When this failed, they placed waterproof blankets over their poncho liners. When that failed, they were wet. Their cots and the wood ammo boxes, that held their possessions, sunk into the mud. They placed C-ration cans under them to prop them up. As each can disappeared into the mud they would add another can. They joked that they could eat for a year just by digging them up. Outside, the trenches and bunkers the Bru called home filled with water. Ever resourceful, they pried the locks off the steel conex containers, removed the camp's supplies and moved in.

Typhoon Bess came ashore at Phu Bai during the first week of September 1968. It dumped almost twenty inches of rain on the northeast corner of South Vietnam over a three day period. Much of the area between the coast and the low foothills, about ten kilometers to the west, was inundated with water. Bridges and roads were washed out and at military facilities bunkers collapsed. Luckily, none of the SOG units were trapped in the field. Combat operations had been temporarily suspended, not in anticipation of the storm, but by the disruption caused by the attack on Da Nang. At Mai Loc, the Seabees had just bulldozed the beginnings of a permanent triangle shaped camp across the runway where Dawson's platoon had held their rifle practice. It and the runway dissolved into a sea of mud. For two weeks, after the typhoon passed through, low clouds would enter the valley from the east, get trapped by the mountains on the south and west, dumping rain on the camp day and night.

"You know Charlie is sitting in his houch, nice and dry, with his feet up, roasting marshmallows, laughing at us, LT." They were hidden in the forest just south of Bang Son. The rice paddies were flooded and the big road entering the village was barely above water. The rain was steady, but not hard. The kind of rain that makes you want to lean up against a tree and go to sleep.

"Somebody has to see if anything is going on around the camp."
"Maybe somebody besides us could do it for a change."
"This is better that hanging around in the tents."
"Even the Bru are getting sick of this. LT."
"Getting sick of what?"
"The rain. No operations."
"How do you know?"
"Thoung told me."
"You talk to Thoung?"
"Yeah. Why?"
"Don't do that. I don't want him catching any of your bad

habits," Dawson laughed. They watched nothing happen in the village for another half hour.

"How long are you planning on staying out here, LT?"

"Until you stop complaining."

"We didn't bring enough rations for that."

When they returned to camp Dawson sat on the ammo box next to his bunk and removed his socks. Big chunks of spongy white skin that used to be calluses fell off his foot. He powdered his feet and took a semi-dry pair of socks down form the clothes line he had rigged under the poncho and put them on. He shook pieces of skin out of his wet socks and hung them over the line pretending they would dry. Then he put his wet boots back on and sloshed through the mud to the mess tent. He ate with Rogers. When they finished they got a couple of drinks.

"Let's get out of here, LT. They put the top up on the jeep."

"The seats will be wet."

"Your ass is wet. What difference does it make?" Inside the jeep Rogers asked, "How come you haven't asked me what happened at DaNang, LT?"

"I wanted to give you time to make up a good story." They laughed at that. "Ok, so tell me."

"There's really not much to tell. I found a bunk in one of the team houses and had just gotten to sleep when the explosions went off. I thought we were taking incoming. Most of the explosions happened in the first couple of minutes up around the TOC. I rolled out of the rack and lay on the floor pulling on my pants and web gear. I stayed on the floor because I couldn't remember how far up the sides the building was sand bagged. There was a fair amount of gun fire but it wasn't hitting the houch. We heard a couple more explosions that, I know now, were satchel charges. It didn't seem to be getting any closer so we decided to stay put. Then they started firing illumination from the hatchet force mortar pit, so we went outside and lay on the ground to see what was happening. That's pretty much what everybody did. We thought there was a better chance of getting shot by other Americans or the hatchet force than by the enemy if we started moving around. After awhile a spooky C-47 gunship arrived and started dropping flares. Then they fired their miniguns right into the camp. That scared the hell out of everybody. They must have been ordered to stop because they only did it twice. Things began to calm down with only a burst of fire every once in a while. The ambulance and a couple of jeeps took the wounded to the aid station. Just before dawn, kingbees landed with a hatchet force from Phu Bai. They swept the place and fired up a couple of sappers that were hiding in the latrine. That's about it."

"From what I heard it sounded like there was a lot more fighting than that."

"You know how it is, LT. Four different people see the same thing and it becomes four different stories."

"Doesn't sound like you'll be getting any hero medals," Dawson prodded.

"They'll be too busy writing them for the all people that got killed."

"It's hard to believe the FOB had so little security."

"Yeah, well, this place isn't any better. Charlie wouldn't even need a can opener to get in here."

"That's why I took you on that little stroll in the rain. The one you bitched about all afternoon."

"What the hell, LT. I know the area has to be patrolled just not always by us."

"Listen, the more we're out on patrol the less the chance we'll be in camp if it gets attacked," Dawson quipped.

"That's some logic. Did they teach you that in Officer's Candidate School?"

"It's my motto for this war. Don't be there when it happens."

It stopped raining. The sun didn't come out, but it did stop raining. They spent a couple of days repairing the trenches and bunkers to get the Bru out of the conex containers and back on the line. Then they built a makeshift walkway out of wood pallets, boards and sandbags that ran from the airstrip to the operations tent. The first helicopters in three weeks were on their way with VIPs coming to check out the construction of their new camp. The Bru were looking very professional, standing guard and cleaning their weapons.

"How'd you get the Bru so straight, LT?"

"I told Thoung a general was coming," Dawson replied as a pair of helicopters appeared out of the east, approached, landed on the runway and shut down. Soldiers placed a sheet of plywood on the ground by the strut so the passengers didn't have to step in the mud to get to the new walkway.

"Somebody better remember to move that so it doesn't blow up into the rotors when the helicopters take off," Jennings observed. The passengers started to get off. Dawson didn't recognize the first two. The third was Major Capra. Then Major Barton. The majors turned and helped the last passenger onto the plywood. Dressed in a light purple áo dài?, black pants and a conical hat, Major Barton's Vietnamese girlfriend appeared.

"You can't make this shit up," Dawson laughed quietly.

"Who is she?" Jennings asked.

"Shut up!" Rogers hissed as the group made their way through the gate within earshot. The Bru stopped cleaning their weapons and stared.

"Mai Loc beaucoup mud," they clearly heard the woman complain. After they entered the operations tent, Thoung said,

"No have general."

"The woman's the general," Rogers joked.

"No general," Thoung shook his head. "Boom boom."

CHAPTER TWENTY-THREE

THE SUN FINALLY came out. They rolled up the sides of the tents and things began to dry. The platoon received a mission order. Route 9, the same Route 9 that had been used to move FOB 3 out of Khe Sanh to Mai Loc, began at Hwy 1 on the east coast of Vietnam and ran generally west past Khe Sanh into Laos and continued completely across the country to Savannakhet on the Thai border. There is a river that runs parallel to and just south of Route 9 in Laos. Aerial reconnaissance had discovered a short, new road running from Route 9 to the river a few kilometers west of the border. It was suspected that the North Vietnamese were moving supplies on the river and loading them on trucks, bound for their forces in South Vietnam. The platoon's mission was to find out.

Dawson briefed Rogers on the operation.

"Are we going to go in here?" Rogers asked, pointing to a fairly steep ridge line northwest of the target on the map.

"I don't see anywhere else unless you want to save a lot of walking and just land on the intersection of the roads."

"The pilots would probably have a problem with that. There's still a lot of flat ground we'd have to cover once we get down off the ridge."

"That's what we have to do, unless you know someone who lives in the neighborhood."

"What?"

"Yeah, you could just call them up. Hey, Mr. Laotian. How you doing? That's good. Me? I'm fine too. Question for you. Are the North Vietnamese taking supplies off boats on the river and loading them onto trucks there? They are. Hey, thanks for the information. Bye now."

"You know, LT, sometimes I think you're nuts. Other times I'm absolutely sure of it."

"Yeah, it makes a lot more sense to put millions of dollars worth of aircraft at risk, not to mention a bunch of lives, to find out rather than just giving some local five bucks and telling him to walk down to the river and take a look. And you think I'm the one that's nuts?"

Except for one of the Bru who sprained his ankle during the insertion and had to be evacuated, the first three days of the operation were uneventful. Having progressed down the hills to the north of Route 9, they were now on flatter ground and having difficulty finding a spot that allowed them to overlook the road.

"If we head south we're going to run into the road within a couple of hundred meters, LT."

"Yeah, but the problem is we won't know if we're east or west of the new road that runs to the river. Once we get to Route 9 we don't want to spend a lot of time dicking around trying to find it."

"There aren't any signs of the enemy, sir," Jennings observed. Dawson called Thoung over.

"VC stay here?" He asked.

"Tahan don't know."

"Ask RaLang." Toung went and got RaLang. The two had a long conversation with a lot of pointing.

"Maybe have VC here," Thoung summed it up, pointing to the southwest.

"What do you say we go locate Route 9?" Dawson asked Rogers.

"It's getting a little late in the day, LT. If we get into a fight it will be dark by the time we get any air support." The platoon moved north and spent a quiet night hidden in the ridgeline.

Covey flew over just after 0900 hrs. The platoon had moved back to the flat area and set up a perimeter. Dawson had him up on the radio.

"Can you see the road that runs from Route 9 to the river?" Dawson asked in the clear.

"I need your location. Over."

"Wait one." He motioned to Rogers. "See if you can get a mirror on Covey." Rogers did and in a few seconds Covey came back up.

"I got you. You're right on top of it! Over."

"Give me azimuth and distance."

"In the clear? Over," Covey asked.

"In the clear. It's not going to be any secret where we are in a couple of minutes." That done Dawson radioed, "I need you to stick around for a while. Just in case."

"Roger that. We were just going to RTB for coffee and donuts."

"Not this morning. Unless you run out of gas."

"This is No Neck standing by. Good hunting. Be safe." Dawson conferred with Rogers, Jennings and Thoung. They moved the troops into position.

"You OK with this?" Dawson quietly asked Rogers.

"So long as it works, LT."

With a nod RaLang headed out, leading the point squad, followed by two lines in assault formation. The head high scrub did not impede their movement. In minutes they were at Route 9. They slid west for thirty meters and found the intersection. Recent truck and cart tracks, approaching from the west, turned south on the road toward the river. With little hesitation the point squad crossed Route 9 and moved south clinging to the west side of the road. To their right was a heavily wooded area. They pressed forward, the assault squads quickly following. As the road curved a building came into view. A man jumped up to run. RaLang cut him down. The rest of the point squad opened fire. Enemy soldiers began running for their lives. Some dropped their weapons, others turned and fired. The assault squads moved up and engaged. The firing ended as quickly as it had started.

"I'm gonna go check out the river," Dawson told Rogers.

"You better take one of my gunners with you. I'll make sure Jennings covers our back door," Rogers said, as he pulled a Bru with a machine gun forward, gesturing for him to follow Dawson.

It only took a minute to reach the river. The road ran right down into the water and emerged on the other side in dense jungle. Dawson snapped pictures with his half-frame camera and returned within five minutes.

"Find anything, LT?"

"They built a pretty cool underwater bridge. Let's check this place out." As the first squad began to move into the camp they were forced to the ground by heavy fire. The enemy, over the initial shock, had abandoned their camp and was reorganizing from the wooded area behind.

"Get everybody back north. We don't want to get trapped between the road and the river."

"You better get air support," Rogers responded. Dawson was already on the radio. The assault squads crossed Route 9 while the NVA were still concentrating their fire back into camp. As the point element crossed, the enemy began to fire on the road. A Bru went down. Dawson and RaLang grabbed him under the arms and pulled him across. He was unhurt. Bullets had hit his back pack knocking him to the ground.

"Jennings, put two guns west in case they try to flank us," Rogers ordered as he was setting up the perimeter. The enemy was sweeping the area with small arms fire. "Hold your fire. They don't know where we are." Dawson popped a yellow smoke grenade to show their position to Covey. "What the hell, LT, you can't use a panel?" They pushed their bodies harder into the ground as the NVA fired into the smoke.

Covey launched a white phosphorous marker rocket into the wooded area. The yellow smoke drifted north clearing Dawson's view. He raised up to see where the rocket had landed. A single bullet skimmed off the ground and flew by his head. He slammed himself down and felt a sharp surge of adrenalin. Someone had aimed directly at him.

"Give me some cover," he yelled. Thoung called out to the Bru and a roar of indiscriminate fire erupted. He moved back and a few feet to his left. Fearing the shooter wouldn't miss a second time, he forced his head up and took a quick look. Relieved he was still alive, he confirmed the rockets location to Covey. Low and slow, a single propeller driven A1E Skyraider approached from the east and strafed the wooded area with its 20 millimeter cannons. It was followed by another. The Spads, as they are called, are airborne dump trucks. Capable of delivering a vast amount of ordinance accurately on target. They are the infantry's best friend.

"Get your heads down," Covey advised. He repeated, "Get your heads down." Doing exactly the opposite, every man in the platoon stopped firing and watched as two large silver canisters were released from beneath the wings of the Spad and tumbled into the trees. There was a slight pause, then the forest erupted in a flaming inferno. The Bru grinned widely and many gave the thumbs up sign. The rejoicing didn't last long. Enemy fire still poured out of the firestorm. Rogers crawled over to Dawson.

"Time to pull the plug."

"Not yet," he replied.

"No! Our job's done. The assets are here now to get us out. If you wait this whole thing could go sideways. Pull the plug, LT," Rogers demanded. Dawson hesitated, as if to say something more, then keyed the handset.

"I am declaring a Prairie Fire Emergency."

"When I went to call in the air strike somebody shot right at my head. Not some stray round. Somebody had me right in their sights and was waiting for me to stick my head up. It scared the shit out of me and at the same time it pissed me off. It was personal." The top had been removed from the jeep and the windshield lowered. Dawson slumped in the shotgun seat with his legs draped over the hood. He had had too many beers.

"I saw it, LT. Your head was stuck in the ground long enough for me to think you were hit. You got your shit back together quick enough. That's all that matters. The next time it happens the guy will probably hit you. Then you won't have to worry about it anymore."

"That's real encouraging." Dawson opened another beer. "Hey, who's that guy No Neck? The Covey rider who always says he's going to RTB for coffee and donuts."

"He's was the Cambode platoon leader you replaced back at Phu Bai."

"The guy who got hit with the Chinese claymore?"

"Yeah. Why?"

"I should probably get to know him."

"What for?"

"So he knows who he's talking to on the ground. You know, if he knows who we are he may work harder to keep us alive."

"What happens when he finds out you're an asshole?"

CHAPTER TWENTY-FOUR

WITH BETTER WEATHER, the pace of both combat operations and camp construction picked up at Mai Loc. There was an historic shortage of supplies in Northern I Corps because everything was being diverted to build the McNamara Line. A series of outposts which sought to disrupt NVA infiltration of men and material across the DMZ. The fact that the enemy was using Laos for infiltration, not the DMZ, didn't deter the Secretary of Defense. Fortunately, for the troops at Mai Loc, there was an insatiable market for captured enemy weapons among the rear echelon American support troops. Especially prized were the semi-automatic SKS carbine rifles and Russian Tokarev pistols which could be brought home as war souvenirs along with hair-raising tales of their capture. As the recon teams and hatchet forces accumulated enemy weapons from the battlefield, they were bartered at the port of Dong Ha for everything from concertina wire and plywood to pallets of beer and the trucks and manpower to transport them.

While captured weapons solved the problem of moving camp construction forward, the shortage of personnel caused another. Units were scrambled and unscrambled in order to conduct combat operations. Dawson was lent to a recon team to replace the assistant team leader who was on R & R. Unlike his experience with Peterson, he didn't go through any training with the team. The target preparation consisted of little more than here's the map, there's the helicopter. He returned seven days later without a shot being fired.

"You have to get us out of here, LT. This construction work is killing me."

"This is probably the only place in Vietnam where people actually want to get out of camp to go fight," Dawson laughed.

"Easy for you to say after a week long camping trip. How'd it go?"

"It was a dry hole. Which is probably a good thing."

"Why?"

"I don't know. The whole mission was weird. We hit the LZ and made a beeline for the woods. Which is normal. But, then the one-zero takes off towards the target like he's on a compass course at Ft. Bragg. I'm trying to convince myself that this guy has figured out that the NVA know recon teams move slowly and carefully. So he's plowing through the jungle to fool them. But I know he's just being reckless."

"So did you put a stop to it?"

"No. He was the one-zero. Mostly I just followed along. I was watching the Bru and they didn't seem worried. There was a point when he started to walk down a trail and we had a little discussion."

"Oh, I can just picture one of your discussions, LT."

"I was pretty tactful."

" No. Your weren't."

"Anyway, we moved over three kilometers the first day and ran right into the road and the little bridge we were supposed to recon. I've got to give the guy credit, he could read a map and compass. We found a bomb crater about sixty meters up the hill that overlooked the bridge and set up." Dawson took a pause to drink some of his beer.

"Then what did you do?"

"Nothing. We just sat in the bomb crater for six fricken days and watched the bridge."

"That's it?"

"No it gets even weirder. While we're sitting there the one-zero keeps telling us about how he was in the army and met this beautiful girl. So he got out of the service and married her. She was really loaded with daddy's money. The biggest decision he had to make was whether to drive the Cadillac or the Mercedes when they went out to dinner. Then her father got arrested and went to jail. The money was gone. He got divorced and rejoined the army."

"This goes on for six days?"

"Yeah."

"How did you get out?"

"We ran out of water and the Bru started bitching so he called an extraction."

"Sounds like he's a little distracted to be running recon."

"That thought crossed my mind."

The next day, the paymaster arrived by helicopter. The Bru lined up and with a thumbprint collected their pay. Through years of experience Thoung knew the drill. He, RaLang and two others carefully cleaned their thumbs by rubbing them with dirt, put on bush hats and with a lot of laughing and joking went through the line a second time collecting the pay of soldiers that didn't exist. Then he dutifully gave the money to Dawson who turned it in at the TOC tent. The fraud may have seemed risky, but since the Bru had no written language, there were no identifiable names to go with faces or thumbprints. The forms listed them as SCU-01, SCU-02, etc. SCU standing for Special Commando Unit. The phonetic names next to each were meaningless. It was inconceivable that anyone would ever go to the trouble of checking for duplicate thumbprints in a war where millions of dollars were wasted bombing trees every day.

While the troops were being paid, two Vietnamese Kingbee helicopters landed on the airstrip. The pilots got out and waited, each holding a clipboard. Some of the Bru left the camp and gave them money.

"What's this all about?" Dawson asked Rogers.

"Beats the hell out of me LT." They watched for a while and saw Thoung returning from the runway.

"Hey, Thoung. What's going on?"

"Trung uy?"

"Why are the tahan giving the Vietnamese pilots money?"

"Maybe tahan die in helicop. Vietnam pay money to mama-son, baby-son." Rogers and Dawson exchanged looks.

"How do you know the Vietnamese will pay?" Rogers asked.

"Vietnam no pay, tahan shoot," Thoung said with a grin.

"It's the wild west with flight insurance," Dawson laughed.

Later that afternoon, the Bru got time off to go to the village and give money to their families. That evening they all played cards. The next morning none of them had any money.

"We got a mission and a captain," Dawson announced.

"A captain?" Jennings questioned.

"A West Point captain."

"A West Pointer in SOG? He's gotta be on somebody's shit list. What's he doing here, LT?"

"He's new. Going out with us to get his feet wet."

"We really don't need to babysit some West Point captain," Rogers complained.

"Hopefully, you won't have to. I'm Captain Tillerson," He entered the tent wearing a jungle fatigue shirt with full color patches. Special Forces, captain's bars, jump wings and most obvious a big blue jungle expert badge. Noticeably absent was the combat infantryman's badge.

"Have a seat," Dawson said pointing to a bunk. "This is Rogers, our platoon sergeant. He's the one who's not interested in babysitting you. This is Jennings. He does all the work."

"Don't worry. I'm only here to learn. The major says you guys know what you're doing."

"Oh, we're not worried, sir," Rogers explained. "This is like the TV show 'Combat!' You ever see that show?" he continued without waiting for an answer. "Dawson's the Lieutenant. I'm Sergeant Sanders and Jennings is Little John. We survive every episode. It's the new guy who always gets killed." To say the captain was a little taken aback would be an understatement.

"Why did you volunteer for SOG?" Dawson asked getting past the awkward moment.

"I didn't. They assigned me."

"That makes two of us. Do you have your field gear, sir?"

"No," the captain replied, relieved that Dawson had shown him a little respect.

"Jennings, how about helping the captain get set up and if Sergeant Rogers doesn't have a TV audition, we'll run a patrol to Bang Son tomorrow so he can get it settled in and learn some of our basics."

"That story about the TV show 'Combat!' was perfect. Did you make it up?" Dawson asked Rogers that evening.

"You never heard that before?"

"No."

"My team sergeant told me that when I got here for my first tour. I've been waiting almost two years to use it, LT."

The training exercise went well the next day. They decided to add a machine gun to the point squad since Rogers had lent one of his gunners to Dawson when he checked out the river on their last mission. Unlike Phu Bai, where weapons were scarce, at Mai Loc it was accomplished by opening a conex container and taking one. They instructed the new captain to walk directly in front of Rogers with his assault squad. He was cooperative if not helpful. At the beginning of the exercise, he questioned why Dawson carried the radio instead of using an RTO.

"He knows if he ever gave the radio to someone else we'd sneak off and leave him in the middle of the night," Rogers joked.

Two days later, they were inserted into Laos for what turned out to be a pretty uneventful mission. On the fourth day, while they were moving along a ridgeline, they received fire from an adjacent ridge. As the captain turned to look, Rogers reached up, grabbed his web gear and slammed him to the ground. The Bru hit the ground and responded immediately with a tremendous volley of fire. It was over in a few seconds. The ridgelines were too far apart and the draw between them too deep to make it a serious encounter.

"Are you OK, sir?," Rogers asked the captain.

"Yeah, fine," he replied, getting back on his feet. "I guess you had a reason to make me walk in front of you." After a pause, "Thanks."

"Wouldn't look good if we sent you home in a body bag, sir."

The next few days were quiet. The NVA may have been keeping tabs on the platoon but they showed no interest in getting into a fight. Dawson figured that meant the enemy didn't have anything worth protecting in the area. He told Covey as much and they scheduled an extraction. On the way to the LZ they ran into an unmarked high speed trail. RaLang came to a halt, and signaled with his hand to his throat. Dawson pointed and his new machine gunner and ammo bearer moved forward and set up. They all quietly dropped to the ground. Instead of gunfire he heard RaLang call out.

"Papa nai. Den day." Bru and Vietnamese for come here. Thoung moved forward. Dawson signaled for a perimeter. Now he could hear another man speaking. He cautiously moved forward. An unarmed NVA soldier was standing in the trail. A prisoner, he thought. By far, the biggest prize of any mission. Thoung and RaLang pulled him off the trail and into the quickly forming perimeter. The man was dressed in green fatigues and some kind of a floppy cloth hat. He was barefoot but his belt had an NVA red star buckle. Problem was he was old.

"VC?" he asked Thoung.

"No VC. Papa son," Thoung laughed.

"What's he saying."

"No speak Bru. No speak Vietnam."

"Laotian?"

"Maybe Lao."

"What have you got, LT?" Rogers came up.

"I don't know," he replied. Then to Thoung, "You sure no VC."

"No VC, trung uy. For sure no VC."

"OK. Give him a couple of rations and some cigarettes. Let him go. Let's get to the LZ."

"You can't do that, LT," Rogers said, nodding toward the captain who was watching. "You gotta call it in."

"What the fuck. Yeah, you're right. Make sure Jennings has guns on the flanks of the trail."

"They're already set up."

"Good," Dawson said. He took off his back pack and flipped up the whip antenna. "Give the guy something to eat."

It took forty minutes to raise Covey.

"They want us to bring him in." The platoon moved to the LZ.

"Do you want us to tie his hands, sir?" Jennings asked.

"Yeah. I guess we have to. Take him on the first ship with you. Be careful he doesn't do a face plant on the skid with his hands tied."

If Mai Loc was Rome there would have been rose pedals scattered on the runway. Word had obviously spread that they were bringing in a prisoner. A crowd gathered as Jennings led him, hands tied, into the camp. The West Point captain walked proudly beside them. Rogers and Dawson hung to the rear. The old man seemed to be enjoying himself as if it were a celebration just for him. And, in fact, it was.

Dawson was sitting on his bunk cleaning his weapon. He had already eaten. Rogers appeared.

"They want us to put him back, LT."

"You're shitting me."

"Nope. They want us to put him back."

"Just fly back to the same LZ and drop him off. Sounds like a good way to get killed. The NVA are probably scouring the LZ right now. Can't they just put him on a bus?" he joked. "Tell the captain to take him back. If he wasn't there we never would have brought him here in the first place."

"Want me to go with you?"

"No, you're too valuable," Dawson grinned. "I'll do it."

An hour later Dawson helped the old man out of the helicopter with a back pack full of rations and cigarettes and the story of a life time.

CHAPTER TWENTY-FIVE

MOVIE NIGHT CAME to Mai Loc. They lined up two rows of folding chairs, set up a projector and a pull-up screen. Things got off to an inauspicious start when a sergeant sat on one of the chairs and, as he told it, a banded krait, the deadly two step snake, was coiled on the seat. As luck would have it, his wallet crushed the snake's head saving his life. The story was made even better as word got out that the sergeant's tour of duty ended in a week. He wore the snake around his neck as a trophy for the rest of the evening. Dawson, Rogers, Jennings and Thoung sat together in the second row. There were a few comments that the seats were for Americans only, but since no one said anything to them directly, they ignored them. It looked like every Bru in the camp was crowded in behind the chairs. Dawson, of course, worried if anyone was guarding the place.

"Where'd they get this stuff?" Jennings asked, referring to the movie equipment..

"One of the traveling captains brought it in this morning," Rogers replied.

"What's a traveling captain?"

"One of those guys that's assigned here, but never is here."

"Probably only brought it because he has to take it back to

Saigon in the morning," Dawson laughed. "They better start the movie before Sergeant Rogers has to get another drink."

"Why do you think I'm sitting in the back row, LT? Hey, speaking of traveling captains, what ever happened to the guy from West Point who went out with us?"

"He's gone. Got his ticket punched for a Combat Infantyman's Badge, so he's probably back in the states teaching the fine art of hatchet force operations."

The movie began with a full color travelogue featuring the Golden Gate Bridge. There were oohs and aahs from the Bru.

"I must have flown over that bridge four times in the last six months," Sergeant Nolan, the medic who had yanked out Dawson's stitches, called out. Then, seeing the major, wished he had kept his big mouth shut. The feature film "They Died with Their Boots On" starring Errol Flynn as General George Armstrong Custer began. Made in the forties, it was in black and white. Thoung kept trying to ask him something, but Dawson was having trouble understanding what he meant. He finally realized Thoung wanted to know why the movie wasn't in color. How do you explain to a mountain tribesman that color is an advanced technology when you naturally see in color? He had no idea so he just told Thoung not to talk. The film was long. He knew because Rogers left four times to reload his drink. He only came back twice with a beer for Dawson. The movie was coming to an end. The Indians had Custer surrounded at the Little Big Horn and the massacre began. The Bru behind him were grumbling.

"General same, same shit," Thoung said loud, enough for everyone to hear. "Why he no get helicop, get jet, come shoot

Indian?" Everybody around him burst out laughing.

With the movie over Dawson decided to walk the perimeter to make sure the Bru had returned to their positions. Jennings went with him.

"Do you think the Bru don't know that that Indian stuff happened a long time ago, sir?"

"No, of course, they don't. How would they know?"

"What do you mean, sir?"

"They don't live all that different in the mountains today than the Indians did in the 1800's. Bare feet, loin clothes, grass huts, little handmade crossbows. Yet they travel a few miles and they're walking around with machine guns and riding in helicopters. It all exists at the same time for them so why would they think it's different for the Indians?"

"I never thought of it that way, sir."

"Matter of fact, they think our job as soldiers is to go fight the Indians when we return to the states. You've heard Thoung say 'Trung uy beaucoup sweat Indian.' He says it all the time when I tell him to do something he doesn't want to do."

"Yeah. I have heard him say that, but I didn't know what he meant."

"He's making fun of me. He thinks I'm here because I'm afraid of the Indians and would rather fight the VC."

"Really, sir?"

"Yep. Really."

Construction on the camp was progressing. The protective berm was in place. Concertina and tangle foot wire were being installed around the perimeter. Concrete slabs, which would become the floors of hardback buildings, were laid and a massive hole had been dug for the new TOC. The Americans were checking the Bru's equipment. Not to be confused with the formal inspections U. S. troops routinely undergo, the Bru were sitting around on sandbags with their gear scattered out around them. Rogers and Jennings where making sure they each had the right number of magazines for their M-16's and that the magazines actually had bullets in them. Dawson was checking to make sure that they hadn't cut up any of the blocks of C-4 explosive or removed the C-4 from the claymore mines and used it to cook with.

"Sir, there's a Vietnamese guy at the gate." It was one of the radio operators from the TOC.

"OK. Why are you telling me?"

"He wants to talk to somebody and as far as I can tell you're the highest ranking person in the camp."

"Oh. God help us," Rogers said, feigning exasperation. Jennings laughed.

"Does he speak English?" Dawson asked.

"I don't think so, sir."

"Hey Thoung?"

"Trung uy," he responded.

"There's a Vietnamese at the gate. I need you to tell me what he's saying." Outside the gate Thoung and the Vietnamese talked back and forth until Dawson grew impatient.

"What's he saying?"

"Man speak VC come village take food."

"What village?" More chatter.

"Village here," Thoung said pointing east.

"The one right down the road with the little rice paddy?"

"Yes."

"When did they come?"

"One night."

"Last night?"

"Yes, trung uy. Before sleep."

"How many were there?"

"He say maybe three man VC come."

"Yeah, maybe six man come," Dawson said, testing. Thoung asked again.

"No, six man. Three man."

"Did they have weapons? AK's?" This took a lot of back and forth with Thoug making the sounds of different guns."

"Have rifle. Vietnam don't know AK."

"OK. Did they give them food?"

"No have food ready. VC come back tonight get food. Maybe bring more VC to carry."

"See if he knows which way they came into and left the village. I'll be right back." When he returned, Dawson gave the man five hundred piasters and thanked him.

"No can do give Vietnam money," Thoung complained as they walked back to join the platoon.

"Wanna go shoot some people tonight?" Dawson told Rogers and Jennings the villager's story.

"If there are NVA in the area they'll be watching and see us leave the camp. They'll never show if they know we have a platoon out, LT."

"I have a plan."

"Here we go. There's nothing more dangerous than a lieutenant with a plan," Jennings laughed. He was getting to sound more like Rogers everyday. The good part was he was acting more like him too.

"Go find an extra radio," Dawson told him.

Later that afternoon, the platoon left the camp, moving around the construction and continuing on a few hundred meters east to an open area just in front of the tree line. There they held live fire drills, shouting commands, firing their weapons and drawing a lot of attention to themselves. At the first sign of sunset they regrouped by the tree line. From there, Jennings marched them right down the road back to camp. Only the keenest observer would have noticed the nine men who slipped into the forest.

Silently, blending in with the lengthening shadows they moved through the woods until they were just south of the road that entered the village and set up a perimeter. They ate their evening rations and waited for nightfall. There was no conversation. Everyone knew his job. They had practiced over and over that afternoon while the platoon exercise went on around them. It was dark. It was time. They moved across the road to the bank that formed the southern border of the rice paddy. Dawson and Rogers traded weapons with the machine gunners and set up the guns on top of the bank overlooking the rice paddy. RaLang was between them. His job was to spot the enemy. Outside of the machine guns, two Bru with grenade launchers moved into place. With a little luck and Jennings' training, they could lob grenades over the dike as the enemy scattered. Thoung, behind RaLang, directed their flank and rear security. Then they waited.

Dawson was braced behind his machine gun second guessing his decisions. Was the story the villager told true? Did Thoung understand what he had said? Could it be a trap? They had too much firepower to worry about that. He had thought of all of this before. As he told Rogers, odds were the NVA would not show up and nothing would happen. After a while his mind began to wander. He thought about Linh, the bargirl in Saigon. He could see her smooth skin and hear her quiet laugh. He remembered when she pulled his hand back to touch her.

"VC," RaLang whispered. Dawson searched the rice paddy. He didn't see them. RaLang slid back to warn Thoung and returned. Dawson still didn't see them. Then he did. They were there. Right there in front of him. Not twenty meters away. He had been looking toward the center of the paddy. Now he clearly saw weapons.

"Got them?" He said softly to Rogers.

"On you, LT." Dawson waited. His heart rate increasing with every step they took. He waited until he could see the last man in line. Moving his shoulder, he focused back on their point man, pulled the trigger, and slowly swept the gun back to the center of the line. Rogers was doing the same, beginning at the back. The enemy was too close for the grenadiers to lob their rounds so they reverted to firing them like shot guns. Some of enemy fell off the dike toward them. More dropped on top. A couple jumped behind it seeking safety. He heard them cry out as he expended the remainder of the hundred round belt of ammunition.

"Let's go." He slid down the bank and gave the Bru back the machine gun in exchange for his CAR-15. They formed up exactly as they had practiced that afternoon and moved quickly down the road toward the camp. By the time the enemy managed to return any meaningful fire on their ambush position they were fifty meters away. A half hour later, outside the wire of the new camp, Dawson radioed Jennings. He came to the gate with a flashlight. They called back and forth making sure the Bru in their bunkers wouldn't shoot them by accident, crossed the runway and entered the camp.

They dropped off their equipment and went to the mess tent.

"You're a little late this evening," a sergeant said to Rogers.

"Yeah, I had to get the lieutenant straightened out. You know how that is." He poured a rum and coke and handed Dawson a beer. "Good one, LT."

The next morning they were back working with the Bru on the camp's defenses when the radio operator approached.

"Sir, there's about twenty Vietnamese at the gate looking for you."

"All hail the conquering hero," Jennings laughed. Dawson climbed down off the bunker.

"Wish I had a clean shirt to put on," He joked.

"Not as much as we do, LT. That thing you've been wearing stinks."

"That's what happens when you actually do some work, sergeant."

"I'm surprised the Vietnamese have the balls to come here to thank us," Rogers said.

"Get Thoung. You guys come with me. I don't want to take all the credit," Dawson laughed. They walked to the gate. Thoung listened while all of the villagers talked at once. The Americans stood back assuming their best aw shucks, it was nothing poses.

"Hey, Thoung. What are they saying?" Rogers asked.

"Vietnam say see VC. Want trung uy give money."

The major returned to Mai Loc and summoned Dawson to his tent.

"You know we're in the Marine's area of operation?" He asked.

"Yes, sir."

"You know that offensive operations have to be approved?"

"I guess so, sir. I never really thought about it."

"Well, did you run an operation a couple of nights ago?"

"We were out training and got into a little scuffle, sir."

"OK, here's how this works. I'm going to tell you what I know. Then you're going to tell me what happened. Then we're going to decide what to report. Is that all right with you, lieutenant?"

"Yes, sir."

"Good then. I was in a meeting with the FOB commander and a Marine colonel shows up. Seems the Marines found the bodies of an NVA platoon in a rice paddy near here. They don't have any records of the contact. He wanted to know if we knew anything about it and, of course, we didn't. He didn't believe us. This has gone all the way up the chain to the I Corp Commander. Now it's your turn." Dawson told him exactly what happened.

"It wasn't any platoon, sir. Maybe ten, fifteen tops."

"Probably depends what the Marine's casualty multiplier is this week," the major laughed. "Forget about the tip from the Vietnamese and it's just a routine training operation with an accidental encounter. You good with that?" Dawson nodded. "Now you get to go to Phu Bai and tell them exactly that."

"I should probably take Sergeant Rogers with me, sir."

"Yeah, that's fine."

"Oh, and sir. Could we take a couple of extra days? Maybe go to Nha Trang. We've been working seven days a week for months without a break."

"You have anything scheduled?"

"Camp construction is all, sir."

"Sure, go ahead."

"Thanks, sir."

"Nice job Dawson. Just make sure the next time you do something like this you report it."

"I will, sir."

"Hey, Sergeant Rogers. You and I are going to the FOB this afternoon for an after action report."

"I already heard we're in trouble. Why do you have to drag me along?"

"We're not in trouble. Besides, you're a hero."

"I didn't do anything."

"Oh, that's not how I told the story," Dawson laughed. "Bring your civies. I got us a couple of days off."

"What about me, lieutenant?" Jennings asked.

"Sorry, you have to stay here and watch the kids."

CHAPTER TWENTY-SIX

ROGERS AND DAWSON were in the S-2 shack at Phu Bai. After listening to Sergeant Fallon describe how extraordinarily angry Major Barton was about being caught off-guard by the Marine colonel, they described their training operation in detail. He meticulously wrote it all down. As they were finishing up a specialist showed up and told Dawson to report to the commander's office.

"Off to the principle's office, LT," Rogers laughed.

"I've got broad shoulders," He replied. After Dawson left Fallon said to Rogers,

"You better watch out for that lieutenant. It's one thing to get orders for a mission, you don't need some lieutenant getting you killed by taking you out on some unauthorized ambush."

"He's pretty careful. Besides, we had plenty of firepower to handle the situation."

"Yeah, that's what's wrong with this war."

"What?" Rogers asked.

"Firepower. From the joint chiefs on down that's all you hear. There's no strategic plan. In World War Two everything was if you take this, then you can take that and the final result was victory. Here all anybody cares about is if they have enough firepower to win each little battle, but no idea how each little battle adds up to a big win." They sat in silence until Dawson returned.

"You don't look any the worse for wear, LT."

"The major took a chunk out of my ass. Hope he feels better now. We done here?"

"I've got everything I need," Fallon replied.

"Oh, by the way, I meant to ask you. Have you heard anything new about Lieutenant Zobel?"

"Yeah, he thinks he's getting out of Valley Forge Hospital soon and then going to the 1st Group on Okinawa. I told him you were here, sir. Have you written him?"

"No, it's one of those things I keep meaning to do but never get around to. I have enough trouble writing my parents once a month. Thanks for the update."

"So, how are you and the FOB commander getting along, LT?"

"Jesus, you can't even wait till I get a beer?"

"That bad, huh?"

"Yeah. He kept going on and on about reporting and the chain of command and I had to just stand there like an idiot because I can't tell him there's nobody to report to at Mai Loc. He told me never to do it again and I got sick of it so I told him I wouldn't go out and shoot anybody ever again."

"You didn't say that!"

"Yeah, I did. Pretty much."

"What did he say?"

"He went ballistic. I thought I was going to have to scrape him off the ceiling with a spatula."

"You gotta learn how to keep your mouth shut, LT."

"I probably should have tried to get in his good graces by asking him how his Vietnamese girlfriend liked Mai Loc."

"Yeah, that would have done it," Rogers laughed.

When they finished eating and got a couple more drinks Dawson asked,

"Did Fallon ever tell you how many NVA the marines said we killed?"

"No. Why?"

"I was going to get Major Capra to put you in for a medal."

"You were not."

"Yeah, I was. Since you're a lifer it would be good for your career."

"Major Capra's not here. He's on R&R. Besides at the rate you're going, you have enough problems with your own career."

"Believe me, the only way this is going to be my career is if I get killed."

"Speaking of getting killed, LT, Sergeant Fallon says you're going to get me killed."

"Is this your way of asking for a transfer? Why'd he say that?"

"He basically said our job's risky enough without some lieutenant going out and trying to start his own war."

"What did you say?"

"Oh, I totally agreed with him," Rogers laughed.

"You should have told him he's never been to Mai Loc where you can be soaking wet for a month or dig in the dirt all day every day. The only fun we have is to go out and shoot people. If I was stationed in some civilized place with hot and cold running hookers you'd never get me out in the field."

"Amen to that, LT. "

Two bare-headed men walked past the headquarters building of the 5th Special Forces Group in Nha Trang, wearing jungle fatigues with no insignia whatsoever, combat loaded web gear and carrying CAR-15 rifles. A tall blonde captain in pressed fatigues and a green beret moved to intercept them.

"This asshole's gonna tell us to put on our headgear," Dawson said, remembering his first day in Nha Trang.

"Just don't shoot him, LT," Rogers joked.

"Are you from SOG?" the captain asked.

"Who wants to know?" Dawson answered.

"Colonel Aaron."

"Who's Colonel Aaron?"

"The commander of the 5th Special Forces Group."

"In that case the answer's yes." They followed the captain to the headquarters entrance, where the colonel was standing beside a short, red-headed man with big ears. Dawson didn't know if he was expected to let go of this rife and salute, but the colonel spoke before he made up his mind.

"You men from SOG?"

"Yes, sir. FOB 1."

"This is Ross Perot. He asked to meet you."

"I know exactly what you men do," Perot said, pausing to let them know he was privy to top secret information. "On behalf of the millions of Americans, that you never hear much about, I'd like to thank you for the job you're doing," he continued in a funny southern twang. "You men are warriors. The best we have. If you ever need anything, I want you to know, I'm the man you should call.

And I mean that. Give your names to my assistant." He turned and walked into the building followed by the colonel.

"I wonder who that Ross Perot guy is?"

"I don't know, LT. But I was gonna ask him if he could get me the hell out of Mai Loc."

"I got a feeling you save him for when you need something a lot more important than that."

Splitting up, Rogers headed for the NCO barracks and he went to the BOQ.

"Need a room, sir?"

"Yes. Thanks. Hey, do you know if Sergeant Johnson, the guy who got shot in the leg is still here?"

"When was he here, sir?" Dawson paused counting months on his fingers.

"It would be six months," he replied feeling foolish.

"No, sir. This gig only lasts a month or two."

"Oh, sorry," he said, turning to look at the empty matching furniture. He remembered the day he met Miller, with his cocky self-confidence. Miller had been dead for five months. By now, his family's life was probably getting back to normal, he thought. Entering the room he dropped his equipment on the rack and sat down. The air around him felt heavy. He went back out to the street. Rogers wasn't in sight and he was hungry so he walked to the officer's club. Inside he was surprised to see how busy it was. He sat at the bar and got two fried egg sandwiches and a beer. No one questioned his rank or uniform. He imagined they knew he was from SOG. But, of course, they were just there to have fun and hadn't even noticed him. He wasn't having fun. He felt out of place and uncomfortably alone. Irrationally, he was irritated by the people enjoying themselves. After another beer he returned to the BOQ.

"Wanna go down town to the blow bath?" Dawson asked Rogers the next morning.

"No, I don't fuck around on my wife on purpose."

"On purpose? What, the hell, does that mean?"

"I just don't go out looking for it."

"She must be real proud of you," Dawson laughed. Rogers punched his arm. "You never told me you were married. Most of these guys kiss their wives goodbye at Ft. Bragg and thirty six hours later they arrive in Vietnam and act like they haven't been laid in six months."

"Yeah, well, I don't do that."

"That's very admirable of you," he said sarcastically. "But, it probably disqualifies you from Special Forces. I'm going down town. Did you bring a pistol?"

"Just the 45 on my rig."

"Let me borrow it. I don't want to go out of the camp unarmed."

"Didn't you bring your Browning?"

"No, I gave it to RaLang."

"You did. Why."

"He's a great point man. Absolutely fearless. If we're out in the field or digging trenches, he works his ass off and never complains. I thought it was a good way to show him our appreciation. He took it as a really great honor."

"He's a stone cold killer, LT."

"Yeah, I'd love to have thirty more just like him."

Dressed in his bush jacket and jeans, Rogers' 45 shoved in the waistband, Dawson paid the Lambretta driver and entered the massage pallor. Soon he was standing in the steam room with the bleach stinging his eyes and lungs. The girl was attractive, but not as pretty as the one when he was there with Sergeant Johnson. She didn't giggle. When it was time to pay her, she got out of her pajamas, climbed up on the table and continued with the same detached expertise she had demonstrated during the massage. The adventure he had been looking forward to for months turned out to be just another task to be completed. He was glad to return to the familiar surrounds of Mai Loc.

"Beaucoup Marine come Mai Loc, trung uy," Thoung told Dawson.
"When?"
"Maybe one day."
"How do you know?"
"Speak village."

The following night Dawson, Rogers and Jennings set up four strobe lights near the southern end of the runway. At precisely 2100 hours a Marine CH-46 appeared. Dawson waved a flashlight, more to identify his position than to direct the big helicopter. It landed and Marines rushed out past him forming a security perimeter. Helicopter after helicopter landed. The Marines formed up in platoon size units and double timed to the south. An hour later it was quiet. The Marines had completed their first night time combat helicopter assault in history. Or at least that's what he was told.

"That went off without a hitch," Jennings remarked as the three walked back to camp. "Wait till Charlie wakes up tomorrow morning and finds out a few hundred Marines moved into the neighborhood."

"Probably won't be much of a surprise."

"Why not, LT?"

"Thoung told me they were coming yesterday."

With the Marines in the valley, the Bru were confined to camp so they were stuck working on the camp's defenses.

"Hey, Sarge. They're looking for volunteers to go on a mission to insert some pole bean. OK if I go?" Jennings asked, sounding like a kid who just got invited to Disneyland.

"When?" Rogers asked.

"Now."

"We're going to need you here today. We have to finish sandbagging the last of the conex containers.

"What's pole bean?" Dawson asked, overhearing the conversation.

"Exploding NVA ammo. They take cases of Chinese 82 millimeter mortar rounds to Okinawa open the cases and fix one of the rounds to explode when it's dropped down the tube. Then they put the case back together so it looks like it's never been touched. It kills the mortar crew and is supposed to make them afraid to use their ammo," Rogers explained.

"Did it used to be called Project Eldest Son?"

"Yeah, and it was also called Italian Green for a while, LT."

"We planted a phony document about it on a dead NVA officer on that recon mission I ran with Peterson."

"Can I go, lieutenant?" Jennings asked.

"What do you think this is? If daddy says no you go ask mommy," Rogers said.

"What part of flying around with booby trapped mortar rounds sounds like a good idea?," Dawson asked. "You heard the sergeant. You're going to play in the dirt with us today."

The Seabees had cut firing ports into the backs of conex containers. Then they dug holes and buried them in the berm so that the firing ports were about a foot above the ground to provide grazing fire. They tried to get them level, but were mostly unsuccessful. It was left to the Hatchet force to sandbag them in place and dig steps down to the large steel doors. They also had to sandbag the insides in order to protect the soldiers' ears when firing a weapon inside a metal box. It was hard work and they had been at it for over a week. The Bru labored with a minimum of complaining. The same couldn't be said for the Americans. Dawson, while not the least little bit happy with the job, tried to lead by example, digging steps and helping the Bru set sandbags to keep them from collapsing. Rogers and Jennings were doing as little as possible. By early afternoon, after watching them fool around with the sandbags on the top of one of the containers and accomplishing little, Dawson grew irritated.

"You know, if I had three of me this job would be done," he said, letting his mouth overrule his better judgment.

"If there were three of you, LT, this war would be over and we wouldn't have to build these goddamn bunkers," Rogers replied sarcastically.

"It wouldn't take three of me to beat your sorry ass."

"Any time, lieutenant." Overreacting, Dawson threw his shovel, almost hitting a Bru by accident, and started up the steps he had just built.

"Whoa guys," Jennings called out. "This isn't worth a fight." A sudden commotion on the airstrip took their attention. Dawson climbed up on the conex container to take a look. He came back down, found his tee shirt, pulled it on over his grimy, sweat-soaked skin and took a drink from a canteen.

"I'll go check it out. We need a break anyway." Defusing the situation. he walked back to the camp.

"The lieutenant's really pissed," Jennings said to Rogers.

"Fuck him. He can be a hothead. He'll get over it."

A half hour later, Dawson returned. He noticed the roof of the conex container had been completed and another one started.

"Well, Jennings you can thank Sergeant Rogers big time."

"Why, sir?"

"That helicopter you wanted to go out on got shot down and exploded. No survivors," he abruptly informed them. There was silence as Jennings realized his life was as fragile as a simple yes or no. Rogers just stared at him.

"They were like real people this morning," Jennings said in shock.

"How many people got killed, LT?"

"Seven of ours and the crew."

"Are we going to take the Bright Light?"

"There's nothing left to rescue."

CHAPTER TWENTY-SEVEN

THEY WERE FINALLY moving to the new camp. The hardback buildings were complete and the defensive system was in place. The TOC was still mostly a hole in the ground, but the big wooden beams used to support the roof had been built out. Had they been moving a greater distance, they would have broken down the camp, loaded it on vehicles and set it up in the new location in one single operation. But since they were only moving across the runway it was being done piecemeal, carrying their equipment and supplies by hand. As a result, it was taking forever. Nobody could find anything. At one point, they were forced to eat field rations because they had two half equipped non-functioning mess halls. It was the definition of what military personnel call a cluster-fuck. But eventually, they were done and living in plywood buildings with corrugated metal roofs that smelled of curing concrete. All that was left of the old camp were some strands of barbed wire, hundreds of engineer stakes protruding out of the ground and thousands of C-Ration cans that had sunk into the mud.

"Here comes the lieutenant," Jennings said. Rogers looked up and saw Dawson carrying maps.

"We've got a mission."

"We can see that, LT."

"Wait till you hear this. Our mission, if we choose to accept it, is to infiltrate the Demilitarized Zone, capture an NVA prisoner and photograph him in front of an identifiable terrain feature. This tape will self destruct in ten seconds," Dawson said mimicking the popular TV show "Mission Impossible."

"Oh, bullshit, LT."

"Swear to God. That's just what they said at the briefing. They want evidence to present at the U. N. that proves the North has troops in the DMZ."

"OK, let me see if I got this straight, LT. We going into the DMZ to prove the NVA are in the DMZ. Now suppose we're successful, what's to stop the North Vietnamese from saying that the only reason they were in the DMZ was to prove that the Americans are in the DMZ?"

"Exactly. It took a staff sergeant two seconds to figure that out. That's way too logical for all the people with stars on their shoulders, running this war, to figure out."

"That's ridiculous. Nobody's going to capture a prisoner. Everybody knows that. They expect us to risk our lives so some asshole can make political points at the U. N. You should get us out of this one, LT."

"I can't. They're even sending teams from Phu Bai and DaNang to try to pull this off."

"Most of the troops are coming in through Laos," Jennings said.

"I can see it now. This will get screwed up. The North Vietnamese will show up at the U. N. with your picture and you'll be famous, LT." They all laughed at that.

"You should never have put that prisoner back. We could have just taken his picture," Jennings added.

"Actually, we could just take one of the Bru who looks Vietnamese and dress him up," Dawson said, only half-kidding.

"And send the picture to the National Security Council," Rogers laughed. "Even you don't have the balls to do that. Besides, they'll probably want the prisoner to testify."

"What if he won't talk?" Jennings asked.

"That's so much crap," Rogers said. "Don't believe all those stories about taking three prisoners up in a helicopter and throwing one out to get the other two to talk. I dealt with prisoners on my last tour. You capture a prisoner you have a lot bigger problem getting him to shut up than you do making him talk."

"OK guys," Dawson interrupted. "Let's just worry about our job. I haven't told you the best part yet."

"Can't wait to hear this, LT."

"We can't take a full platoon because they think that would be too big of a footprint. Mission size is limited to twelve. They want us to take the Bru from the recon team that lost their Americans in the pole bean crash."

"That's not good. They don't know how we work. We'd have to do some training. Besides, from what you said, that team didn't sound that great anyway."

"OK. We'll take our own guys. That's settled."

"Settled? Just like that?" Jennings asked. "You can't just disobey an order, sir."

"It wasn't an order. It was a briefing. Do I look smart enough to remember everything they said?"

"No, sir," Rogers said quickly.

"I didn't think you'd have any problem agreeing with that," Dawson laughed. "So who are we going to take. The three of us, RaLang, Thoung, a machine gunner and ammo bearer. That's seven. We've going in northwest of the Rockpile. The hills are only a couple of hundred meters high. We can easily put five or six on each chopper."

"Now that you have a machine gun in the point squad, why not just take them and add Jennings and me?" Rogers asked.

"Yeah. That works. You know, there was one Bru from the recon team that was pretty good. His name is Pong. If Thoung says he's decent we can take him as the tail gunner. That way if anybody asks we can cover our ass by saying we took what we could use from the recon team."

For the next three weeks teams went back and forth across the DMZ. Dawson's team went twice. A couple of teams got into small firefights. Thankfully, there weren't any casualties. To no one's surprise, they didn't capture any prisoners. Then, without any announcement, the missions stopped. You had to get pretty high up in the Army chain of command to find people who were out of touch enough to think they would succeed. Of course, no one had the courage to tell that to whoever concocted the mission.

The straps on the cheap back packs they carried were constantly breaking. They were inspecting and replacing them when a Vietnamese National Police jeep pulled up to the gate. It was followed by an ARVN three-quarter ton truck. Two QC got out of the jeep. They held 45 caliber pistols in their hands and were trying to look menacing. A feat not easily accomplished when facing Bru mercenaries armed with machine guns. A group of civilians got out of the truck.

"What did you do now, LT?" Rogers joked.

"I'm not sure. Hey, Thoung go find out what they want." Thoung went to the gate and returned shortly.

"Vietnam want sell money."

"Why?" Dawson asked.

"Tahan don't know. Maybe tahan shoot Vietnam take money," Thoung grinned.

"Nobody is going to shoot anybody."

"Not so fast. That depends on how much money they have, sir." Jennings and a couple of other Americans gathered around to watch.

"Can anybody tell me what's going on?" Dawson asked.

"I can, sir." Sergeant Nolan, the medic, who had yanked the stitches out of Dawson's head came trotting up with an empty duffle bag. "They pulled the script. Their money is worthless."

"What script? I have no idea what you're talking about."

"OK, sir. You know the script, the MPC, Military Payment Certificates we use instead of green backs?"

"Yeah."

"Well, last week all the U. S. military personnel in Vietnam were confined to base. They took their old MPC and exchanged it for a new version. Now the old script, the MPCs are worthless."

"So, you're telling me my money is worthless?."

"Yes. But, no. We're in the middle of nowhere. The paymaster hasn't gotten here yet. In a couple of days they'll show up and exchange our money. Before that happens we can buy it from the Vietnamese.

"Why are they changing the MPCs?"

"Because it takes money out of the black market."

"But, how are we going to buy the money from the Vietnamese when all we have are the old MPCs and some piasters?"

"That's easy," Nolan said, flashing a roll of hundred dollar bills.

"Where, the hell, did you get that?"

"My girlfriend sends me a hundred dollar bill in every letter she writes. After my last tour, I got out of the army and started med school. I ran out of money. So I re-signed and came back to get money for tuition. Can you guys cover me so I don't get robbed?"

"I guess," Dawson replied. He and Rogers got their CAR-15s and followed Nolan out the gate.

"You could probably get in a lot of trouble for this, LT."

"Yeah, That would be something new." As they passed the gate, Dawson motioned for the QC to holster their pistols. One of them had something angry to say but they did it.

"Try not to shoot anybody. Will you?" Rogers said laughing. Nolen was speaking Vietnamese, handing out hundred dollar bills and dumping wads of script into his duffle bag. In quick order he was done.

"OK, guys. Let's go," he said. Back in the camp, he gave them each five hundred dollars in MPCs.

"Hey thanks. How'd you make out?" Dawson asked.

"I go two thousand dollars worth of script for each hundred dollar bill."

"Holy shit," Both Dawson and Rogers said almost simultaneously. A half an hour later they watched as two of the camp's captains walked through the gate and bought MPCs from the Vietnamese. They were probably using the payroll money from the Bru that didn't exist. And just as Sergeant Nolan had predicted a couple of days later the paymaster arrived and exchanged their money without a hitch.

"So what are you going to do for Christmas, Sarge?"

"Open presents in the morning then have family over in the afternoon. I think my wife will cook a turkey," Rogers replied, playing along. They were sitting in the jeep drinking. The berm around the camp blocked their view of Camp Carroll. "How about you, LT?"

"Oh, I'll probably take the platoon out and break the holiday truce," he laughed.

It was busy at Mai Loc with teams flying in from Phu Bai and being inserted across the fence. As Dawson had predicted, he received a mission order. Once again the team size was limited to twelve personnel. This time the reason was more obvious. With all of the teams being deployed they simply didn't have enough helicopters to airlift an entire platoon. After a delay of a couple of days, they were given the go ahead and woke up Christmas morning high on a Laotian hilltop just 12 kilometers north of where they had run the Route 9 river operation. Dawson was listening to the radio.

"Ready to mount up?" Rogers asked.

"There's so many teams out I can hear Covey talking to them," he replied stowing the handset and slipping the antennae into his backpack.

"Maybe today isn't a good day to get into a fight, LT."

"That's what I'm thinking. If a couple of teams declare an emergency at the same time they aren't going to have the assets to support them."

"What do you want to do?"

"Hide. We can patrol around here and make sure we're alone."

Late that afternoon, a team got into trouble. They could hear Covey's side of the conversation. The next morning they listened to the extraction. For a week the team avoided contact while listening to teams being inserted and extracted. On New Year's morning Covey called for a Bright Light. A team was in serious trouble. The next night it rained. Running low on water they placed their palms on tree trunks and let water run off their thumb to fill the canteens. The mountains were socked in and the team moved like ghosts through dense fog. They ran out of food. Two days later, Covey found a hole in the cloud cover and directed them to an LZ. The slicks came in. Jennings and half the team on the first. Dawson, Rogers and the rest on the second. As they climbed to altitude, the choppers were enveloped in clouds. Everyone had the same thought. They were going to slam into a mountain. The expressionless backs of the pilots' helmets offered no sign of confidence. By the look on the crew chief's face it was obvious that if he had a rosary he would be flipping beads. Totally at the mercy of the pilot's skill, they sat there for horrifying minute after horrifying minute. Dawson looked at Rogers and quickly turned away not wanting him to see the terror he knew was reflected in his face. Finally, they broke through into bright sunshine. They were flying over a cloud bank. It was a view you would expect to see from the safety of a commercial airliner not through the open doors of a little helicopter.

"How high are we?" Dawson yelled at the crew chief.

"Ten thousand feet," he yelled back, more composed now.

"I didn't know these things could go that high." The crew chief nodded his head in response. They were freezing at this altitude.

Teeth chattering and shaking. Dawson wondered if the Bru had ever experienced cold like this. The crew chief motioned them to pull their legs back into the helicopter and slid the doors closed.

"Thanks," Dawson called.

"I did it to save fuel. We're running low." Dawson checked his compass. They were heading due east. He could see the other helicopter just ahead of them. The clouds thinned out, a road and then the ocean became visible. They followed the first helicopter down, flew along the road for a minute and landed on a small marked pad. The choppers took off immediately leaving them standing there.

"Where are we?" Jennings yelled, the noise of the rotors still in his ears.

"North Vietnam," Dawson joked. The relief from the fear left him giddy. He dropped his back pack with the radio. "Wait here. I'll find out."

"See if you can find a McDonald's, LT. The little guys are starving."

CHAPTER TWENTY-EIGHT

"WERE'RE IN QUANG Tri. There's a Vietnamese Army compound a block away. They'll have a mess hall." They walked down the road and approached a sleepy looking sentry at the gate. Dawson asked where the mess hall was. Of course, the guard didn't understand. "Chop, chop," Dawson said making scooping motions toward his mouth. The guard just stared. Thoung called out something that sounded like a demand. The Guard nodded, forgetting his weapon, he led them into the camp and down a street full of ARVN soldiers. The Bru, always wary of the Vietnamese, instinctively moved into a combat formation. They entered the mess hall and dropped their heavy gear. Following a lead from the Bru, the Americans kept their weapons with them. They heard the Vietnamese in the kitchen repeating the word moi. The pejorative term for montagnyard, meaning savage. Dawson and Thoung approached the kitchen workers. Thoung told them they needed food. Dawson got out his map case, pulled out a few five hundred piaster notes he always carried and paid them. In minutes they were eating hot rice mixed with some kind of vegetables out of bowls with their fingers.

"Who are you people?" a loud voice demanded. Dawson had a flashback. He recognized the voice. He knew what the man would look like before he slowly raised his head. A short, round-faced lieutenant came into view. He wore pressed fatigues with lots of bright patches and a maroon beret. Without reading his name tag Dawson knew it would say Oberlong. His TAC officer from OCS. The one who had trashed his room. "I'm asking you again. Who are you people?" he boomed.

"We've been out in the field and haven't eaten in a few days. Thanks for the food," Dawson replied slowly in a soft voice. "We paid for it," he added.

"What is your unit? Where's your insignia?"

"Sorry, lieutenant, I'm not authorized to give you that information."

"Not authorized? I didn't say you could eat in my mess hall. Get your people out of my compound right now or I'll have you arrested."

"All you had to do was let us eat in peace, lieutenant," Dawson said, without raising his voice, as he stood and picked up his CAR-15. Instantly, the Bru grabbed their weapons. Moving quickly around the table, he took a chair and kicked it up against the wall. Oberlong froze. Dawson grabbed him by the front of his shirt, pulled him over and shoved him down into the chair.

"Sit there. Don't move, and keep your big fucking mouth shut," Dawson said. His reaction was motivated more by the anger he felt at himself for his fear in the helicopter than from some past injustice. "RaLang," he said motioning him to come over. "Thoung. Tell RaLang to shoot him if he moves or speaks." The only thing more terrifying than being blinded by fog in a helicopter was RaLang pointing a Browning 9mm pistol at your face. Dawson felt better.

233

They finished eating and took Lt. Oberlong with them as they walked through a gauntlet of Vietnamese soldiers. They didn't offer any resistance, in fact, they seemed to think it was funny. The team, with their hostage, passed through the gate.

"When you get back inside, don't cause us any more trouble. These guys are very, very good at what they do. Your Vietnamese won't stand a chance. Do you understand?"

"Yes," Oberlong stammered.

"Oh, and to answer a question you once asked me, yes, I think I am better than you," Oberlong looked up a scared, questioning expression on his face, as Dawson released him. When he was gone Rogers asked,

"What the hell was that all about, LT?"

"That was the payback of a lifetime. I'll fill you in later."

"Maybe we should get off the main street. Just in case he gets the Vietnamese to come after us."

"Sure, if you want to, but that's not gonna happen. He may be an asshole, but he's not suicidal. Besides, I think he has to change his pants," Dawson, calmed down now, laughed. They found the airbase, without any trouble, and got a hop to Phu Bai.

"Not now," Major Capra barked. The operations room was in turmoil. Dawson left, went down the hall and entered the S-2.

"Hey, Sergeant Fallon."

"Lieutenant Dawson. What did you do now, sir? Pull another unauthorized ambush?"

"Not this time," he replied, remembering Fallon had told Rogers he was reckless. "We just got back in from the field. I thought you might want to do the debriefing."

"That's all I've been doing," he said tapping a stack of folders on his desk. "Guess one more wouldn't kill me." For the next hour, Dawson went over all the mundane details of the mission. When they finished Fallon said, "So, you just basically wandered around the area doing nothing."

"Yep. That's pretty much it. We could hear other teams getting into trouble and figured they wouldn't have enough assets if we needed support. Is that a problem?"

"No, nobody ever reads this stuff anyway."

"That's encouraging."

"How did you hear that other teams were getting into trouble?"

"We could hear Covey on the radio." Fallon looked puzzled. "Covey has been on frequency 54.40 since the day I got here. You can hear him whenever he's in range which is a lot longer air to ground than ground to ground," Dawson explained. "You didn't know that?"

"No. I didn't. That means the NVA can just sit there with a big old antennae and listen to everything we're doing without even hunting for frequencies. You know we lost a team last Wednesday?"

"I heard some chatter about a Bright Light. Were they from Mai Loc?"

"No. Recon team from FOB 4. All the Americans were killed. The Nungs didn't have a scratch."

"Did the Nungs kill them?"

"No. We suspected that too, at first. The Nungs said the Americans were drinking and making a lot of noise. So they left them. Their story checked out. We found AK rounds in their bodies and the Nungs were polygraphed to make sure." Dawson raised his eyebrows.

As they finished up, Dawson asked,

"Why dump all the teams in the field at the same time?"

"To meet the quota." Fallon replied.

"What quota?"

"Well, it's not a real quota. SOG's effectiveness is basically measured by how many operations we run." Fallon began to explain.

"Not by what we find?" Dawson interrupted.

"Well, they would like to think so but they really don't know how to quantify that. It's almost impossible to value the results of an operation. If your team kills six NVA is it more valuable than another team that kills three? Depends on who the NVA are and nobody knows that. If a Hatchet Force runs into a battalion of NVA and we have to bomb the hell out of the place to get them out, do you think anybody follows up and keeps bombing once the Hatchet Force is safe? Never happens. Oh, they may schedule a B-52 strike two weeks later. But by then who knows what's still there. So how valuable was that operation? Nobody knows. Unless you actually go shoot Ho Chi Minh nobody knows. So the only way they have to define success is by the number of teams they put on the ground. They put all of the teams in at the end of the month to make the reports look good."

"You sound like you've thought about this a lot," Dawson said.

"Yeah. I have."

"But how about all the supplies we stop from coming down the trail?"

"The NVA moves tons a day. We don't make a dent in that."

"Then what's the point in going out and getting our asses shot off?"

"That's a good question, maybe it's why SOG is classified for twenty years. By the time your kids are grown up and you can tell them what you did, I'm sure they'll have come up with something."

"Lieutenant!" It was Major Capra.

"Sir," Dawson replied. He hadn't gotten ten steps out of the S-2 shack.

"You didn't accomplish much out there."

"No, sir. It was quiet."

"It usually is, if you stay in the mountain tops. I expect that from some of these other people, but not from you."

"Well, sir, to be honest, from what I was hearing on the radio, it didn't sound like we'd be able to get much help if we got into trouble."

"Next time, you do your job. I'll take care of the support. Do you understand?"

"Yes, sir."

"That's all." Dawson turned to leave. "Oh, Dawson."

"Sir?"

"I heard you destroyed an NVA platoon while I was on R & R."

"It wasn't a platoon, sir."

"That's what the after action report says."

"Yeah, well, nobody was particularly happy about that either, sir."

"You're dismissed, lieutenant."

Dawson went to the club, expecting to find Rogers and Jennings. He wasn't disappointed.

"Looks like you guys have a pretty good head start," he observed.

"We have faith you'll catch up. Did you hear they lost a team

New Year's day?" Jennings asked. "They said they got drunk in the field."

"Yes, I heard. I wouldn't say much about the drinking. I'm sure they cleaned up the report."

"How'd the debriefing go, LT?"

"Oh, just great. First Fallon tells me SOG's not accomplishing anything, then Capra tells me I'm not accomplishing anything."

"I'm surprised. You're the major's fair-haired boy," Rogers said.

"Yeah, right. Why would you ever say that?"

"He sent me to Mai Loc to take care of you."

"Holy shit, talking about rewriting history," Dawson laughed.

"Did you tell the major you kidnapped a lieutenant in Quang Tri because he wouldn't buy us lunch?" Jennings asked getting a big kick out of himself.

"Yeah, that's exactly what I told him. You guys are having too much fun. I better get a beer. What's the bartender's name?"

"I think it's Linh, LT."

"Of course, it's Linh. What else would it be?" Later, after a few beers, Dawson told Rogers and Jennings an exaggerated version of his experiences with TAC officer Oberlong in Officers Candidate School.

Back at Mai Loc, Dawson was in the fancy new aid station. Sergeant Nolan was cleaning debris out of a scrape he had gotten on the operation. A couple of Bru were waiting to be treated for similar injuries, when Thoung entered.

"Trung uy. Wife Thoung sick. Need bac si."

"Your wife's sick and needs a doctor," Dawson translated out of habit.

"Yes, trung uy. Bac si can come?"

"Want to take a walk down to the village, sergeant?" Nolan talked to Thoung in Vietnamese.

"Sounds like his wife has a high fever," Nolan said, as he taped a piece of gauze to Dawson's knee. "Let me finish up with these two and we'll go."

Dawson waited outside the hut while Sergeant Nolan examined Thoung's wife.

"She's got malaria," he announced and started talking to Thoung in Vietnamese. He took out a small note pad and started drawing pictures of the face of a clock, explaining to Thoung when she should take her medication.

"Have you got a watch?" Dawson asked, pointing to his. Thoung shook his head, no. He took off his field watch and gave it to him. "Stay here with your wife tonight. I hope she's OK.

"Thank you, trung uy. Thank you bac si,"

"She gonna be OK?" Dawson asked Nolan as they walked back to camp.

"She should be in a hospital, but the Vietnamese won't treat her. So, she's better off here. I gave her chloroquine phosphate. It's similar to what we take but, a lesser dose because of their body weight. If she follows the schedule she should be OK. I'll come back tomorrow and check on her, sir."

"Thanks. I appreciate that. Thoung's a good friend."

"Yeah, the Bru are easy to bond with. She'll be OK."

With only the point squad participating in the last three operations, the platoon needed to work together again. Fighting skills are quickly lost when not constantly practiced. In the morning they worked on marksmanship, firing off half of the ammunition they carried. Then spent the afternoon on formations and immediate action drills. As they returned to camp Dawson was surprised to see Thoung.

"Hey, how's your wife?" he called out.

"Wife Thoung die." Dawson was staggered by the news.

"What happened?"

"Bac si no can do help."

"Jesus. That's terrible. You can go back to the village."

"Thoung tahan," he said proudly, tapping his chest with his fist. "Stay here now," his eyes brimming. So were Dawson's.

"What the fuck happened?" Dawson confronted Nolan.

"She felt better after I gave her the first two pills so she took the rest all at one time. Turns out she was pregnant. I asked her and she said she wasn't. You can't take that stuff when you're pregnant. That killed the baby and she hemorrhaged internally. I went down to check on her, but there was nothing I could do. I'm sorry, sir."

"I was really impressed with the way you drew the clocks to explain how to take the pills. It's not your fault, but it is a goddamn shame."

CHAPTER TWENTY-NINE

HOT WATER HIT the back of his neck and shoulders in a powerful spray. He could feel muscles relaxing that had been tense for months. The window was open and curtain pulled back so he could breathe the cool air off the ocean. Pragmatically, he wondered how long it would be before he ran out of hot water. The door opened and a woman intruded. He quickly wiped the water out of his eyes. She was tall, twenty something, very white skin and very naked. With her thin waist and large breasts she was, by any standard, breathtaking. At first she pretended to be shocked, but then shrugged and stood to her full height, pushing her breasts out posing for him. Then she brazenly sat and peed. When she was through she washed her hands, then turned, smiled and walked out giving him a lingering view of her ass. Finally, the water was getting cold. Toweled off, he returned to the room and looked out over the crescent beach. It was full of people even though it was early. Rogers was snoring, something he never did in the field, probably a result of alcohol poisoning. He returned to his bed and went back to sleep.

When Dawson, Rogers and Jennings boarded the Pan Am flight in Saigon to go to Australia they had no idea it would take thirteen hours before they would arrive at the R&R center in the Kings Cross section of Sydney. Dawson had a slight fever and slept through large portions of the trip. Rogers complained about his sleeping. Jennings was well-behaved. At the center someone gave them a card recommending a hotel on Bondi Beach. It was supposed to be owned by an ex-Special Forces sergeant. After a twenty minute cab ride they checked in and got a two room suite, separated by a bathroom, overlooking the beach and ocean. Rogers headed to a local pub. Jennings went back to Kings Cross for the night clubs and women. Dawson went to bed. When the pub closed, at ten o'clock Rogers returned and went right to sleep. After midnight, Jennings showed up with a girl in tow causing a commotion.

The room had a TV which was a treat for the soldiers. They were surprised that the shows started and ended at odd times not adhering to the hour, half-hour rule they were used to in the states and amused that the broadcasts were interrupted with special announcements about horse racing results. Later they all went to the beach. When they returned the girl walked around naked. Rogers was shocked. Dawson had had a preview in the shower. By the time they would have to leave they would be used to it. That night was a repeat of the first.

"How you feeling, LT?"
"Better. I was good last night, but I didn't want to push it. How was the pub?"
"It was OK. I met a guy there last night."
"I don't want to here this," Dawson interrupted. "At least Jennings picks up girls," he laughed. They could hear them screwing

in the next room.

"Fuck you, LT. No, I met this guy. He said he's a garbo. That's what they call a trash collector. He said it's one of the most prized jobs because it starts early and ends just as the pubs open. Seems like for most of the men here, life revolves around the pub."

"Well, they must be doing something other than going to the pub. Every girl I see is pushing a baby carriage."

"What do you want to do today?"

"Go sightseeing."

The ferry ride across Sydney Harbor to the zoo was, by far, the highlight of their R&R. Well, at least it was for Dawson and Rogers. Jennings may have put it in second place. With the big steel arch bridge in the background, Dawson asked,

"What's that?" Pointing to a cluster of huge concrete shells surrounded by construction cranes.

"It's going to be the opera house. They have been building it for years," the girl replied.

"What's her name?" Rogers quietly asked.

"I don't know. I haven't asked."

"Why not?"

"I'm afraid it might be Linh."

"Lynn?"

"It's a long story."

After the ferry ride, the zoo was a let down. A bunch of wild animals standing around in cordoned off areas not looking very wild. There was a large two story high cage holding lots of monkeys. The girl took particular glee in pointing out all of the dirty things they were doing. Dawson insisted they see the duck-billed platypus. After a long walk down a hill they came to its pen only to find out it was hidden away somewhere. On the way out Rogers bought a stuffed koala bear at the souvenir shop.

"That's gonna look real cute lying on your poncho liner back at Mai Loc." Dawson mocked.

"Fuck you, LT."

"Well, at least you got a box for it so nobody sees you hugging it on the ferry ride back."

The next morning, after the girl paraded around naked for a while, Jennings announced they were going to the beach.

"We'll catch up with you later," Rogers informed him, drawing a sideways glance from Dawson. As soon as they left Dawson asked,

"What's up?" Rogers walked across the room, picked up the box and took out the koala bear. Then went to his bag, shuffled around, and pulled out a stack of bills wrapped in rubber bands.

"Holy shit. That's more money than I make in a year!"

"This is more money than we both make in a year, LT."

"Where, the hell, did you get it?"

"It's Nolan's. Remember the money exchange?"

"Yeah. How'd he convert it to greenbacks?"

"I have no idea, but he said he lost his contact to get it out of the country so he gave it to me to mail to his girlfriend."

"His contact is probably in Leavenworth."

"Probably. Got a knife?"

With the money inside the bear and the box secured with tape from the front desk, Rogers and Dawson got out of a cab in front of a huge stone building with a three story clock tower.

"Looks more like a prison than a post office," Dawson observed.

"That's reassuring. All the way down here I've been picturing alarms going off and ending up in an Australian jail. I'd be a lot more comfortable in a fire fight than doing this."

"When I was in intelligence school."

"You weren't in intelligence school," Rogers nervously joked.

"Yeah. I was. They taught us how to go through foreign customs with a forged passport and how to steal stuff. The problem is you think you're too important. They used the example of a high school kid walking around with a "Playboy Magazine" in his notebook. The kid thinks every teacher in the school is looking for him, but in fact, he's not important and nobody gives a shit what he's doing. The trick is to convince yourself of that."

"Sorry I didn't take that class."

"You want me to do it?"

"No, I'll do it, or you'd never let me hear the end of it, LT."

"No I won't. Give me the box." Rogers paced the sidewalk for almost a half hour before Dawson returned.

"Where the hell you been?"

"Let's get out of here!"

"What happened?" Rogers asked anxiously.

"Nothing. I'm just screwing with you. It was a long line."

"So it went OK?"

"Yeah, up until the clerk asked me how much I wanted to insure it for."

"What'd you say?"

"Twenty thousand dollars," Dawson laughed.

Their last two days went quickly. During the day they all hung out on the beach. At night Dawson joined Rogers at the pub. Jennings kept banging the girl. After the long miserable flight back to Saigon they stopped to visit a friend of Rogers. He was an ARVN Ranger advisor stationed at a small compound on the traffic circle just next to the main gate of Tan Son Nhut Airbase. They all went out for dinner at a pretty decent local seafood place and stayed the night with the Rangers. The next day they bounced up the coast, hitching rides on whatever aircraft were going in the right direction, finally arriving at Mai Loc a day or two late. But, of course, at Mai Loc nobody was counting.

CHAPTER THIRTY

"LOOKS LIKE WE'RE going to have to find a new spot," Rogers said. R&R was over and they were sitting in the jeep at Mai Loc.

"This whole deal sucks. How many sandbags did we fill? How many bunkers did we build? This place is perfect for combat operations. No distractions. Train whenever you want. Everybody stays sharp. Nobody messes with you."

"You're definitely going to get some adult supervision now, LT."

SOG was completely reorganized. Mai Loc and FOB 1 were closing. Everyone was being relocated to FOB 4 at Da Nang which had been renamed Command and Control North or CCN for short. The FOB at Kontum became Command and Control Central (CCC). Ban Me Thuot was now Command and Control South (CCS). Headquarters remained on Pasteur Street in Saigon.

While Dawson was on R&R the Bru were on leave. He sent a message to the village asking them to return to camp. Once assembled, he told Thoung what was happening and had him relay the information to the platoon. Not surprisingly, they weren't thrilled.

He gave them two days off to get their families squared away.

"You should have told them it was temporary, LT. You might not get them back," Rogers said.

"I'm not going to lie to them. Besides there's an ARVN ranger battalion taking over the camp. They'd figure it out pretty quick. They'll come back."

"Yeah, at least enough for a recon team," Rogers laughed.

"What do you think, Thoung? Will the tahan come back?" Dawson asked.

"No worry, trung uy, tahan come back," He assured.

"They're pretty loyal, lieutenant," Jennings added.

"Yeah, well I'd rather rely on the sixty bucks a month we pay them." Over the next couple of days the Bru returned, every one of them. They packed up and made the move to Da Nang.

"Any of you guys Lieutenant Dawson?"

"I am, sir," Dawson replied to a man about his height wearing a beret with captain's bars.

"I'm Captain Henry. Your company commander."

"How ya doing, sir? This is Sergeant Rogers and soon to be Sergeant Jennings. And this is Thoung our Bru platoon leader."

"Dai uy," Thoung acknowledged bowing his head slightly.

"Major Capra tells me you guys are pretty good."

"Don't believe everything you hear, sir," Rogers said.

"Capra's here?" Dawson asked.

"Yep. That guy's never going home."

"How about Major Barton?"

"No, he didn't get reassigned here. We have a new base commander. You guys have everything you need?"

"So far, sir," Dawson replied.

"Come with me, Dawson. I'll show you around."

"I was here with the platoon after the August attack. I know my way around pretty well."

"Humor me, lieutenant." The Bru were in a new barracks between supply and Marble mountain. From there they walked to the center of the camp and then east on towards the ocean. "I hear things were pretty lax up at Mai loc. You guys pretty much just did what you wanted."

"Well, sir, if you mean camp construction, training and combat operations, we did what had to be done. We didn't have much adult supervision if that's what you mean," Dawson replied borrowing Rogers' words.

"I heard the uniform of the day was cut off jeans and tee shirts."

"Yes, sir, if we were digging ditches."

"Well, you won't be digging any ditches here so keep your troops in proper uniform."

"Yes, sir. Where's the training area?"

"They told me your troops are combat ready. This is a combat zone not basic training."

"We always practice movements and marksmanship between operations, sir."

"I've seen the recon teams use the beach to run drills. Maybe you can train there if need be." They walked in silence for a while, then Captain Henry said, "When you're out in the field you'll have complete control. I have three platoons to run. If one is out and the other two are here I have to stay with the majority of the troops. If two platoons are on operation I keep them separate and control things from the air. Is that what you're used to?"

"Yes, sir. We didn't have a company commander at Mai Loc." From what Dawson just heard, it didn't sound like he would have much of a company commander here either.

"This isn't as comfortable as the jeep."

"The jeep didn't have an ocean view, LT." The were drinking at a picnic table down by the beach.

"I'd rather watch Camp Carroll get shelled."

"How'd your little tour go with the captain?"

"He's worried we'll show up in cut off jeans."

"This place is a little too civilized for that. They have maid service for the barracks and they wash our clothes in real washing machines rather than pounding them on a rock."

"It feels strange to actually live here. I got up this morning and it's like everything is done and there's nothing to do."

"The captain will probably think of something."

"I'm not so sure about that. He seems pretty disinterested. He told me he doesn't go out in the field."

"What?"

"Yeah, some bullshit about he stays with the majority of his troops so he never runs operations with more than one platoon."

"A little risk adverse, maybe?"

"That's what it sounded like, but he said it like he was proud of it. I asked him where we train and he acted like I was nuts. Told me we were supposed to be combat ready."

"The little guys will be perfectly happy to sit around playing cards and eating. I'm worried that you'll find some creative way to get into trouble. LT."

"We could always go sightseeing," Dawson laughed.

"Oh Jesus, I knew that was coming. Hopefully, they'll find something for us to do before it comes down to that.

They didn't have to wait long. Dawson was summoned to the TOC. Sergeant Fallon had made the move from FOB 1 to CCN. He was seated behind a desk piled high with target folders and after action reports, the picture of his wife in her blue bathing suit prominently displayed. After they both agreed that they didn't like the new camp, Fallon began the briefing.

"You're going into the area where only the Americans were killed on a recon operation that we talked about before." The target was in Laos just southwest of the DMZ. From the map, the terrain looked hilly, but not the steep mountain jungle they were used to. In the Northeast corner it dropped down to a river that ran out of the DMZ. A recon team had reported seeing Chinese advisors and a pipeline there last summer. Fallon then went on to detail the surviving Nungs' report on the deadly operation. He didn't sugarcoat the drinking. When he was finished Dawson observed,

"That doesn't add up."

"Why not?"

"The fact that the Nungs left the Americans because they were drunk and loud makes sense. Then, you say, the Americans were killed by NVA, maybe even sappers. We know this because AK rounds were recovered from the bodies and the Nungs passed a polygraph. Right?" Fallon nodded. "The Nungs never engaged the enemy. Then after the Americans were dead the Nungs contacted Covey with the team's radio and were extracted. Correct?"

"Yeah. What's your problem with that?"

"There's no way NVA troops, let alone highly trained sappers, would leave a PRC-25 radio behind."

"Maybe they just got sloppy."

"Don't bet your life on that one."

Next, Dawson went to operations for a reunion with Major Capra. The first thing the major did was chastise him for hiding in the hills on the last mission.

"This target is really important," he said. "We have good intelligence that there's a pipeline running along the river. We need to find it. It's important. We also have reports of Chinese troops in the area."

"Yes, sir."

"You know we lost a team in here?"

"I just had the briefing, sir."

"Yeah, well, it's important. But it's not worth getting killed over. If you run into something you can't handle don't push it, just get out. I don't want to lose anymore people in there. Do you understand?"

"Yes, sir. We carry a lot of firepower. If we can get in clean we should be able to move around. At least for a while."

"Good. Find that pipeline and don't get killed doing it."

"Where you been, LT?"

"Briefing. We have a very important mission."

"What makes it important?"

"Because Capra said it was three times."

Two mornings later, they assembled the platoon by the chopper pad. Jennings stayed with them while Dawson and Rogers went to the TOC for a pre-mission briefing. It was very impressive. First, Sergeant Fallon, addressing the camp commander, described the target. Next Major Capra explained the objectives of the mission. Then one of the pilots explained that they had two troop carries on the pad that would transport the team to Quang Tri where the protection package was waiting, then they would fly to the target area and rendezvous with Covey.

"Somebody fuck up," Dawson whispered to Rogers.

"Yeah, I heard it, too. We sure can't move a platoon on only two helicopters. You know they're going to blame it on you, LT."

"Very good, gentlemen," the camp commander said. "Are the troops prepared to carry out this mission?" Captain Henry stood up,

"Yes, sir. My platoon is ready to accomplish this mission," he stated firmly. That's when the shit hit the fan.

"This is a recon mission, captain," Major Capra said as he jumped to his feet. Henry had no idea what to say. He had tried to take credit for something he knew nothing about. Now he was stuck with it. The camp commander, not the least little bit amused, got up and said,

"You people better get this straightened out," and walked out of the room. Dawson and Rogers avoided looking at each other knowing they would burst out laughing.

Finally, after recriminations all around, the shit, as Major Capra would say, rolled down hill to Dawson. He calmly explained that on three occasions, when they were short-handed at Mai Loc, his point squad had been used on recon operations.

"When you were at the FOB, you and Peterson found the road," Major Capra pointed out.

"Why can't the lieutenant just take his point squad out for this mission?" Captain Henry volunteered. Dawson shot him a look.

"You wanna take this one, Dawson?" the major asked.

"I'll do what I'm ordered to do. But, I'm not raising my hand. If I did and Rogers got shot he'd blame me."

"What about you, Sergeant Rogers?"

"I'm with the LT on this one, sir."

"Is your team or point squad or whatever you want to call it ready to go?"

"Yes, sir."

"Put them on the choppers."

"Yes, sir. Is ten OK? We go heavier than a recon team. We carry a machine gun."

"Yeah, that's fine." As they left the major called, "Don't get hurt out there."

"Yes, sir," they both answered.

Returning to the chopper pad, Dawson explained to Thoung what happened.

"No good," Thoung said.

"Yeah, no good." Two squads returned to their barracks shaking their heads.

"Hey, Thoung," Rogers said. "Tell them not to eat all their rations in one day."

"Tahan no eat all."

"Yes they will," Dawson laughed.

CHAPTER THIRTY-ONE

RALANG CAME TO a halt and motioned for Dawson to come up. They had been inserted about four kilometers from where the pipeline was reported and had spent the first two days moving carefully up hill through dense jungle. There was no sign of enemy activity. Now, early on the morning of the third day, they were at a point where the jungle turned into a flat pine forest. The floor was a layer of pine needles with very few bushes. The branches of the trees began about ten feet above the ground. Looking through the forest, all you could see was hundreds, maybe thousands of tree trunks until they disappeared into the darkness. Rogers joined them.

"This is eerie," Dawson said. "You ever see anything like this?"

"Yeah, in North Carolina. Somebody could shoot you from a hundred meters away, LT. Is there a way around it?"

"I can't tell where the jungle ends and the forest begins from the map. If we move to the east it drops down and we'd have to climb back up again. We could work our way around to the north and see if it ends."

"Let's try. We don't wanna cross it unless we absolutely have to." They spent an hour looking without success, then took a break in the safety of the jungle. Questions to RaLang and Thoung about enemy presence were met with shrugs.

"What are you going to do, LT?"

"It's like crossing a rice paddy with a roof over it. Once we get in there, we'll be exposed and Covey won't be able to find us so we won't have air support," Jennings pointed out.

"It can't be more than a kilometer wide because then it drops off down to the river," Dawson said.

"A lot can happen in a kilometer, LT."

"It's either that or head west and try to find somebody to get in a fight with so we can get out of here. So far we haven't seen any signs of the enemy. If were going to find the major's pipeline we have to cross it. You guys OK with this?"

They moved silently like ghosts from tree to tree in the dim light. The trunks weren't wide enough to provide complete cover. A couple of times Dawson thought he saw movement but RaLang didn't react. The had to be half way across by now. One of the Bru behind him to his left fired a short burst. They hit the ground. No more shots were fired.

"Keep moving," Dawson called quietly, motioning RaLang forward. A minute later another burst, this time from his right. Again they hit the ground.

"Go," Rogers yelled. "Go." Up now and moving, the enemy appeared in small groups. Most turned to flee. Some dropping their rifles. A few returned fire. It didn't matter, they were all shot down. No more diving for cover. Pausing only to reload behind trees the team pushed forward. Faster now, almost running. Jennings was free-handing the machine gun. Enemy soldiers were falling. Their blood soaking the pine needles. Less firing now, they were running out of people to shoot. Breathing hard they left the forest and plunged into the jungle. Pausing only to count heads, they moved forward a hundred meters. Two hundred meters. Exhausted, they fell to the ground then formed a quick perimeter on a little rise.

"Those guys really sucked," Jennings said. "Half of them ran."

"Lucky for us. There must have been a hundred of them. Who were they, LT?"

"I don't know. Fallon said a team saw Chinese here. These guys had floppy hats with little brims. Maybe they were Chinese. They sure weren't NVA. I didn't hear an AK or an RPD. I think they only had SKS carbines. Hey Thoung."

"Trung uy?"

"Tahan fight Chinese?"

"No China. Lao."

"You sure?"

"For sure, trung uy. Have VC, China tahan die."

"What did he say, sir?" Jennings asked.

"He said they were Pathet Loa. If they were NVA or Chinese they would have killed us." That shut everybody up for a while. Dawson took off his back pack and screwed in the long whip antennae.

"You know you're bleeding, LT."

"Let me call this in." He contacted Hillsboro and was told Covey was launching.

"Tahan need bac si," Thoung said. One of the Bru had broken his arm. Jennings cut a couple of twigs and splinted it as best he could. Dawson had a crease along the side of his head, Rogers cut off a piece of his bandanna and used it to stop the bleeding.

Covey came on station and after a long conversation Dawson announced,

"They're pulling us. We gotta blow a tree to make some room. We're going out on strings."

"I hate that string shit. Can't we move to an LZ?" Rogers asked.

"What do you think I've been arguing about for the last five minutes? Just blow a tree." They watched Rogers tape blocks of C-4 explosive to a tree trunk. Without a kicker charge they had no idea which way the tree was going to fall. So, of course, when Rogers set off the explosives the tree fell back toward the team sending them scrambling. A helicopter hovered over the opening and dropped four ropes anchored by ammo cans filled with sand. The ropes ended with a loop covered with green padding. They detached the ammo cans and put the Bru in the seats, doubling up two of them, and clipped the snap links from their web gear to the ropes. Jennings and five Bru were pulled up and out of the jungle. The second helicopter hovered and Dawson, Rogers, Thoung and RaLang repeated the process. As they were being pulled out, Dawson's back pack caught on a tree branch. He hung there, stuck for a second, as the rope stretched, then lurched upward as one of his straps broke swinging the back pack with the radio sideways taking Dawson with it. Struggling as the helicopter gained altitude he finally freed himself by sending the back pack plummeting to the ground. Upright now, he regained his composure. Looking at the jungle far below then up at the helicopter. Dawson felt as secure as someone possibly could dangling from a helicopter a half mile high on hundred foot long rope. Beside him, off the other side of the chopper, he saw Rogers and behind him Thoung. It wasn't until they were dumped on the familiar dirt of the Mai Loc runway that he realized the rope behind him was empty.

"Hey, Thoung. Where's RaLang?" Dawson yelled. They were off the ropes and back inside the helicopter.

"Maybe go here," He yelled pointing toward the other helicopter.

"No, I saw him get on the string."

"Tahan don't know," Thoung shrugged. While the helicopters were being refueled at Quang Tri Dawson kept asking about RaLang.

"Did you clip him in, LT?"

"No. To be honest, I was too busy trying to figure out how the thing worked."

"You never had any training?"

"I've never even seen one of those things before."

"So, that's why you came out upside down?"

"You saw that? The strap on my back pack broke. Scared the shit out of me. Thought I was going to fall."

"You're not going to die that easy, LT. Maybe RaLang fell out?"

"Jesus, I hope not. We need him."

"He keeps you alive."

"Yeah. It's a whole different deal without him. No way I'm walking point behind somebody else. It's like he has a sixth sense. Even before he signals I can tell, just by the way he moves, when we are going to make contact. If we have to break in a new guy you and I will have to switch places."

"That's not gonna happen, LT."

"Then I guess Jennings is next up."

"You know he is getting pretty good at this?"

"He's a little bit reckless. Still thinks he's bulletproof. But, you're right."

"Have you noticed the Bru don't seem too upset about RaLang?"

"The Bru never seem to get upset about anything."

It was still early in the day when they landed back at Da Nang. Dawson dropped off his gear and headed to the Bru Barracks. There he confronted Thoung again.

"Maybe die. Maybe no die. No sweat, trung uy."

"That's great. No have RaLang, Thoung be point man." Dawson was starting to talk like a Montagnard.

"Thoung no can do be point man. Tam be point man."

"Hey sir, they want us for the debriefing," Jennings called into the barracks.

"Yeah, I'm coming." As he turned to leave Thoung said,

"Maybe RaLang come back, trung uy," Dawson thought he detected a sly smile. Or maybe he just hoped he did.

The debriefing was wrapping up. They had detailed all of the boring stuff about their movement from the landing zone to where they made contact. Each gave his own version of the firefight. Dawson had a much lower estimate of the number of enemy soldiers and of the casualties they inflicted than Rogers and Jennings. That wasn't unusual. Each had their own perspective of the battle. In fact, they held the debriefings as soon as the teams came off the ground just to prevent them from rehearsing their stories.

"Are you sure the soldiers you encountered were Pathet Lao and not Chinese? You know another team reported seeing Chinese troops in this area," Fallon asked.

"The Bru said they were Pathet Lao and they should know," Dawson replied.

"They were pretty far east to be Pathet Lao," Fallon challenged.

"They were pretty far south to be Chinese," Jennings offered sarcastically. Rogers put his hand on his shoulder to quiet him.

"It's just that it would be a lot bigger deal and the operation would be a lot more successful if they were Chinese," Fallon said defensively. "I'm just making sure."

"Actually, it makes sense," Dawson said.

"What makes sense?"

"Remember, when the Americans, who were drinking, were killed the enemy didn't take their radio?"

"Yeah, so?"

"Well these guys were really poorly trained. Like we said, most of them turned and ran. They were the kind of troops who wouldn't even know to take the radio."

"But the Americans were killed with AKs and you said these guys only had SKS carbines."

"Both rifles fire the same cartridge," Rogers said.

"If we had the platoon, can you imagine how much money we could have made if we scrafed up all of those SKSs," Dawson said as they left the TOC.

"Speaking of making money, you better go see Nolan."

"What are you talking about?"

"You know, Nolan the medic, the stuffed bear, Australia, the hole in the side of your head. This RaLang thing really has you off your game, LT."

"Yeah, yeah. I just forgot his name is all. OK with you if I get a beer first?"

When Dawson entered the aid station, the first thing he saw was the injured Bru from his platoon. He was sitting on a table without a shirt, his arm in a new cast. He looked so little, almost frail. He was one of the young ones. Seeing him like this it was hard to believe he was a mercenary soldier able to carry sixty pounds of gear. At that moment, it didn't seem fair. Dawson walked over to him.

"Trung uy," the boy said.

"Tahan, OK?" Dawson asked taking and holding his good hand. It was a Bru tradition. He sat up a little straighter and shook his head yes, a look of pain or fear or both in his eyes.

"He'll be OK, lieutenant." Sergeant Nolan entered the room.

"Have you got something for his pain?"

"Right here." Holding up a glass of water and a couple of darvon. "What did you do to your head this time?"

"It's just a knick," he said taking off his bandanna.

"This is nothing. Just bled a lot. I'll clean it out. Doesn't need sutures. It's pretty straight, looks like a bullet just creased you. That's the second time you've been lucky. Probably time you learn to keep your head down." As he was cleaning the wound he said, "By the way, thanks for your help in Australia. Rogers told me about the post office."

"If I had any brains I would have taken it and gone AWOL," Dawson joked.

"I've got something for you for you're trouble. Wait here." He went in the back and returned with a small automatic pistol, a screw on suppressor and extra magazines. "Here, this will come in handy when you're in town. It's not silent, but it's pretty quiet."

"Hey thanks. This is pretty neat."

"No problem."

After, once again, checking on the injured Bru, Dawson left the aid station and returned to the barracks. Thoung had the tahan cleaning their weapons. There was no sign of Rogers or Jennings. He found them, in an animated discussion about shooting Pathet Lao, at the picnic table.

"You don't look any the worse for wear, LT."

"Nah, It's just a scratch."

"How many Pathet Lao did you kill, sir?" Jennings asked.

"I don't have any idea. We ran into a few small groups. From the debriefing it sounds like you had a lot more action behind me on the flanks."

"It was like a shooting gallery back there, sir."

"If they ran, I mostly let them go. I was concentrating on the ones that tried to fight," Dawson replied.

"Your a real humanitarian, LT."

"Oh, bullshit. RaLang and the others took care of the runners."

"Now that you brought him up, who are you going to replace him with?" Rogers asked.

"Thoung says some guy named Tam. I don't know who he is."

"He's in my squad. He's pretty good," Jennings offered.

"I was thinking Pong, the guy we brought over from the recon team to be our tail gunner. He has that hard edge like RaLang. Whoever we pick the first thing we have to do is make sure he can see."

"Can see what, LT?"

"Vision. When's the last time you had thirty-six people and none of them needed glasses?"

"Don't you think they check them before they get hired?"

"No, I don't think they check them before they get hired. I better get started on this before they assign us another target. I'll be back later."

"What did you do, get hit in the head again already, sir?" Sergeant Nolan laughed.

"No, not yet. Listen, can you check the Bru's vision?"

"Yeah, like for injuries or removing something stuck in their eyes?"

"No, like to see how well they can see."

"They actually make an indig eye chart with arrows instead of letters."

"Good. Can I go get a couple of Bru and test them?"

"I don't have a chart. I've got cardboard and magic markers if you want to make one." It took Dawson about a half hour to make the chart. It came out pretty good. Then he went to the Bru barracks got Pong and Tam and took them to the dispensary to get tested.

"Did they pass, LT?"

"Yep. They did fine."

"So you just wasted a perfectly good hour of drinking time," Rogers mocked. "Are you going to test the rest of them?"

"Yeah, I guess we should."

"What are you going to do with the ones that fail?"

"I don't know. Replace them. I guess."

"I can see it now," Jennings said. "You're going to be famous as the chicken lieutenant who wouldn't take his platoon in the field because he didn't have an ophthalmologist."

"You guys are great. I'm gonna get cleaned up, eat and get some sleep."

The next morning they gathered some of the white plastic egg-shaped containers that each held three M-79 rounds, threw them in the ocean and had Tam and Pong fire at them while they bobbed around. Pong was clearly the best shot. He became the point man.

Late that afternoon they were sitting at the picnic table. Captain Henry approached, looked at them disapprovingly, and said,

"Dawson, Major Capra wants to see you."

"Think we got another mission already?" Jennings asked.

"No, I know what this is about."

"What, LT?"

"He probably wants the Pathet Lao turned into Chinese. Nothing like an international incident to spice up an after action report."

Dawson was back in less than twenty minutes.

"So did the major get his Chinese, LT?"

"Nope." Dawson smiled.

"You gonna tell us or what?"

"RaLang turned himself in to the Marines."

CHAPTER THIRTY-TWO

"RALANG'S ALIVE AND safe. That's great news LT. When did this happen?"

"Just an hour or so ago."

"Where?" Jennings asked.

"OK, here's what I know. RaLang found some Marines near the Rockpile.

"The Rockpile? That's not that far from Mai Loc," Jennings interrupted.

"Do you wanna hear this or not?" Dawson asked. Then continued. "So he took off his equipment and surrendered. Then he showed them his gear. And when they saw the equipment he had, they were smart enough to figure out he was somebody important. They had a re-supply chopper take him to the artillery base on the Rockpile. There's also some kind of secret Army signal intercept unit there with Vietnamese speakers. They figured out he was with SOG pretty quick. He's probably in the air to Quang Tri right now and he'll be here tomorrow."

"How far did he walk, LT?"

"Over twenty miles through the jungle in what? Twenty-eight hours. He's really something."

"I'll drink to that, LT."

"I won't even say it," Dawson laughed.

The next afternoon a slick landed on the chopper pad. RaLang emerged. He was the only passenger. The helicopter took off.

"He travels better than we do," Jennings remarked.

"He's more important," Rogers said. As they approached the barracks the Bru poured out and greeted him. All smiles. All chattering at once.

The prodigal son returns," Dawson said. Rogers and Jennings looked at him. "What you never went to Sunday School." Dawson walked over to Thoung. "Ask him where his rifle and web gear are." That started a minute long conversation.

"RaLang speak Marine take."

"Hey, Jennings how about taking RaLang to supply and replace his equipment."

"We could just give him the guy's stuff who broke his arm."

"No. RaLang needs a CAR-15. Besides that kid feels bad enough I don't want to take his gear away."

"Aren't you going to ask him, LT?"

"Ask him what? About the extract?"

"Yeah."

"I don't want to get in the middle of his homecoming. Besides. I'm pretty sure I know."

"What happened?" Dawson drew Rogers aside and quietly told him that RaLange was afraid to get on the string.

"I didn't know he was afraid of anything. If I knew we had the option of walking home I'd of gone with him."

"Yeah, like you'd walk twenty miles."

"What are you going to do about it, LT?"

"Nothing."

"You can't just do nothing."

"Of course, I can."

That evening Captain Henry joined them in the mess hall. He wasn't happy that they had insisted the enemy they encountered were Pathet Lao and not Chinese. He, actually, had a certain logic. If they had reported they were Chinese, their superiors would have deemed the operation a great success. And since nobody was going to do anything about it anyway, why not just tell them what they wanted to hear. Dawson was only half listening. He was busy giving Jennings a stare that told him to keep his mouth shut. But, he heard it loud and clear when the captain said,

"You know, it's CCN policy that you get one day off for every day you're in the field for up to five days."

After he left, they settled in for some serious drinking at the picnic table.

"Do you think we can really take four days off, LT?"

"I have a rule. If a superior officer tells you to do something you want to do, never question it. Just do it."

"I'm gonna have to start writing down all these rules you have," Rogers laughed. "Does that mean Nha Trang here we come?"

"No. That means Eden Rock Hotel, Saigon here we come."

"That's pretty far, LT."

"There's a lot more planes leaving Da Nang for Saigon than Nha Trang. By the time we hang around for a flight to Nha Trang we can be in Saigon."

Can I go with you guys?" Jennings asked.

"Absolutely," Dawson assured him.

"What about the Bru?"

"That's Captain Henry's problem." They each had another drink then Dawson ordered two more beers. "I've got something I have to do. Let's meet up at 0900 hours in the morning. Pack some civilian clothes and don't forget your side arms."

"Aren't you going to tell the captain, LT?"

"Hell no." They all laughed. "I'm sure we all heard him order us to take four days off."

Dawson took the two beers to the aid station. As he expected, Sergeant Nolan was there tending to his patients.

"What can I do for you, lieutenant?"

"Question for you," he said handing him a beer.

"Thanks. Ask away."

"We're going to Saigon tomorrow and all we have is MPC should we change it into piasters?"

"Oh, definitely. If you pay a bar tab, five dollars MPC is the same as five hundred piasters. If you exchange it in the PX the rate is one hundred eighteen to one. But, if you exchange it on the black market the rate is one-fifty, one-sixty to one."

"That's a big difference."

"Yeah, it is."

"So, how to we change it on the black market?"

"What time are you leaving?"

"Early. 0900 hours."

"Ah. That's too soon for me to get a hold of my guy. Here's what you do. When you go into any Vietnamese bar there is always a guy that works there who watches the girls."

"Yeah, I've seen that."

"Tell him you want to change money. Now, he's gonna tell you to just give it to him. Don't do that. Tell him you have to do it in person. He may act like he doesn't understand. Don't be fooled. He'll understand what you want. Just go back and sit at the bar. Be patient and somebody will show up and ask if you want to change money. Follow him outside and he'll take you to the guys with the money. They'll make the exchange."

"Sounds risky."

"They may try to rob you. Just don't go alone and make sure you take the pistol I gave you."

The next morning they gathered in the mess hall and, of course, as luck would have it, they ran into Captain Henry. Rogers and Jennings kept looking at Dawson to see what he was going to do. Henry was still going on about the Chinese. When he finally quieted down Dawson asked,

"Can we bring you anything back from Saigon, sir?" trying to keep a straight face. The captain hemmed and hawed around for a while. Then he told them to be back in four days about a dozen times.

"I almost spit my coffee right across the room when you asked him if he wanted anything from Saigon," Jennings said.

"Thought you weren't going to tell him, LT."

"Give me a break. What choice did I have?"

As Dawson predicted, they didn't have to wait long to catch a flight to Saigon. From the terminal at Ton San Nhut they hitched a ride to the main gate and walked down the street to the ARVN Ranger compound. They decided to split up. Rogers would stay the night with his buddy from Bragg, while Dawson and Jennings headed downtown, agreeing to meet up at the Eden Rock Hotel in the morning. Dressed in civilian clothes, they caught a Lambretta taxi. Rounding the big traffic circle Dawson pointed to a crowded, run down looking area.

"That's Hundred P Alley."

"Why do they call it that, sir?"

"Because you're supposed to be able to get laid there for a hundred piasters."

"I'm still spoiled by Elaine."

"That was her name? The girl in Australia?"

"Yeah."

"She didn't look like an Elaine. What was the deal with her anyway?"

"What do you mean?"

"Was she a hooker?"

"No."

"What, she just feel in love with you?"

"Well, not exactly. I bought her some groceries before we left. Actually, I bought her a lot of groceries."

They went to the rooftop of the Rex Hotel. Sitting at the bar, Dawson starting thinking back. Something he didn't do much of in Vietnam. The last time he was here, he was with Peterson after they found the road on his first recon operation. He had barely been in country two months. Now he was three-quarters of the way through his tour. A lot had happened. A lot of people had been killed. But his little group had managed to avoid tragedy. Mostly by luck. Dawson knew that if Jennings had asked him to go on the failed Pole Bean mission, instead of Rogers, he would have let him go. They had managed to avoid being in a helicopter crash and hadn't been inserted into the middle of an overwhelming enemy force. They had been careful on the ground. Most of the credit for that went to Rogers who had the good sense to know when to get out. And now RaLang had returned. The shrimp was still on the menu. They ordered it.

"What time is it?" Dawson asked.
"You still haven't gotten a watch?"
"No. I keep forgetting."
"It's 1730. Good thing this isn't World War Two. The soldiers were always synchronizing their watches in the movies."
"There's a press briefing downstairs. They'll be coming up here soon."
"How do you know, sir?"
"I've been here before."
"Think we should leave?"
"No. Our GI haircuts are long gone. We'll blend in."

On cue, the bar filled up. Most of the reporters, correspondents or whatever they were, sat quietly at tables. A gray-haired man had a small group of fawning younger people surrounding him as he pontificated importantly. It grew dark and a few were getting drunk, pawing at the waitresses. Dawson could hear them cursing about it, in Vietnamese, at the service bar. Beyond them he saw the guy he was looking for.

"I'll be right back." Jennings watched as he walked over and had a short conversation and returned. "I'm going to exchange some money," Dawson said and explained what was going to happen as he paid the check. A skinny kid, dressed in a white linen shirt and slicked down hair came up to them.

"You come now." They followed him out of the hotel, down the street and into an alley. There they met two other men. Dawson counted out a hundred dollars in MPC notes. The Vietnamese carefully counted out thirty five-hundred piaster notes rolled them up and wrapped them in a rubber band.

"MP come!" The other Vietnamese shouted excitedly. "MP come!" The first man shoved the rolled up bills into Dawson's hand, took his money and disappeared into the alley. Dawson and Jennings quickly walked back to the lighted street.

"Jeez! I'm glad we didn't get caught," Jennings said.

"Yeah. That wouldn't have been good. I never even thought about MPs."

They walked down the street past the Rex then over a block and entered the lobby of the Eden Rock Hotel. It was crowded with GIs and bar girls.

"I like this place already, sir."

"Yep. They had you in mind when they built it. Let's get a couple of rooms." They moved to the front desk. "Shit!" he exclaimed under his breath.

"What's the matter?" Jennings asked. Dawson showed him the roll of money he had gotten from the Vietnamese. It contained one five-hundred piaster note wrapped around a bunch of twenties.

"Those sons of bitches switched the money. I got robbed."

They checked into their rooms, met back downstairs in the disco and with luck found seats at the bar. The tough-looking guy he had seen hassling the girls seven months ago was still working at the end of the bar. He wondered if Linh was there. When the band took a break and he could hear himself think, Dawson stood up and leaned over Jennings.

"I'm going to set up another money exchange."

" Are you crazy, sir?"

"Yes."

This exchange went down exactly like the last one, except with a different kid and different Vietnamese in the alley. Well, not exactly, exactly. This time when the man counted out the five-hundred piaster notes Dawson shoved the pistol Nolan had given him in the man's face.

"No can shoot. MP come," the man sneered, clutching the money to his chest. Dawson lowered the pistol and fired a round into the ground. It only made a little more noise than a cap gun. The man got the idea real fast and handed over the money. Dawson pushed the phony roll of notes into his hand hoping he'd understand the Americans were just getting even.

"Di Di mau. Get out of here," He ordered. As the Vietnamese began to walk down the alley one drew his finger across his throat. Dawson pointed the pistol at him and he turned and ran. He looked at Jennings. For once he was speechless.

"Let's go get laid."

Dawson watched the girl shower. He hadn't realized how pretty she was the night before. Now, he wished he had paid more attention to her when they woke up this morning. Sex was like combat, there were always things you'd do differently given a second chance. After she left, he got cleaned up, dressed and went to Jennings' room. He wasn't exactly astonished to see a naked girl on his bed.

"I'm going down to the coffee shop. Rogers will be here anytime now."

"OK, sir. I'll finish up here and be down in about 20 if that's alright."

"Yeah, fine. Take your time. But not all day," he laughed.

He exited the elevator, walked across the lobby and looked out the open double doors, noticing a group of Vietnamese cowboys, street thugs, sitting on their little Honda motor bikes. Entering the coffee shop, he got a cup and went to a table. Paranoid after the previous night's adventure, he started to think the cowboys were waiting for him to get revenge for the money changers. He had heard plenty of stories about these motor bike gangs. They fancied themselves Vietnamese Hell's Angles. People were warned not to hang their arm carelessly out of taxi windows because they would ride by and chop their hand off with a machete to steal rings. He told himself he was over-reacting like the kid with the Playboy Magazine. But, he also knew to trust his instincts. He left the coffee shop and found a place in the lobby where he could watch the street without being seen. He counted ten that were definitely together. There were a few more he wasn't sure about. He returned to his table. After a while, Jennings joined him. Dawson explained the situation.

"Let me go take a look," he said getting up and walking toward the lobby.

"Don't let them see you. Maybe they'll get tired of waiting and leave."

"I can't tell. Maybe this is just where they hang out," he said when he returned.

Finally, Rogers appeared. He waved, got a cup of coffee and joined them.

"This coffee's terrible. Can't you find a better place than this, LT?"

"Yeah. I can but there's a problem." He told him what may or may not be going on.

"How long have they been there?"

"Almost an hour and a half now."

"We're all armed. Why don't we just walk out the front and see what happens," Jennings proposed.

"What do you think you are? A fucking Green Beret?" Rogers laughed.

"If we shoot the place up we'll spend the rest of our tours explaining it to CID at the Long Binh Jail," Dawson said.

"Let's find out if they really are waiting for you. LT. Why don't you walk out front and see if you get their attention. We'll back you up." Dawson got up.

"Let's do it." They were back at the table in thirty seconds.

"Well, that certainly got their attention. What do you want to do now, sir?"

"Here's what you're going to do," Rogers responded. "You and the lieutenant are going to stay put and I'm going to go get the calvary. They aren't looking for me. That OK with you, LT?"

"Yeah. That's good. Thanks. But we won't be here. I can't drink anymore of this coffee. We'll be in the bar."

Dawson ordered his second beer and laughed out loud.

"What's so funny, sir?"

"I was just thinking about what a big deal this would be if we were back in the states, trapped in a bar, surrounded by bikers who wanted to kill us. Here it's about as exciting as waiting for the rain to stop so we don't get wet." They had just paid for their third beer when they heard a heavy truck pull up outside.

"That will be our ride," Dawson said. Taking the beer with them, they left the hotel and climbed into the back of a deuce-and-a-half joining half a dozen combat loaded ARVN rangers. They waved goodbye to the cowboys and went to the Ton San Nhut terminal. From there, they flew to Nha Trang and returned to Da Nang two days later. Captain Henry was happy. They were back on time.

CHAPTER THIRTY-THREE

DAWSON WAS CLEANING his little pistol when he was told to report to the TOC. Captain Henry was already there.

"We've been waiting for you, lieutenant," he said.

"They just told me five minutes ago."

"How you doing, Dawson?" Major Capra asked.

"Not bad, sir."

"How's Rogers?"

"Aw, you know, sir. He runs on rum and keeps me out of trouble." Henry threw him a look.

"I've got a job for the two of you." Major Capra went on to explain their mission. Captain Henry interrupted to ask a couple of questions. Dawson could tell Capra thought he was annoying. Henry was oblivious. "That's it," the major finished up. "You can get with Fallon for the intel. You guys be careful out there."

"We will, sir. Thanks." On the way out Henry said,

"You and the major seem to get along."

"Yeah, he was here when I got here. Rogers was one of his platoon sergeants when he commanded a hatchet force out of FOB 2."

"Well, if you need anything for the mission let me know," the captain said. Dawson thought he sounded a little like a kid who didn't get picked for the ball team.

"We're going out the day after tomorrow."

"No rest for the weary, huh, LT. Do they know we have a platoon this time?"

"Oh, God I hope so. No, they do. The 1st platoon's been out for eight days, pretty far west, north of Base Area 611. They found a bunch of food and medical supplies. We're going to relieve them and continue to search the area."

"So everybody in the world will know where we are?"

"The platoon's reported all kinds of signs of the enemy, but so far they have been avoiding a fight. Probably just waiting for us," Dawson said seriously.

"Why don't they just re-supply them and leave 'em on the ground with us?" Jennings asked. "We could do a bigger search and have twice as many guns."

"Probably because that makes too much sense."

"No. I know why," Rogers said. "Because then the captain would have to come with us."

Two days later a Marine CH-46 landed on a small cleared hill top in an area that had been heavily bombed. As the Bru piled out, Rogers placed them in a perimeter as the departing platoon took their place on the troop carrier. Dawson knelt and spoke to their platoon leader. As the helicopter took off, the second one came in low with the rest of the platoon.

As the big helicopter lost altitude, Jennings took a couple of steps down the ramp. Gone was the blue sky as the jungle came closer. Preparing for the landing he took another step. His feet hit a large spot of grease. He started to slide. Skillfully, he bent his knees, arms out for balance, and surfed right out of the helicopter. He wasn't that high, a couple of body lengths, but he fell long enough to see the sky and twist his body. He landed in a bomb crater, partially filled with water, on his back. The water and his back pack absorbing most of the impact. The wind was knocked out of him and he was blinded by the sediment now stirred from the bottom as he sank under water. With his lungs involuntarily heaving he fought to keep himself from inhaling. He tried to lean forward but the weight of his gear was too much. He tried a second time. Finally, he rolled to his side, pushed himself up and got his head out of the water. Gasping, his lungs convulsing, he fought his way out of the back pack. He could hear the sound of the helicopter.

"Trung si, trung si," the Bru were calling as they exited the second helicopter. Recognizing the word for sergeant, Dawson yelled for Thoung.

"What's going on?"

"Tahan speak Trung si Jennings fall helicop."

"Where?"

"Maybe here," Thoung said pointing. As Dawson turned to look a figure covered in mud entered the perimeter.

"Are you OK?" He called running toward Jennings.

"Yes, sir."

"What the hell happened?"

"There was a slick spot on the ramp. I fell."

"Are you sure you're OK? Tell me now while I can still get you out of here."

"Yeah, I'm fine."

"What, the fuck happened to you?" Rogers said, as he came rushing over.

"I fell out of the helicopter."

"You OK?"

"I'm fine. It wasn't that high."

"Your rifle's full of mud. Get it cleaned up. I can't believe the shit you and the lieutenant can get into."

"Don't make me a part of this," Dawson said. Then to Jennings, "Clean it and test fire it now. I want to get moving."

The 1st platoon had found enemy caches of equipment at the base of a ridgeline that flanked a well-camouflaged road. They picked up where the other platoon had stopped. Dawson had them zigzagging up and down the ridge. There were foxholes and empty storage bunkers all over the place. It was definitely an abandoned enemy base area. At least, they hoped it was abandoned.

"Tahan go up. Tahan go down. No good," Thoung complained.

"Yeah, why do we have to keep climbing up and down this ridge, sir?" Jennings wasn't happy about it either. "All the stuff we're finding is down here by the road."

"You got an opinion?" Dawson asked Rogers.

"Probably wouldn't do me any good if I did, LT," he said laughing.

"Look, see how the terrain drops off on the other side of the road before it rises up that steep hill? If the enemy wanted to attack us from there he'd have to be a hundred, a hundred and fifty meters away. We could just sit behind a tree and he could shoot at us all day and not do any damage. He couldn't advance because we'd cut him to pieces in the low area. But if he came over that ridge behind us we'd be screwed. So we keep going back up to make sure that doesn't happen."

"No have VC, trung uy."

"No have VC? You sure no have VC?" Dawson replied.

"Tahan don't know."

"Yep. That's for sure. Tahan don't know." They loaded up and climbed back up the ridge. Dawson started replacing RaLang with Pong on point when they were returning down the ridge. They both started grumbling.

"Why RaLang no go point, Trung uy?"

"In case he decides to walk home again." Thoung had a quick conversation with him.

"RaLang no walk home."

"For sure?"

"For sure, Trung uy."

"OK. Tell RaLang to move up and teach Pong to be point man."

"Why teach?"

"In case VC shoot RaLang."

Around noon of the fifth day, as they approached the road, Pong fell through the jungle floor. They set up security and scrambled to the road. The North Vietnamese had dug a small cavern into the side of the hill and hidden it behind a massive tangle of vines. Inside they found a three-quarter ton Russian truck, two Czech motorcycles and Pong. Dawson called it in and was told to take photos and destroy them.

" I'm running out of film. Can you destroy this stuff?" Dawson asked Rogers.

"We don't have any thermite grenades, LT. Hey, Jennings see if there's gas in the vehicles." As they talked, Jennings kick started a bike with a roar and drove it down the road, skidded into a U-turn and returned.

"You fucking moron!" Dawson yelled. Rogers put his arm across his chest, restraining him."

"I got this, LT."

After Rogers rigged some explosives and disabled the vehicles, they climbed back to the top the ridge and set up for the night.

"What did you say to Steve McQueen, over there? He's been pretty quiet."

"I told him the next time he pulled a stunt like that I'd let you kill him."

"Every time I start to think he's really getting his shit together he goes off and pulls a stunt like that."

"That's funny, I feel the same way about you, LT."

"Oh, bullshit."

"What do you think they were doing with those motorcycles?" Rogers asked.

"I don't know. They abandoned this place in a hurry. Couldn't have been more than a couple of weeks ago. Maybe the war ended and they forgot to tell us?"

"Well, if it did, they're going to start it up again real soon. They took all their ammunition with them, LT."

They found a couple of bamboo hooches tucked into the woods. "Check this out, LT," Rogers said, handing him a large green shoulder bag. "Do you think it's important?"

"Believe me, other than not getting killed, I have no idea what's important in this war."

"Sir, I found a tunnel," Jennings said excitedly. "In here." There was a hole in the dirt floor.

"It's probably just a bunker," Rogers said.

"No. Look." Jennings shined a big Army flashlight down the hole. "See there's a shaft dug out of the side." Indeed. there was. "There could be a hospital or a command center down there."

"Maybe Ho Chi Minh's down there," Rogers said.

"Aren't we going to check it out?" Dawson and Rogers exchanged looks. Rogers shook his head.

"No. It's just a bunker," Dawson said.

"At least let me go down and shine the light down the tunnel and see if I can see anything, sir."

"OK, go ahead, But stay out of the tunnel." Dawson said, relenting. Jennings dropped his back pack and web gear and climbed down into the hole. Dramatically, he held the flashlight and pistol together, crouched and thrust them into the tunnel.

"I can't see anything. It curves around. Maybe if I just move down it a little bit."

"Get out of the hole," Rogers cut him off. "It's a bunker. And when you get debriefed, it's still a bunker. Do you have any problems with that?"

"No," Jennings replied, remembering when Rogers had stopped him from getting on the helicopter that got shot down.

Dawson finished up with Covey.

"They want us to stay in. They're bringing us a food and battery resupply in the morning. I asked them for more film."

"What are we going to do with this?" Rogers asked, holding up the document bag.

"They're going to lower a rope and I'm going to send it out."

Overnight, something changed. The platoon was ordered to move to an LZ. They were extracted just before noon.

CHAPTER THIRTY-FOUR

"TOOK YOU LONG enough, LT."

"That's the last time I'm ever gonna take seventy pictures on an operation," Dawson said, as he slumped down at the picnic table.

"Why don't you go get the lieutenant a beer? Better make it two," Rogers told Jennings. After he left, Rogers asked, "What's wrong, LT?"

"Fallon brought the pictures out in a box. They weren't even in order. I had to sort them out and put descriptions and locations on each one."

"No. What's wrong? You look like somebody just shot your puppy."

"I just found out a friend of mine got killed."

"From here?"

"No. Fort Bragg."

"What happened?"

"He got here just before I did and got assigned to FOB 2. He was on an operation and stepped on a toe popper. Just went through months of surgeries and rehab then they sent him to the 1st Group on Okinawa. They wanted to get him qualified for his parachute pay, but didn't want to risk hurting his foot, so they set him up with a water jump. The plane crashed into the bay. He was the only one that didn't survive."

"That's too bad. How good a friend was he?"

"We shared a house at Bragg. Went diving in the Bahamas together. I met his father and brother. Really nice people. This is going to be tough on them."

"I sorry, LT. I don't know what to say."

"Just don't say: Fuck it. Don't mean nothing." Jennings returned with the beers. Dawson opened one and changed the subject. "I still don't know why they pulled us off the target."

"I just heard they're putting parts of the Nung Company into the A Shau Valley. Has something to do with some big operation the Marines are running," Jennings said.

"Better them than us."

"The captain's coming up behind you, LT." Dawson didn't bother to turn around.

"Still duty hours gentlemen." Captain Henry said, referring to the fact they were drinking. Dawson opened his second beer. Rogers rolled his eyes. It was silent for a moment. The captain decided to drop it. "Major Capra said you did a good job out there."

"We always do, sir," Jennings said.

"Apparently you do because you got promoted. Congratulations Sergeant E-5 Jennings."

"Thank you, sir."

"You want a beer, sir? Jennings is buying," Dawson offered.

Over the next few days Command and Control North became

rumor control north. Word was spreading that a large Marine force had crossed the border into Laos from the A Shau Valley and had sustained heavy casualties. All kinds of scenarios were floated about what role SOG would have in the action. Even the Bru were infected. As Dawson was checking on the young soldier who had broken his arm, Thoung asked,

"Tahan go A Shau?"

"I don't know," Dawson replied.

"Trung uy know."

"No, I don't. If I did I would tell you."

"A Shau no good. Beaucoup VC. Tahan no can do go A Shau."

"You keep telling me, 'Maybe die. Maybe no die. No sweat.' Isn't that right?"

"Thoung no sweat VC," Thoung replied with false pride. "Maybe some man Tahan sweat VC."

"It's OK for tahan to sweat VC. I sweat VC. That makes us careful."

"VC no can do shoot trung uy. Tahan know trung uy kametai." Dawson put his hand on Thoung's shoulder and shook him gently.

"Tahan take care trung uy. Trung uy take care tahan. I promise."

"What are you hearing, LT?"

"Nothing solid. I went to the TOC this afternoon. Everybody was running around. Capra told me to leave."

"Two platoons from the Nung Company are going out tomorrow."

"Where?"

"I don't know. I asked one of the platoon sergeants and he told me they weren't being told until the pre-insertion briefing."

"That's weird. You'd think if it was important they'd get more briefing time. Not less. I'm gonna go get a beer. I'll bring you a drink. Where's Jennings?"

"Da Nang. He went downtown with a couple guys from a recon team."

"Good for him. He could find a way to get laid in the middle of a fire fight. The Bru think we're going to the A Shau Valley."

"I thought you were going to get me a drink?"

"They're not real happy about it."

"If that's where we're going, I'm not real happy about it either."

"Don't worry. You can just stand behind me."

"What good is that gonna do me?"

"Thoung says the Bru think I'm kametai."

"What, the hell, does that mean?"

"It means they believe VC can't shoot me."

"Lucky you. They didn't happen to include me did they?"

"Nope, sorry. Only one kametai guy at a time," Dawson laughed. "The problem with their theory is that I've already got a couple of scars in my head."

"Yeah, well, just don't get anymore, LT." Rogers said seriously. "You gonna get us something to drink or what."

"On my way."

Each afternoon, after their insertion, lightly wounded men from the Nung Company kept returning to the camp. Dawson had no idea whether there were more serious casualties evacuated to the hospital or even worse. No Americans were killed. They would have heard that. On Wednesday one of the Americans returned, injured. Dawson and Rogers stood in the club, listening to him recount the horrors of the operation for a while, then took their drinks to the picnic table.

"That guy's pretty shook up," Dawson said.

"I know who he is. He's a young Spec. 4. Hasn't been in country long. From what he says the NVA are just fucking with them, shooting at the point to slow them down waiting for medevacs. Sounds like they could use RaLang."

"Sounds like they could use an experienced old sergeant like you."

"Fuck you, LT."

"Here comes Captain Courageous." That made Rogers laugh, spilling some of his drink down his chin.

"Don't you people do anything other than sit around drinking?"

"It's after 1700 hours, sir," Dawson said checking his empty wrist. He still hadn't replaced his watch.

"We're going out the day after tomorrow to link up with the Nung company."

"Who's we, sir?" Rogers inquired.

"All of us. The whole company. How much ammunition do your men carry?"

"Riflemen carry seventeen magazines plus one in the gun. Machine gunners, eight hundred rounds. Grenadiers, eighteen plus one. Eight claymores total," Dawson rattled off.

"They're going to need to carry more than that. Much more than that. The Nung company is in constant contact!"

"Yes, sir. Where is the Nung company?"

"Supporting the Marines."

"That covers a lot of territory."

"Someplace near the A Shau Valley. I have to go inform the 1st platoon. Make sure you draw extra ammo and be ready to go by the end of the day tomorrow."

"Yes, sir," Dawson answered.

"Sounds like the captain is going with us, LT."

"Yeah. It does."

"He doesn't even know how much ammo we carry. You and him on the ground together. This is going to be beautiful."

"Let's get another drink. Oh, and make sure I get a watch from supply tomorrow."

As the Bru were getting their rations and extra ammo for the next day's operation, they were uneasy. The rumor that they were going to the A Shau Valley was now taken as a fact. Thoung kept asking Dawson where they were going and Dawson kept saying that he didn't know. It was pretty obvious Thoung didn't believe him.

"Can't you go find out where we're going, LT?"

"Now you're going to start busting by balls too? The captain doesn't know. He said we won't be told until just before we get on the choppers. The colonel wants total operational security."

"Well, they already said we're going out to join the Nung company. The NVA know where they are. So who are they keeping it a secret from?"

"Just us I guess. Listen, I'm gonna go see what I can find out. Have Jennings get a half dozen entrenching tools from supply and pass them out to the Bru."

"You think we're going to need them, LT?"

"I certainly hope not."

Dawson entered the TOC, walked quickly past operations and slipped into the intel office.

"What's the big secret?" He asked as he dropped into a chair across from Fallon.

"I can't tell you, sir."

"Give me a hint." Fallon looked around the empty room as if he was afraid someone was watching and slid an after action report across his desk. Dawson opened the folder. He only glanced at it for a couple of seconds, looked up and said,

"I wrote this."

"No, I wrote it. You did it."

"So, this is it?"

"In the last week of January the Marines starting building artillery support bases in the area. After a bunch of bad weather they started pushing an entire regiment to the south. Last week they crossed the border and are running company size ambushes on the road."

"Who's winning?"

"The Marines, but they're paying a big price. SOG's been tasked to take some of the pressure off them."

"We're bait."

"I doubt they'd call it that. Now, would you please get out of here, sir, before you get me in trouble."

After he left, he went to the Bru barracks and found Thoung.

"We are not going to A Shau." He told him.

"Tahan no go A Shau?"

"No."

"For sure, trung uy?"

"For sure."

"Where Tahan go?"

"South of our last mission."

Dawson took his CAR-15 and a beer and joined Rogers and Jennings at the picnic table.

"Anybody got any goose grease?" he asked.

"I do, sir," Jennings said, jumping up from the table. "I'll get it."

"He's got everything," Dawson laughed.

"What'd you find out, LT?"

"Let's wait for Jennings," he replied as he broke down his rifle.

"Jesus, don't you ever clean that thing?"

"I think I did once. It fires better when it's loaded up with sludge."

"Oh, I got you a little present from supply," Rogers said, and handed Dawson a watch.

"Hey, thanks. I forgot all about it," he said, strapping it on.

"Here you go, sir."

"Thanks." Dawson stuck his finger in the little container of white grease and spread a thin layer on the bolt. Then he put the rifle back together, wiped his finger on his pants and pulled three map cases out of his side pocket. Inside were carefully folded maps of their target area. He passed them around.

"How'd you get these?" Rogers asked.

"People feel sorry for me, so they give me stuff."

"That's how Jennings gets laid, LT."

"Aw, come on guys," Jennings said, as they laughed.

"Don't worry. We're just jealous," Dawson assured him. "Ok, see how the border runs east and west and just to the south in Laos is Route 922." He went on to explain the area and about the Marines. "Just to the south of where we're going in, there's an unmarked road that runs east toward the top end of the A Shau."

"How do you know so much about this place, sir?"

"I went on a little camping trip there about nine months ago."

"The recon mission with Peterson's team. That was a big deal. You guys found some road. I remember you got back on the day we fired the Cambodes. That was probably the last time you cleaned your weapon, LT."

"Probably. Yeah, we had to go to SOG Headquarters in Saigon for a debriefing. They told us the road we found didn't mean shit."

"Here comes the captain."

"Get rid of the maps."

"Too late, LT."

"I wouldn't drink too much tonight gentleman. We have a big day tomorrow. What are you doing with the maps?"

"Just a little map reading class, sir," Dawson answered.

"Is that our target area?"

"I don't know, sir. They haven't told us yet."

"Is it in the A Shau Valley?"

"No, sir. The A Shau would be over here," Dawson said, pointing to a spot on the picnic table.

"You probably shouldn't have those maps."

"It never hurts to be prepared. Just might keep some people alive. And remember, sir, you're going with us."

"Yeah, you're probably right. See you in the morning. Don't drink too much." They were quiet for a while.

"Think Captain Henry is gonna be a problem, LT?"

"No, he's basically a decent guy. Just doesn't have a lot of ground experience so he's not comfortable around us."

How can he be a Special Forces captain and not have a lot of ground experience?" Jennings asked.

"Just look at all the other officers we have here. The only reason the lieutenant isn't sitting behind a desk is because he's on somebody's shit list."

"Yeah, lucky for you guys. We've been together for what, nine months? I know what you're going to do before you do it. Same with the Bru. Jennings, you're still a mystery."

"No I'm not."

"Yeah, like I expected you to gun that motorcycle up and down the trail. It's not only all the operations we've run, think about the hundreds of hours we spent patrolling around Mai Loc."

How could I ever forget, LT."

"Yeah, and you bitched about every one of them. All I'm saying is that most of the platoon leaders run a couple of missions and get reassigned. They don't get a chance to learn what they're doing. I hate to admit it, because I can't stand the guy, but when Major Barton made me carry the radio, on my first few operations, it was the best thing that ever happened to me. Gave me a chance to get a feel for this place without being in charge."

"We just let you think you're in charge, LT," Rogers laughed. "Seriously, though, what are you going to do if Henry starts making mistakes out there?"

"I'll just tell him. He'll be OK."

'But what if he's not?"

"Then," Dawson paused, "I'll send him home."

At 0900 hours the next morning they were briefed on the operation. It was a real dog and pony show. Chief SOG was there from Saigon along with a Marine major and someone from I Corps headquarters. The intelligence summary was almost as informative as the Bru's claims of beacoup VC. The operation was pretty straightforward. They would be inserted into Laos, meet up with the Nung company, move north, cross the border back into Vietnam and link up with the Marines. The distance was only about eight klicks in a straight line. They would probably have to walk double that when you counted in the mountains. The aviation briefing was long and complicated. The ground forces weren't very interested. After all, they were only going to get on, hope for the best and get off. Preferably in the correct location. For the first time, they heard that they would be inserted in two lifts. Apparently, there weren't enough helicopters available for this extremely important operation to take them all at once. The camp commander gave a rah-rah speech and the briefing ended.

"So, we're part of a task force, LT. That makes it sound like a big deal," Rogers said sarcastically.

"That S-2 major they chose for ground commander doesn't look like he's in any shape to hump the mountains," Dawson replied.

"Yeah well, if the colonel said 'We' one more time I was gonna to ask him if he was going with us."

"That's all we'd need is somebody else out there who has no idea what they're doing. I've got a feeling we're going to be glad when this one is over."

CHAPTER THIRTY-FIVE

THE PLATOON LAY in the grass in a circle, sweating without any overhead cover. The helicopters had dropped them off and returned to get the rest of the company. Every once in a while, a bullet cracked by. The shooter was far enough away that his firing wasn't dangerous, just annoying. The Bru ignored him. Dawson got up, walked to an opening in the jungle and fired a couple of short bursts in the general direction of the enemy and returned to lying in the grass.

"Get him?" Rogers asked.

"Of course, not."

"You probably shouldn't take this Bru idea that the enemy can't shoot you too seriously, LT."

"I'm just getting tired of waiting. What it's been, over two hours?"

"You got a watch."

"Oh, yeah. I forgot," Dawson laughed.

"Maybe they put them in on the wrong LZ?"

"No. I would have heard something on the radio."

A half hour later the second lift came in and the captain sat in the field looking at his map and compass. After a few minutes he moved near the jungle opening and directed the 1st Platoon to move out.

"Guess we'll bring up the rear, LT."

"Looks that way." Dawson ran over to the captain and returned.

"What was that about?"

"I just wanted to let him know we took a little fire from where they're headed."

"That was nice of you," Rogers laughed.

The 1st platoon was moving quickly single file down a well-worn trail. Dawson tried to move in two columns parallel to the trail with the point squad taking up the rear guard, but they couldn't keep up. So after a while, they had to move onto the trail and hope that if anything happened, it happened up front.

They entered a big bamboo and elephant grass field and stopped. It was hot.

"What's going on, LT?"

"They were radioing back and forth with the Nungs. I think they made the link up. Are the Bru carrying their two quart bladders?"

"Just like you said."

"Hey, Thoung. Tell the tahan to conserve water." Thoung didn't understand. "No drink beaucoup," Dawson said, holding up his canteen.

"Where are we, sir?" Jennings asked, handing him his map.

"We're here about a klick north of the road we found with the recon team. Now we're on this marked trail that runs due north up over the highest point of the ridge then down to Route 922. That's probably where we're going. When we move out of this field into the tree line there's going to be an unmarked east-west trail. We got into a fight on it just east of this deep draw," Dawson said, pointing to places on the map.

Bang! Then a scream from ahead of them, where the Nungs were. The Bru brought their weapons up.

"Toe popper mine. One down. Two to go," Dawson said, disgust in his voice.

"You plant it, LT?"

"No. A recon team that was here a few months before us did. We stayed pretty far east of here because we didn't trust the coordinates in the after-action report."

"Maybe they should have read that report." Another bang. Another scream.

"Yeah, maybe. Hope they don't find the third one the hard way. Have the Bru kick down some of this vegetation and set up a perimeter. We're going to be here for a while." The Bru made a game out of swinging their new entrenching tools at the sticks of bamboo. They never would have made anybody's little league baseball team. And, of course, while they were fooling around, Captain Henry appeared.

"Two people were just seriously wounded by booby-traps. Maybe you should be taking this more seriously."

"We have security out, sir." The captain could see about half of the platoon lying prone behind their weapons. "The enemy would have to be right up on top of us to do any damage. You can't shoot through this stuff, sir. It's too thick."

"Well, have them be quiet."

"Yes, sir. Oh, and sir, the Nungs are stepping on toe poppers that a recon team planted about a year and a half ago. There's one left."

Late in the afternoon a Marine CH-46 came and took out the wounded. As it pulled out it dumped fuel all over the LZ.

"That's great," Jennings said. "Now all the NVA have to do is throw a match at us." It was an exaggeration, but they could taste and smell the fuel. The platoon stayed in place and waited for orders. Finally, just before dark, they were told to move about thirty meters as the task force set up an overnight perimeter. Thoung asked how many of the Bru should stay awake guarding their position. Dawson told him three.

"Do you think that's enough, LT?"

"The NVA would have to make a hell of a lot of noise moving through this shit to get close enough to be effective. But if you want more just let me know."

"No, you're probably right."

"Hey, Jennings did you hear that?"

"Hear what, sir?"

"For the first time ever, Rogers said I was right."

"No, I said you were probably right, LT."

From the other side of the perimeter someone started screaming and yelling.

"What the fuck is that?" Jennings asked.

"It's one of the Nungs. He's having a religious experience. It happened a couple of times when I was here on my last tour," Rogers said, as he rolled over and sat up. The screaming continued. "What are you laughing about, LT?"

"When I was in the Special Forces Officers Course they put me in charge when somebody went nuts like this. I sent a couple of people out to get the guy and quiet him down. Apparently, they thought I made the right decision because I graduated."

"So what's funny about that?"

"Now, I'd just shoot the fucker."

"You've been in Vietnam too long, LT."

Dawson woke up with a start. At first he thought he was awakened by the enemy approaching. He listened intently, then slid over and kicked Rogers. Rogers instinctively pulled his rifle to his shoulder as he opened his eyes and rolled over facing the perimeter.

"Listen," Dawson whispered.

"Trucks."

"Yeah."

"You gonna tell the captain?"

"No, I'm going to tell Moonbeam." Moonbeam was the airborne command and control plane that controlled all of the airpower in their area.

"You're gonna get your ass in a sling, LT." Dawson crawled away and spoke on his radio, then returned.

"What did they say?" Rogers asked.

"They said they'd send a Voodoo."

"What's that?"

"I have no idea." Twenty minutes later a jet flew directly over their position firing explosions of light and ten minutes after that, jets dropped bombs south and just west of their location. Dawson got back on the radio.

"What did they say, LT?"

"They got three trucks pulling into a truck park. I guess the road Peterson and I found wasn't such bullshit after all."

In the morning Dawson told Captain Henry what happened. At first he questioned Dawson's authority to take the action, but after realizing he could take credit for destroying three trucks, Henry was more than happy to report it to the major. They formed up to move out when a Nung stepped on the final toe popper. So they sat around for two hours waiting for a medevac.

"Saddle up. We've got the point. Hey, Jennings."

"Sir?"

"Make sure the guys with the entrenching tools aren't making a racket." They moved from the rear to the front, past the Nungs. Taller and leaner than the Bru, they looked fierce in comparison. Giving the toe popper area a wide berth, they moved out of the field and began to make their way up the steep, heavily wooded slope. With the point squad in front, the assault squads flanked either side of the trail. Slowly and silently they made their way forward. To the untrained eye they were invisible. To the trained it was, of course, a different story. Behind them, the rest of the unit walked on the trail in single file, stretching out over a couple of hundred meters. The going was difficult. Like climbing a saw blade. Up twenty meters then down ten and repeat. Dawson brought their advance to a halt, sat down on the ground, took off his boot and rolled down his sock. Rogers came up quickly and watched as he squirted insect repellent on a leech that was sucking blood from his ankle.

"We stopped because you got a leech?"

"Yep. One of the few privileges bestowed on the officer corps," Dawson grinned. The radio squelched then came to life. The volume was too loud. A stupid mistake. Rogers reached into his back pack and turned it down while Dawson listened and replied.

"He wants to know what the hold up is." They continued on just as before.

An hour and two radio messages later, RaLang came to a halt. Dawson moved up. Thoung, Rogers and Jennings joined him. The trail, perfectly straight, dropped down gently then rose back up again. The woods were sparse on the right side.

"Good place to get shot, LT."

"Perfect. Shift everything to the left side?"

"Nothing else you can do. Bring the machine guns up?"

"Yeah. I better keep the rest of the people from running up our ass." Dawson radioed a request that the unit stay in place until they secured the area.

"What'd he say?" Rogers asked.

"He told me to make it snappy."

They were almost up the other side when RaLang put his hand to his throat. Just above them bunkers had been recently dug on each side of the trail connected by a narrow trench. They could see the fresh dirt that had not yet been camouflaged. No enemy soldiers were visible. Dawson signaled for two machine guns to come forward. He put them on line and they crawled forward on their hands and knees. The machine gunners extended the bipods and silently picked them up and put them down as they moved. They were within five meters of the bunkers when RaLang opened fire, immediately followed by their machine guns. Then the assault squads kicked in firing over their heads. A single B-40 rocket round, fired wildly exploded in the trees. Inaccurate AK fire was returned as the enemy attempted to flee. The firing tapered off. Dawson threw a grenade into a bunker as Rogers and his squad moved up.

"See if you can get to the end of the bunkers," Dawson yelled. Jennings moved his squad across the trail trying to trap the enemy. Suddenly, firing from their rear sent them diving to the ground, crawling for cover. M-79 rounds exploded in the trees. Dawson tried to reach for his handset as a chunk of a tree hit him in the head driving his face into the ground.

"Cease fire. Cease fire," he yelled joined by Rogers and Jennings. Getting to his radio he screamed. "Cease fire. You've got us pinned down for Christ sakes." Finally the firing stopped. "Everybody OK? Count heads. Everybody good? Let's go. Check the bunkers."

There was some blood. Enemy equipment, back packs, web gear, rice bag rolls, shovels were scattered throughout the bunkers. They found the rocket launcher and an AK.

"Are you sure everybody's OK?"

"Everybody but you. You got nicked in the head again, LT."

"How's it look?"

"Didn't bleed much. Pretty good lump. You'll live."

"RaLang, Thoung let's go." At the end of the row of bunkers they found an escape trail that curved around a big tree affording the enemy cover. They followed it a short way then returned to the main trail.

"Nice setup," Jennings observed.

"They're good at this. Hey, LT. You wanna wait for the rest of them to catch up?"

"No, let's keep moving. It's getting late. We need to find a place to RON." They moved off flanking the trail just as they had earlier.

"They want us to come back," Dawson said shoving the handset into his back pack.

"This is a pretty good spot to RON, LT."

"I told them that. We gotta go back. This is fucked up."

They stayed on the radio, as they entered the perimeter, to make sure nobody shot them.

"Who's in charge of this mess?" Dawson said.

"I am." He turned to see the major sitting on a poncho surrounded by a recon team for protection. Rogers squeezed his arm.

"I radioed for you guys to stay back while we cleared the area," Dawson continued, the anger in his voice coming through loud and clear. "Sir," he added.

"Did you get ambushed?" Captain Henry asked.

"No, we didn't get fucking ambushed! We owned them. Just as we were about to sweep the bunkers your clowns opened up and pinned us down. That gave them a chance to escape. Didn't you see their blood and equipment?"

"Anybody get hurt?"

"No, sir."

"The lieutenant got clipped in the back of the head when some asshole fired an M-79 round into the trees," Rogers corrected.

"Let me take a look at that." Dawson recognized the voice.

"Sergeant Nolan. I didn't know you made house calls," Dawson said calming down.

CHAPTER THIRTY-SIX

"WHAT THE HELL are they doing, sir?"

"How would I know? This is probably what it's like to be a regular infantryman. Spending all your time wandering around the jungle not knowing what's going on."

"We're not even wandering around. The longer we sit in one place, LT, the more time it gives the NVA to get their shit together."

Once again the platoon was bringing up the rear. The task force had been stopped long enough that they set up a perimeter and let the Bru eat.

"I wish we'd get going," Jennings said. "They kept bitching at us for moving too slow yesterday."

"Why you got a hot date waiting for you?" Rogers laughed.

"They were talking about a rice cache on the radio earlier. Maybe they're trying to destroy it," Dawson said.

"How do you destroy," Jennings words were cut off by the sound of gunfire someplace up ahead of them.

"RPD, LT."

"Yeah, it stopped pretty quick." Now all they heard was the crackling of M-16s. It was over in a few seconds. "Sounds like they taught the Nungs what cease fire means," Dawson said as he reached for his hand set to listen. After a few seconds, "Oh, shit!"

"What, LT?"

"They have KIAs."

"Americans?"

"Two. Here, take the radio," he said pushing his back pack to Rogers. "I'm gonna go check it out. "RaLang pa pa nai. Let's go."

They left their perimeter and started picking their way down the hill past a long line of soldiers sitting on the trail.

"Where are you going, Dawson?"

"Sorry, sir. I didn't see you," he replied, as he stepped over Captain Henry. "I'm gonna go check it out."

"Shouldn't you be with your platoon?"

"Sergeant Rogers has got it. Maybe, you should come with us, sir?" The captain followed with his RTO. They continued down the trail till they reached a spot were people were milling around like the enemy had run out of bullets. The major was seated talking on the radio. Bodies, now partially covered with ponchos, had been moved from where they had fallen. He saw where the column had stopped, but he didn't see any rice. Dawson tapped RaLang's shoulder, pointed at his eyes and motioned him forward. RaLange immediately switched to point man mode. As they passed the bodies the unforgettable smell of drying blood filled Dawson's nostrils. He quickly turned his head. A few meters away there was a bomb crater right up against the right side of the trail. The blast of the bomb had blown down a large tree that blocked their way. They climbed over it and came to a gully. An American was standing there holding an AK-47.

"They left this," he said, in obvious distress. Dawson nodded in sympathy, walked closer and quietly said,

"You better go back up with the others. There's no security here." As the man walked away RaLang inspected the gully and pointed out four bent grass spots where the enemy had lay in wait. Dawson found the machine gunner's position, dropped to his knees and looked back up the trail. From his vantage point anyone passing the bomb crater was slowed by the fallen tree and silhouetted. When the recon team moved out, it didn't have a chance.

"Trung uy," RaLang motioned him over to the west side of the trail. "VC," he said pointing to a large clump of bushes. Dawson leaned over and looked into a small opening that revealed a foot path tunneled through the thick vegetation.

"Yeah, VC go here," he agreed. They walked back up the trail, past the bomb crater, to the main group. Dawson borrowed the captain's radio and told Rogers to bring the platoon down.

Rogers went to work blowing trees to create an LZ for the medevac. Again and again he carried claymore bags filled with blocks of C-4 explosive down the side of the steep hill, taped them to tree trunks, climbed back up and set them off. It was tiring work. He discarded his rifle and web gear and continued unprotected. When Dawson saw, he sent Pong to guard him. Finally, Rogers was finished, he lay on the ground, soaked with sweat, guzzling water.

"If you worked that hard at Mai Loc we would have been living in a palace."

"Fuck you, LT."

Rogers did a good job clearing the area. With the trees down, the view was breathtaking. Towering behind them was the mountain they had just traversed. Now they were at the beginning of a ridge that sloped down to the valley. On each side it dropped off steeply into deep gorges then rose up again to parallel ridgelines. A great place for a cabin, but not a position any army would choose to defend. If they could stop getting held up by medevacs and continue their mission long enough to cross the border back into Vietnam, they wouldn't have to worry so much about defense.

Nolan was sitting next to the wounded Nungs, filing out Field Medical Cards and wiring them to what was left of their uniforms. On the back of each one KEEP IN US CHANNELS was stamped in big red letters. Dawson and Rogers walked over.

"You told me about these," Dawson said pointing to the stamp.

"It's not so important for the Nungs but if your Bru wind up in a Vietnamese hospital they won't treat them."

"That's what you told me. I've just never seen them before."

"That's because you've been pretty good at not getting your Bru shot up," Nolan said. "I hope I brought enough of these cards."

"I hope you have way more than you need. When's the medevac coming in?" he asked.

"Supposed to be on its' way." An artillery round whizzed overhead and slammed into the side of the hill behind them. They ducked reflexively.

"I hope that was ours," Dawson joked.

"Yeah. Looks like the major is trying to set a registration point. Maybe he should wait until after the medevac comes in. The pilot probably won't be too happy dodging 155 shells," Rogers said. "You better go tell him, LT." Dawson walked over and told the major. He wasn't very appreciative of the advice, but he stopped. The medevac came in and removed the dead and wounded.

It was getting late in the day so they were ordered to RON right where they were. Captain Henry ordered the platoon to form a line across the ridge, protecting the south section of the perimeter from the overlooking mountain.

"If we get attacked here, they'll be shooting right down our throat," Dawson complained. "Guess it was too much trouble to walk a couple hundred meters back up the hill."

"It they attack, I guarantee you, it will be from here, LT." Pushing out of the clearing they set up security and started digging, in the concealment of the woods. They dug narrow and deep just like the NVA. Rogers had them pile the dirt to the rear on the side away from the enemy.

"Good thing I was smart enough to bring shovels," Dawson joked. The other platoons were struggling with knives and canteen cups trying to make a dent in the red clay.

"Yeah, you're a real genius, LT."

"Why are you having them pile the dirt behind them?"

"If the enemy fires down this hill, they'll probably shoot over our heads. If the Nungs return fire they'll shoot us right in the back of the head."

"Now, who's the genius? Make sure they prop up the bipods on the machine guns so they don't just fire into the ground in front of them."

"Hey, sir, want me to have them dig you a hole behind the line?" Jennings asked.

"Yeah, and put a flag on it so the NVA know exactly where to shoot. Just set me up some place in the middle." When they were done, their thirty dug-in rifles and five machine guns were a formidable obstacle for any enemy.

"Hey, Jennings. Let the other platoons use our E-tools."

"Yes, sir."

"Just make damn sure you get them back."

The night was quiet. Dawson couldn't sleep in his cramped little hole so he got his gear and lay on the ground behind his position.

"Thought everybody was supposed to stay in their holes, LT."

"What are you doing out here?"

"Same thing you are."

"Wonder how the major's sleeping without a recon team to protect him?"

"Don't even go there, LT. That sergeant that got killed was a decent guy."

"I didn't mean any disrespect. Except for the major."

"Maybe you should try thinking first."

"Sorry. But you know if they put out security when they stopped, it wouldn't have happened."

"A little late to think of that now. They still planning on moving out in the morning?"

"As far as I know."

"Think the NVA will try to stop us?"

"If they move single file like they've been doing the NVA will keep hitting the point."

"Yeah, I figure the same thing. What if they put us on point?"

"Then we'll walk the artillery in front of us, if they'd let us, recon it by fire and blast our way down the hill. They don't have enough people to stop us."

"How do you know?"

"Because if they did, we'd be getting hit with mortars."

"Mortars! That's what I like about you, LT. Always thinking on the bright side."

Just by luck most of the Bru were in their deep holes when the NVA struck at exactly 0800 hours the next morning. The first B-40 rockets exploded in the trees, immediately followed by RDPs and AKs. Their sound was quickly drowned out by a tremendous volume of fire unleashed by the platoon toward the unseen enemy. Three artillery rounds exploded too high up the hill to do any damage, but they added shock effect. The firing subsided. In the best case scenario, the NVA were dragging off their dead and wounded.

"Hey, sir. Two of my guys got hit," Jennings reported.

"Thoung." No answer. "Hey, Thoung," Dawson called.

"Trung uy. One man tahan need bac si."

"Take them down to Sergeant Nolan."

Rogers and Dawson moved cautiously along the line making sure all of the Bru were OK.

"They fired off a lot of ammo, LT."

"Yeah, maybe that was the NVA's idea. I'm going to go check on the wounded."

"Thank God the artillery broke up the attack," Captain Henry said.

"Yeah, that's what did it, sir," Dawson replied. "Listen, sir, this is really important. Make sure that the medevac brings in a resupply of ammo and water." Henry didn't reply. He seemed distracted. "Sir, make sure the medevac brings in a resupply of ammo and water," he repeated.

"What? Oh, yes, I will. Do you have any wounded?"

"Three that I know of. I'm going to check now, sir."

"What have we got?" Dawson asked Nolan.

"These yours, sir?"

"I'm afraid so."

"This one's OK. You can have him back. A bullet shattered this one's ankle." Dawson looked at him curled up on the ground with his eyes closed. "And this one isn't going to make it. He got hit in the armpit into his chest. I mainlined him with morphine. You know him?"

"Of course, I do."

Finally, word came that the medevac was inbound. Dawson took four of his men to the edge of the LZ to unload the resupply and carry the wounded on board. As it landed, the Bru ran to the chopper and returned empty-handed.

"No have," one said. Then they loaded the wounded. The chopper took off to the west. As it turned north, it took a little ground fire.

"Where, the hell's, the resupply?" Dawson demanded. Captain Henry just looked at him. "We didn't get the resupply. Did you request it.?"

"I . . . of course, I did. It didn't come?

"No. It didn't come."

"You better go back to your troops, lieutenant."

"I hope you got water along with the ammo, LT. The little guys are getting pretty low."

"We didn't get shit."

"What do you mean?"

"I mean, we didn't get a resupply."

"Did you request it?" Dawson didn't dignify that question with a response.

"Did the captain request it?"

"Says he did."

"Do you believe him?"

"No."

For the rest of the afternoon they sat around waiting. Dawson got sick and tired of being asked when they were moving out. At exactly 1700 hours the enemy attacked down the hill again. Attacked is too strong a word. Probably chastened by the volume of fire the platoon returned in the morning, the NVA seemed more concerned with self-preservation than inflicting casualties. The platoon responded with a minimum of fire. Once again, three artillery rounds were fired into the hillside. When it was over the platoon returned to doing what it had been doing. Which was nothing.

bad. You're not planning on medevacing yourself, are you?"

"No sir. Don't worry."

"That's good. Sergeant Nolan, I'll be with the major. Come get me when you can tend to my wound."

"Yes, sir."

"Oh, Dawson, you'll be glad to know I have a resupply coming in."

"What an asshole," Nolan said, after the captain left. "I'm going to put a couple of sutures in your shoulder just to hold it together for now. I'll have to open it up and re-clean it when we get back."

"You carry sutures?"

"Yeah, I got everything in this bag, sir."

"You do? Then I have a job for you," Dawson explained what he wanted done.

"I can't do that, sir."

"You can't? Who risked going to jail sending money to your girlfriend from Australia?"

"You and Rogers did, sir, and I appreciate it. I gave you that pistol. But . . ."

"No buts. If you wanna get your ass out of here alive, you'll do what I tell you."

The resupply came in. Dawson and Rogers watched the Nungs unload it. When they were done Sergeant Nolan led Captain Henry to the chopper and helped him on. Then the major climbed aboard. The chopper took off.

"What the hell just happened?" Rogers asked.

"The captain got medevaced."

"He only had a scratch."

"Guess he went into shock."

"What'd you do, LT? This has your name written all over it."

"I had Nolan shoot him up and put him in la-la land."

"He did that?"

"Yeah, after I reminded him about Australia."

"What about the major?"

"I have no idea. I had nothing to do with that."

The ammo inventory Jennings prepared was pretty grim. They were down to about twenty-five percent of their basic load.

"This doesn't include the resupply, does it?

"No. sir."

"What'd we get?

"They brought in about 5 cans of water. The Nungs got most of that, but they need it worse than us. Radio batteries. A couple of days rations for the Nungs and Bru. Same for the Americans. They're breaking it down now, but it looks like five or six magazines each.

"What about machine gun ammo?"

"There wasn't any, sir."

"Go get Rogers, will ya." he said, shaking his head in disgust.

Dawson attempted to put on his web gear. Grimacing, he succeeded on the second try. He stood there thinking about all the people in movies who got the shit kicked out of them and were up running around, like nothing happened, in a matter of minutes. Realizing the Bru were staring at him, he gave them the thumbs up. They grinned and returned the gesture.

"Trung uy no can do carry radio," Thoung said. "Maybe have

one man tahan carry?"

'Thanks. I may take you up on that if we ever get out of here." Thoung didn't understand. Rogers approached.

"Where you been?"

"Down with Nolan, LT."

"Yeah, he tell you any good stories?"

"He's worried he's gonna get court-martialed."

"Did you tell him that's the least of his worries?"

"Don't even say that."

"Let's go to the ammo store."

A half hour later, they returned accompanied by three Nungs lugging ammo.

"Where'd you get all that?" Jennings asked.

"We bought it from the NVA," Rogers joked.

"The Nungs just gave it to you?"

"Yeah, after LT told them that if they didn't they could switch positions with us."

"I got something from them that's even better," Dawson said. "I got the call-signs for the artillery."

"Are we staying here, sir?"

"Looks that way for now. From what I could hear, it sounds like the higher-ups are pretty upset that the major bugged out. The Nung company commander, I just found out his name's Gardner, Captain Gardner, is in charge now and he's not volunteering to go anywhere. Why don't you guys pass out the ammo?"

"You need any, LT?"

"No, by the time I need it there will be plenty of it laying around."

Captain Gardner made his first visit to the platoon. Shocked, he observed the area.

"Jesus, the jungle is shot to hell up here. But, you're dug in pretty well," he added.

"Yes, sir. Starting to feel like home," Dawson replied.

"Don't get too used to it. We've been ordered to attack to the north tomorrow."

"With what, sir?"

"I requested another resupply of ammo and water. They're sending twenty thousand rounds of machine gun ammo. Do you think that will be enough?"

"If I can have half of it, sir."

"It's being air dropped. Do you know how to handle an air drop?"

"Yes, sir."

"Good. Here's the call-signs. I'll have my people recover the bundles."

"Thank you, sir."

"Don't thank me lieutenant. When we head out tomorrow you're taking the point."

They sat around waiting. Rogers was, apparently, an expert in aerial resupply.

"There're gonna have to fly straight up this ridge. Really low to make sure the parachutes don't blow into the gorge. Then pull up hard to keep from slamming into the mountain. It will feel like they're driving a car a hundred and thirty miles an hour straight at a brick wall. Plus, they're gonna be a huge target. No way the NVA won't fire on them. This will never work."

"Then, I guess, we should call it off," Dawson said sarcastically.

"I'm just saying, that's what's going to happen, LT. The only people who are going to get these bundles are the NVA."

Their position wasn't going to be hard to spot from the air, but they marked it with an orange panel anyway. When they heard the plane Dawson got on the radio.

"You're not going to believe this," he said.

"Believe what, LT?"

"The major's on the plane."

"What major?"

"Our task force commander. Major Cut and Run Chicken Shit. I'm talking to him."

"You're kidding?"

"Honest to God." The plane flew over, high above, located their position and circled around.

"Do they have an air escort."

"Nope. No Covey. No Spads. Just a big fat C-130." They made the first run low and slow, dropped a bundle and pulled up sharply just as Rogers had described. "The major is practically begging me to tell him if they're taking fire."

"What'd you tell him?"

"The truth. There're making a second run." This one was met with a volley of small arms fire from north-west of their position. "The major's crapping his pants."

"Did you tell him they took fire that time?"

"What fire?" he laughed. The plane made it's third and final run and departed. They watched as the parachute drifted across the landing zone and landed in the bottom of the deep gorge, just like the first two. "I really hate it when you're right," Dawson told Rogers.

"What are we going to do now, LT?"

"When we get out of here. If we get out of here. I'm going to get the words I DON'T FUCKING KNOW tattooed on my forehead."

They went back up the hill and prepared for the evening attack. 1700 hours came and went. 1730 hours came and went. By 1800 hours it was dark, so they gave up on the enemy and ate.

"After that air drop the Bru are starting to complain that we don't know what we're doing, LT."

"I'm surprised it took them this long to figure that out."

"How's your back?"

"You know that class where they teach you that rather than trying to ignore pain, you should focus right into it and ask yourself why you think the sensation is unpleasant?"

"No."

"If you ever have the chance to take it, don't. It doesn't work. Let's get some sleep. Charlie will probably be up bright and early in the morning."

At 0730 hours the next morning Dawson made a commo check with the artillery support base. He held the hand set and looked at his watch until the enemy's first B-40 rockets exploded at exactly 0800 hours.

"Fire Mission!" he called into the hand set. Speaking slowly he went through the commands, ending with "Danger Close." When he heard the "Shot Out" reply he yelled, "Get your Heads down!" several times then made himself as small as possible in the bottom of his hole. When artillery shells explode at a safe distance they make a two stage sound, something like Ka-Wumph. These rounds exploded twenty-five meters up the hill in front of the platoon with a shattering Wam, tearing through the attackers. Shards of steel tore branches off the trees above them, continued at deadly speed across the landing zone and over the Nung company. All firing stopped. As he gathered himself, Dawson heard the screams of enemy soldiers. He rose and took a look. One by one he watched Bru heads pop out of their holes like prairie dogs. Rogers looked at him. For once he didn't say a word.

As he cautiously picked his way down to the Nung position, Dawson remembered the heavy piece of shrapnel he had cut his hand on in orientation and how, with all of the world's amazing accomplishments and inventions, the kill or be killed cycle still remained an unsolvable problem. He snapped back. A wandering mind could bring his role in that cycle to an abrupt end.

"Are you crazy lieutenant? You could have gotten us all killed." Captain Gardner was more than a little upset.

"Did anyone get hurt sir?"

"No, but." Dawson interrupted by pointing up at the scars in the trees.

"It was pretty far above you, sir."

"Did you hit the enemy?"

"They stopped shooting and started screaming, sir."

"Get everybody saddled up we're moving out in twenty," Dawson called out to no one in particular.

"You want me to take the radio, LT.? It'll be tough on your

back."

"No, that's OK. I'm switching back packs with Thoung. I appreciate the thought," He quipped.

"Why don't you get one of the Bru to carry Thoung's?"

"I'd rather be a little uncomfortable than look different and be a target." Twenty minutes came and went.

"What are we waiting for, sir?" Jennings asked.

"Hey, Rogers. I can't get that tattoo soon enough," he laughed. "I don't know," he told Jennings. They continued to sit. The Bru, used to filling their spare time with eating, didn't know what to do. Dawson had them move back into their positions for security.

"So, how'd the captain like your artillery strike, LT?"

"He's not of big fan of precision."

"Yeah, well, you scared the hell out of me too." Thoung came over and handed Dawson the handset. Rogers watched intently as Dawson listened, nodding his head as if the captain could see him. The conversation ended.

"We're going home!"

CHAPTER THIRTY-EIGHT

"TAHAN GO DA NANG?" Thoung asked.

"Maybe go. Maybe no go. Trung uy don't know," Dawson laughed. Thoung grinned.

"Hey, LT, Captain Gardner wants to see you. Wants to know why you're not answering the radio."

"Did you tell him it's because the radio is in the bottom of my hole and unlike him, I actually get out of the hole once in a while?"

"Oh, it's going to be one of those days. I better go with you to keep you out of trouble."

Captain Gardner briefed them on the extraction. Because his company had come in to the area first, they were going out first. He'd run the communications then turn it over to Dawson.

"No sense changing horses in the middle of the stream. We'll run it," Rogers said.

"I saw what your lieutenant did with the artillery. No way I'm letting him take charge of the air power," Gardner replied as if Dawson wasn't even there.

"The lieutenant saved your ass."

"Changing horses in the middle of the stream. Where the hell did you get that?" Dawson laughed.

"What, were you just going to sit there and let him run the show?"

"Of course not, but I would have done it with a little more tact."

"No you wouldn't have." They stopped and told Nolan to pack up, then moved up to their positions.

"Hey, tahan go Da Nang?" Dawson called out as they reached the platoon. The Bru were all smiles and laughter and chatter.

"What time are we leaving, sir?" Jennings asked.

"1400 hours."

"That means 1500 hours."

"Probably. Listen, keep these guys in their positions and alert. After all we've been through, I don't want to lose anybody because we get stupid."

"Yes, sir."

"You got a spare battery? I don't want the radio to go south in the middle of this."

He sat by his position changing the radio battery, thinking that they were probably going to get hero medals for this operation. He remembered that old army saying: Give a guy a paycheck and he'll work for you. Give a guy a medal and he'll die for you. When he was done he made a commo check with Captain Gardner to make sure it worked. Jennings was right, it was 1500 hours when Covey came on station. Dawson and Rogers had moved down near Nolan's position.

"Where the hell you been, on R&R?" he called into the handset. He listened and then said to Rogers. "It's not No Neck. This guy's more serious." He carefully explained to Covey that they needed

Dawson's War

suppressive fire on the parallel ridge to the west and a lot of fire at the base of it three hundred meters to his northwest.

"Get your heads down," Covey advised. A Phantom jet roared out of the north and dropped 500 pound bombs into the gorge between the ridgelines, shaking the earth. Way too close. It scared the hell out of them.

"The captain's going to be real thrilled he gave you this job, LT." Dawson was back on the radio adjusting the fire. The first Marine CH-46 was inbound.

"Make sure the chopper approaches from the east and leaves back to the east. You will take fire if you fly out to the west. I repeat, you will take fire if you fly out to the west." The big helicopter landed. The Nungs broke ranks rushing to board, but Captain Gardner and his Americans got them under control quickly. When loaded, it took off toward the west and drew fire.

"I told you to exit back to the east. Charlie has a 51 caliber antiaircraft gun three hundred meters northwest of my position," Dawson warned. The next helicopter came in loaded, turned around and flew off to the east. Spads started working the antiaircraft position with their 20 mm cannons. The two helicopters were ferrying them, one platoon at a time to a nearby forward artillery base and returning.

"The NVA just brought in that antiaircraft gun, LT."

"Yeah, who knows what else is on it's way. Good thing we're getting out now."

Covey was careful to stay east while the Spads continued to duel with the antiaircraft gun. Eventually it went silent. A machine gun opened up from the west ridge placing accurate fire on the LZ. The

Spads quickly took care of it too. The rest of the extraction went smoothly. Finally, only the platoon was left. Jennings brought the Bru down from their positions and they waited for the helicopters to return.

"I'm gonna miss this place."

"You're getting drunk just thinking about getting drunk, LT."

"Here we go," he said as Covey was back on the radio. He listened and put the hand set down.

"What's the matter, LT."

"The motherfuckers are leaving us here."

CHAPTER THIRTY-NINE

THE BRU KNEW exactly what had happened the moment they were told to go back to their positions. Their grins faded and the chatter ended. Every eye in the platoon watched Dawson as he listened on the radio.

"What the hell happened, LT?"

"They said they had to refuel and couldn't get back before dark."

"This really sucks."

"You know sir, the NVA might not know we're here. They might think everybody got out," Jennings said.

"You know, you could be right." He stopped and thought for a moment. "If they come to see if we left any equipment behind they aren't going to walk all the way up the ridge like they do to attack us. They're just gonna to take that little footpath they used to ambush the recon team. Get a machine gun on it," he told Jennings.

"We gonna stay here?" Rogers asked.

"They said they'll send spooky gun ships from Thailand to box us in all night if we get into trouble and pull us in the morning."

"They'll probably find a way to fuck that up too."

"I don't know what other choice we have."

"We could slide down the east side of the ridge and disappear into the jungle," Jennings suggested.

"I thought of that, but we're too low on ammo. For now, I think we're better off here. The artillery is dialed in. If they try to hit us from above it will tear them to shreds and they know it. We'll go over the side as a last resort, but I think we're better off here for now. You good with this?" he asked Rogers.

"I don't like the idea of just sitting here all night. I'd much rather be on the move. But, we'd still have to set up another extraction and who knows how much shit we'd get into then? So, yeah, I guess I'm OK with this. I just hope they don't set up a helicopter trap, LT."

They braced for a early evening attack. Dawson checked in with the artillery support base, but it stayed quiet. Then it got dark.

"That was good news."

"What was good news, LT?"

"Just made contact with Moonbeam. Says he's got a Spooky sitting on the runway with our name on it."

"Does it have any gas?"

"Probably not."

"How's your back?"

"I'm too worried about everything else to worry about it."

"Don't worry, LT. Here's how this is gonna play out. Charlie's gonna attack in the morning. You're gonna blow the shit out of him with artillery. Then we're going to sit around for five hours until the choppers come and take us home. This time tomorrow night, we'll be drinking at the picnic table telling war stories."

"I can handle that."

"Besides, we've been holding off the NVA on our own this whole operation. The others were here, but they weren't in any position to help."

"You're forgetting one thing."

"What's that?"

"We used to have bullets."

Dawson lay behind his position staring off into the darkness until he finally fell asleep just before dawn. Something hit his glasses. Then on the side of his face. He opened his eyes. He was hit twice more on his head. Rain! Helicopters don't fly in the rain.

They didn't talk much that morning. There was nothing to say. They went about their business preparing for the enemy attack. At the fire support base, howitzers were loaded and locked into position. Their deadly projectiles would be fired in the time it took to pull the lanyard. They waited. The attack never came.

The Bru collected water that ran off the trees and ate. Some sharing the last of their rations. Dawson was arguing with someone on the radio when one of their machine guns fired. Carefully, in two round bursts, preserving the precious ammunition. It was joined by a couple of dozen single shot M-16 rounds. Dawson, caught off guard, dived into his hole for safety and stayed there for the seconds it took to be over. Four NVA lay on the LZ. Jennings was right, the enemy didn't know the platoon had been left behind. As predicted, they had come up the little path to search the position for abandoned equipment.

"Want me to collect their guns and ammo, sir?" Jennings asked. Dawson nodded yes. Rogers came over.

"You OK, LT?"

"Yeah."

"What's the matter?"

"I just froze up."

"Couldn't have been for long."

"No, but I couldn't get my head out of the hole."

"This ain't the movies, LT. Nobody's a hero all the time. Probably not a bad idea for you to keep your head down once in a while anyway. Here comes Jennings."

"There was a fifth body down behind the log. We got their AKs and magazine vests. Some are damaged where they got hit," Jennings reported.

"Thanks. Have your guys get the bodies off the LZ," Dawson said.

"Where do you want me to put them, sir?"

"I don't care just get them off the LZ and be careful not to get shot doing it. Oh, and make sure that gun is still focused on our back door in case they send anybody else."

"We got five AKs and six hundred rounds of ammunition, LT. That's a help."

"Yeah. Better than any resupply we got from our side. Thoung," Dawson called.

"Trung uy?"

"Have five tahan can shoot AK-47?"

"For sure. RaLang, Pong, Tam. Many tahan can do."

"OK good. Let RaLang keep his CAR-15. Give these out to the tahan who used to be VC."

"Tahan no VC."

"I know just trying to make a joke here."

Dawson was back on the radio. He purposely didn't tell them about the captured weapons and ammo, afraid they'd get some brilliant idea. Turned out it didn't matter.

"You're not going to believe this shit."

"What, LT?"

"We just got ordered to attack to the north."

"Who ordered you?"

"None other than the CCN commander, himself."

"What's he nuts?"

"Yes. Sounds like nobody bothered to tell him the resupply failed."

"What'd you say?"

"I asked him if he wanted us to throw rocks at the NVA. Then I declared a Prairie Fire Emergency."

"I thought Captain Gardner did that?"

"So did I."

"Won't make any difference if it doesn't stop raining."

"They say it's gonna clear up by late this afternoon."

"Now they start reading the fucking weather report?"

It was still early in the day. Dawson noticed the Bru were animated. They seemed to be speaking quietly looking around to make sure the Americans didn't hear. Or maybe he was just paranoid.

"Do you have any instantaneous grenade fuses?" he asked Rogers.

"Yeah. I've got a half dozen wrapped up in trip wire that I've been carrying around since I got here. Why?"

"We could use them to booby-trap the area about ten meters past the claymores."

"Thought we were getting out of here this afternoon."

"Maybe."

"What about the artillery?"

"I can't get it any closer than it is. If we get attacked and they get inside the artillery they'll trip the grenades and we'll know it's time to blow the claymores. After that it's up to our rifles."

"So you want me to set them up, LT?"

"Yeah."

"I hate the goddamn things. One false move and they'll go off on you."

"I thought you just turned them sideways or something."

"If you think it's so easy, I'll give them to you and you can do it."

"You're the demo expert."

"Those things scare the shit out of me."

"You know we should do it."

"Oh, what the fuck. If I blow myself up it's on you, LT."

"Take RaLang with you. Tell him not to step on the trip wire."

"That's real funny."

Dawson sat around for an hour waiting to hear a bang, watching the Bru. Finally, Rogers returned.

"Get them set up OK?"

"Yeah, Took ten years off my life, LT."

"Maybe it added fifty." After a while he said, "Hey, thanks."

The Bru heard it first. They quickly got into their positions. The Americans followed, not knowing why. There was an explosion from someplace down in the gorge. They waited and heard a faint 'thunk' from the west. Probably on the reverse slope of the parallel ridge.

Then an explosion, maybe closer, but still in the gorge. The third mortar round was also short. Then it stopped.

"Hand-held Chinese sixty millimeter mortar," Rogers said. Those things don't have any range without fin charges." He no sooner finished speaking when two enemy machine guns began placing fire on the landing zone. Dawson got on the radio. By the time he finished the firing had stopped.

"You gonna call a fire mission?" Jennings asked.

"No. We wouldn't hit anything. Covey's trying to get up."

"Are they gonna extract us, sir?"

"Don't get you're hopes up. Even if they can get the choppers in, we're too socked in for air support."

With no more enemy activity, the Bru were quietly talking again. Dawson moved along the line checking each position. His back was really starting to bother him. Most of the Bru grinned and gave him the thumbs up. Others wouldn't look him in the eye. He sat beside Thoung and took some darvon.

"Bac si no fix?" Thoung asked.

"I'll be OK. What's going on with the tahan?"

"Tahan Ok, trung uy."

"No they're not."

"Maybe one man tahan speak tahan fini war, go home."

"And leave the Americans?"

"Yes, trung uy."

"What do the tahan say?"

"Beaucoup tahan say no. Some man tahan say maybe."

"Who's telling the tahan to go?"

"One man Pong." Dawson got up and moved to Pong's

position. He unsnapped his CAR-15, took out three of his last magazines and made a big deal out of presenting them to Pong. He gestured for the AK-47 and ammo vest. Pong handed them over.

"Pong number one tahan," Dawson said as he smiled, patted him on the shoulder and gave him the thumbs up. Pong returned the thumbs up, but he couldn't quite get to the smile. Rogers had watched the whole thing.

"What the hell was that all about?"

"With a little luck, I just put down a revolt."

"Why'd you give Pong your CAR-15?"

"Because, if the sneaky little bastard had an AK, he might think he could shoot me and get away with it."

The Bru seemed to settle down. Quietly speaking among themselves. The Americans just sat around waiting, for what they didn't know, as long minutes turned into hours.

"You know what's funny about this?" Dawson asked.

"There's nothing funny about this, LT. He moved closer to listen. "OK, tell me what's so funny."

"We want the same thing the NVA want."

"What?"

"All we want to do is get the fuck out of here. All Charlie wants us to do is get out of here so he can go back to moving his supplies. He's trying to figure out what we're doing. Probably thinks we're part of some diabolical stay-behind operation. No way he thinks the only reason we're here is because the Marines ran out of gas."

"Yeah, so why don't you just tell them?"

"If it was that simple we probably wouldn't be here in the first place."

Late in the afternoon, the weather cleared and Covey got airborne. Rogers and Jennings watched as Dawson had a long and angry conversation on the radio. When it ended he turned and said,

"Two things. One, we're not being extracted today. Two, the Marines pulled out."

"What does that mean for us, sir?"

"We get to stay here another night with no artillery support."

CHAPTER FORTY

"YOU EVER THINK about getting killed, LT?"

"You mean besides now?"

"Yeah."

"Not really. I mean, of course, I know I can get killed. Everybody does. But when we get in a fire fight I always think we're gonna win."

"We've been pretty lucky."

"Actually, we're pretty careful. No, I always thought that if I was gonna buy it, it would be because they stuck us into a loaded LZ and we'd get overwhelmed immediately. You know, just a big frenzy and I'd be dead before I had a chance to think about it."

"Yeah, not this drip, drip shit. You run out of food. You run out of water. You run out of bullets. They take away the artillery. It's one thing if you fuck up and get yourself killed. But this thing's been screwed up since day one. How do you think it's gonna turn out, LT?"

"I don't know. I feel like I'm at the fucking Alamo."

There were reports that the enemy was massing around them so a rotation of C-47 Spooky gunships had boxed them in all night long.

They set up a strobe light in the middle of the LZ. The planes, flying low beneath the clouds, with only the darkness to conceal them, used it as a guide to fire stream after stream of red tracers into the surrounding jungle. Every time the firing stopped, a lone NVA soldier would pop up and fire a few rounds from his AK at the plane. They dubbed him the bravest man in the North Vietnamese Army. The last plane departed just before 0600 hours as it started to get light through the heavy cloud cover. The men of the platoon braced themselves, their backs against the dirt walls, rifles at their shoulders, pointing up the hill. They were hungry, tired and thirsty, but compared to the lack of ammunition, those were now minor inconveniences. Make every bullet count was no longer just a military cliché. Today it would be a matter of survival.

At exactly 0800 hours the battle began as mortar rounds exploded on the LZ sending deadly shrapnel into their positions. The piles of dirt they had put behind their holes to protect them from the Nungs allowed them to keep their heads up, watching the hill. After thirty or forty rounds the barrage ended. One of Rogers' booby-trapped grenades went off. Then silence. They heard an NVA shouting commands. All at once, the enemy opened up with B-40 rockets, machine guns and AKs, driving the platoon deep into their holes. The rocket fire stopped, but the light weapons fire continued as the enemy began to move forward. They started throwing hand grenades, but they were coming up short. Another of Rogers' booby-traps exploded. The NVA ignored it. Then a third went off. The firing slowed for a few seconds then resumed. They started firing rocket propelled grenades again, but they were high in the trees for fear of hitting their comrades. Now, for the first time Dawson saw the enemy. He blew two claymores sending hundreds of steel pellets effectively into the advancing troops causing them to fall back. The platoon began to fire their weapons. Carefully aiming, one bullet at a time, they shot the enemy soldiers as they tried to retrieve those wounded by the claymores. The enemy fell back. It became silent.

"Casualties," Dawson called.
"We're OK here, LT."
"I got two. Minor no big deal," Jennings replied.
"Thoung, you OK?"
"OK, trung uy. Maybe VC no come back. Get helicop."

The day was getting brighter as the clouds burned off. Dawson tried to raise Covey. Failing, He got Hillsboro and requested air support.
"Any good news, LT?
"Hillsboro is trying to get Covey up," he said as mortar rounds exploded in the trees over their heads, driving them down in their holes. The barrage continued for minutes, causing casualties. The second they stopped, B-40 rockets began exploding low in the trees, quickly replaced by RPDs and Aks and simultaneously a booby-trapped grenade exploded. Knowing the enemy was close, Dawson blew two more claymores without even looking. He rose with the AK and began firing. The enemy was advancing. The brave ones, running forward, were easily shot. The ones firing from behind trees, more difficult. All up and down the line soldiers fought their own individual battles, alone in their little hole in the ground, unaware of what was going on around him. See. Aim. Kill. Ducking from rounds that had already passed by. Rogers blew two claymores. The enemy

fell to the ground, then got back up and continued moving forward. Every instinct in Dawson's body was telling him to get down in the hole, if only for a moment of safety. But, he knew, if he did, he wouldn't have the courage to rejoin the fight. Even as fear buckled his knees, his training took over. His mind slowed the battle down, as if the enemy was moving in slow motion and he was at full speed. As targets appeared he shot them, but they just kept coming. Resigned to death, fear was replaced with ferocity. The heavy AK-47 felt powerful in his hands with its deep sound. He kept aiming and firing, as enemy bullets slammed into the dirt pile behind his head. Every time he thought they had beaten them back more would appear. How, the hell, many men were they willing to lose? A whistle blew. The enemy stopped firing and moved back up the hill. Insanely, he still wanted to kill. He gathered himself. Adrenaline caused his body to tremble.

"You OK?" Dawson called to Rogers.

"Yeah."

"Jennings?"

"Little ding, sir. No big deal." he replied.

"We can't take another shot like that. You think they've gonna try round three, LT?"

"I don't know. How are you fixed for ammo?"

"My last magazine is in the gun."

"I've still got almost sixty rounds for the AK. Here I'll throw you two magazines for your M-16."

"Where'd you get them?"

"I held them back from Pong." They braced and waited.

"I can hear them moving, LT. Do you think this is it?"

Dawson ignored the question. He bent down and spoke on the

radio. In a moment he raised back up.

"Let' em fucking come. I've got Covey and two Spads on station." Rogers looked at him.

"Thank God," he said softly.

"Don't tell the little guys. Keep them sharp."

A marker rocket slammed into the hillside. Within seconds 20mm cannon ripped through the forest above them. Keeping their heads down, little hands appeared above the holes flashing the thumbs up signal. He imagined he could see them grinning.

For the next hour and a half Dawson viciously directed air strikes. Constantly claiming to be under fire, he demanded more and more sorties of Spads. Saturating the hillside above and to the west with cannon fire, napalming the parallel ridge and finally dropping 500 pound bombs on the area to their north-west he believed to be the enemy's base camp. The transports arrived from the east. Jennings took half the platoon on the first. It turned and flew back out to the east as directed. Quickly the second landed. Dawson stood on the ground at the base of the tailgate, watching the Bru helping the wounded aboard. Rogers stopped beside him.

"Go ahead, LT," he called into his ear over the noise of the rotors.

"No, for the first time in this fucked up operation, the commander is going to be the last man off the ground." He followed Rogers up the ramp. The helicopter turned around and rose. Dawson looked down on the still smoking carnage below. No one would want to build a mountain cabin there now, he thought.

The crew chief busied himself getting the Bru to point their weapons toward the floor. He needn't have bothered. Most of them were out of bullets. They off-loaded at Quang Tri. A Marine captain approached along with one of the pilots.

"Who's in charge here?" he asked.

"I am," Dawson said.

"Who are you?"

"Captain Dawson," he lied.

"Where you going?'

"Da Nang. Marble Mountain."

"It may be a while before you can get a flight. We can send your seriously wounded to the ARVN hospital. The others we can treat at the aid station."

"I can't let these guys go to a Vietnamese hospital, Can't we get some quicker transportation? "

"Give us a chance to refuel and we'll take you," the pilot offered.

"That would be great, Thanks a lot."

"Don't thank me. This is a story I'm going to tell my grandchildren. How I flew into Laos and rescued, I don't know, whoever you people are."

"SOG," Dawson said. You'll be able to tell them about it in about twenty years, when it gets declassified." It took a long time to refuel, but finally they got airborne and landed on the CCN helipad before dark. Dawson thanked the pilots and gave each an AK-47. They were thrilled.

They didn't exactly expect a parade, but maybe a couple of people could have bothered to greet them. They walked through the camp helping the wounded to the aid station. On the way, they ran into Major Capra dressed in civilian clothes.

"Got a date, sir?" Dawson said sarcastically. Gesturing with his rifle.

"Dawson, Rogers what are you doing here?"

"Yeah, I guess it's a surprise after you guys did all you could to get us killed."

"Watch what you say lieutenant. Heads are already rolling over this operation."

"Yeah, well let me know if there's anything I can do to help with that."

"Remember what I told you lieutenant. Shit rolls down hill."

"It ain't rolling this far and after what we've just been through I'm not about to take any of it either." He added, "Sir."

"Sergeant Rogers, maybe you should calm the lieutenant down a bit."

"Oh, I hope he's just getting started, sir." They continued on, leaving Major Capra standing there.

They got to the aid station and, of course Nolan was there. He quickly checked out the Bru.

"Only two are serious, but they'll live. The rest are just pulling shrapnel, cleaning and stitching. Can you have some of your men get their equipment out of here? I'll get a couple of other medics and we'll have them all fixed up in a few hours."

"How about taping up Jennings' arm so we can go get a drink?" Rogers asked. They agreed to go dump their gear and meet at the picnic table.

The table was littered with beer cans, glasses and half-eaten cheeseburgers.

"What was the shit about you telling that Marine you were a captain, LT?"

"I didn't need him trying to give me orders. So I equaled out the ranks. Besides, I only lied by a couple of months."

"Whoa! There's a news flash. I thought you couldn't wait to get out of this man's army?"

"I'm thinking about it. I'm not sure. I shouldn't have said anything." They talked and drank and replayed the battle.

"So, I shot this one guy three times and he keeps coming and all I can think is, come on, fall down, I'm running out of ammo for Christ sakes," Jennings recounted.

CHAPTER FORTY-ONE

DAWSON MADE HIS way back to his billet. He was filthy and didn't want to dirty his rack so he propped his back pack up against it, sat on the concrete floor, took off his boots, leaned back and fell asleep quickly. He opened his eyes slowly the next morning, not knowing which hurt more his shoulder or his head. A girl in black pajamas came into focus. She was reaching up cleaning something. Her pants had slid down low on her hips which tapered to a small waist of smooth skin and cute belly button. She lowered her arms, her shirt dropped and the view disappeared. Realizing he was awake she said,

"Trung uy beaucoup dinky dou."

"No, I don't think I'm drunk anymore. But I stink."

"Linh wash," she said.

"Linh?" he laughed.

"Yes, Linh. What so funny?"

"Nothing. You speak good English."

"I go school one year English," she said proudly as she gathered up soap and towels.

"Why are you working here as a maid?"

"No hieu biet, no understand." She didn't want to tell him.

Dawson got to his feet. Linh took his hand and led him to the shower. He stood under the almost warm water and leaned his arms against the wall. Linh gently washed him. Beneath the water streaming down his face tears flowed. The transition from brutality to kindness overwhelmed him. When she was done, he dried himself and they returned to his room. As she gathered up her cleaning supplies and began to leave Dawson said,

"Thank you. I hope I see you again."

"Trung uy see Linh again," she assured.

The Bru stopped cleaning their weapons as the Americans entered the barracks and starting calling out trung uy, trung si, displaying their bandaged wounds with pride. Dawson, Rogers and Jennings walked around thanking and congratulating them. They didn't understand the words, but they got the point.

"What's the casualty count?" Dawson asked.

"We had one killed, three seriously wounded, that we probably won't get back, and twenty-four lightly wounded, sir," Jennings replied. "Could have been a lot worse, sir." Dawson walked over and spoke with RaLang and Thoung, then he stopped by Pong who didn't look up.

"As usual RaLang, Thoung and Rogers came out without a scratch," he joked.

"That's the difference between amateurs and professionals, LT," Rogers laughed. "The idea is not to get a purple heart, not see how many oak leaf clusters you can stick on it."

"At least the lieutenant got himself cleaned up for a change," Jennings joined in good-naturedly.

"Got a hot date, LT?" repeating what Dawson had asked Capra

the night before. Dawson, of course, initially thought he was talking about Linh, before he got it.

"You're gonna have to take care that they get their bandages changed so we don't end up with a lot of infections."

"Maybe you should take your own advice, LT, and go see Nolan."

"I'll take care of getting the Bru reloaded with ammunition, sir."

"No hurry. We're not going anywhere for a while."

"When's the debriefing, LT?"

"I haven't heard a thing."

"That's weird."

Dawson went to the S-2. Fallon told him they weren't going to be debriefed. The after-action report was closed. Dawson read it.

"This is garbage," he said tossing it on the desk when he finished. The only true part is about the trucks on the first night. Rogers and I did that. The major didn't even know about it till the next morning. You remember that's the road Peterson and I found back in June or July?" Fallon opened the report and checked the coordinates on a map.

"You're right. The road that leads to the top of the A Shau."

"Yeah, the road that SOG said was just a diversion."

"They're using it?"

"Well, they blew up trucks on it. Do you think it's important?"

"Probably. But nobody's going to do anything about it anyway."

On the way out, he ran into Major Capra.

"Dawson. In my office." Once inside Capra slammed the door. "Who the fuck do you think you are, lieutenant, waving your rife around in my face last night?"

"I didn't wave my rifle around in your face, sir. That was the most fucked-up operation I've ever seen."

"So, you had to sit there an extra couple of days. I got you extracted."

"A couple of extra days! In those extra days, all but six of my Bru were wounded. We probably shot a hundred NVA. None of us had more than a half magazine left when we finally got airpower. How would you know? Fallon says you don't even want an after-action report, for Christ's sake." Dawson was furious, but he remembered to add, "Sir."

"No, I don't know any of this. Go get Sergeant Rogers. I'll instruct Fallon to include an annex in the after-action report. You know the two company commanders and the major were relieved. They've been sent back to 5th Group."

"Yeah, well, they're probably not too unhappy about that."

"They will be when they read their efficiency reports. Their careers are done."

"Whoever was stupid enough to put that desk jockey major on the ground, in the first place, is the one who ought to get shit canned."

"You definitely don't want to go there, lieutenant."

The debriefing was short.

"OK. So when they extracted the task force they left you on the ground because it got too dark to continue helicopter operations. They next day it rained. You were short of ammo. The artillery support was withdrawn. On the last day you repelled numerous enemy attacks sustaining one KIA and twenty-six WIA. You were extracted by helicopter. Is that accurate?" Fallon asked.

"Doesn't sound like we did much when you say it that way," Rogers said.

"When it hits the intelligence annex for distribution all it's gonna to say is that an indigenous, platoon size paramilitary unit of unknown origin encountered a superior enemy force at the location and date. Rating A6. Impeccable source. Information cannot be verified."

"It can be verified by Covey and the pilots who got us out," Dawson said.

"Not if they don't exist."

"Did we take the pressure off the Marines? That was our mission."

"They pulled the Marines out the day you hit the ground."

"Fuck this. This is bullshit. I'm going to see Nolan and get patched up."

"See you at the picnic table, LT."

"What do you people think you're doing drinking during duty hours," Dawson said, mocking Captain Henry.

"Guess we won't have to worry about him anymore. Want me to get you a beer, sir?" Jennings asked.

"Yeah, thanks. Get a couple of rounds," he replied reaching for some money.

"We don't need that. Major Capra's buying."

"Guess I should wave a gun around in his face more often."

"How's you're back, LT?"

"Hurts a lot more now that Nolan fixed it," he said sliding onto the bench. Their conversation was a lot more subdued than the night before. After a few drinks they returned to talking about the battle.

"We were really lucky to get out of there," Jennings observed.

"No, if we were lucky we wouldn't have gotten stuck in that position in the first place," Rogers replied. "What do you think, LT?"

"I don't know."

"I thought you were going to get that tattooed on your forehead," Rogers laughed.

"I'm not a big fan of luck," Dawson continued. "This was all on the Bru. I don't think one of them hid in the bottom of their hole. They just aimed and fired. They were absolutely fearless. We've got one hell of a platoon here."

"Well, don't get too used to it, LT. I'm outta here in a month."

"I've still got three months," Jennings said. "When you leaving, sir?"

"I don't know." He repeated. They laughed. "My tour's up in about a month and a half."

"Don't tell me you're gonna extend, LT?"

"Maybe. I'm thinking about it.."

"That's crazy. Why would you do that?"

"Well, if you asked my father, he'd probably say it's because I want to walk around profiling in my Green Beret." Dawson smiled.

"How's that working out for you, LT?"

"Not so good. No, I feel like I belong here. I'm comfortable. But, most of all, I don't want some asshole taking over and getting the Bru killed."

"You're gonna have to leave them sooner or later and you know they're going to get killed anyway. That's just a fact, LT."

"Yeah, unfortunately you're right."

"So, why stay?"

"Do you think they would have attacked the third time, sir?" Jennings asked wanting to change the subject.

"No, I think they were done. They lost too many people and with the sky clearing they had to know that we'd get air support. There wasn't going to be a third attack."

"Did you really believe that at the time, LT?"

"Yeah. Of course, then it was more of a hope than a belief. Their commander may have ordered them to attack again, but they already lost all their good fighters. What was left would have gotten half way down the hill and quit.

"So we won, sir?"

"Yeah, we won in the sense that if they knew how it was going to end they would have never started it in the first place."

"Sounds like you just summed up this whole goddamned war, LT."

CHAPTER FORTY-TWO

AFTER A FEW welcomed days off, sitting around waiting for everyone to heal up became tedious. The Bru could only clean their weapons and equipment so many times. Jennings had a weird gunshot wound. A bullet had entered his forearm just below the elbow, slid along, just under the skin and came to a stop with a visible lump in his wrist, doing little damage. It had obviously gone through something before hitting him. He spent a couple of hours each day taking the Bru to the dispensary to get their wounds cleaned and bandages changed.

They sat around the picnic table drinking every evening. By the time it got dark, the conversation always returned to the last two days of the operation. Though separated by little more than a half-dozen body lengths, they had each fought very different battles. Jennings, on the right flank, didn't receive the heavy infantry rush. His biggest threat were the mortars bursting in the trees. Dawson in the center, with the luxury of four thirty-round AK magazines, concentrated on shooting every enemy he could target. While Rogers, counting down his ammunition with each pull of the trigger, dared fire only at the enemy who could overrun their line. Word of their action had spread around the camp. During the evening, soldiers would drop by to hear tales of the battle. Rogers became the unlikely spokesman for the group. The number of enemy they had faced was directly proportional to the number of rum and cokes he had consumed. When they were drunk they'd return to their billets.

Nolan had determined that Dawson's wound was infected, so he had debrided and sutured it. Dawson thought it would have healed just as well if he had left it alone. Now it hurt constantly. But with the pain, there was opportunity. He used it as an excuse to lie around each morning waiting anxiously for Linh to arrive and clean his room. They would chat, mostly about her school. He wanted to ask her about the war. But, real or imagined, he perceived she had a sense of pride or purpose not normally associated with someone tasked to clean rooms. He knew the fishing village she came from was full of VC or, at the least, sympathizers. The attack on the camp had been staged there. So he didn't ask, thinking he wouldn't get the truth, that he didn't want to hear, anyway. Nevertheless, one morning he patted the side of his bed and motioned her over. She looked away long enough that he thought he a made a mistake. Then she walked to him and sat. After an awkward moment, she said,

"Trung uy want boom boom?"

The Bru were healing up. Rogers was getting short. Linh was a lot of fun. Dawson went to TOC to see Major Capra.

"If I extend for six months can I keep my platoon, sir?"

"When's your tour up?"

"May 1, sir."

"Is that the same as your date of rank?"

"Yes, sir."

"So, you'll make captain."

"Depends on my efficiency report," Dawson laughed.

"Don't worry about that. You've been on the ground long enough. If you extend I'll make you my assistant operations officer."

"I appreciate that, sir. But I'd only extend to stay with the platoon."

"You'd be the company commander. You can do whatever you want with the platoon."

"So I can definitely do this? Same company? Same platoon? I don't want to extend then find out I'm getting stuck behind a desk. No offense, sir."

"Yeah. I'm here for almost another four months. I can't guarantee anything after that."

"Thanks, sir. I'm gonna need a replacement for Rogers. He has less than twenty days left."

"I'm going to have to put you back out in the field before then."

"It'll be a few days before the Bru, Jennings and I get the stitches out from the last operation. Rogers is too short." Major Capra picked up a piece of paper from his desk.

"I have you scheduled for a Base Area 607 target. I can move you to a tango target north of Route 9. Area recon. Not much more than training, but we have the mission. Five days in and out."

"Rogers is too short to go across the street."

"A tour is three-hundred sixty-five days, lieutenant. Oh, and by the way, Rogers, Jennings and you are being decorated Saturday morning. A Marine general is presenting. See if you can find a clean fatigue jacket with insignia."

"That was quick. Thank you, sir."

Saturday morning arrived. The Hatched Force companies were to assemble in formation on the helipad. It should have been simple. But it wasn't.

Hey, sir. The Bru want to carry their web gear and weapons," Jennings called.

"Why?"

"I don't know." Dawson walked with him to the barracks.

"Where's Rogers?"

"He's inside, sir." They climbed the steps and entered.

"They want to carry their weapons, LT."

"Thoung."

"Trung uy."

"Why tahan take M-16, machine gun?"

"Be tahan!" he replied, making a fist and thumping his chest.

"OK."

"You're going to let them carry their weapons, sir?"

"Sure. Why not? They want to look like soldiers. They earned it. Get'em to the helipad."

"This is going to be beautiful, LT."

"I know," Dawson laughed.

When they got to the helipad the other platoons were already there. It was obvious that the Nungs had been taught what a formation was. The Americans with the other Bru platoon were keeping them in ranks, but with difficulty. They moved the Bru into the gap in the formation. Jennings tried to get them lined up, failing miserably. Rogers and Dawson watched and laughed.

"Sir, as soon as we go up front to get our medals this is going to turn into a real shit show." Jennings was laughing now. Dawson walked toward the Bru and gave out a short, sharp whistle to get their attention. He pointed two fingers toward the ground then raised his hand pointing the same two fingers toward his eyes. The Bru immediately fell silent and moved into a fighting formation. Weapons at the ready, two columns back with the V-shaped point squad forward.

"Thoung, have tahan stay. Tahan stay. Stay." It sounded like he was talking to a dog.

"You gonna leave them like that, LT?"

"Yep. I think they look kinda cool."

"I'm sure the colonel will agree with you."

The ceremony began. First a major, who had been the liaison with the Marines at the fire support base, got the Silver Star. As Dawson, Rogers and Jenning received Bronze Stars for Valor, the Bru called out trung uy, trung si. Other than that, they were well-behaved as a few other medals were passed out. The ceremony ended. As they took the Bru back to the barracks, they walked right past the colonel, who, of course, couldn't keep his mouth shut.

"Your troops don't know how to stand in formation, lieutenant?"

"No, sir. They're combat troops," Dawson replied, and kept walking, listening to hear if the colonel wanted to press it. But he didn't.

"You know why we got these medals so fast, don't you, LT?"

"Yeah, we were cover for the major's bullshit Silver Star."

Dawson lay on his bed, his head propped up by his elbow, looking down over Linh's smooth body. He thought about their first time and how she had protested,

"No good! No good! Chop, chop glick same, same dog," He laughed out loud. "What so funny?" she asked

"You," he said tickling her. As if reading his mind she said, "Ruff-ruff."

Later he told her he was going away for a few days.
"Where go?"
"To do my job."
"Where?"
"Wanna see on a map?"
"You have map?"
"No. I no have map," he laughed, tickling her again.

"So I told Linh I was going out and she wanted to know where," Dawson said opening another beer.
"What'd you tell her, LT?"
"I showed her on a map."
"You showed her on a map?" Jennings got excited. Rogers laughed.
"No, of course, not."
"Do you think she's a VC, sir?"
"How would I know? About the best you can hope for is that they're on whichever side is winning."
"Maybe you should tell somebody, sir."
"Tell them what? That maybe she's a VC. They'd probably replace her with some fat, hardcore commie who doesn't put out." They laughed.

The last helicopter departed. Jennings moved his squad into the tree line. Dawson and Rogers knelt at the edge of the LZ, checking the map and waiting for their ears to clear before contacting Covey to verify their position. Two short bursts of fire sent them sprawling flat on the ground.

"What the fuck. Not already."

"Thought this was supposed to be a dry hole, LT." There was no more firing.

"VC shoot! VC shoot," Thoung called out as he came running over.

"What happened?" Dawson asked.

"Trung uy come see." They followed him a short way into the wooded area. RaLang and Tam were milling around. Dawson noticed that the cover over RaLang's ejector port of this CAR-15 was open.

"VC shoot Pong," he said. Dawson took a look and contacted Covey.

"I've got a kilo india alpha down here. I need you to turn one of the slicks around to get the body out."

"Straw hat?" Covey asked, using the deliberately misleading code word for American.

"They're all the same to me. Let's do this fast so we can get moving."

"Is the LZ hot?"

"No we just bumped heads. The enemy scattered." The task was completed in fifteen minutes and they were ready to move out. Dawson stood by Thoung and said softly,

"So, RaLange VC, huh?" Thoung grinned. Later when they took a break Jennings asked,

What the hell happened on the LZ, sir?"

"Just a little Bru justice," Dawson replied.

They worked their way up the steep mountain and meandered around the high ground for three days effectively turning an area recon into a search and avoid operation. The Bru had carried four of the entrenching tools with them. Each night they wanted to dig in. But, because there were no signs of the enemy Dawson wouldn't let them, preferring to stay stealthy. At the end of the third day they found a perfect little hill top and set up their RON.

"You should let them dig about a hundred holes and really confuse the hell out of Charlie, LT."

"Only problem is we're so far up this mountain that it could be years before Charlie finds them."

"The major's not going to be real proud of you for this operation."

"All we gotta do is get you out of here in one piece. How many days will you have left when we get back?"

"When are we getting extracted?"

"I figure we'll get water tomorrow and set up near an LZ tomorrow night. Get out the next day."

"That will leave me with eight days then. How about you?"

"My tour's up fourteen days after yours. But I'm going to hang around a little longer to make sure I get promoted to captain before I leave."

"So you can go profiling around home in your green beret. Captain?"

"Exactly." They quietly laughed.

"You going back to Bragg?"

"No, LT. I'm going to the 10th Special Forces Group in Bad Tolz, Germany."

"Whoa, lock up the frauleins. Why didn't I already know that?"

"Because you never asked. It's an accompanied tour. I'm taking my wife."

"That's a waste."

"Yeah, well, I wish I'd get promoted. I could use the extra money."

"They tend to hold a grudge when you smack an officer around."

"Yeah, it's really not fair."

"Why?"

"Because if I punched you, LT, they'd not only promote me, they'd give me a medal."

They broke camp and moved silently down the mountain. After about an hour and a half they found the small stream they were looking for, near its source.

"Let's make sure we do this right. Today's not a day for fuckups," Dawson admonished. They placed machine gun teams on the flanks and to the rear, bringing the last two guns along with an assault squad parallel facing the creek. "All set?" he asked.

"Ready as we'll ever be, LT." As RaLang went to move forward, they took fire from deep in the jungle on the other side of the creek. The Bru responded furiously. Sending hundreds and hundreds of rounds toward the unseen enemy. Shredding the jungle and cutting down small trees. Their firing began to subside. Dawson listened carefully through the noise. He didn't hear any enemy fire, but the crackle of the platoons M-16s and the occasional burst of their machine guns continued.

"Cease fire," he shouted. "Cease fire." The Bru kept shooting.

"You'd think they'd have learned to conserve ammo from the last time, LT," Rogers called out from about six feet away.

"Cease fire." Dawson rose to one knee. Suddenly, a volley of AK rounds ripped past him. He slammed himself back to the ground. The Bru responded quickly, silencing the gun. Finally, the Bru stopped firing. "That was a little too close," Dawson said, pushing himself off the ground. As he moved to observe, he was hit with a tremendous pain. Rogers stared at him. The pain burned his heart and tore through his guts. Staggering him. He dropped to his knees and cried out in anguish. Rogers still stared. Rogers was dead.

CHAPTER FORTY-THREE

"TRUNG UY SAD?" she asked.

"Yeah, I'm sad."

"Because trung si die?"

"Yes."

"Maybe Linh can fix?"

"Maybe I can fix," he corrected.

"What mean I?"

"I. It's a pronoun," he said sharply.

"Maybe not so sad. Maybe trung uy angry?"

"It's hard to tell the difference." Dawson tried to console himself. Rogers would have been leaving in ten days. He probably would have never seen him again anyway. It made perfect sense in his head, but it wasn't working worth a damn in his heart.

Drinking alcohol from a 105mm artillery shell casing at special events is a long honored military tradition. For Lieutenant Alan Dawson it resulted in an almost total memory loss of the night he was promoted to captain. By the next afternoon, with the aid of several darvon capsules and a couple of warm beers, he was able to perform rudimentary tasks like walking and talking. He joined

Jennings in the Bru barracks.

"Trung uy, tahan want go Da Nang," Thoung informed him.

"No trung uy. Dai uy," Dawson replied, pointing to the new captain's bars pinned to his otherwise blank fatigue shirt.

"Trung uy. Dai uy. Dai uy," Thoung called out. The rest of the Bru stood and called out dai uy over and over.

"You got promoted, sir?"

"That's what they tell me," he joked.

"Congratulations! Rough night?"

"Brutal."

"Tahan can do go Da Nang, dai uy?" Thoung asked.

"I'm not getting anybody out of jail," Dawson replied. The simple mountain tribesmen had discovered that they could get things for free by pointing a 45 caliber pistol at shop clerks.

"Tahan no go jail," Thoung smiled slyly, as if any such thing was out of the question.

"You gonna get them, if they get in trouble?" he asked Jennings.

"Sure, sir."

"OK. Ten man tahan can go," Dawson said, holding up ten fingers.

"RaLang can go?"

"Of course, he's the only one who can throw the pistol over the wire." They were searched for weapons at the gate.

"RaLang no throw pistol."

"Take a pistol. Stay together. Do not take things with the pistol. Understand?" Vietnamese thugs would beat the Bru up if they were alone or unarmed. All these lessons had been learned the hard way.

Drinking at the picnic table left them feeling hollow since Rogers had been killed, but they kept it up anyway.

"I'm starting my thirty day leave the day after tomorrow."

"They're liable to put someone in charge while you're gone, sir."

"Yeah, that's what I want to talk to you about. I told Major Capra that if he assigned anybody, a lieutenant, senior sergeant or whatever, to the platoon, while I'm gone, you were to remain in command."

"What he say?"

"I got one of those non-committal, don't worry about it answers. I had S-1 type this up for you," Dawson said, fishing in his pocket for a folded up piece of paper. "It, basically, says what I told you, signed by me, for whatever that's worth. You know, before you got here, all I did was carry the radio around. It gave me a chance to learn before I could get a lot of people killed. Now SOG feels more like the regular army."

"Even with this letter, If someone tries to pull rank there won't be much I can do about it, sir."

"You'll need at least two more people to go out. There's not much chance of that happening. I'll probably be back before the end of my thirty day leave anyway."

Dawson parked the rental car at the curb. There was a new Chevy Impala in the driveway. For as long as he could remember his father prided himself on getting a new car every two years. He walked past the car, up to the porch and rang the bell. His mother answered the door.

"Alan's home," she called excitedly, as she pushed open the screen door and hugged him. His father appeared behind her.

"What are we doing keeping the electric company? Don't just

stand there come on in." He shook his son's hand and wrapped his other arm around him. "Good to have you home." He stepped back, his eyes focusing on the rows of ribbons and badges displayed on the khaki shirt. "Three Purple Hearts. Looks like your letters left a few things out. Thank God you're done with it."

Going on a thirty day leave after a year of combat is something every soldier looks forward to, until they actually do it. For Dawson, it was mostly a problem of space. He was a very large presence in the tiny ranch house. His parents wanted to make him feel at home, but the harder they tried the more awkward it became. After a few days, he put on his uniform and drove to Pope Air Force Base in New Jersey. The people on the base were eager to help the young Special Forces captain and after a few inquiries he was directed to his destination.

He entered the small building and removed his beret. About a dozen civilians were working in cubicles. One approached nervously and asked if he could help.

"I'd like to speak to Master Sergeant Zobel," Dawson replied.

"He retired. Works here as a contractor now. Is this about his son?"

"Yes, he was a friend. I want to pay my respects."

"His son's death hit him very hard. Didn't work for a couple of months. He's still not right. I'll get him." Dawson waited. Every worker in the place stared at him. Anxiety in their faces. A couple of long minutes passed and Walter Zobel, Sr. appeared from a back office. By the time he was close, tears were brimming in his eyes. He was a broken man. Dawson expressed his regrets. Zobel mumbled something about how his son's body was almost unrecognizable in the casket. Realizing his presence was causing great pain, Dawson left quickly. Outside, he took a deep breath. He should have known better. When people had expressed sorrow about Rogers he didn't find it helpful. He thought they were a pain in the ass.

Other than their deep belief that being Protestant was better than being Catholic or Jewish, Dawson never considered his parents very religious. But they did attend church every Sunday. His father made it plain that he was expected to join them. He put on an old suit from high school, found a pair of black loafers and cleaned the dust off them with a green army tee shirt. Dressed, he joined his parents in the living room.

"What are you doing? Trying to embarrass me?" his father asked angrily. The suit jacket was a little tight across the back and the pants loose in the waist, but the jacket hid it. Humping the jungle with sixty pounds of gear had changed his body.

"It doesn't look that bad."

"You're supposed to wear your uniform."

"I thought I was going to church not show and tell," he replied sharply, sounding more like Captain Dawson than somebody's kid. But he went back to the bedroom and changed. They rode to church in the shiny Chevrolet his father meticulously washed every Saturday morning.

The church was familiar. Someplace in the little ranch house, was a Sunday School pin Dawson had received with row after row of perfect attendance bars. He sat through the service, not really listening, thinking about Jennings and Thoung and, of course,

Rogers. When it was over, they filed out, shaking hands with the pastor. Then the dog and pony show began.

"This is my son. He's a green beret," his father said. "Just got back from Vietnam," he told another. "Three Purple Hearts. That's a Bronze Star the V is for valor." He went on and on. "He got a battlefield promotion to captain." Battlefield promotion? Dawson guessed the real story wasn't good enough. "Hey, Charlie, Have you met my son?" Dawson was getting annoyed. Enough was enough. He recognized this guy. His junior high school gym teacher. Sadistic, sneaky, little prick. Liked to cheap shot his students then pretend nothing happened. He remembered he'd kneed him a couple of times in that painful spot between the muscles of his thigh.

"Look at you. All grown up." Charlie thrust out his chest and approached to shake hands.

"I remember you," Dawson said. "Tough guy. Real tough with little kids." The dog and pony show ended.

The next Thursday, Dawson walked through the living room in front of the TV as Walter Cronkite announced,

"Tonight American paratroopers are battling for control of a key mountain in the area." Behind him a map displayed Dong Ap Bai, Hill 937, a solitary mountain just northwest of the A Shau Valley. He stopped to listen.

"You'd make a better door than you would a window," he father said from behind him. Dawson followed the battle carefully on the TV and in the newspaper. The fighting raged for days and the press coverage increased each day. The following Wednesday, the Associated press reported in detail that the mountain had been taken the day before. U.S. losses totaled 72 killed and 381 wounded. In addition the U.S. Air Force flew 258 missions expending more than 500 tons of ordinance. North Vietnamese losses included 630 bodies recovered. Many enemy soldiers escaped into Laos. Not reported was the fact that the North Vietnamese supplied their fortified mountain base using a road that ran out of Laos, 8 kilometers south of Route 922. The road that had been discovered by Peterson and Dawson in July of 1968 and dismissed as a diversion. The next day, the press started calling the encounter the Battle of Hamburger Hill.

For three weeks, Dawson had waited for his father to ask the question. But it never came. Here we go, he thought as he zipped up his kitbag and walked into the living room.

"So, you're off to Ft. Bragg?" his father asked. The answer sparked a half hour of drama.

Dawson sat on the beach at Cam Ranh Bay. Someone blew a whistle, a white banner was lowered from the flag staff and replaced by a large red ball. Swimmers exited the ocean. A strange looking helicopter flew out over the sea, past the shark net, and hovered. A shooter leaned out of the cabin and fired two rifle rounds into the ocean.

EPILOGUE

December 17, 1992

The arrivals area at Palm Beach International Airport was busy. He loaded his wife's suitcase into the trunk and opened the door for her.

"Long flight?"

"Full of snowbirds. Newark's always a mess."

"How's your sister?"

"Not good." He could see she was wringing her hands. "She still has a few months at best. Did you have any luck with Tsongas's doctor?" Senator Paul Tsongas of Massachusetts suffered from the same deadly form of cancer as her sister. His doctor had become famous for keeping him alive.

"No. They're nice enough in the senator's office, but I can't get the doctor on the phone and no one from his office is returning my calls."

"There's nothing you can do?"

"Not that I can think of."

January 15, 1993

His wife sat at her small desk almost in tears. She had just gotten off the phone with her sister.

"Let me sit there," he said.

"Why?"

"Just give me the chair. I'm gonna try something." He called information and got connected.

"What are you doing?" she interrupted. He waved her off. After a few minutes he hung up. "What did you do?" she asked.

"Just wait. He asked me to keep this line clear." They didn't have to wait long. In less than five minutes the phone rang. Caller ID showed Boston, MA. He tapped the speaker button. "Hello," he said.

"Captain Dawson?"

"Speaking."

"This is Doctor Ronald Takvorian from the Dana-Farber Cancer Institute. Ross Perot instructed me to call you."

April 4, 2001

Twenty-nine years after the Studies and Observation Group was disbanded, the unit was awarded the Presidential Unit Citation. It read in part:

The Studies and Observations Group is cited for extraordinary heroism, great combat achievement, and unwavering fidelity while executing unheralded top secret missions deep behind enemy lines across Southeast Asia. . . Despite casualties that sometimes became universal, Special Operations Group's operators never wavered but fought throughout the war with the same flair, fidelity and intrepidity that distinguished Special Operation Group from its beginning. The Studies and Observations Group's combat prowess, martial skills and unacknowledged sacrifices saved many American lives, and provide a paragon for American future special operation forces.

As Dawson read it, one sentence stood out.

Special Operations Group's cross-border operations proved an effective economy-of-force, compelling the North Vietnamese Army to divert 50,000 soldiers to rear area security duties, far from the battlefields of South Vietnam.

He remembered a conversation he had had with Sergeant Fallon many years before.
" . . . how about all the supplies we stop from coming down the trail?" Dawson asked.
"The NVA moves tons a day. We don't make a dent in that," Fallon replied.
"Then what's the point in going out and getting our asses shot off?"
"That's a good question. By the time your kids are grown up and you can tell them what you did, I'm sure they'll have come up with something."

Dawson turned off his computer. He had to change clothes. He and his wife were attending his sister-in-law's fifty-fifth birthday party that evening.

February 20, 2019

As was his habit, the old man was having a beer and a rum and coke at a local bar in Jupiter, Florida. A young fellow, big, well-built, late twenties, put his hand on the next bar stool and asked,

"Mind if I sit here, sir?"

"No, go ahead. You a ball player?" Spring training had just started and the Cardinals and Marlins were in town.

"No. Air Force."

"Oh, yeah, what do you do?"

"Special Operations. Combat controller."

"Really, that's a tough job." They sat in silence for a while. "You ever heard of SOG?"

"Every special operator has heard of SOG. We don't take those kind of risks anymore. Why, did you serve in SOG, sir?"

"No," the old man lied. "I had a friend who was a sergeant in SOG. He was about your age."

Made in the USA
Middletown, DE
30 July 2020